T. Tembar

Frances Hodgson Burnett

Alpha Editions

This edition published in 2024

ISBN : 9789362514530

Design and Setting By
Alpha Editions
www.alphaedis.com
Email - info@alphaedis.com

As per information held with us this book is in Public Domain.
This book is a reproduction of an important historical work. Alpha Editions uses the best technology to reproduce historical work in the same manner it was first published to preserve its original nature. Any marks or number seen are left intentionally to preserve its true form.

Contents

CHAPTER I: .... - 1 -
CHAPTER II .... - 7 -
CHAPTER III .... - 20 -
CHAPTER IV .... - 29 -
CHAPTER V .... - 40 -
CHAPTER VI .... - 47 -
CHAPTER VII .... - 65 -
CHAPTER VIII .... - 71 -
CHAPTER IX .... - 81 -
CHAPTER X .... - 88 -
CHAPTER XI .... - 95 -
CHAPTER XII .... - 101 -
CHAPTER XIII .... - 117 -
CHAPTER XIV .... - 134 -
CHAPTER XV .... - 145 -
CHAPTER XVI .... - 159 -
CHAPTER XVII .... - 172 -
CHAPTER XVIII .... - 184 -
CHAPTER XIX .... - 191 -
CHAPTER XX .... - 204 -
CHAPTER XXI .... - 215 -
CHAPTER XXII .... - 224 -
CHAPTER XXIII .... - 230 -
CHAPTER XXIV .... - 239 -
CHAPTER XXV .... - 248 -
CHAPTER XXVI .... - 257 -

- CHAPTER XXVII ....- 266 -
- CHAPTER XXVIII ....- 271 -
- CHAPTER XXIX ....- 283 -
- CHAPTER XXX ....- 291 -
- CHAPTER XXXI ....- 301 -
- CHAPTER XXXII ....- 315 -
- CHAPTER XXXIII ....- 330 -
- CHAPTER XXXIV ....- 343 -
- CHAPTER XXXV ....- 354 -
- CHAPTER XXXVI ....- 363 -
- CHAPTER XXXVII ....- 372 -
- CHAPTER XXXVIII ....- 388 -
- CHAPTER XXXIX ....- 397 -
- CHAPTER XL ....- 413 -

CHAPTER I:

The boys at the Brooklyn public school which he attended did not know what the "T." stood for. He would never tell them. All he said in reply to questions was: "It don't stand for nothin'. You've gotter have a' 'nitial, ain't you?" His name was, in fact, an almost inevitable school-boy modification of one felt to be absurd and pretentious. His Christian name was Temple, which became "Temp." His surname was Barom, so he was at once "Temp Barom." In the natural tendency to avoid waste of time it was pronounced as one word, and the letter p being superfluous and cumbersome, it easily settled itself into "Tembarom," and there remained. By much less inevitable processes have surnames evolved themselves as centuries rolled by. Tembarom liked it, and soon almost forgot he had ever been called anything else.

His education really began when he was ten years old. At that time his mother died of pneumonia, contracted by going out to sew, at seventy-five cents a day, in shoes almost entirely without soles, when the remains of a blizzard were melting in the streets. As, after her funeral, there remained only twenty-five cents in the shabby bureau which was one of the few articles furnishing the room in the tenement in which they lived together, Tembarom sleeping on a cot, the world spread itself before him as a place to explore in search of at least one meal a day. There was nothing to do but to explore it to the best of his ten-year-old ability.

His father had died two years before his mother, and Tembarom had vaguely felt it a relief. He had been a resentful, domestically tyrannical immigrant Englishman, who held in contempt every American trait and institution. He had come over to better himself, detesting England and the English because there was "no chance for a man there," and, transferring his dislikes and resentments from one country to another, had met with no better luck than he had left behind him. This he felt to be the fault of America, and his family, which was represented solely by Tembarom and his mother, heard a good deal about it, and also, rather contradictorily, a good deal about the advantages and superiority of England, to which in the course of six months he became gloomily loyal. It was necessary, in fact, for him to have something with which to compare the United States unfavorably. The effect he produced on Tembarom was that of causing him, when he entered the public school round the corner, to conceal with determination verging on duplicity the humiliating fact that if he had not been born in Brooklyn he might have been born in England. England was not popular among the boys in the school. History had represented the country to them in all its tyrannical rapacity and bloodthirsty oppression of the humble free-born. The manly and admirable attitude was to say, "Give me liberty or give me death"—and there was the Fourth of July.

Though Tembarom and his mother had been poor enough while his father lived, when he died the returns from his irregular odd jobs no longer came in to supplement his wife's sewing, and add an occasional day or two of fuller meals, in consequence of which they were oftener than ever hungry and cold, and in desperate trouble about the rent of their room. Tembarom, who was a wiry, enterprising little fellow, sometimes found an odd job himself. He carried notes and parcels when any one would trust him with them, he split old boxes into kindling-wood, more than once he "minded" a baby when its mother left its perambulator outside a store. But at eight or nine years of age one's pay is in proportion to one's size. Tembarom, however, had neither his father's bitter eye nor his mother's discouraged one. Something different from either had been reincarnated in him from some more cheerful past. He had an alluring grin instead—a grin which curled up his mouth and showed his sound, healthy, young teeth,—a lot of them,—and people liked to see them.

At the beginning of the world it is only recently reasonable to suppose human beings were made with healthy bodies and healthy minds. That of course was the original scheme of the race. It would not have been worth while to create a lot of things aimlessly ill made. A journeyman carpenter would not waste his time in doing it, if he knew any better. Given the power to make a man, even an amateur would make him as straight as he could, inside and out. Decent vanity would compel him to do it. He would be ashamed to show the thing and admit he had done it, much less people a world with millions of like proofs of incompetence. Logically considered, the race was built straight and clean and healthy and happy. How, since then, it has developed in multitudinous less sane directions, and lost its normal straightness and proportions, I am, singularly enough, not entirely competent to explain with any degree of satisfactory detail. But it cannot be truthfully denied that this has rather generally happened. There are human beings who are not beautiful, there are those who are not healthy, there are those who hate people and things with much waste of physical and mental energy, there are people who are not unwilling to do others an ill turn by word or deed, and there are those who do not believe that the original scheme of the race was ever a decent one.

This is all abnormal and unintelligent, even the not being beautiful, and sometimes one finds oneself called upon passionately to resist a temptation to listen to an internal hint that the whole thing is aimless. Upon this tendency one may as well put one's foot firmly, as it leads nowhere. At such times it is supporting to call to mind a certain undeniable fact which ought to loom up much larger in our philosophical calculations. No one has ever made a collection of statistics regarding the enormous number of perfectly sane, kind, friendly, decent creatures who form a large proportion of any mass of human beings anywhere and everywhere—people who are not vicious or cruel or depraved, not as a result of continual self-control, but simply because they do not want to be, because it is more natural and agreeable to be exactly the opposite things; people who do not tell lies because they could not do it with any pleasure, and would, on the contrary, find the exertion an annoyance and a bore; people whose manners and morals are good because their natural preference lies in that direction. There are millions of them who in most essays on life and living are virtually ignored because they do none of the things which call forth eloquent condemnation or brilliant cynicism. It has not yet become the fashion to record them. When one reads a daily newspaper filled with dramatic elaborations of crimes and unpleasantness, one sometimes wishes attention might be called to them—to their numbers, to their decencies, to their normal lack of any desire to do violence and their equally normal disposition to lend a hand. One is inclined to feel that the majority of persons do not believe in their existence. But if an accident occurs in the street, there are always several of them who appear to spring out of the earth to give human sympathy and assistance; if a national calamity, physical or social, takes place, the world suddenly seems full of them. They are the thousands of Browns, Joneses, and Robinsons who, massed together, send food to famine-stricken countries, sustenance to earthquake-devastated regions, aid to wounded soldiers or miners or flood-swept homelessness. They are the ones who have happened naturally to continue to grow straight and carry out the First Intention. They really form the majority; if they did not, the people of the earth would have eaten one another alive centuries ago. But though this is surely true, a happy cynicism totally disbelieves in their existence. When a combination of circumstances sufficiently dramatic brings one of them into prominence, he is either called an angel or a fool. He is neither. He is only a human creature who is normal.

After this manner Tembarom was wholly normal. He liked work and rejoiced in good cheer, when he found it, however attenuated its form. He was a good companion, and even at ten years old a practical person. He took his loose coppers from the old bureau drawer, and remembering that he had several times helped Jake Hutchins to sell his newspapers, he went forth into the world to find and consult him as to the investment of his capital.

"Where are you goin', Tem?" a woman who lived in the next room said when she met him on the stairs. "What you goin' to do?"

"I'm goin' to sell newspapers if I can get some with this," he replied, opening his hand to show her the extent of his resources.

She was almost as poor as he was, but not quite. She looked him over curiously for a moment, and then fumbled in her pocket. She drew out two ten-cent pieces and considered them, hesitating. Then she looked again at him. That normal expression in his nice ten-year-old eyes had its suggestive effect.

"You take this," she said, handing him the two pieces. "It'll help you to start."

"I'll bring it back, ma'am," said Tem. "Thank you, Mis' Hullingworth."

In about two weeks' time he did bring it back. That was the beginning. He lived through all the experiences a small boy waif and stray would be likely to come in contact with. The abnormal class treated him ill, and the normal class treated him well. He managed to get enough food to eat to keep him from starvation. Sometimes he slept under a roof and much oftener out-of-doors. He preferred to sleep out-of-doors more than half of the year, and the rest of the time he did what he could. He saw and learned many strange things, but was not undermined by vice because he unconsciously preferred decency. He sold newspapers and annexed any old job which appeared on the horizon. The education the New York streets gave him was a liberal one. He became accustomed to heat and cold and wet weather, but having sound lungs and a tough little body combined with the normal tendencies already mentioned, he suffered no more physical deterioration than a young Indian would suffer. After selling newspapers for two years he got a place as "boy" in a small store. The advance signified by steady employment was inspiring to his energies. He forged ahead, and got a better job and better pay as he grew older. By the time he was fifteen he shared a small bedroom with another boy. In whatsoever quarter he lived, friends seemed sporadic. Other boy's congregated about him. He did not know he had any effect at all, but his effect, in fact, was rather like that of a fire in winter or a cool breeze in summer. It was natural to gather where it prevailed.

There came a time when he went to a night class to learn stenography. Great excitement had been aroused among the boys he knew best by a rumor that there were "fellows" who could earn a hundred dollars a week "writing short." Boyhood could not resist the florid splendor of the idea. Four of them entered the class confidently looking forward to becoming the recipients of four hundred a month in the course of six weeks. One by one they dropped off, until only Tembarom remained, slowly forging ahead. He had never meant anything else but to get on in the world—to get as far as he could. He kept at his "short," and by the time he was nineteen it helped him to a place in a newspaper office. He took dictation from a nervous and harried editor, who, when he was driven to frenzy by overwork and incompetencies, found that the long-legged, clean youth with the grin never added fuel to the flame of his wrath. He was a common young man, who was not marked by special brilliancy of intelligence, but he had a clear head and a good temper, and a queer aptitude for being able to see himself in the other man's shoes—his difficulties and moods. This ended in his being tried with bits of new work now and then. In an emergency he was once sent out to report the details of a fire. What he brought back was usable, and his elation when he found he had actually "made good" was ingenuous enough to spur Galton, the editor, into trying him again.

To Tembarom this was a magnificent experience. The literary suggestion implied by being "on a newspaper" was more than he had hoped for. If you have sold newspapers, and slept in a barrel or behind a pile of lumber in a wood-yard, to report a fire in a street-car shed seems a flight of literature. He applied himself to the careful study of newspapers—their points of view, their style of phrasing. He believed them to be perfect. To attain ease in expressing himself in their elevated language he felt to be the summit of lofty ambition. He had no doubts of the exaltation of his ideal. His respect and confidence almost made Galton cry at times, because they recalled to him days when he had been nineteen and had regarded New York journalists with reverence. He liked Tembarom more and more. It actually soothed him to have him about, and he fell into giving him one absurd little chance after another. When he brought in "stuff" which bore too evident marks of utter ignorance, he actually touched it up and used it, giving him an enlightening, ironical hint or so. Tembarom always took the hints with gratitude. He had no mistaken ideas of his own powers. Galton loomed up before him a sort of god, and though the editor was a man with a keen, though wearied, brain and a sense of humor, the situation was one naturally productive of harmonious relations. He was of the many who unknowingly came in out of the cold and stood in the glow of Tembarom's warm fire, or took refuge from the heat in his cool breeze. He did not know of the private, arduous study of journalistic style, and it was not unpleasing to see that the nice young cub was gradually improving. Through pure modest fear or ridicule, Tembarom kept to himself his vaulting ambition. He practised reports of fires, weddings, and accidents in his hall bedroom.

A hall bedroom in a third-rate boarding-house is not a cheerful place, but when Tembarom vaguely felt this, he recalled the nights spent in empty trucks and behind lumber-piles, and thought he was getting spoiled by luxury. He told himself that he was a fellow who always had luck. He did not know, neither did any one else, that his luck would have followed him if he had lived in a coal-hole. It was the concomitant of his normal build and outlook on life. Mrs. Bowse, his hard-worked landlady, began by being calmed down by his mere bearing when he came to apply for his room and board. She had a touch of grippe, and had just emerged from a heated affray with a dirty cook, and was inclined to battle when he presented himself. In a few minutes she was inclined to battle no longer. She let him have the room. Cantankerous restrictions did not ruffle him.

"Of course what you say GOES," he said, giving her his friendly grin. "Any one that takes boarders has GOT to be careful. You're in for a bad cold, ain't you?"

"I've got grippe again, that's what I've got," she almost snapped.

"Did you ever try Payson's 'G. Destroyer'? G stands for grippe, you know. Catchy name, ain't it? They say the man that invented it got ten thousand dollars for it. 'G. Destroyer.' You feel like you have to find out what it means when you see it up on a boarding. I'm just over grippe myself, and I've got half a bottle in my pocket. You carry it about with you, and swallow one every half-hour. You just try it. It set me right in no time."

He took the bottle out of his waistcoat pocket and handed it to her. She took it and turned it over.

"You're awful good-natured,"—She hesitated,—"but I ain't going to take your medicine. I ought to go and get some for myself. How much does it cost?"

"It's on the bottle; but it's having to get it for yourself that's the matter. You won't have time, and you'll forget it."

"That's true enough," said Mrs. Bowse, looking at him sharply. "I guess you know something about boarding-houses."

"I guess I know something about trying to earn three meals a day—or two of them. It's no merry jest, whichever way you do it."

CHAPTER II

When he took possession of his hall bedroom the next day and came down to his first meal, all the boarders looked at him interestedly. They had heard of the G. Destroyer from Mrs. Bowse, whose grippe had disappeared. Jim Bowles and Julius Steinberger looked at him because they were about his own age, and shared a hall bedroom on his floor; the young woman from the notion counter in a down-town department store looked at him because she was a young woman; the rest of the company looked at him because a young man in a hall bedroom might or might not be noisy or objectionable, and the incident of the G. Destroyer sounded good-natured. Mr. Joseph Hutchinson, the stout and discontented Englishman from Manchester, looked him over because the mere fact that he was a new-comer had placed him by his own rash act in the position of a target for criticism. Mr. Hutchinson had come to New York because he had been told that he could find backers among profuse and innumerable multi-millionaires for the invention which had been the haunting vision of his uninspiring life. He had not been met with the careless rapture which had been described to him, and he was becoming violently antagonistic to American capital and pessimistic in his views of American institutions. Like Tembarom's father, he was the resentful Englishman.

"I don't think much o' that chap," he said in what he considered an undertone to his daughter, who sat beside him and tried to manage that he should not be infuriated by waiting for butter and bread and second helpings. A fine, healthy old feudal feeling that servants should be roared at if they did not "look sharp" when he wanted anything was one of his salient characteristics.

"Wait a bit, Father; we don't know anything about him yet," Ann Hutchinson murmured quietly, hoping that his words had been lost in the clatter of knives and forks and dishes.

As Tembarom had taken his seat, he had found that, when he looked across the table, he looked directly at Miss Hutchinson; and before the meal ended he felt that he was in great good luck to be placed opposite an object of such singular interest. He knew nothing about "types," but if he had been of those who do, he would probably have said to himself that she was of a type apart. As it was, he merely felt that she was of a kind one kept looking at whether one ought to or not. She was a little thing of that exceedingly light slimness of build which makes a girl a childish feather-weight. Few girls retain it after fourteen or fifteen. A wind might supposably have blown her away, but one knew it would not, because she was firm and steady on her small feet. Ordinary strength could have lifted her with one hand, and would have been tempted to do it. She had a slim, round throat, and the English daisy face it upheld caused it to suggest to the mind the stem of a flower. The roundness of her cheek, in and out of which totally unexpected dimples flickered, and the forget-me-not blueness of her eyes, which were large and rather round also, made her look like a nice baby of singularly serious and observing mind. She looked at one as certain awe-inspiring things in perambulators look at one—with a far and clear silence of gaze which passes beyond earthly obstacles and reserves a benign patience with follies. Tembarom felt interestedly that one really might quail before it, if one had anything of an inferior quality to hide. And yet it was not a critical gaze at all. She wore a black dress with a bit of white collar, and she had so much soft, red hair that he could not help recalling one or two women who owned the same quantity and seemed able to carry it only as a sort of untidy bundle. Hers looked entirely under control, and yet was such a wonder of burnished fullness that it tempted the hand to reach out and touch it. It became Tembarom's task during the meal to keep his eyes from turning too often toward it and its owner.

If she had been a girl who took things hard, she might have taken her father very hard indeed. But opinions and feelings being solely a matter of points of view, she was very fond of him, and, regarding him as a sacred charge and duty, took care of him as though she had been a reverentially inclined mother taking care of a boisterous son. When his roar was heard, her calm little voice always fell quietly on indignant ears the moment it ceased. It was her part in life to act as a palliative: her mother, whose well-trained attitude toward the ruling domestic male was of the early Victorian order, had lived and died one. A nicer, warmer little woman had never existed. Joseph Hutchinson had adored and depended on her as much as he had harried her. When he had charged about like a mad bull because he could not button his collar, or find the pipe he had mislaid in his own pocket, she had never said more than "Now, Mr. Hutchinson," or done more than leave her sewing to button the collar with soothing fingers, and suggest quietly that sometimes he DID chance to carry his pipe about with him. She was of the class which used to call its husband by a respectful surname. When she died she left him as a sort of legacy to her daughter, spending the last weeks of her life in explaining affectionately all that "Father" needed to keep him quiet and make him comfortable.

Little Ann had never forgotten a detail, and had even improved upon some of them, as she happened to be cleverer than her mother, and had, indeed, a far-seeing and clear young mind of her own. She had been called "Little Ann" all her life. This had held in the first place because her mother's name had been Ann also, and after her mother's death the diminutive had not fallen away from her. People felt it belonged to her not because she was especially little, though she was a small, light person, but because there was an affectionate humor in the sound of it.

Despite her hard needs, Mrs. Bowse would have faced the chance of losing two boarders rather than have kept Mr. Joseph Hutchinson but for Little Ann. As it was, she kept them both, and in the course of three months the girl was Little Ann to almost every one in the house. Her normalness took the form of an instinct which amounted to genius for seeing what people ought to have, and in some occult way filling in bare or trying places.

"She's just a wonder, that girl," Mrs. Bowse said to one boarder after another.

"She's just a wonder," Jim Bowles and Julius Steinberger murmured to each other in rueful confidence, as they tilted their chairs against the wall of their hall bedroom and smoked. Each of the shabby and poverty-stricken young men had of course fallen hopelessly in love with her at once. This was merely human and inevitable, but realizing in the course of a few weeks that she was too busy taking care of her irritable, boisterous old Manchester father, and everybody else, to have time to be made love to even by young men who could buy new boots when the old ones had ceased to be water-tight, they were obliged to resign themselves to the, after all, comforting fact that she became a mother to them, not a sister. She mended their socks and sewed buttons on for them with a firm frankness which could not be persuaded into meaning anything more sentimental than a fixed habit of repairing anything which needed it, and which, while at first bewildering in its serenity, ended by reducing the two youths to a dust of devotion.

"She's a wonder, she is," they sighed when at every weekend they found their forlorn and scanty washing resting tidily on their bed.

In the course of a week, more or less, Tembarom's feeling for her would have been exactly that of his two hall-bedroom neighbors, but that his nature, though a practical one, was not inclined to any supine degree of resignation. He was a sensible youth, however, and gave no trouble. Even Joseph Hutchinson, who of course resented furiously any "nonsense" of which his daughter and possession was the object, became sufficiently mollified by his good spirits and ready good nature to refrain from open conversational assault.

"I don't mind that chap as much as I did at first," he admitted reluctantly to Little Ann one evening after a good dinner and a comfortable pipe. "He's not such a fool as he looks."

Tembarom was given, as Little Ann was, to seeing what people wanted. He knew when to pass the mustard and other straying condiments. He picked up things which dropped inconveniently, he did not interrupt the remarks of his elders and betters, and several times when he chanced to be in the hall, and saw Mr. Hutchinson, in irritable, stout Englishman fashion, struggling into his overcoat, he sprang forward with a light, friendly air and helped him. 'He did not do it with ostentatious politeness or with the manner of active youth giving generous aid to elderly avoirdupois. He did it as though it occurred to him as a natural result of being on the spot.

It took Mrs. Bowse and her boarding-house less than a week definitely to like him. Every night when he sat down to dinner he brought news with him—news and jokes and new slang. Newspaper-office anecdote and talk gave a journalistic air to the gathering when he was present, and there was novelty in it. Soon every one was intimate with him, and interested in what he was doing. Galton's good-natured patronage of him was a thing to which no one was indifferent. It was felt to be the right thing in the right place. When he came home at night it became the custom to ask him questions as to the bits of luck which befell him. He became "T. T." instead of Mr. Tembarom, except to Joseph Hutchinson and his 'daughter. Hutchinson called him Tembarom, but Little Ann said "Mr. Tembarom" with quaint frequency when she spoke to him.

"Landed anything to-day, T. T.?" some one would ask almost every evening, and the interest in his relation of the day's adventures increased from week to week. Little Ann never asked questions and seldom made comments, but she always listened attentively. She had gathered, and guessed from what she had gathered, a rather definite idea of what his hard young life had been. He did not tell pathetic stories about himself, but he and Jim Bowles and Julius Steinberger had become fast friends, and the genial smoking of cheap tobacco in hall bedrooms tends to frankness of relation, and the various ways in which each had found himself "up against it" in the course of their brief years supplied material for anecdotal talk.

"But it's bound to be easier from now on," he would say. "I've got the 'short' down pretty fine—not fine enough to make big money, but enough to hold down a job with Galton. He's mighty good to me. If I knew more, I believe he'd give me a column to take care of—Up-town Society column perhaps. A fellow named Biker's got it. Twenty per. Goes on a bust twice a month, the fool. Gee! I wish I had his job!"

Mrs. Bowse's house was provided with a parlor in which her boarders could sit in the evening when so inclined. It was a fearsome room, which, when the dark, high-ceilinged hall was entered, revealed depths of dingy gloom which appeared splashed in spots with incongruous brilliancy of color. This effect was produced by richly framed department-store chromo lithographs on the walls, aided by lurid cushion-covers, or "tidies" representing Indian maidens or chieftains in full war paint, or clusters of poppies of great boldness of hue. They had either been Christmas gifts bestowed upon Mrs. Bowse or department-store bargains of her own selection, purchased with thrifty intent. The red-and-green plush upholstered walnut chairs arid sofa had been acquired by her when the bankruptcy of a neighboring boarding-house brought them within her means. They were no longer very red or very green, and the cheerfully hopeful design of the tidies and cushions had been to conceal worn places and stains. The mantelpiece was adorned by a black-walnut-and-gold-framed mirror, and innumerable vases of the ornate ninety-eight-cents order. The centerpiece held a large and extremely soiled spray of artificial wistaria. The end of the room was rendered attractive by a tent-like cozy-corner built of savage weapons and Oriental cotton stuffs long ago become stringy and almost leprous in hue. The proprietor of the bankrupt boarding-house had been "artistic." But Mrs. Bowse was a good-enough soul whose boarders liked her and her house, and when the gas was lighted and some one played "rag-time" on the second-hand pianola, they liked the parlor.

Little Ann did not often appear in it, but now and then she came down with her bit of sewing,—she always had a "bit of sewing,"—and she sat in the cozy-corner listening to the talk or letting some one confide troubles to her. Sometimes it was the New England widow, Mrs. Peck, who looked like a spinster school-ma'am, but who had a married son with a nice wife who lived in Harlem and drank heavily. She used to consult with Little Ann as to the possible wisdom of putting a drink deterrent privately in his tea. Sometimes it was Mr. Jakes, a depressed little man whose wife had left him, for no special reason he could discover. Oftenest perhaps it was Julius Steinberger or Jim Bowles who did their ingenuous best to present themselves to her as energetic, if not successful, young business men, not wholly unworthy of attention and always breathing daily increasing devotion. Sometimes it was Tembarom, of whom her opinion had never been expressed, but who seemed to have made friends with her. She liked to hear about the newspaper office and Mr. Galton, and never was uninterested in his hopes of "making good." She seemed to him the wisest and most direct and composed person he had ever known. She spoke with the broad, flat, friendly Manchester accent, and when she let drop a suggestion, it carried a delightfully sober conviction with it, because what she said was generally a revelation of logical mental argument concerning details she had gathered through her little way of listening and saying nothing whatever.

"If Mr. Biker drinks, he won't keep his place," she said to Tembarom one night. "Perhaps you might get it yourself, if you persevere."

Tembarom reddened a little. He really reddened through joyous excitement.

"Say, I didn't know you knew a thing about that," he answered. "You're a regular wonder. You scarcely ever say anything, but the way you get on to things gets me."

"Perhaps if I talked more I shouldn't notice as much," she said, turning her bit of sewing round and examining it. "I never was much of a talker. Father's a good talker, and Mother and me got into the way of listening. You do if you live with a good talker."

Tembarom looked at the girl with a male gentleness, endeavoring to subdue open expression of the fact that he was convinced that she was as thoroughly aware of her father's salient characteristics as she was of other things.

"You do," said Tembarom. Then picking up her scissors, which had dropped from her lap, and politely returning them, he added anxiously: "To think of you remembering Biker! I wonder, if I ever did get his job, if I could hold it down?"

"Yes," decided Little Ann; "you could. I've noticed you're that kind of person, Mr. Tembarom."

"Have you?" he said elatedly. "Say, honest Injun?"

"Yes."

"I shall be getting stuck on myself if you encourage me like that," he said, and then, his face falling, he added, "Biker graduated at Princeton."

"I don't know much about society," Little Ann remarked,—"I never saw any either up-town or down-town or in the country,—but I shouldn't think you'd have to have a college education to write the things you see about it in the newspaper paragraphs."

Tembarom grinned.

"They're not real high-brow stuff, are they," he said. "'There was a brilliant gathering on Tuesday evening at the house of Mr. Jacob Sturtburger at 79 Two Hundredth Street on the occasion of the marriage of his daughter Miss Rachel Sturtburger to Mr. Eichenstein. The bride was attired in white peau de cygne trimmed with duchess lace.'"

Little Ann took him up. "I don't know what peau de cygne is, and I daresay the bride doesn't. I've never been to anything but a village school, but I could make up paragraphs like that myself."

"That's the up-town kind," said Tembarom. "The down-town ones wear their mothers' point-lace wedding-veils some-times, but they're not much different. Say, I believe I could do it if I had luck."

"So do I," returned Little Ann.

Tembarom looked down at the carpet, thinking the thing over. Ann went on sewing.

"That's the way with you," he said presently: "you put things into a fellow's head. You've given me a regular boost, Little Ann."

It is not unlikely that but for the sensible conviction in her voice he would have felt less bold when, two weeks later, Biker, having gone upon a "bust" too prolonged, was dismissed with-out benefit of clergy, and Galton desperately turned to Tembarom with anxious question in his eye.

"Do you think you could take this job?" he said.

Tembarom's heart, as he believed at the time, jumped into his throat.

"What do you think, Mr. Galton?" he asked.

"It isn't a thing to think about," was Galton's answer. "It's a thing I must be sure of."

"Well," said Tembarom, "if you give it to me, I'll put up a mighty hard fight before I fall down."

Galton considered him, scrutinizing keenly his tough, long-built body, his sharp, eager, boyish face, and especially his companionable grin.

"We'll let it go at that," he decided. "You'll make friends up in Harlem, and you won't find it hard to pick up news. We can at least try it."

Tembarom's heart jumped into his throat again, and he swallowed it once more. He was glad he was not holding his hat in his hand because he knew he would have forgotten himself and thrown it up into the air.

"Thank you, Mr. Galton," he said, flushing tremendously. "I'd like to tell you how I appreciate your trusting me, but I don't know how. Thank you, sir."

When he appeared in Mrs. Bowse's dining-room that evening there was a glow of elation about him and a swing in his entry which attracted all eyes at once. For some unknown reason everybody looked at him, and, meeting his eyes, detected the presence of some new exultation.

"Landed anything, T. T.?" Jim Bowles cried out. "You look it."

"Sure I look it," Tembarom answered, taking his napkin out of its ring with an unconscious flourish. "I've landed the up-town society page—landed it, by gee!"

A good-humored chorus of ejaculatory congratulation broke forth all round the table.

"Good business!" "Three cheers for T. T.!" "Glad of it!" "Here's luck!" said one after another.

They were all pleased, and it was generally felt that Galton had shown sense and done the right thing again. Even Mr. Hutchinson rolled about in his chair and grunted his approval.

After dinner Tembarom, Jim Bowles, and Julius Steinberger went upstairs stairs together and filled the hall bedroom with clouds of tobacco-smoke, tilting their chairs against the wall, smoking their pipes furiously, flushed and talkative, working themselves up with the exhilarated plannings of youth. Jim Bowles and Julius had been down on their luck for several weeks, and that "good old T. T." should come in with this fairy-story was an actual stimulus. If you have never in your life been able to earn more than will pay for your food and lodging, twenty dollars looms up large. It might be the beginning of anything.

"First thing is to get on to the way to do it," argued Tembarom. "I don't know the first thing. I've got to think it out. I couldn't ask Biker. He wouldn't tell me, anyhow."

"He's pretty mad, I guess," said Steinberger.

"Mad as hops," Tembarom answered. "As I was coming down-stairs from Galton's room he was standing in the hall talking to Miss Dooley, and he said: 'That Tembarom fellow's going to do it! He doesn't know how to spell. I should like to see his stuff come in.' He said it loud, because he wanted me to hear it, and he sort of laughed through his nose."

"Say, T. T., can you spell?" Jim inquired thoughtfully.

"Spell? Me? No," Tembarom owned with unshaken good cheer. "What I've got to do is to get a tame dictionary and keep it chained to the leg of my table. Those words with two m's or two l's in them get me right down on the mat. But the thing that looks biggest to me is how to find out where the news is, and the name of the fellow that'll put me on to it. You can't go up a man's front steps and ring the bell and ask him if he's going to be married or buried or have a pink tea."

"Wasn't that a knock at the door?" said Steinberger.

It was a knock, and Tembarom jumped up and threw the door open, thinking Mrs. Bowse might have come on some household errand. But it was Little Ann Hutchinson instead of Mrs. Bowse, and there was a threaded needle stuck into the front of her dress, and she had on a thimble.

"I want Mr. Bowles's new socks," she said maternally. "I promised I'd mark them for him."

Bowles and Steinberger sprang from their chairs, and came forward in the usual comfortable glow of pleasure at sight of her.

"What do you think of that for all the comforts of a home?" said Tembarom. "As if it wasn't enough for a man to have new socks without having marks put on them! What are your old socks made of anyhow—solid gold? Burglars ain't going to break in and steal them."

"They won't when I've marked them, Mr. Tembarom," answered Little Ann, looking up at him with sober, round, for-get-me-not blue eyes, but with a deep dimple breaking out near her lip; "but all three pairs would not come home from the wash if I didn't."

"Three pairs!" ejaculated Tembarom. "He's got three pairs of socks! New? That's what's been the matter with him for the last week. Don't you mark them for him, Little Ann. 'Tain't good for a man to have everything."

"Here they are," said Jim, bringing them forward. "Twenty-five marked down to ten at Tracy's. Are they pretty good?"

Little Ann looked them over with the practised eye of a connoisseur of bargains.

"They'd be about a shilling in Manchester shops," she decided, "and they might be put down to sixpence. They're good enough to take care of."

She was not the young woman who is ready for prolonged lively conversation in halls and at bedroom doors, and she had turned away with the new socks in her hand when Tembarom, suddenly inspired, darted after her.

"Say, I've just thought of something," he exclaimed eagerly. "It's something I want to ask you."

"What is it?"

"It's about the society-page lay-out." He hesitated. "I wonder if it'd be rushing you too much if—say," he suddenly broke off, and standing with his hands in his pockets, looked down at her with anxious admiration, "I believe you just know about everything."

"No, I don't, Mr. Tembarom; but I'm very glad about the page. Everybody's glad."

One of the chief difficulties Tembarom found facing him when he talked to Little Ann was the difficulty of resisting an awful temptation to take hold of her—to clutch her to his healthy, tumultuous young breast and hold her there firmly. He was half ashamed of himself when he realized it, but he knew that his venial weakness was shared by Jim Bowles and Steinberger and probably others. She was so slim and light and soft, and the serious frankness of her eyes and the quaint air of being a sort of grown-up child of astonishing intelligence produced an effect it was necessary to combat with.

"What I wanted to say," he put it to her, "was that I believe if you'd just let me talk this thing out to you it'd do me good. I believe you'd help me to get somewhere. I've got to fix up a scheme for getting next the people who have things happening to them that I can make society stuff out of, you know. Biker didn't make a hit of it, but, gee! I've just got to. I've got to."

"Yes," answered Little Ann, her eyes fixed on him thoughtfully; "you've got to, Mr. Tembarom."

"There's not a soul in the parlor. Would you mind coming down and sitting there while I talk at you and try to work things out? You could go on with your marking."

She thought it over a minute.

"I'll do it if Father can spare me," she made up her mind. "I'll go and ask him."

She went to ask him, and returned in two or three minutes with her small sewing-basket in her hand.

"He can spare me," she said. "He's reading his paper, and doesn't want to talk."

They went down-stairs together and found the room empty. Tembarom turned up the lowered gas, and Little Ann sat down in the cozy-corner with her work-basket on her knee. Tembarom drew up a chair and sat down opposite to her. She threaded a needle and took up one of Jim's new socks.

"Now," she said.

"It's like this," he explained. "The page is a new deal, anyhow. There didn't used to be an up-town society column at all. It was all Fifth Avenue and the four hundred; but ours isn't a fashionable paper, and their four hundred ain't going to buy it to read their names in it. They'd rather pay to keep out of it. Uptown's growing like smoke, and there's lots of people up that way that'd like their friends to read about their weddings and receptions, and would buy a dozen copies to send away when their names were in. There's no end of women and girls that'd like to see their clothes described and let their friends read the descriptions. They'd buy the paper, too, you bet. It'll be a big circulation-increaser. It's Galton's idea, and he gave the job to Biker because he thought an educated fellow could get hold of people. But somehow he couldn't. Seems as if they didn't like him. He kept getting turned down. The page has been mighty poor—no pictures of brides or anything. Galton's been sick over it. He'd been sure it'd make a hit. Then Biker's always drinking more or less, and he's got the swell head, anyhow. I believe that's the reason he couldn't make good with the up-towners."

"Perhaps he was too well educated, Mr. Tembarom," said Little Ann. She was marking a letter J in red cotton, and her outward attention was apparently wholly fixed on her work.

"Say, now," Tembarom broke out, "there's where you come in. You go on working as if there was nothing but that sock in New York, but I guess you've just hit the dot. Perhaps that was it. He wanted to do Fifth Avenue work anyway, and he didn't go at Harlem right. He put on Princeton airs when he asked questions. Gee! a fellow can't put on any kind of airs when he's the one that's got to ask."

"You'll get on better," remarked Little Ann. "You've got a friendly way and you've a lot of sense. I've noticed it."

Her head was bent over the red J and she still looked at it and not at Tembarom. This was not coyness, but simple, calm absorption. If she had not been making the J, she would have sat with her hands folded in her lap, and gazed at the young man with undisturbed attention.

"Have you?" said Tembarom, gratefully. "That gives me another boost, Little Ann. What a man seems to need most is just plain twenty-cents-a-yard sense. Not that I ever thought I had the dollar kind. I'm not putting on airs."

"Mr. Galton knows the kind you have. I suppose that's why he gave you the page." The words, spoken in the shrewd-sounding Manchester accent, were neither flattering nor unflattering; they were merely impartial.

"Well, now I've got it, I can't fall down," said Tembarom. "I've got to find out for myself how to get next to the people I want to talk to. I've got to find out who to get next to."

Little Ann put in the final red stitch of the letter J and laid the sock neatly folded on the basket.

"I've just been thinking something, Mr. Tembarom," she said. "Who makes the wedding-cakes?"

He gave a delighted start.

"Gee!" he broke out, "the wedding-cakes!"

"Yes," Little Ann proceeded, "they'd have to have wedding-cakes, and perhaps if you went to the shops where they're sold and could make friends with the people, they'd tell you whom they were selling them to, and you could get the addresses and go and find out things."

Tembarom, glowing with admiring enthusiasm, thrust out his hand.

"Little Ann, shake!" he said. "You've given me the whole show, just like I thought you would. You're just the limit."

"Well, a wedding-cake's the next thing after the bride," she answered.

Her practical little head had given him the practical lead. The mere wedding-cake opened up vistas. Confectioners supplied not only weddings, but refreshments for receptions and dances. Dances suggested the "halls" in which they were held. You could get information at such places. Then there were the churches, and the florists who decorated festal scenes. Tembarom's excitement grew as he talked. One plan led to another; vistas opened on all sides. It all began to look so easy that he could not understand how Biker could possibly have gone into such a land of promise, and returned embittered and empty-handed.

"He thought too much of himself and too little of other people," Little Ann summed him up in her unsevere, reasonable voice. "That's so silly."

Tembarom tried not to look at her affectionately, but his voice was affectionate as well as admiring, despite him.

"The way you get on to a thing just in three words!" he said. "Daniel Webster ain't in it."

"I dare say if you let the people in the shops know that you come from a newspaper, it'll be a help," she went on with ingenuous worldly wisdom. "They'll think it'll be a kind of advertisement. And so it will. You get some neat cards printed with your name and Sunday Earth on them."

"Gee!" Tembarom ejaculated, slapping his knee, "there's another! You think of every darned thing, don't you?"

She stopped a moment to look at him.

"You'd have thought of it all yourself after a bit," she said. She was not of those unseemly women whose intention it is manifestly to instruct the superior man. She had been born in a small Manchester street and trained by her mother, whose own training had evolved through affectionately discreet conjugal management of Mr. Hutchinson.

"Never you let a man feel set down when you want him to see a thing reasonable, Ann," she had said. "You never get on with them if you do. They can't stand it. The Almighty seemed to make 'em that way. They've always been masters, and it don't hurt any woman to let 'em be, if she can help 'em to think reasonable. Just you make a man feel comfortable in his mind and push him the reasonable way. But never you shove him, Ann. If you do, he'll just get all upset-like. Me and your father have been right-down happy together, but we never should have been if I hadn't thought that out before we was married two weeks. Perhaps it's the Almighty's will, though I never was as sure of the Almighty's way of thinking as some are."

Of course Tembarom felt soothed and encouraged, though he belonged to the male development which is not automatically infuriated at a suspicion of female readiness of logic.

"Well, I might have got on to it in time," he answered, still trying not to look affectionate, "but I've no time to spare. Gee! but I'm glad you're here!"

"I sha'n't be here very long." There was a shade of patient regret in her voice. "Father's got tired of trying America. He's been disappointed too often. He's going back to England."

"Back to England!" Tembarom cried out forlornly, "Oh Lord! What shall we all do without you, Ann?"

"You'll do as you did before we came," said Little Ann.

"No, we sha'n't. We can't. I can't anyhow." He actually got up from his chair and began to walk about, with his hands thrust deep in his pockets.

Little Ann began to put her first stitches into a red B. No human being could have told what she thought.

"We mustn't waste time talking about that," she said. "Let us talk about the page. There are dressmakers, you know. If you could make friends with a dressmaker or two they'd tell you what the wedding things were really made of. Women do like their clothes to be described right."

CHAPTER III

His work upon the page began the following week. When the first morning of his campaign opened with a tumultuous blizzard, Jim Bowles and Julius Steinberger privately sympathized with him as they dressed in company, but they heard him whistling in his own hall bedroom as he put on his clothes, and to none of the three did it occur that time could be lost because the weather was inhuman. Blinding snow was being whirled through the air by a wind which had bellowed across the bay, and torn its way howling through the streets, maltreating people as it went, snatching their breath out of them, and leaving them gaspingly clutching at hats and bending their bodies before it. Street-cars went by loaded from front to back platform, and were forced from want of room to whizz heartlessly by groups waiting anxiously at street corners.

Tembarom saw two or three of them pass in this way, leaving the waiting ones desperately huddled together behind them. He braced himself and whistled louder as he buttoned his celluloid collar.

"I'm going to get up to Harlem all the same," he said. "The 'L' will be just as jammed, but there'll be a place somewhere, and I'll get it."

His clothes were the outwardly decent ones of a young man who must perforce seek cheap clothing-stores, and to whom a ten-dollar "hand-me-down" is a source of exultant rejoicing. With the aid of great care and a straight, well-formed young body, he managed to make the best of them; but they were not to be counted upon for warmth even in ordinarily cold weather. His overcoat was a specious covering, and was not infrequently odorous of naphtha.

"You've got to know something about first aid to the wounded if you live on ten per," he had said once to Little Ann. "A suit of clothes gets to be an emergency-case mighty often if it lasts three years."

"Going up to Harlem to-day, T. T.?" his neighbor at table asked him as he sat down to breakfast.

"Right there," he answered. "I've ordered the limousine round, with the foot-warmer and fur rugs."

"I guess a day wouldn't really matter much," said Mrs. Bowse, good-naturedly. "Perhaps it might be better to-morrow."

"And perhaps it mightn't," said Tembarom, eating "break-fast-food" with a cheerful appetite. "What you can't be stone-cold sure of to-morrow you drive a nail in to-day."

He ate a tremendous breakfast as a discreet precautionary measure. The dark dining-room was warm, and the food was substantial. It was comfortable in its way.

"You'd better hold the hall door pretty tight when you go out, and don't open it far," said Mrs. Bowse as he got up to go. "There's wind enough to upset things."

Tembarom went out in the hall, and put on his insufficient overcoat. He buttoned it across his chest, and turned its collar up to his ears. Then he bent down to turn up the bottoms of his trousers.

"A pair of arctics would be all to the merry right here," he said, and then he stood upright and saw Little Ann coming down the staircase holding in her hand a particularly ugly tar-tan-plaid woolen neck-scarf of the kind known in England as a "comforter."

"If you are going out in this kind of weather," she said in her serene, decided little voice, "you'd better wrap this comforter right round your neck, Mr. Tembarom. It's one of Father's, and he can spare it because he's got another, and, besides, he's not going out."

Tembarom took it with a sudden emotional perception of the fact that he was being taken care of in an abnormally luxurious manner.

"Now, I appreciate that," he said. "The thing about you. Little Ann, is that you never make a wrong guess about what a fellow needs, do you?"

"I'm too used to taking care of Father not to see things," she answered.

"What you get on to is how to take care of the whole world—initials on a fellow's socks and mufflers round his neck." His eyes looked remarkably bright.

"If a person were taking care of the whole world, he'd have a lot to do," was her sedate reception of the remark. "You'd better put that twice round your neck, Mr. Tembarom."

She put up her hand to draw the end of the scarf over his shoulder, and Tembarom stood still at once, as though he were a little boy being dressed for school. He looked down at her round cheek, and watched one of the unexpected dimples reveal itself in a place where dimples are not usually anticipated. It was coming out because she was smiling a small, observing smile. It was an almost exciting thing to look at, and he stood very still indeed. A fellow who did not own two pairs of boots would be a fool not to keep quiet.

"You haven't told me I oughtn't to go out till the blizzard lets up," he said presently.

"No, I haven't, Mr. Tembarom," she answered. "You're one of the kind that mean to do a thing when they've made up their minds. It'll be a nice bit of money if you can keep the page."

"Galton said he'd give me a chance to try to make good," said Tembarom. "And if it's the hit he thinks it ought to be, he'll raise me ten. Thirty per. Vanastorbilts won't be in it. I think I'll get married," he added, showing all his attractive teeth at once.

"I wouldn't do that," she said. "It wouldn't be enough to depend on. New York's an expensive place."

She drew back and looked him over. "That'll keep you much warmer," she decided. "Now you can go. I've been looking in the telephone-book for confectioners, and I've written down these addresses." She handed him a slip of paper.

Tembarom caught his breath.

"Hully gee!" he exclaimed, "there never were TWO of you made! One used up all there was of it. How am I going to thank you, anyhow!"

"I do hope you'll be able to keep the page," she said. "I do that, Mr. Tembarom."

If there had been a touch of coquetry in her earnest, sober, round, little face she would have been less distractingly alluring, but there was no shade of anything but a sort of softly motherly anxiety in the dropped note of her voice, and it was almost more than flesh and blood at twenty-five could stand. Tembarom made a hasty, involuntary move toward her, but it was only a slight one, and it was scarcely perceptible before he had himself in hand and hurriedly twisted his muffler tighter, showing his teeth again cheerily.

"You keep on hoping it all day without a let-up," he said. "And tell Mr. Hutchinson I'm obliged to him, please. Get out of the way, Little Ann, while I go out. The wind might blow you and the hat-stand upstairs."

He opened the door and dashed down the high steps into the full blast of the blizzard. He waited at the street corner while three overcrowded cars whizzed past him, ignoring his signals because there was not an inch of space left in them for another passenger. Then he fought his way across two or three blocks to the nearest "L" station. He managed to wedge himself into a train there, and then at least he was on his way. He was thinking hard and fast, but through all his planning the warm hug of the tartan comforter round his neck kept Little Ann near him. He had been very thankful for the additional warmth as the whirling snow and wind had wrought their will with him while he waited for the cars at the street corner. On the "L" train he saw her serious eyes and heard the motherly drop in her voice as she said, "I do hope you'll be able to keep the page. I do that, Mr. Tembarom." It made him shut his hands hard as they hung in his overcoat pockets for warmth, and it made him shut his sound teeth strongly.

"Gee! I've got to!" his thoughts said for him. "If I make it, perhaps my luck will have started. When a man's luck gets started, every darned thing's to the good."

The "L" had dropped most of its crowd when it reached the up-town station among the hundredth streets which was his destination. He tightened his comforter, tucked the ends firmly into the front of his overcoat, and started out along the platform past the office, and down the steep, iron steps, already perilous with freezing snow. He had to stop to get his breath when he reached the street, but he did not stop long. He charged forth again along the pavement, looking closely at the shop-windows. There were naturally but few passers-by, and the shops were not important-looking; but they were open, and he could see that the insides of them looked comfortable in contrast with the blizzard-ruled street. He could not see both sides of the street as he walked up one side of the block without coming upon a confectioner's. He crossed at the corner and turned back on the other side. Presently he saw that a light van was standing before one place, backed up against the sidewalk to receive parcels, its shuddering horse holding its head down and bracing itself with its forelegs against the wind. At any rate, something was going on there, and he hurried forward to find out what it was. The air was so thick with myriads of madly flying bits of snow, which seemed whirled in all directions in the air, that he could not see anything definite even a few yards away. When he reached the van he found that he had also reached his confectioner. The sign over the window read "M. Munsberg, Confectionery. Cakes. Ice-Cream. Weddings, Balls and Receptions."

"Made a start, anyhow," said Tembarom.

He turned into the store, opening the door carefully, and thereby barely escaping being blown violently against a stout, excited, middle-aged little Jew who was bending over a box he was packing. This was evidently Mr. Munsberg, who was extremely busy, and even the modified shock upset his temper.

"Vhere you goin'?" he cried out. "Can't you look vhere you're goin'?"

Tembarom knew this was not a good beginning, but his natural mental habit of vividly seeing the other man's point of view helped him after its usual custom. His nice grin showed itself.

"I wasn't going; I was coming," he said. "Beg pardon. The wind's blowing a hundred miles an hour."

A good-looking young woman, who was probably Mrs. Munsberg, was packing a smaller box behind the counter. Tembarom lifted his hat, and she liked it.

"He didn't do it a bit fresh," she said later. "Kind o' nice." She spoke to him with professional politeness.

"Is there anything you want?" she asked.

Tembarom glanced at the boxes and packages standing about and at Munsberg, who had bent over his packing again. Here was an occasion for practical tact.

"I've blown in at the wrong time," he said. "You're busy getting things out on time. I'll just wait.. Gee! I'm glad to be inside. I want to speak to Mr. Munsberg."

Mr. Munsberg jerked himself upright irascibly, and broke forth in the accent of the New York German Jew.

"If you comin' in here to try to sell somedings, young man, joost you let that same vind vat blew you in blow you right out pretty quick. I'm not buyin' nodings. I'm busy."

"I'm not selling a darned thing," answered Tembarom, with undismayed cheer.

"You vant someding?" jerked out Munsberg.

"Yes, I want something," Tembarom answered, "but it's nothing any one has to pay for. I'm only a newspaper man." He felt a glow of pride as he said the words. He was a newspaper man even now. "Don't let me stop you a minute. I'm in luck to get inside anywhere and sit down. Let me wait."

Mrs. Munsberg read the Sunday papers and revered them. She also knew the value of advertisement. She caught her husband's eye and hurriedly winked at him.

"It's awful outside. 'T won't do harm if he waits—if he ain't no agent," she put in.

"See," said Tembarom, handing over one of the cards which had been Little Ann's businesslike inspiration.

"T. Tembarom. New York Sunday Earth," read Munsberg, rather grudgingly. He looked at T. Tembarom, and T. Tembarom looked back at him. The normal human friendliness in the sharp boyish face did it.

"Vell," he said, making another jerk toward a chair, "if you ain't no agent, you can vait."

"Thank you," said Tembarom, and sat down. He had made another start, anyhow.

After this the packing went on fast and furious. A youth appeared from the back of the store, and ran here and there as he was ordered. Munsberg and his wife filled wooden and cardboard boxes with small cakes and larger ones, with sandwiches and salads, candies and crystallized fruits. Into the larger box was placed a huge cake with an icing temple on the top of it, with silver doves adorning it outside and in. There was no mistaking the poetic significance of that cake. Outside the blizzard whirled clouds of snow-particles through the air, and the van horse kept his head down and his forelegs braced. His driver had long since tried to cover him with a blanket which the wind continually tore loose from its fastenings, and flapped about the creature's sides. Inside the store grew hot. There was hurried moving about, banging of doors, excited voices, irascible orders given and countermanded. Tembarom found out in five minutes that the refreshments were for a wedding reception to be held at a place known as "The Hall," and the goods must be sent out in time to be ready for the preparations for the wedding supper that night.

"If I knew how to handle it, I could get stuff for a column just sitting here," he thought. He kept both eyes and ears open. He was sharp enough to realize that the mere sense of familiarity with detail which he was gaining was material in itself. Once or twice he got up and lent a hand with a box in his casual way, and once or twice he saw that he could lift some-thing down or up for Mrs. Munsberg, who was a little woman. The natural casualness of his way of jumping up to do the things prevented any suspicion of officiousness, and also prevented his waiting figure from beginning to wear the air of a superfluous object in the way. He waited a long time, and circumstances so favored him as to give him a chance or so. More than once exactly the right moment presented itself when he could interject an apposite remark. Twice he made Munsberg laugh, and twice Mrs. Munsberg voluntarily addressed him.

At last the boxes and parcels ware all carried out and stored in the van, after strugglings with the opening and shutting of doors, and battlings with outside weather.

When this was all over, Munsberg came back into the store, knocking his hands together and out of breath.

"Dot's all right," he said. "It'll all be there plenty time. Vouldn't have fell down on that order for twenty-vive dollars. Dot temple on the cake was splendid. Joseph he done it fine."

"He never done nothin' no finer," Mrs. Munsberg said. "It looked as good as anything on Fift' Avenoo."

Both were relieved and pleased with themselves, their store, and their cake-decorator. Munsberg spoke to Tembarom in the manner of a man who, having done a good thing, does not mind talking about it.

"Dot was a big order," he remarked.

"I should smile," answered Tembarom. "I'd like to know whose going to get outside all that good stuff. That wedding-cake took the tart away from anything I've ever seen. Which of the four hundred's going to eat it?"

"De man vot ordered dot cake," Munsberg swaggered, "he's not got to vorry along on vun million nor two. He owns de biggest brewery in New York, I guess in America. He's Schwartz of Schwartz & Kapfer."

"Well, he 's got it to burn!" said Tembarom.

"He's a mighty good man," went on Munsberg. "He's mighty fond of his own people. He made his first money in Harlem, and he had a big fight to get it; but his own people vas good to him, an' he's never forgot it. He's built a fine house here, an' his girls is fine girls. De vun's goin' to be married to-night her name's Rachel, an' she's goin' to marry a nice feller, Louis Levy. Levy built the big entertainment-hall vhere the reception's goin' to be. It's decorated vith two thousand dollars' worth of bride roses an' lilies of de valley an' smilax. All de up-town places vas bought out, an' den Schwartz vent down Fift' Avenoo."

The right moment had plainly arrived.

"Say, Mr. Munsberg," Tembarom broke forth, "you're giving me just what I wanted to ask you for. I'm the new up-town society reporter for the Sunday Earth, and I came in here to see if you wouldn't help me to get a show at finding out who was going to have weddings and society doings. I didn't know just how to start."

Munsberg gave a sort of grunt. He looked less amiable.

"I s'pose you're used to nothin' but Fift' Avenoo," he said.

Tembarom grinned exactly at the right time again. Not only his good teeth grinned, but his eyes grinned also, if the figure may be used.

"Fifth Avenue!" he laughed. "There's been no Fifth Avenue in mine. I'm not used to anything, but you may bet your life I'm going to get used to Harlem, if you people'll let me. I've just got this job, and I'm dead stuck on it. I want to make it go."

"He's mighty different from Biker," said Mrs. Munsberg in an undertone.

"Vhere's dod oder feller?" inquired Munsberg. "He vas a dam fool, dot oder feller, half corned most de time, an' puttin' on Clarence airs. No one was goin' to give him nothin'. He made folks mad at de start."

"I've got his job," said Tembarom, "and if I can't make it go, the page will be given up. It'll be my fault if that happens, not Harlem's. There's society enough up-town to make a first-class page, and I shall be sick if I can't get on to it."

He had begun to know his people. Munsberg was a good-natured, swaggering little Hebrew.

That the young fellow should make a clean breast of it and claim no down-town superiority, and that he should also have the business insight to realize that he might obtain valuable society items from such a representative confectioner as M. Munsberg, was a situation to incite amiable sentiments.

"Vell, you didn't come to de wrong place," he said. "All de biggest things comes to me, an' I don't mind tellin' you about 'em. 'T ain't goin' to do no harm. Weddings an' things dey ought to be wrote up, anyhow, if dey're done right. It's good for business. Vy don't dey have no pictures of de supper-tables? Dot'd be good."

"There's lots of receptions and weddings this month," said Mrs. Munsberg, becoming agreeably excited. "And there's plenty handsome young girls that'd like their pictures published.

"None of them have been in Sunday papers before, and they'd like it. The four Schwartz girls would make grand pictures. They dress splendid, and their bridesmaids dresses came from the biggest place in Fift' Avenoo."

"Say," exclaimed Tembarom, rising from his chair, "I'm in luck. Luck struck me the minute I turned in here. If you'll tell me where Schwartz lives, and where the hall is, and the church, and just anything else I can use, I'll go out and whoop up a page to beat the band." He was glowing with exultation. "I know I can do it. You've started me off."

Munsberg and his wife began to warm. It was almost as though they had charge of the society page themselves. There was something stimulating in the idea. There was a suggestion of social importance in it. They knew a number of people who would be pleased with the prospect of being in the Sunday Earth. They were of a race which holds together, and they gave not only the names and addresses of prospective entertainers, but those of florists and owners of halls where parties were given.

Mrs. Munsberg gave the name of a dressmaker of whom she shrewdly guessed that she would be amiably ready to talk to a society-page reporter.

"That Biker feller," she said, "got things down all wrong. He called fine white satin 'white nun's-veiling,' and he left out things. Never said nothing about Miss Lewishon's diamond ring what her grandpa gave her for a wedding-present. An' it cost two hundred and fifty."

"Well, I'm a pretty big fool myself," said Tembarom, "but I should have known better than that."

When he opened the door to go, Mrs. Munsberg called after him:

"When you get through, you come back here and tell us what you done. I'll give you a cup of hot coffee."

He returned to Mrs. Bowse's boarding-house so late that night that even Steinberger and Bowles had ended their day. The gas in the hall was turned down to a glimmering point, and the house was silent for the night. Even a cat who stole to him and rubbed herself against his leg miauwed in a sort of abortive whisper, opening her mouth wide, but emitting no sound. When he went cautiously up the staircase he carried his damp overcoat with him, and hung it in company with the tartan muffler close to the heater in the upper hall. Then he laid on his bedside table a package of papers and photographs.

After he had undressed, he dropped heavily into bed, exhausted, but elate.

"I'm dog-tired," he said, "but I guess I've got it going." And almost before the last word had uttered itself he fell into the deep sleep of worn-out youth.

CHAPTER IV

Mrs. Bowse's boarding-house began to be even better pleased with him than before. He had stories to tell, festivities to describe, and cheerful incidents to recount. The boarders assisted vicariously at weddings and wedding receptions, afternoon teas and dances, given in halls. "Up-town" seemed to them largely given to entertainment and hilarity of an enviably prodigal sort. Mrs. Bowse's guests were not of the class which entertains or is entertained, and the details of banquets and ball-dresses and money-spending were not uncheering material for conversation. Such topics suggested the presence and dispensing of a good deal of desirable specie, which in floating about might somehow reach those who needed it most. The impression was that T. Tembarom was having "a good time." It was not his way to relate any incidents which were not of a cheering or laughter-inspiring nature. He said nothing of the times when his luck was bad, when he made blunders, and, approaching the wrong people, was met roughly or grudgingly, and found no resource left but to beat a retreat. He made no mention of his experiences in the blizzard, which continued, and at times nearly beat breath and life out of him as he fought his way through it. Especially he told no story of the morning when, after having labored furiously over the writing of his "stuff" until long after midnight, he had taken it to Galton, and seen his face fall as he looked over it. To battle all day with a blizzard and occasional brutal discouragements, and to sit up half the night tensely absorbed in concentrating one's whole mental equipment upon the doing of unaccustomed work has its effect. As he waited, Tembarom unconsciously shifted from one foot to another, and had actually to swallow a sort of lump in his throat.

"I guess it won't do," he said rather uncertainly as Galton laid a sheet down.

Galton was worn out himself and harried by his nerves.

"No, it won't," he said; and then as he saw Tembarom move to the other foot he added, "Not as it is."

Tembarom braced himself and cleared his throat.

"If," he ventured—"well, you've been mighty easy on me, Mr Galton—and this is a big chance for a fellow like me. If it's too big a chance—why—that's all. But if it's anything I could change and it wouldn't be too much trouble to tell me—"

"There's no time to rewrite it," answered Galton. "It must be handed in to-morrow. It's too flowery. Too many adjectives. I've no time to give you—" He snatched up a blue pencil and began to slash at the paper with it. "Look here—and here—cut out that balderdash—cut this—and this—oh,—"

throwing the pencil down,—"you'd have to cut it all out. There's no time." He fell back in his chair with a hopeless movement, and rubbed his forehead nervously with the back of his hand. Ten people more or less were waiting to speak to him; he was worn out with the rush of work. He believed in the page, and did not want to give up his idea; but he didn't know a man to hand it to other than this untrained, eager ignoramus whom he had a queer personal liking for. He was no business of his, a mere stenographer in his office with whom he could be expected to have no relations, and yet a curious sort of friendliness verging on intimacy had developed between them.

"There'd be time if you thought it wouldn't do any harm to give me another chance," said Tembarom. "I can sit up all night. I guess I've caught on to what you DON'T want. I've put in too many fool words. I got them out of other papers, but I don't know how to use them. I guess I've caught on. Would it do any harm if you gave me till to-morrow?"

"No, it wouldn't," said Galton, desperately. "If you can't do it, there's no time to find another man, and the page must be cut out. It's been no good so far. It won't be missed. Take it along."

As he pushed back the papers, he saw the photographs, and picked one up.

"That bride's a good-looking girl. Who are these others? Bridesmaids? You've got a lot of stuff here. Biker couldn't get anything." He glanced up at the young fellow's rather pale face. "I thought you'd make friends. How did you get all this?"

"I beat the streets till I found it," said Tembarom. "I had luck right away. I went into a confectionery store where they make wedding-cakes. A good-natured little Dutchman and his wife kept it, and I talked to them—"

"Got next?" said Galton, grinning a little.

"They gave me addresses, and told me a whole lot of things. I got into the Schwartz wedding reception, and they treated me mighty well. A good many of them were willing to talk. I told them what a big thing the page was going to be, and I—well, I said the more they helped me the finer it would turn out. I said it seemed a shame there shouldn't be an up-town page when such swell entertainments were given. I've got a lot of stuff there."

Galton laughed.

"You'd get it," he said. "If you knew how to handle it, you'd make it a hit. Well, take it along. If it isn't right tomorrow, it's done for."

Tembarom didn't tell stories or laugh at dinner that evening. He said he had a headache. After dinner he bolted upstairs after Little Ann, and caught her before she mounted to her upper floor.

"Will you come and save my life again?" he said. "I'm in the tightest place I ever was in in my life."

"I'll do anything I can, Mr. Tembarom," she answered, and as his face had grown flushed by this time she looked anxious. "You look downright feverish."

"I've got chills as well as fever," he said. "It's the page. It seems like I was going to fall down on it."

She turned back at once.

"No you won't, Mr. Tembarom," she said "I'm just right-down sure you won't."

They went down to the parlor again, and though there were people in it, they found a corner apart, and in less than ten minutes he had told her what had happened.

She took the manuscript he handed to her.

"If I was well educated, I should know how to help you," she said, "but I've only been to a common Manchester school. I don't know anything about elegant language. What are these?" pointing to the blue-pencil marks.

Tembarom explained, and she studied the blue slashes with serious attention.

"Well," she said in a few minutes, laying the manuscript down, "I should have cut those words out myself if—if you'd asked me which to take away. They're too showy, Mr. Tembarom."

Tembarom whipped a pencil out of his pocket and held it out.

"Say," he put it to her, "would you take this and draw it through a few of the other showy ones?"

"I should feel as if I was taking too much upon myself," she said. "I don't know anything about it."

"You know a darned sight more than I do," Tembarom argued. "I didn't know they were showy. I thought they were the kind you had to put in newspaper stuff."

She held the sheets of paper on her knee, and bent her head over them. Tembarom watched her dimples flash in and out as she worked away like a child correcting an exercise. Presently he saw she was quite absorbed. Sometimes she stopped and thought, pressing her lips together; sometimes she changed a letter. There was no lightness in her manner. A badly mutilated stocking would have claimed her attention in the same way.

"I think I'd put 'house' there instead of 'mansion' if I were you," she suggested once.

"Put in a whole block of houses if you like," he answered gratefully. "Whatever you say goes. I believe Galton would say the same thing."

She went over sheet after sheet, and though she knew nothing about it, she cut out just what Galton would have cut out. She put the papers together at last and gave them back to Tembarom, getting up from her seat.

"I must go back to father now," she said. "I promised to make him a good cup of coffee over the little oil-stove. If you'll come and knock at the door I'll give you one. It will help you to keep fresh while you work."

Tembarom did not go to bed at all that night, and he looked rather fagged the next morning when he handed back the "stuff" entirely rewritten. He swallowed several times quite hard as he waited for the final verdict.

"You did catch on to what I didn't want," Galton said at last. "You will catch on still more as you get used to the work. And you did get the 'stuff'."

"That—you mean—that goes?" Tembarom stammered.

"Yes, it goes," answered Galton. "You can turn it in. We'll try the page for a month."

"Gee! Thank the Lord!" said Tembarom, and then he laughed an excited boyish laugh, and the blood came back to his face. He had a whole month before him, and if he had caught on as soon as this, a month would teach him a lot.

He'd work like a dog.

He worked like a healthy young man impelled by a huge enthusiasm, and seeing ahead of him something he had had no practical reason for aspiring to. He went out in all weathers and stayed out to all hours. Whatsoever rebuffs or difficulties he met with he never was even on the verge of losing his nerve. He actually enjoyed himself tremendously at times. He made friends; people began to like to see him. The Munsbergs regarded him as an inspiration of their own.

"He seen my name over de store and come in here first time he vas sent up dis vay to look for t'ings to write," Mr. Munsberg always explained. "Ve vas awful busy—time of the Schwartz vedding, an' dere vas dat blizzard. He owned up he vas new, an' vanted some vun vhat knew to tell him vhat vas goin' on. 'Course I could do it. Me an' my vife give him addresses an' a lot of items. He vorked 'em up good. Dot up-town page is gettin' first-rate. He says he don' know vhat he'd have done if he hadn't turned up here dot day."

Tembarom, having "caught on" to his fault of style, applied himself with vigor to elimination. He kept his tame dictionary chained to the leg of his table—an old kitchen table which Mrs. Bowse scrubbed and put into his hall bedroom, overcrowding it greatly. He turned to Little Ann at moments of desperate uncertainty, but he was man enough to do his work himself. In glorious moments when he was rather sure that Galton was far from unsatisfied with his progress, and Ann had looked more than usually distracting in her aloof and sober alluringness,—it was her entire aloofness which so stirred his blood,—he sometimes stopped scribbling and lost his head for a minute or so, wondering if a fellow ever COULD "get away with it" to the extent of making enough to—but he always pulled himself up in time.

"Nice fool I look, thinking that way!" he would say to himself. "She'd throw me down hard if she knew. But, my Lord! ain't she just a peach!"

It was in the last week of the month of trial which was to decide the permanency of the page that he came upon the man Mrs. Bowse's boarders called his "Freak." He never called him a "freak" himself even at the first. Even his somewhat undeveloped mind felt itself confronted at the outset with something too abnormal and serious, something with a suggestion of the weird and tragic in it.

In this wise it came about:

The week had begun with another blizzard, which after the second day had suddenly changed its mind, and turned into sleet and rain which filled the streets with melted snow, and made walking a fearsome thing. Tembarom had plenty of walking to do. This week's page was his great effort, and was to be a "dandy." Galton must be shown what pertinacity could do.

"I'm going to get into it up to my neck, and then strike out," he said at breakfast on Monday morning.

Thursday was his most strenuous day. The weather had decided to change again, and gusts of sleet were being driven about, which added cold to sloppiness. He had found it difficult to get hold of some details he specially wanted. Two important and extremely good-looking brides had refused to see him because Biker had enraged them in his day. He had slighted the description of their dresses at a dance where they had been the observed of all observers, and had worn things brought from Paris. Tembarom had gone from house to house. He had even searched out aunts whose favor he had won professionally. He had appealed to his dressmaker, whose affection he had by that time fully gained. She was doing work in the brides' houses, and could make it clear that he would not call peau de cygne "Surah silk," nor duchess lace "Baby Irish." But the young ladies enjoyed being besought by a society page. It was something to discuss with one's bridesmaids and friends, to protest that "those interviewers" give a person no peace. "If you don't want to be in the papers, they'll put you in whether you like it or not, however often you refuse them." They kept Tembarom running about, they raised faint hopes, and then went out when he called, leaving no messages, but allowing the servant to hint that if he went up to Two Hundred and Seventy-fifth Street he might chance to find them.

"All right," said Tembarom to the girl, delighting her by lifting his hat genially as he turned to go down the steps. "I'll just keep going. The Sunday Earth can't come out without those photographs in it. I should lose my job."

When at last he ran the brides to cover it was not at Two Hundred and Seventy-fifth Street, but in their own home, to which they had finally returned. They had heard from the servant-girl about what the young gentleman from the Sunday Earth had said, and they were mollified by his proper appreciation of values. Tembarom's dressmaker friend also proffered information.

"I know him myself," she said, "and he's a real nice gentle-manlike young man. He's not a bit like Biker. He doesn't think he knows everything. He came to me from Mrs. Munsberg, just to ask me the names of fashionable materials. He said it was more important than a man knew till he found out" Miss Stuntz chuckled.

"He asked me to lend him some bits of samples so he could learn them off by heart, and know them when he saw them. He's got a pleasant laugh; shows his teeth, and they're real pretty and white; and he just laughed like a boy and said: 'These samples are my alphabet, Miss Stuntz. I'm going to learn to read words of three syllables in them.'"

When late in the evening Tembarom, being let out of the house after his interview, turned down the steps again, he carried with him all he had wanted—information and photographs, even added picturesque details. He was prepared to hand in a fuller and better page than he had ever handed in before. He was in as elated a frame of mind as a young man can be when he is used up with tramping the streets, and running after street-cars, to stand up in them and hang by a strap. He had been wearing a new pair of boots, one of which rubbed his heel and had ended by raising a blister worthy of attention. To reach the nearest "L" station he must walk across town, through several deserted streets in the first stages of being built up, their vacant lots surrounded by high board fencing covered with huge advertising posters. The hall bedroom, with the gas turned up and the cheap, red-cotton comfort on the bed, made an alluring picture as he faced the sleety wind.

"If I cut across to the avenue and catch the 'L,' I'm bound to get there sometime, anyhow," he said as he braced himself and set out on his way.

The blister on his heel had given him a good deal of trouble, and he was obliged to stop a moment to ease it, and he limped when he began to walk again. But he limped as fast as he could, while the sleety rain beat in his face, across one street, down another for a block or so, across another, the melting snow soaking even the new boots as he splashed through it. He bent his head, however, and limped steadily. At this end of the city many of the streets were only scantily built up, and he was passing through one at the corner of which was a big vacant lot. At the other corner a row of cheap houses which had only reached their second story waited among piles of bricks and frozen mortar for the return of the workmen the blizzard had dispersed. It was a desolate-enough thoroughfare, and not a soul was in sight. The vacant lot was fenced in with high boarding plastered over with flaring sheets advertising whiskies, sauces, and theatrical ventures. A huge picture of a dramatically interrupted wedding ceremony done in reds and yellows, and announcing in large letters that Mr. Isaac Simonson presented Miss Evangeline St. Clair in "Rent Asunder," occupied several yards of the boarding. As he reached it, the heel of Tembarom's boot pressed, as it seemed to him, a red-hot coal on the flesh. He had rubbed off the blister. He was obliged to stop a moment again.

"Gee whizz!" he exclaimed through his teeth, "I shall have to take my boot off and try to fix it."

To accomplish this he leaned against the boarding and Miss Evangeline St. Clair being "Rent Asunder" in the midst of the wedding service. He cautiously removed his boot, and finding a hole in his sock in the place where the blister had rubbed off, he managed to protect the raw spot by pulling the sock over it. Then he drew on his boot again.

"That'll be better," he said, with a long breath.

As he stood on his feet again he started involuntarily. This was not because the blister had hurt him, but because he had heard behind him a startling sound.

"What's that?" broke from him. "What's that?"

He turned and listened, feeling his heart give a quick thump. In the darkness of the utterly empty street the thing was unnatural enough to make any man jump. He had heard it between two gusts of wind, and through another he heard it again—an uncanny, awful sobbing, broken by a hopeless wail of words.

"I can't remember! I can't—remember! O my God!"

And it was not a woman's voice or a child's; it was a man's, and there was an eerie sort of misery in it which made Tembarom feel rather sick. He had never heard a man sobbing before. He belonged to a class which had no time for sobs. This sounded ghastly.

"Good Lord!" he said, "the fellow's crying! A man!"

The sound came directly behind him. There was not a human being in sight. Even policemen do not loiter in empty streets.

"Hello!" he cried. "Where are you?"

But the low, horrible sound went on, and no answer came. His physical sense of the presence of the blister was blotted out by the abnormal thrill of the moment. One had to find out about a thing like that one just had to. One could not go on and leave it behind uninvestigated in the dark and emptiness of a street no one was likely to pass through. He listened more intently. Yes, it was just behind him.

"He's in the lot behind the fence," he said. "How did he get there?"

He began to walk along the boarding to find a gap. A few yards farther on he came upon a broken place in the inclosure—a place where boards had sagged until they fell down, or had perhaps been pulled down by boys who wanted to get inside. He went through it, and found lie was in the usual vacant lot long given up to rubbish. When he stood still a moment he heard the sobbing again, and followed the sound to the place behind the boarding against which he had supported himself when he took off his boot.

A man was lying on the ground with his arms flung out. The street lamp outside the boarding cast light enough to reveal him. Tembarom felt as though he had suddenly found himself taking part in a melodrama,—"The Streets of New York," for choice,—though no melodrama had ever given him this slightly shaky feeling. But when a fellow looked up against it as hard as this, what you had to do was to hold your nerve and make him feel he was going to be helped. The normal human thing spoke loud in him.

"Hello, old man!" he said with cheerful awkwardness. "What's hit you?"

The man started and scrambled to his feet as though he were frightened. He was wet, unshaven, white and shuddering, piteous to look at. He stared with wild eyes, his chest heaving.

"What's up?" said Tembarom.

The man's breath caught itself.

"I don't remember." There was a touch of horror in his voice, though he was evidently making an effort to control him-self. "I can't—I can't remember."
"What's your name? You remember that?" Tembarom put it to him.

"N-n-no!" agonizingly. "If I could! If I could!"

"How did you get in here?"

"I came in because I saw a policeman. He wouldn't understand. He would have stopped me. I must not be stopped. I MUST not."

"Where were you going?" asked Tembarom, not knowing what else to say.

"Home! My God! man, home!" and he fell to shuddering again. He put his arm against the boarding and dropped his head against it. The low, hideous sobbing tore him again.

T. Tembarom could not stand it. In his newsboy days he had never been able to stand starved dogs and homeless cats. Mrs. Bowse was taking care of a wretched dog for him at the present moment. He had not wanted the poor brute,—he was not particularly fond of dogs,—but it had followed him home, and after he had given it a bone or so, it had licked its chops and turned up its eyes at him with such abject appeal that he had not been able to turn it into the streets again. He was unsentimental, but ruled by primitive emotions. Also he had a sudden recollection of a night when as a little fellow he had gone into a vacant lot and cried as like this as a child could. It was a bad night when some "tough" big boys had turned him out of a warm corner in a shed, and he had had nowhere to go, and being a friendly little fellow, the unfriendliness had hit him hard. The boys had not seen him crying, but he remembered it. He drew near, and put his hand on the shaking shoulder.

"Say, don't do that," he said. "I'll help you to remember."

He scarcely knew why he said it. There was something in the situation and in the man himself which was compelling. He was not of the tramp order. His wet clothes had been decent, and his broken, terrified voice was neither coarse nor nasal. He lifted his head and caught Tembarom's arm, clutching it with desperate fingers.

"Could you?" he poured forth the words. "Could you? I'm not quite mad. Something happened. If I could be quiet! Don't let them stop me! My God! my God! my God! I can't say it. It's not far away, but it won't come back. You're a good fellow; if you're human, help me! help me! help me!" He clung to Tembarom with hands which shook; his eyes were more abject than the starved dog's; he choked, and awful tears rolled down his cheeks. "Only help me," he cried—"just help, help, help—for a while. Perhaps not long. It would come back." He made a horrible effort. "Listen! My name—I am—I am—it's—"

He was down on the ground again, groveling. His efforts had failed. Tembarom, overwrought himself, caught at him and dragged him up.

"Make a fight," he said. "You can't lie down like that. You've got to put up a fight. It'll come back. I tell you it will. You've had a clip on the head or something. Let me call an ambulance and take you to the hospital."

The next moment he was sorry he had said the words, the man's terror was so ill to behold. He grew livid with it, and uttered a low animal cry.

"Don't drop dead over it," said Tembarom, rather losing his head. "I won't do it, though what in thunder I'm going to do with you I don't know. You can't stay here."

"For God's sake!" said the man. "For God's sake!" He put his shaking hand on Tembarom again, and looked at him with a bewildered scrutiny. "I'm not afraid of you," he said; "I don't know why. There's something all right about you. If you'll stand by me—you'd stand by a man, I'd swear. Take me somewhere quiet. Let me get warm and think."

"The less you think now the better," answered Tembarom. "You want a bed and a bath and a night's rest. I guess I've let myself in for it. You brush off and brace yourself and come with me."

There was the hall bedroom and the red-cotton comfort for one night at least, and Mrs. Bowse was a soft-hearted woman. If she'd heard the fellow sobbing behind the fence, she'd have been in a worse fix than he was. Women were kinder-hearted than men, anyhow. The way the fellow's voice sounded when he said, "Help me, help me, help me!" sounded as though he was in hell. "Made me feel as if I was bracing up a chap that was going to be electrocuted," he thought, feeling sickish again. "I've not got backbone enough to face that sort of thing. Got to take him somewhere."

They were walking toward the "L" together, and he was wondering what he should say to Mrs. Bowse when he saw his companion fumbling under his coat at the back as though he was in search of something. His hands being unsteady, it took him some moments to get at what he wanted. He evidently had a belt or a hidden pocket. He got something out and stopped under a street light to show it to Tembarom. His hands still shook when he held them out, and his look was a curious, puzzled, questioning one. What he passed over to Tembarom was a roll of money. Tembarom rather lost his breath as he saw the number on two five-hundred-dollar bills, and of several hundreds, besides twenties, tens, and fives.

"Take it—keep it," he said. "It will pay."

"Hully gee!" cried Tembarom, aghast. "Don't go giving away your whole pile to the first fellow you meet. I don't want it."

"Take it." The stranger put his hand on his shoulder, the abject look in his eyes harrowingly like the starved dog's again.

"There's something all right about you. You'll help me."

"If I don't take it for you, some one will knock you upon the head for it." Tembarom hesitated, but the next instant he stuffed it all in his pocket, incited thereto by the sound of a whizzing roar.

"There's the 'L' coming," he cried; "run for all you're worth." And they fled up the street and up the steps, and caught it without a second to spare.

CHAPTER V

At about the time Tembarom made his rush to catch the "L" Joseph Hutchinson was passing through one of his periodical fits of infuriated discouragement. Little Ann knew they would occur every two or three days, and she did not wonder at them. Also she knew that if she merely sat still and listened as she sewed, she would be doing exactly what her mother would have done and what her father would find a sort of irritated comfort in. There was no use in citing people's villainies and calling them names unless you had an audience who would seem to agree to the justice of your accusations.

So Mr. Hutchinson charged up and down the room, his face red, and his hands thrust in his coat pockets. He was giving his opinions of America and Americans, and he spoke with his broadest Manchester accent, and threw in now and then a word or so of Lancashire dialect to add roughness and strength, the angrier a Manchester man being, the broader and therefore the more forcible his accent. "Tha" is somehow a great deal more bitter or humorous or affectionate than the mere ordinary "You" or "Yours."

"'Merica," he bellowed—"dang 'Merica! I says—an' dang 'Mericans. Goin' about th' world braggin' an' boastin' about their sharpness an' their open-'andedness. 'Go to 'Merica,' folks'll tell you, 'with an invention, and there's dozens of millionaires ready to put money in it.' Fools!"

"Now, Father,"—Little Ann's voice was as maternal as her mother's had been,—"now, Father, love, don't work yourself up into a passion. You know it's not good for you."

"I don't need to work myself up into one. I'm in one. A man sells everything he owns to get to 'Merica, an' when he gets there what does he find? He canna' get near a millionaire. He's pushed here an scuffled there, an' told this chap can't see him, an' that chap isn't interested, an' he must wait his chance to catch this one. An' he waits an' waits, an' goes up in elevators an' stands on one leg in lobbies, till he's broke' down an' sick of it, an' has to go home to England steerage."

Little Ann looked up from her sewing. He had been walking furiously for half an hour, and had been tired to begin with. She had heard his voice break roughly as he said the last words. He threw himself astride a chair and, crossing his arms on the back of it, dropped his head on them. Her mother never allowed this. Her idea was that women were made to tide over such moments for the weaker sex. Far had it been from the mind of Mrs. Hutchinson to call it weaker. "But there's times, Ann, when just for a bit they're just like children. They need comforting without being let to know they are being comforted. You know how it is when your back aches, and some one just slips a pillow under it in the right place without saying anything. That's what women can do if they've got heads. It needs a head."

Little Ann got up and went to the chair. She began to run her fingers caressingly through the thick, grizzled hair.

"There, Father, love, there!" she said. "We are going back to England, at any rate, aren't we? And grandmother will be so glad to have us with her in her cottage. And America's only one place."

"I tried it first, dang it!" jerked out Hutchinson. "Every one told me to do it." He quoted again with derisive scorn: "'You go to 'Merica. 'Merica's the place for a chap like you. 'Merica's the place for inventions.' Liars!"

Little Ann went on rubbing the grizzled head lovingly.

"Well, now we're going back to try England. You never did really try England. And you know how beautiful it'll be in the country, with the primroses in bloom and the young lambs in the fields." The caressing hand grew even softer. "And you're not going to forget how mother believed in the invention; you can't do that."

Hutchinson lifted his head and looked at her.

"Eh, Ann," he said, "you are a comfortable little body. You've got a way with you just like your poor mother had. You always say the right thing to help a chap pull himself together. Your mother did believe in it, didn't she?"

She had, indeed, believed in it, though her faith was founded more upon confidence in "Mr. Hutchinson" than in any profound knowledge of the mechanical appliance his inspiration would supply. She knew it had something important to do with locomotive engines, and she knew that if railroad magnates would condescend to consider it, her husband was sure that fortune would flow in. She had lived with the "invention," as it was respectfully called, for years.

"That she did," answered Little Ann. "And before she died she said to me: 'Little Ann,' she said, 'there's one thing you must never let your father do. You must never let him begin not to believe in his invention. Your father's a clever man, and it's a clever invention, and it'll make his fortune yet. You must remind him how I believed in it and how sure I was.'"

Hutchinson rubbed his hands thoughtfully. He had heard this before, but it did him good to hear it again.

"She said that, did she?" he found vague comfort in saying. "She said that?"

"Yes, she did, Father. It was the very day before she died."

"Well, she never said anything she hadn't thought out," he said in slow retrospection. "And she had a good head of her own. Eh, she was a wonderful woman, she was, for sticking to things. That was th' Lancashire in her. Lancashire folks knows their own minds."

"Mother knew hers," said Ann. "And she always said you knew yours. Come and sit in your own chair, Father, and have your paper."

She had tided him past the worst currents without letting him slip into them.

"I like folks that knows their own minds," he said as he sat down and took his paper from her. "You know yours, Ann; and there's that Tembarom chap. He knows his. I've been noticing that chap." There was a certain pleasure in using a tone of amiable patronage. "He's got a way with him that's worth money to him in business, if he only knew it."

"I don't think he knows he's got a way," Little Ann said. "His way is just him."

"He just gets over people with it, like he got over me. I was ready to knock his head off first time he spoke to me. I was ready to knock anybody's head off that day. I'd just had that letter from Hadman. He made me sick wi' the way he pottered an' played the fool about the invention. He believed in it right enough, but he hadn't the courage of a mouse. He wasn't goin' to be the first one to risk his money. Him, with all he has! He's the very chap to be able to set it goin'. If I could have got some one else to put up brass, it'd have started him. It's want o' backbone, that's the matter wi' Hadman an' his lot."

"Some of these days some of them 're going to get their eyes open," said Little Ann, "and then the others will be sorry. Mr. Tembarom says they'll fall over themselves to get in on the ground floor."

Hutchinson chuckled.

"That's New York," he said. "He's a rum chap. But he thinks a good bit of the invention. I've talked it over with him, because I've wanted to talk, and the one thing I've noticed about Tembarom is that he can keep his mouth shut."

"But he talks a good deal," said Ann.

"That's the best of it. You'd think he was telling all he knows, and he's not by a fat lot. He tells you what you'll like to hear, and he's not sly; but he can keep a shut mouth. That's Lancashire. Some folks can't do it even when they want to."

"His father came from England."

"That's where the lad's sense comes from. Perhaps he's Lancashire. He had a lot of good ideas about the way to get at Hadman."

A knock at the door broke in upon them. Mrs. Bowse presented herself, wearing a novel expression on her face. It was at once puzzled and not altogether disagreeably excited.

"I wish you would come down into the dining-room, Little Ann." She hesitated. "Mr. Tembaron's brought home such a queer man. He picked him up ill in the street. He wants me to let him stay with him for the night, anyhow. I don't think he's crazy, but I guess he's lost his memory. Queerest thing I ever saw. He doesn't know his name or anything."

"See here," broke out Hutchinson, dropping his hands and his paper on his knee, "I'm not going to have Ann goin' down stairs to quiet lunatics."

"He's as quiet as a child," Mrs. Bowse protested. "There's something pitiful about him, he seems so frightened. He's drenched to the skin."

"Call an ambulance and send him to the hospital," advised Hutchinson.

"That's what Mr. Tembarom says he can't do. It frightens him to death to speak of it. He just clings to Mr. Tembarom sort of awful, as if he thinks he'll save his life. But that isn't all," she added in an amazed tone; "he's given Mr. Tembarom more than two thousand dollars."

"What!" shouted Hutchinson, bounding to his feet quite unconsciously.

"What!" exclaimed Little Ann.

"Just you come and look at it," answered Mrs. Bowse, nodding her head. "There's over two thousand dollars in bills spread out on the table in the dining-room this minute. He had it in a belt pocket, and he dragged it out in the street and would make Mr. Tembarom take it. Do come and tell us what to do."

"I'd get him to take off his wet clothes and get into bed, and drink some hot spirits and water first," said Little Ann. "Wouldn't you, Mrs. Bowse?"

Hutchinson got up, newspaper in hand.

"I say, I'd like to go down and have a look at that chap myself," he announced.

"If he's so frightened, perhaps—" Little Ann hesitated.

"That's it," put in Mrs. Bowse. "He's so nervous it'd make him worse to see another man. You'd better wait, Mr. Hutchinson."

Hutchinson sat down rather grumpily, and Mrs. Bowse and Little Ann went down the stairs together.

"I feel real nervous myself," said Mrs. Bowse, "it's so queer. But he's not crazy. He's quiet enough."

As they neared the bottom of the staircase Little Ann could see over the balustrade into the dining-room. The strange man was sitting by the table, his disordered, black-haired head on his arm. He looked like an exhausted thing. Tembarom was sitting by him, and was talking in an encouraging voice. He had laid a hand on one of the stranger's. On the table beside them was spread a number of bills which had evidently just been counted.

"Here's the ladies," said Tembarom.

The stranger lifted his head and, having looked, rose and stood upright, waiting. It was the involuntary, mechanical action of a man who had been trained among gentlemen.

"It's Mrs. Bowse again, and she's brought Miss Hutchinson down with her. Miss Hutchinson always knows what to do," explained Tembarom in his friendly voice.

The man bowed, and his bewildered eyes fixed themselves on Little Ann.

"Thank you," he said. "It's very kind of you. I—I am—in great trouble."

Little Ann went to him and smiled her motherly smile at him.

"You're very wet," she said. "You'll take a bad cold if you're not careful. Mrs. Bowse thinks you ought to go right to bed and have something hot to drink."

"It seems a long time since I was in bed," he answered her.

"I'm very tired. Thank you." He drew a weary, sighing breath, but he didn't move his eyes from the girl's face. Perhaps the cessation of action in certain cells of his brain had increased action in others. He looked as though he were seeing something in Little Ann's face which might not have revealed itself so clearly to the more normal gaze.

He moved slightly nearer to her. He was a tall man, and had to look down at her.

"What is your name?" he asked anxiously. "Names trouble me."

It was Ann who drew a little nearer to him now. She had to look up, and the soft, absorbed kindness in her eyes might, Tembarom thought, have soothed a raging lion, it was so intent on its purpose.

"My name is Ann Hutchinson; but never you mind about it now," she said. "I'll tell it to you again. Let Mr. Tembarom take you up-stairs to bed. You'll be better in the morning." And because his hollow eyes rested on her so fixedly she put her hand on his wet sleeve.

"You're wet through," she said. "That won't do."

He looked down at her hand and then at her face again.

"Help me," he pleaded, "just help me. I don't know what's happened. Have I gone mad?"

"No," she answered; "not a bit. It'll all come right after a while; you'll see."

"Will it, will it?" he begged, and then suddenly his eyes were full of tears. It was a strange thing to see him in his bewildered misery try to pull himself together, and bite his shaking lips as though he vaguely remembered that he was a man. "I beg pardon," he faltered: "I suppose I'm ill."

"I don't know where to put him," Mrs. Bowse was saying half aside; "I've not got a room empty."

"Put him in my bed and give me a shake-down on the floor," said Tembarom. "That'll be all right. He doesn't want me to leave him, anyhow."

He turned to the money on the table.

"Say," he said to his guest, "there's two thousand five hundred dollars here. We've counted it to make sure. That's quite some money. And it's yours—"

The stranger looked disturbed and made a nervous gesture.

"Don't, don't!" he broke in. "Keep it. Some one took the rest. This was hidden. It will pay."

"You see he isn't real' out of his mind," Mrs. Bowse murmured feelingly.

"No, not real' out of it," said Tembarom. "Say,"—as an inspiration occurred to him,—"I guess maybe Miss Hutchinson will keep it. Will you, Little Ann? You can give it to him when he wants it."

"It's a good bit of money," said Little Ann, soberly; "but I can put it in a bank and pay Mrs. Bowse his board every week. Yes, I'll take it. Now he must go to bed. It's a comfortable little room," she said to the stranger, "and Mrs. Bowse will make you a hot milk-punch. That'll be nourishing."

"Thank you," murmured the man, still keeping his yearning eyes on her. "Thank you."

So he was taken up to the fourth floor and put into Tembarom's bed. The hot milk-punch seemed to take the chill out of him, and when, by lying on his pillow and gazing at the shakedown on the floor as long as he could keep his eyes open, he had convinced himself that Tembarom was going to stay with him, he fell asleep.

Little Ann went back to her father carrying a roll of bills in her hands. It was a roll of such size that Hutchinson started up in his chair and stared at the sight of it.

"Is that the money?" he exclaimed. "What are you going to do with it? What have you found out, lass?"

"Yes, this is it," she answered. "Mr. Tembarom asked me to take care of it. I'm going to put it in the bank. But we haven't found out anything."

CHAPTER VI

His was the opening incident of the series of extraordinary and altogether incongruous events which took place afterwards, as it appeared to T. Tembarom, like scenes in a play in which he had become involved in a manner which one might be inclined to regard humorously and make jokes about, because it was a thousand miles away from anything like real life. That was the way it struck him. The events referred to, it was true, were things one now and then read about in newspapers, but while the world realized that they were actual occurrences, one rather regarded them, when their parallels were reproduced in books and plays, as belonging alone to the world of pure and highly romantic fiction.

"I guess the reason why it seems that way," he summed it up to Hutchinson and Little Ann, after the worst had come to the worst, "is because we've not only never known any one it's happened to, but we've never known any one that's known any one it's happened to. I've got to own up that it makes me feel as if the fellows'd just yell right out laughing when they heard it."

The stranger's money had been safely deposited in a bank, and the stranger himself still occupied Tembarom's bedroom. He slept a great deal and was very quiet. With great difficulty Little Ann had persuaded him to let a doctor see him, and the doctor had been much interested in his case. He had expected to find some signs of his having received accidentally or otherwise a blow upon the head, but on examination he found no scar or wound. The condition he was in was frequently the result of concussion of the brain, sometimes of prolonged nervous strain or harrowing mental shock. Such cases occurred not infrequently. Quiet and entire freedom from excitement would do more for such a condition than anything else. If he was afraid of strangers, by all means keep them from him. Tembarom had been quite right in letting him think he would help him to remember, and that somehow he would in the end reach the place he had evidently set out to go to. Nothing must be allowed to excite him. It was well he had had money on his person and that he had fallen into friendly hands. A city hospital would not have been likely to help him greatly. The restraint of its necessary discipline might have alarmed him.

So long as he was persuaded that Tembarom was not going to desert him, he was comparatively calm, though sunk in a piteous and tormented melancholy. His worst hours were when he sat alone in the hall bedroom, with his face buried in his hands. He would so sit without moving or speaking, and Little Ann discovered that at these times he was trying to remember. Sometimes he would suddenly rise and walk about the little room, muttering, with woe in his eyes. Ann, who saw how hard this was for him, found also that to attempt to check or distract him was even worse. When, sitting in her father's room, which was on the other side of the wall, she heard his fretted, hurried pacing feet, her face lost its dimpled cheerfulness. She wondered if her mother would not have discovered some way of clearing the black cloud distracting his brain. Nothing would induce him to go down to the boarders' dining-room for his meals, and the sight of a servant alarmed him so that it was Ann who took him the scant food he would eat. As the time of her return to England with her father drew near, she wondered what Mr. Tembarom would do without her services. It was she who suggested that they must have a name for him, and the name of a part of Manchester had provided one. There was a place called Strangeways, and one night when, in talking to her father, she referred to it in Tembarom's presence, he suddenly seized upon it.

"Strangeways," he said. "That'd make a good-enough name for him. Let's call him Mr. Strangeways. I don't like the way the fellows have of calling him 'the Freak.'"

So the name had been adopted, and soon became an established fact.

"The way I feel about him," Tembarom said, "is that the fellow's not a bit of a joke. What I see is that he's up against about the toughest proposition I've ever known. Gee! that fellow's not crazy. He's worse. If he was out-and-out dippy and didn't know it, he'd be all right. Likely as not he'd be thinking he was the Pope of Rome or Anna Held. What knocks him out is that he's just right enough to know he's wrong, and to be trying to get back. He reminds me of one of those chaps the papers tell about sometimes—fellows that go to work in livery-stables for ten years and call themselves Bill Jones, and then wake up some morning and remember they're some high-browed minister of the gospel named the Rev. James Cadwallader."

When the curtain drew up on Tembarom's amazing drama, Strangeways had been occupying his bed nearly three weeks, and he himself had been sleeping on a cot Mrs. Bowse had put up for him in his room. The Hutchinsons were on the point of sailing for England—steerage—on the steamship Transatlantic, and Tembarom was secretly torn into fragments, though he had done well with the page and he was daring to believe that at the end of the month Galton would tell him he had "made good" and the work would continue indefinitely.

If that happened, he would be raised to "twenty-five per" and would be a man of means. If the Hutchinsons had not been going away, he would have been floating in clouds of rose color. If he could persuade Little Ann to take him in hand when she'd had time to "try him out," even Hutchinson could not utterly flout a fellow who was making his steady twenty-five per on a big paper, and was on such terms with his boss that he might get other chances.

Gee! but he was a fellow that luck just seemed to chase, anyhow! Look at the other chaps, lots of 'em, who knew twice as much as he did, and had lived in decent homes and gone to school and done their darned best, too, and then hadn't been able to get there! It didn't seem fair somehow that he should run into such pure luck.

The day arrived when Galton was to give his decision. Tembarom was going to hand in his page, and while he was naturally a trifle nervous, his nervousness would have been a hopeful and not unpleasant thing but that the Transatlantic sailed in two days, and in the Hutchinson's rooms Little Ann was packing her small trunk and her father's bigger one, which held more models and drawings than clothing. Hutchinson was redder in the face than usual, and indignant condemnation of America and American millionaires possessed his soul. Everybody was rather depressed. One boarder after another had wakened to a realization that, with the passing of Little Ann, Mrs. Bowse's establishment, even with the parlor, the cozy-corner, and the second-hand pianola to support it, would be a deserted-seeming thing. Mrs. Bowse felt the tone of low spirits about the table, and even had a horrible secret fear that certain of her best boarders might decide to go elsewhere, merely to change surroundings from which they missed something. Her eyes were a little red, and she made great efforts to keep things going.

"I can only keep the place up when I've no empty rooms," she had said to Mrs. Peck, "but I'd have boarded her free if her father would have let her stay. But he wouldn't, and, anyway, she'd no more let him go off alone than she'd jump off Brooklyn Bridge."

It had been arranged that partly as a farewell banquet and partly to celebrate Galton's decision about the page, there was to be an oyster stew that night in Mr. Hutchinson's room, which was distinguished as a bed-sitting-room. Tembarom had diplomatically suggested it to Mr. Hutchinson. It was to be Tembarom's oyster supper, and somehow he managed to convey that it was only a proper and modest tribute to Mr. Hutchinson himself. First-class oyster stew and pale ale were not so bad when properly suggested, therefore Mr. Hutchinson consented. Jim Bowles and Julius Steinberger were to come in to share the feast, and Mrs. Bowse had promised to prepare.

It was not an inspiring day for Little Ann. New York had seemed a bewildering and far too noisy place for her when she had come to it directly from her grandmother's cottage in the English village, where she had spent her last three months before leaving England. The dark rooms of the five-storied boarding-house had seemed gloomy enough to her, and she had found it much more difficult to adjust herself to her surroundings than she could have been induced to admit to her father. At first his temper and the open contempt for American habits and institutions which he called "speaking his mind" had given her a great deal of careful steering through shoals to do. At the outset the boarders had resented him, and sometimes had snapped back their own views of England and courts. Violent and disparaging argument had occasionally been imminent, and Mrs. Bowse had worn an ominous look. Their rooms had in fact been "wanted" before their first week had come to an end, and Little Ann herself scarcely knew how she had tided over that situation. But tide it over she did, and by supernatural effort and watchfulness she contrived to soothe Mrs. Bowse until she had been in the house long enough to make friends with people and aid her father to realize that, if they went elsewhere, they might find only the same class of boarders, and there would be the cost of moving to consider. She had beguiled an armchair from Mrs. Bowse, and had recovered it herself with a remnant of crimson stuff secured from a miscellaneous heap at a marked-down sale at a department store. She had arranged his books and papers adroitly and had kept them in their places so that he never felt himself obliged to search for any one of them. With many little contrivances she had given his bed-sitting-room a look of comfort and established homeliness, and he had even begun to like it.

"Tha't just like tha mother, Ann," he had said. "She'd make a railway station look as if it had been lived in."

Then Tembarom had appeared, heralded by Mrs. Bowse and the G. Destroyer, and the first time their eyes had met across the table she had liked him. The liking had increased. There was that in his boyish cheer and his not-too-well-fed-looking face which called forth maternal interest. As she gradually learned what his life had been, she felt a thrilled anxiety to hear day by day how he was getting on. She listened for details, and felt it necessary to gather herself together in the face of a slight depression when hopes of Galton were less high than usual. His mending was mysteriously done, and in time he knew with amazed gratitude that he was being "looked after." His first thanks were so awkward, but so full of appreciation of unaccustomed luxury, that they almost brought tears to her eyes, since they so clearly illuminated the entire novelty of any attention whatever.

"I just don't know what to say," he said, shuffling from one foot to another, though his nice grin was at its best. "I've never had a woman do anything for me since I was ten. I guess women do lots of things for most fellows; but, then, they're mothers and sisters and aunts. I appreciate it like—like thunder. I feel as if I was Rockefeller, Miss Ann."

In a short time she had become "Little Ann" to him, as to the rest, and they began to know each other very well. Jim Bowles and Julius Steinberger had not been able to restrain themselves at first from making slangy, yearning love to her, but Tembarom had been different. He had kept himself well in hand. Yes, she had liked T. Tembarom, and as she packed the trunks she realized that the Atlantic Ocean was three thousand miles across, and when two people who had no money were separated by it, they were likely to remain so. Rich people could travel, poor people couldn't. You just stayed where things took you, and you mustn't be silly enough to expect things to happen in your class of life—things like seeing people again. Your life just went on. She kept herself very busy, and did not allow her thoughts any latitude. It would vex her father very much if he thought she had really grown fond of America and was rather sorry to go away. She had finished her packing before evening, and the trunks were labeled and set aside, some in the outside hall and some in the corner of the room. She had sat down with some mending on her lap, and Hutchinson was walking about the room with the restlessness of the traveler whose approaching journey will not let him settle himself anywhere.

"I'll lay a shilling you've got everything packed and ready, and put just where a chap can lay his hands on it," he said.

"Yes, Father. Your tweed cap's in the big pocket of your thick topcoat, and there's an extra pair of spectacles and your pipe and tobacco in the small one."

"And off we go back to England same as we came!" He rubbed his head, and drew a big, worried sigh. "Where's them going?" he asked, pointing to some newly laundered clothing on a side table. "You haven't forgotten 'em, have you?"

"No, Father. It's just some of the young men's washing. I thought I'd take time to mend them up a bit before I went to bed."

"That's like tha mother, too—taking care of everybody. What did these chaps do before you came?"

"Sometimes they tried to sew on a button or so themselves, but oftener they went without. Men make poor work of sewing. It oughtn't to be expected of them."

Hutchinson stopped and looked her and her mending over with a touch of curiosity.

"Some of them's Tembarom's?" he asked.

Little Ann held up a pair of socks.

"These are. He does wear them out, poor fellow. It's tramping up and down the streets to save car-fare does it. He's never got a heel to his name. But he's going to be able to buy some new ones next week."

Hutchinson began his tramp again.

"He'll miss thee, Little Ann; but so'll the other lads, for that matter."

"He'll know to-night whether Mr. Galton's going to let him keep his work. I do hope he will. I believe he'd begin to get on."

"Well,"—Hutchinson was just a little grudging even at this comparatively lenient moment,—"I believe the chap'll get on myself. He's got pluck and he's sharp. I never saw him make a poor mouth yet."

"Neither did I," answered Ann.

A door leading into Tembarom's hall bedroom opened on to Hutchinson's. They both heard some one inside the room knock at it. Hutchinson turned and listened, jerking his head toward the sound.

"There's that poor chap again," he said. "He's wakened and got restless. What's Tembarom going to do with him, I'd like to know? The money won't last forever."

"Shall I let him in, Father? I dare say he's got restless because Mr. Tembarom's not come in."

"Aye, we'll let him in. He won't have thee long. He can't do no harm so long as I'm here."

Little Ann went to the door and opened it. She spoke quietly.

"Do you want to come in here, Mr. Strangeways?"

The man came in. He was clean, but still unshaven, and his clothes looked as though he had been lying down. He looked round the room anxiously.

"Where has he gone?" he demanded in an overstrung voice. "Where is he?" He caught at Ann's sleeve in a sudden access of nervous fear. "What shall I do if he's gone?"

Hutchinson moved toward him.

"'Ere, 'ere," he said, "don't you go catchin' hold of ladies. What do you want?"

"I've forgotten his name now. What shall I do if I can't remember?" faltered Strangeways.

Little Ann patted his arm comfortingly.

"There, there, now! You've not really forgotten it. It's just slipped your memory. You want Mr. Tembarom—Mr. T. Tembarom."

"Oh, thank you, thank you. That's it. Yes, Tembarom. He said T. Tembarom. He said he wouldn't throw me over."

Little Ann led him to a seat and made him sit down. She answered him with quiet decision.

"Well, if he said he wouldn't, he won't. Will he, Father?"

"No, he won't." There was rough good nature in Hutchinson's admission. He paused after it to glance at Ann. "You think a lot of that lad, don't you, Ann?"

"Yes, I do, Father," she replied undisturbedly. "He's one you can trust, too. He's up-town at his work," she explained to Strangeways. "He'll be back before long. He's giving us a bit of a supper in here because we're going away."

Strangeways grew nervous again.

"But he won't go with you? T. Tembarom won't go?"

"No, no; he's not going. He'll stay here," she said soothingly. He had evidently not observed the packed and labeled trunks when he came in. He seemed suddenly to see them now, and rose in distress.

"Whose are these? You said he wasn't going?"

Ann took hold of his arm and led him to the corner.

"They are not Mr. Tembarom's trunks," she explained. "They are father's and mine. Look on the labels. Joseph Hutchinson, Liverpool. Ann Hutchinson, Liverpool."

He looked at them closely in a puzzled way. He read a label aloud in a dragging voice.

"Ann Hutchinson, Liverpool. What's—what's Liverpool?"

"Oh, come," encouraged Little Ann, "you know that. It's a place in England. We're going back to England."

He stood and gazed fixedly before him. Then he began to rub his fingers across his forehead. Ann knew the straining look in his eyes. He was making that horrible struggle to get back somewhere through the darkness which shut him in. It was so painful a thing to see that even Hutchinson turned slightly away.

"Don't!" said Little Ann, softly, and tried to draw him away.

He caught his breath convulsively once or twice, and his voice dragged out words again, as though he were dragging them from bottomless depths.

"Going—back—to—England—back to England—to England."

He dropped into a chair near by, his arms thrown over its back, and broke, as his face fell upon them, into heavy, deadly sobbing—the kind of sobbing Tembarom had found it impossible to stand up against. Hutchinson whirled about testily.

"Dang it!" he broke out, "I wish Tembarom'd turn up. What are we to do?" He didn't like it himself. It struck him as unseemly.

But Ann went to the chair, and put her hands on the shuddering shoulder, bending over the soul-wrung creature, the wisdom of centuries in the soft, expostulatory voice which seemed to reach the very darkness he was lost in. It was a wisdom of which she was wholly unaware, but it had been born with her, and was the building of her being.

"'Sh! 'S-h-h!" she said. "You mustn't do that. Mr. Tembarom wouldn't like you to do it. He'll be in directly. 'Sh! 'Sh, now!" And simple as the words were, their soothing reached him. The wildness of his sobs grew less.

"See here," Hutchinson protested, "this won't do, my man. I won't have it, Ann. I'm upset myself, what with this going back and everything. I can't have a chap coming and crying like that there. It upsets me worse than ever. And you hangin' over him! It won't do."

Strangeways lifted his head from his arms and looked at him.

"Aye, I mean what I say," Hutchinson added fretfully.

Strangeways got up from the chair. When he was not bowed or slouching it was to be seen that he was a tall man with square shoulders. Despite his unshaven, haggard face, he had a sort of presence.

"I'll go back to my room," he said. "I forgot. I ought not to be here."

Neither Hutchinson nor Little Ann had ever seen any one do the thing he did next. When Ann went with him to the door of the hall bedroom, he took her hand, and bowing low before her, lifted it gently to his lips.

Hutchinson stared at him as he turned into the room and closed the door behind him.

"Well, I've read of lords and ladies doin' that in books," he said, "but I never thought I should see a chap do it myself."

Little Ann went back to her mending, looking very thoughtful.

"Father," she said, after a few moments, "England made him come near to remembering something."

"New York'll come near making me remember a lot of things when I'm out of it," said Mr. Hutchinson, sitting down heavily in his chair and rubbing his head. "Eh, dang it! dang it!"

"Don't you let it, Father," advised Little Ann. "There's never any good in thinking things over."

"You're not as cheerful yourself as you let on," he said. "You've not got much color to-day, my lass."

She rubbed one cheek a little, trying to laugh.

"I shall get it back when we go and stay with grandmother. It's just staying indoors so much. Mr. Tembarom won't be long now; I'll get up and set the table. The things are on a tray outside."

As she was going out of the room, Jim Bowles and Julius Steinberger appeared at the door.

"May we come in?" Jim asked eagerly. "We're invited to the oyster stew, and it's time old T. T. was here. Julius and me are just getting dippy waiting upstairs to hear if he's made good with Galton."

"Well, now, you sit down and be quiet a bit, or you'll be losing your appetites," advised Ann.

"You can't lose a thing the size of mine," answered Jim, "any more than you could lose the Metropolitan Opera-house."

Ann turned her head and paused as though she were listening. She heard footsteps in the lower hall.

"He's coming now," she announced. "I know his step. He's tired. Don't go yet, you two," she added as the pair prepared to rush to meet him. "When any one's that tired he wants to wash his face, and talk when he's ready. If you'll just go back to your room I'll call you when I've set the table."

She felt that she wanted a little more quiet during the next few minutes than she could have if they remained and talked at the top of elated voices. She had not quite realized how anxiously she had been waiting all day for the hour when she would hear exactly what had happened. If he was all right, it would be a nice thing to remember when she was in England. In this moderate form she expressed herself mentally. "It would be a nice thing to remember." She spread the cloth on the table and began to lay out the plates. Involuntarily she found herself stopping to glance at the hall bedroom door and listen rather intently.

"I hope he's got it. I do that. I'm sure he has. He ought to."

Hutchinson looked over at her. She was that like her mother, that lass!

"You're excited, Ann," he said.

"Yes, Father, I am—a bit. He's—he's washing his face now." Sounds of splashing water could be heard through the intervening door.

Hutchinson watched her with some uneasiness.

"You care a lot for that lad," he said.

She did not look fluttered. Her answer was quite candid.

"I said I did, Father. He's taking off his boots."

"You know every sound he makes, and you're going away Saturday, and you'll never see him again."

"That needn't stop me caring. It never did any one any harm to care for one of his sort."

"But it can't come to anything," Hutchinson began to bluster. "It won't do—"

"He's coming to the door, he's turning the handle," said Little Ann.

Tembarom came in. He was fresh with recent face-washing, and his hair was damp, so that a short lock curled and stood up. He had been uptown making frantic efforts for hours, but he had been making them in a spirit of victorious relief, and he did not look tired at all.

"I've got it!" he cried out the moment he entered. "I've got it, by jingo! The job's mine for keeps."

"Galton's give it to you out and out?" Hutchinson was slightly excited himself.

"He's in the bulliest humor you ever saw. He says I've done first-rate, and if I go on, he'll run me up to thirty."

"Well, I'm danged glad of it, lad, that I am!" Hutchinson gave in handsomely. "You put backbone into it."

Little Ann stood near, smiling. Her smile met Tembarom's.

"I know you're glad, Little Ann," he said. "I'd never have got there but for you. It was up to me, after the way you started me."

"You know I'm glad without me telling you," she answered. "I'm RIGHTDOWN glad."

And it was at this moment that Mrs. Bowse came into the room.

"It's too bad it's happened just now," she said, much flustered. "That's the way with things. The stew'll spoil, but he says it's real important."

Tembarom caught at both her hands and shook them.

"I've got it, Mrs. Bowse. Here's your society reporter! The best-looking boarder you've got is going to be able to pay his board steady."

"I'm as glad as can be, and so will everybody be. I knew you'd get it. But this gentleman's been here twice to-day. He says he really must see you."

"Let him wait," Hutchinson ordered. "What's the chap want? The stew won't be fit to eat."

"No, it won't," answered Mrs. Bowse; "but he seems to think he's not the kind to be put off. He says it's more Mr. Tembarom's business than his. He looked real mad when I showed him into the parlor, where they were playing the pianola. He asked wasn't there a private room where you could talk."

A certain flurried interest in the manner of Mrs. Bowse, a something not usually awakened by inopportune callers, an actual suggestion of the possible fact that she was not as indifferent as she was nervous, somewhat awakened Mr. Hutchinson's curiosity.

"Look here," he volunteered, "if he's got any real business, he can't talk over to the tune of the pianola you can bring him up here, Tembarom. I'll see he don't stay long if his business isn't worth talkin' about. He'll see the table set for supper, and that'll hurry him."

"Oh, gee I wish he hadn't come!" said Tembarom. "I'll just go down and see what he wants. No one's got any swell private business with me."

"You bring him up if he has," said Hutchinson. "We'd like to hear about it."

Tembarom ran down the stairs quickly.

No one had ever wanted to see him on business before. There was something important-sounding about it; perhaps things were starting up for him in real earnest. It might be a message from Galton, though he could not believe that he had at this early stage reached such a distinction. A ghastly thought shot a bolt at him, but he shook himself free of it.

"He's not a fellow to go back on his word, anyhow," he insisted.

There were more boarders than usual in the parlor. The young woman from the notion counter had company; and one of her guests was playing "He sut'nly was Good to Me" on the pianola with loud and steady tread of pedal.

The new arrival had evidently not thought it worth his while to commit himself to permanency by taking a seat. He was standing not far from the door with a businesslike-looking envelop in one hand and a pince-nez in the other, with which Tembarom saw he was rather fretfully tapping the envelop as he looked about him. He was plainly taking in the characteristics of the

- 57 -

room, and was not leniently disposed toward them. His tailor was clearly an excellent one, with entirely correct ideas as to the cut and material which exactly befitted an elderly gentleman of some impressiveness in the position, whatsoever it happened to be, which he held. His face was not of a friendly type, and his eyes held cold irritation discreetly restrained by businesslike civility. Tembarom vaguely felt the genialities of the oyster supper assume a rather fourth-rate air.

The caller advanced and spoke first.

"Mr. Tembarom?" he inquired.

"Yes," Tembarom answered, "I'm T. Tembarom."

"T.," repeated the stranger, with a slightly puzzled expression. "Ah, yes; I see. I beg pardon."

In that moment Tembarom felt that he was looked over, taken in, summed up, and without favor. The sharp, steady eye, however, did not seem to have moved from his face. At the same time it had aided him to realize that he was, to this well-dressed person at least, a too exhilarated young man wearing a ten-dollar "hand-me-down."

"My name is Palford," he said concisely. "That will convey nothing to you. I am of the firm of Palford & Grimby of Lincoln's Inn. This is my card."

Tembarom took the card and read that Palford & Grimby were "solicitors," and he was not sure that he knew exactly what "solicitors" were.

"Lincoln's Inn?" he hesitated. "That's not in New York, is it?"

"No, Mr. Tembarom; in London. I come from England."

"You must have had bad weather crossing," said Tembarom, with amiable intent. Somehow Mr. Palford presented a more unyielding surface than he was accustomed to. And yet his hard courtesy was quite perfect.

"I have been here some weeks."

"I hope you like New York. Won't you have a seat?"

The young lady from the notion counter and her friends began to sing the chorus of "He sut'nly was Good to Me" with quite professional negro accent.

"That's just the way May Irwin done it," one of them laughed.

Mr. Palford glanced at the performers. He did not say whether he liked New York or not.

"I asked your landlady if we could not see each other in a private room," he said. "It would not be possible to talk quietly here."

"We shouldn't have much of a show," answered Tembarom, inwardly wishing he knew what was going to happen. "But there are no private rooms in the house. We can be quieter than this, though, if we go up stairs to Mr. Hutchinson's room. He said I could bring you."

"That would be much better," replied Mr. Palford.

Tembarom led him out of the room, up the first steep and narrow flight of stairs, along the narrow hall to the second, up that, down another hall to the third, up the third, and on to the fourth. As he led the way he realized again that the worn carpets, the steep narrowness, and the pieces of paper unfortunately stripped off the wall at intervals, were being rather counted against him. This man had probably never been in a place like this before in his life, and he didn't take to it.

At the Hutchinsons' door he stopped and explained:

"We were going to have an oyster stew here because the Hutchinsons are going away; but Mr. Hutchinson said we could come up."

"Very kind of Mr. Hutchinson, I'm sure."

Despite his stiffly collected bearing, Mr. Palford looked perhaps slightly nervous when he was handed into the bed-sitting-room, and found himself confronting Hutchinson and Little Ann and the table set for the oyster stew. It is true that he had never been in such a place in his life, that for many reasons he was appalled, and that he was beset by a fear that he might be grotesquely compelled by existing circumstances to accept these people's invitation, if they insisted upon his sitting down with them and sharing their oyster stew. One could not calculate on what would happen among these unknown quantities. It might be their idea of boarding-house politeness. And how could one offend them? God forbid that the situation should intensify itself in such an absurdly trying manner! What a bounder the unfortunate young man was! His own experience had not been such as to assist him to any realistic enlightenment regarding him, even when he had seen the society page and had learned that he had charge of it.

"Let me make you acquainted with Mr. and Miss Hutchinson," Tembarom introduced. "This is Mr. Palford, Mr. Hutchinson."

Hutchinson, half hidden behind his newspaper, jerked his head and grunted:

"Glad to see you, sir."

Mr. Palford bowed, and took the chair Tembarom presented.

"I am much obliged to you, Mr. Hutchinson, for allowing me to come to your room. I have business to discuss with Mr. Tembarom, and the pianola was being played down-stairs—rather loudly."

"They do it every night, dang 'em! Right under my bed," growled Hutchinson. "You're an Englishman, aren't you?"

"Yes."

"So am I, thank God!" Hutchinson devoutly gave forth.

Little Ann rose from her chair, sewing in hand.

"Father'll come and sit with me in my room," she said.

Hutchinson looked grumpy. He did not intend to leave the field clear and the stew to its fate if he could help it. He gave Ann a protesting frown.

"I dare say Mr. Palford doesn't mind us," he said. "We're not strangers."

"Not in the least," Palford protested. "Certainly not. If you are old friends, you may be able to assist us."

"Well, I don't know about that," Hutchinson answered, "We've not known him long, but we know him pretty well. You come from London, don't you?"

"Yes. From Lincoln's Inn Fields."

"Law?" grunted Hutchinson.

"Yes. Of the firm of Palford & Grimby."

Hutchinson moved in his chair involuntarily. There was stimulation to curiosity in this. This chap was a regular top sawyer—clothes, way of pronouncing his words, manners, everything. No mistaking him—old family solicitor sort of chap. What on earth could he have to say to Tembarom? Tembarom himself had sat down and could not be said to look at his ease.

"I do not intrude without the excuse of serious business," Palford explained to him. "A great deal of careful research and inquiry has finally led me here. I am compelled to believe I have followed the right clue, but I must ask you a few questions. Your name is not really Tembarom, is it?"

Hutchinson looked at Tembarom sharply.

"Not Tembarom? What does he mean, lad?"

Tembarom's grin was at once boyish and ashamed.

"Well, it is in one way," he answered, "and it isn't in another. The fellows at school got into the way of calling me that way,—to save time, I guess,—and I got to like it. They'd have guyed my real name. Most of them never knew it. I can't see why any one ever called a child by such a fool name, anyhow."

"What was it exactly?"

Tembarom looked almost sheepish.

"It sounds like a thing in a novel. It was Temple Temple Barholm. Two Temples, by gee! As if one wasn't enough!"

Joseph Hutchinson dropped his paper and almost started from his chair. His red face suddenly became so much redder that he looked a trifle apoplectic.

"Temple Barholm does tha say?" he cried out.

Mr. Palford raised his hand and checked him, but with a suggestion of stiff apology.

"If you will kindly allow me. Did you ever hear your father refer to a place called Temple Barholm?" he inquired.

Tembarom reflected as though sending his thoughts backward into a pretty thoroughly forgotten and ignored past. There had been no reason connected with filial affection which should have caused him to recall memories of his father. They had not liked each other. He had known that he had been resented and looked down upon as a characteristically American product. His father had more than once said he was a "common American lad," and he had known he was.

"Seems to me," he said at last, "that once when he was pretty mad at his luck I heard him grumbling about English laws, and he said some of his distant relations were swell people who would never think of speaking to him,—perhaps didn't know he was alive,—and they lived in a big way in a place that was named after the family. He never saw it or them, and he said that was the way in England—one fellow got everything and the rest were paupers like himself. He'd always been poor."

"Yes, the relation was a distant one. Until this investigation began the family knew nothing of him. The inquiry has been a tiresome one. I trust I am reaching the end of it. We have given nearly two years to following this clue."

"What for?" burst forth Tembarom, sitting upright.

"Because it was necessary to find either George Temple Barholm or his son, if he had one."

"I'm his son, all right, but he died when I was eight years old," Tembarom volunteered. "I don't remember much about him."

"You remember that he was not an American?"

"He was English. Hated it; but he wasn't fond of America."

"Have you any papers belonging to him?"

Tembarom hesitated again.

"There's a few old letters—oh, and one of those glass photographs in a case. I believe it's my grandfather and grandmother, taken when they were married. Him on a chair, you know, and her standing with her hand on his shoulder."

"Can you show them to me?" Palford suggested.

"Sure," Tembarom answered, getting up from his seat "They're in my room. I turned them up yesterday among some other things."

When he left them, Mr. Palford sat gently rubbing his chin. Hutchinson wanted to burst forth with questions, but he looked so remote and acidly dignified that there was a suggestion of boldness in the idea of intruding on his reflections. Hutchinson stared at him and breathed hard and short in his suspense. The stiff old chap was thinking things over and putting things together in his lawyer's way. He was entirely oblivious to his surroundings. Little Ann went on with her mending, but she wore her absorbed look, and it was not a result of her work.

Tembarom came back with some papers in his hand. They were yellowed old letters, and on the top of the package there was a worn daguerreotype-case with broken clasp.

"Here they are," he said, giving them to Palford. "I guess they'd just been married," opening the case. "Get on to her embroidered collar and big breast-pin with his picture in it. That's English enough, isn't it? He'd given it to her for a wedding-present. There's something in one of the letters about it."

It was the letters to which Mr. Palford gave the most attention. He read them and examined post-marks and dates. When he had finished, he rose from his chair with a slightly portentous touch of professional ceremony.

"Yes, those are sufficiently convincing. You are a very fortunate young man. Allow me to congratulate you."

He did not look particularly pleased, though he extended his hand and shook Tembarom's politely. He was rigorously endeavoring to conceal that he found himself called upon to make the best of an extremely bad job. Hutchinson started forward, resting his hands on his knees and glaring with ill-suppressed excitement.

"What's that for?" Tembarom said. He felt rather like a fool. He laughed half nervously. It seemed to be up to him to understand, and he didn't understand in the least.

"You have, through your father's distant relationship, inherited a very magnificent property—the estate of Temple Barholm in Lancashire," Palford began to explain, but Mr. Hutchinson sprang from his chair outright, crushing his paper in his hand.

"Temple Barholm!" he almost shouted, "I dunnot believe thee! Why, it's one of th' oldest places in England and one of th' biggest. Th' Temple Barholms as didn't come over with th' Conqueror was there before him. Some of them was Saxon kings! And him—" pointing a stumpy, red finger disparagingly at Tembarom, aghast and incredulous—"that New York lad that's sold newspapers in the streets—you say he's come into it?"

"Precisely." Mr. Palford spoke with some crispness of diction. Noise and bluster annoyed him. "That is my business here. Mr. Tembarom is, in fact, Mr. Temple Temple Barholm of Temple Barholm, which you seem to have heard of."

"Heard of it! My mother was born in the village an' lives there yet. Art tha struck dumb, lad!" he said almost fiercely to Tembarom. "By Judd! Tha well may be!"

Tembarom was standing holding the back of a chair. He was pale, and had once opened his mouth, and then gulped and shut it. Little Ann had dropped her sewing. His first look had leaped to her, and she had looked back straight into his eyes.

"I'm struck something," he said, his half-laugh slightly unsteady. "Who'd blame me?"

"You'd better sit down," said Little Ann. "Sudden things are upsetting."

He did sit down. He felt rather shaky. He touched himself on his chest and laughed again.

"Me!" he said. "T. T.! Hully gee! It's like a turn at a vaudeville."

The sentiment prevailing in Hutchinson's mind seemed to verge on indignation.

"Thee th' master of Temple Barholm!" he ejaculated. "Why, it stood for seventy thousand pound' a year!"

"It did and it does," said Mr. Palford, curtly. He had less and less taste for the situation. There was neither dignity nor proper sentiment in it. The young man was utterly incapable of comprehending the meaning and proportions of the extraordinary event which had befallen him. It appeared to present to him the aspect of a somewhat slangy New York joke.

"You do not seem much impressed, Mr. Temple Barholm," he said.

"Oh, I'm impressed, all right," answered Tembarom, "but, say, this thing can't be true! You couldn't make it true if you sat up all night to do it."

"When I go into the business details of the matter tomorrow morning you will realize the truth of it," said Mr. Palford. "Seventy thousand pounds a year—and Temple Barholm—are not unsubstantial facts."

"Three hundred and fifty thousand dollars, my lad—that's what it stands for!" put in Mr. Hutchinson.

"Well," said Tembarom, "I guess I can worry along on that if I try hard enough. I mayn't be able to keep myself in the way I've been used to, but I've got to make it do."

Mr. Palford stiffened. He did not know that the garish, flippant-sounding joking was the kind of defense the streets of New York had provided Mr. Temple Barholm with in many an hour when he had been a half-clad newsboy with an empty stomach, and a bundle of unsold newspapers under his arm.

"You are jocular," he said. "I find the New Yorkers are given to being jocular—continuously."

Tembarom looked at him rather searchingly. Palford wouldn't have found it possible to believe that the young man knew all about his distaste and its near approach to disgust, that he knew quite well what he thought of his ten-dollar suit, his ex-newsboy's diction, and his entire incongruousness as a factor in any circumstances connected with dignity and splendor. He would certainly not have credited the fact that though he had not the remotest idea what sort of a place Temple Barholm was, and what sort of men its long line of possessors had been, he had gained a curious knowledge of their significance through the mental attitude of their legal representative when he for a moment failed to conceal his sense of actual revolt.

"It seems sort of like a joke till you get on to it," he said. "But I guess it ain't such a merry jest as it seems."

And then Mr. Palford did begin to observe that he had lost his color entirely; also that he had a rather decent, sharp-cut face, and extremely white and good young teeth, which he showed not unattractively when he smiled. And he smiled frequently, but he was not smiling now.

CHAPTER VII

In the course of the interview given to the explaining of business and legal detail which took place between Mr. Palford and his client the following morning, Tembarom's knowledge of his situation extended itself largely, and at the same time added in a proportionate degree to his sense of his own incongruity as connected with it. He sat at a table in Palford's private sitting-room at the respectable, old-fashioned hotel the solicitor had chosen—sat and listened, and answered questions and asked them, until his head began to feel as though it were crammed to bursting with extraordinary detail.

It was all extraordinary to him. He had had no time for reading and no books to read, and therefore knew little of fiction. He was entirely ignorant of all romance but such as the New York papers provided. This was highly colored, but it did not deal with events connected with the possessors of vast English estates and the details of their habits and customs. His geographical knowledge of Great Britain was simple and largely incorrect. Information concerning its usual conditions and aspects had come to him through talk of international marriages and cup races, and had made but little impression upon him. He liked New York—its noise, its streets, its glare, its Sunday newspapers, with their ever-increasing number of sheets, and pictures of everything on earth which could be photographed. His choice, when he could allow himself a fifty-cent seat at the theater, naturally ran to productions which were farcical or cheerfully musical. He had never reached serious drama, perhaps because he had never had money enough to pay for entrance to anything like half of the "shows" the other fellows recommended. He was totally unprepared for the facing of any kind of drama as connected with himself. The worst of it was that it struck him as being of the nature of farce when regarded from the normal New York point of view. If he had somehow had the luck to come into the possession of money in ways which were familiar to him,—to "strike it rich" in the way of a "big job" or "deal,"—he would have been better able to adjust himself to circumstances. He might not have known how to spend his money, but he would have spent it in New York on New York joys. There would have been no foreign remoteness about the thing, howsoever fantastically unexpected such fortune might have been. At any rate, in New York he would have known the names of places and things.

Through a large part of his interview with Palford his elbow rested on the table, and he held his chin with his hand and rubbed it thoughtfully. The last Temple Temple Barholm had been an eccentric and uncompanionable person. He had lived alone and had not married. He had cherished a prejudice against the man who would have succeeded him as next of kin if he had not died young. People had been of the opinion that he had disliked him merely because he did not wish to be reminded that some one else must some day inevitably stand in his shoes, and own the possessions of which he himself was arrogantly fond. There were always more female Temple Barholms than male ones, and the families were small. The relative who had emigrated to Brooklyn had been a comparatively unknown person. His only intercourse with the head of the house had been confined to a begging letter, written from America when his circumstances were at their worst. It was an ill-mannered and ill-expressed letter, which had been considered presuming, and had been answered chillingly with a mere five-pound note, clearly explained as a final charity. This begging letter, which bitterly contrasted the writer's poverty with his indifferent relative's luxuries, had, by a curious trick of chance which preserved it, quite extraordinarily turned up during an examination of apparently unimportant, forgotten papers, and had furnished a clue in the search for next of kin. The writer had greatly annoyed old Mr. Temple Barholm by telling him that he had called his son by his name—"not that there was ever likely to be anything in it for him." But a waif of the New York streets who was known as "Tem" or "Tembarom" was not a link easily attached to any chain, and the search had been long and rather hopeless. It had, however, at last reached Mrs. Bowse's boarding-house and before Mr. Palford sat Mr. Temple Temple Barholm, a cheap young man in cheap clothes, and speaking New York slang with a nasal accent. Mr. Palford, feeling him appalling and absolutely without the pale, was still aware that he stood in the position of an important client of the firm of Palford & Grimby. There was a section of the offices at Lincoln's Inn devoted to documents representing a lifetime of attention to the affairs of the Temple Barholm estates. It was greatly to be hoped that the crass ignorance and commonness of this young outsider would not cause impossible complications.

"He knows nothing! He knows nothing!" Palford found himself forced to exclaim mentally not once, but a hundred times, in the course of their talk.

There was—this revealed itself as the interview proceeded—just one slight palliation of his impossible benightedness: he was not the kind of young man who, knowing nothing, huffily protects himself by pretending to know everything. He was of an unreserve concerning his ignorance which his solicitor felt sometimes almost struck one in the face. Now and then it quite made one jump. He was singularly free from any vestige of personal vanity. He was also singularly unready to take offense. To the head of the firm of Palford & Grimby, who was not accustomed to lightness of manner, and inclined to the view that a person who made a joke took rather a liberty with him, his tendency to be jocular, even about himself and the estate of Temple Barholm, was irritating and somewhat disrespectful. Mr. Palford did not easily comprehend jokes of any sort; especially was he annoyed by cryptic phraseology and mammoth exaggeration. For instance, he could not in the least compass Mr. Temple Barholm's meaning when he casually remarked that something or other was "all to the merry"; or again, quite as though he believed that he was using reasonable English figures of speech, "The old fellow thought he was the only pebble on the beach." In using the latter expression he had been referring to the late Mr. Temple Barholm; but what on earth was his connection with the sea-shore and pebbles? When confronted with these baffling absurdities, Mr. Palford either said, "I beg pardon," or stiffened and remained silent.

When Tembarom learned that he was the head of one of the oldest families in England, no aspect of the desirable dignity of his position reached him in the least.

"Well," he remarked, "there's quite a lot of us can go back to Adam and Eve."

When he was told that he was lord of the manor of Temple Barholm, he did not know what a manor was.

"What's a manor, and what happens if you're lord of it?" he asked.

He had not heard of William the Conqueror, and did not appear moved to admiration of him, though he owned that he seemed to have "put it over."

"Why didn't he make a republic of it while he was about it?" he said. "But I guess that wasn't his kind. He didn't do all that fighting for his health."

His interest was not alone totally disseverred from the events of past centuries; it was as disseverred from those of mere past years. The habits, customs, and points of view of five years before seemed to have been cast into a vast wastepaper basket as wholly unpractical in connection with present experiences.

"A man that's going to keep up with the procession can't waste time thinking about yesterday. What he's got to do is to keep his eye on what's going to happen the week after next," he summed it up.

Rather to Mr. Palford's surprise, he did not speak lightly, but with a sort of inner seriousness. It suggested that he had not arrived at this conclusion without the aid of sharp experience. Now and then one saw a touch of this profound practical perception in him.

It was not to be denied that he was clear-headed enough where purely practical business detail was concerned. He was at first plainly rather stunned by the proportions presented to him, but his questions were direct and of a common-sense order not to be despised.

"I don't know anything about it yet," he said once. "It's all Dutch to me. I can't calculate in half-crowns and pounds and half pounds, but I'm going to find out. I've got to."

It was extraordinary and annoying to feel that one must explain everything; but this impossible fellow was not an actual fool on all points, and he did not seem to be a weakling. He might learn certain things in time, and at all events one was no further personally responsible for him and his impossibilities than the business concerns of his estate would oblige any legal firm to be. Clients, whether highly desirable or otherwise, were no more than clients. They were not relatives whom one must introduce to one's friends. Thus Mr. Palford, who was not a specially humane or sympathetic person, mentally decided. He saw no pathos in this raw young man, who would presently find himself floundering unaided in waters utterly unknown to him. There was even a touch of bitter amusement in the solicitor's mind as he glanced toward the future.

He explained with detail the necessity for their immediate departure for the other side of the Atlantic. Certain legal formalities which must at once be attended to demanded their presence in England. Foreseeing this, on the day when he had finally felt himself secure as to the identity of his client he had taken the liberty of engaging optionally certain state-rooms on the Adriana, sailing the following Wednesday.

"Subject of course to your approval," he added politely. "But it is imperative that we should be on the spot as early as possible." He did not mention that he himself was abominably tired of his sojourn on alien shores, and wanted to be back in London in his own chambers, with his own club within easy reach.

Tembarom's face changed its expression. He had been looking rather weighted down and fatigued, and he lighted up to eagerness.

"Say," he exclaimed, "why couldn't we go on the Transatlantic on Saturday?"

"It is one of the small, cheap boats," objected Palford.

"The accommodation would be most inferior."

Tembarom leaned forward and touched his sleeve in hasty, boyish appeal.

"I want to go on it," he said; "I want to go steerage."

Palford stared at him.

"You want to go on the Transatlantic! Steerage!" he ejaculated, quite aghast. This was a novel order of madness to reveal itself in the recent inheritor of a great fortune.

Tembarom's appeal grew franker; it took on the note of a too crude young fellow's misplaced confidence.

"You do this for me," he said. "I'd give a farm to go on that boat. The Hutchinsons are sailing on it—Mr. and Miss Hutchinson, the ones you saw at the house last night."

"I—it is really impossible." Mr. Palford hesitated. "As to steerage, my dear Mr. Temple Barholm, you—you can't."

Tembarom got up and stood with his hands thrust deep in his pockets. It seemed to be a sort of expression of his sudden hopeful excitement.

"Why not" he said. "If I own about half of England and have money to burn, I guess I can buy a steerage passage on a nine-day steamer."

"You can buy anything you like," Palford answered stiffly. "It is not a matter of buying. But I should not be conducting myself properly toward you if I allowed it. It would not be—becoming."

"Becoming!" cried Tembarom, "Thunder! It's not a spring bat. I tell you I want to go just that way."

Palford saw abnormal breakers ahead. He felt that he would be glad when he had landed his charge safely at Temple Barholm. Once there, his family solicitor was not called upon to live with him and hobnob with his extraordinary intimates.

"As to buying," he said, still with marked lack of enthusiasm, "instead of taking a steerage passage on the Transatlantic yourself, you might no doubt secure first-class state-rooms for Mr. and Miss Hutchinson on the Adriana, though I seriously advise against it."

Tembarom shook his head.

"You don't know them," he said. "They wouldn't let me. Hutchinson's a queer old fellow and he's had the hardest kind of luck, but he's as proud as they make 'em. Me butt in and offer to pay their passage back, as if they were paupers, just because I've suddenly struck it rich! Hully gee! I guess not. A fellow that's been boosted up in the air all in a minute, as I have, has got to lie pretty low to keep folks from wanting to kick him, anyhow. Hutchinson's a darned sight smarter fellow than I am, and he knows it—and he's Lancashire, you bet." He stopped a minute and flushed. "As to Little Ann," he said—"me make that sort of a break with HER! Well, I should be a fool."

Palford was a cold-blooded and unimaginative person, but a long legal experience had built up within him a certain shrewdness of perception. He had naturally glanced once or twice at the girl sitting still at her mending, and he had observed that she said very little and had a singularly quiet, firm little voice.

"I beg pardon. You are probably right. I had very little conversation with either of them. Miss Hutchinson struck me as having an intelligent face."

"She's a wonder," said Tembarom, devoutly. "She's just a wonder."

"Under the circumstances," suggested Mr. Palford, "it might not be a bad idea to explain to her your idea of the steerage passage. An intelligent girl can often give excellent advice. You will probably have an opportunity of speaking to her tonight. Did you say they were sailing to-morrow?"

To-morrow! That brought it so near that it gave Tembarom a shock. He had known that they sailed on Saturday, and now Saturday had become to-morrow. Things began to surge through his mind—all sorts of things he had no time to think of clearly, though it was true they had darted vaguely about in the delirious excitement of the night, during which he had scarcely slept at all. His face changed again, and the appeal died out of it. He began to look anxious and restless.

"Yes, they're going to-morrow," he answered.

"You see," argued Mr. Palford, with conviction, "how impossible it would be for us to make any arrangements in so few hours. You will excuse my saying," he added punctiliously, "that I could not make the voyage in the steerage."

Tembarom laughed. He thought he saw him doing it.

"That's so," he said. Then, with renewed hope, he added, "Say, I'm going to try and get them to wait till Wednesday."

"I do not think—" Mr. Palford began, and then felt it wiser to leave things as they were. "But I'm not qualified to give an opinion. I do not know Miss Hutchinson at all."

But the statement was by no means frank. He had a private conviction that he did know her to a certain degree. And he did.

CHAPTER VIII

There was a slight awkwardness even to Tembarom in entering the dining-room that evening. He had not seen his fellow boarders, as his restless night had made him sleep later than usual. But Mrs. Bowse had told him of the excitement he had caused.

"They just couldn't eat," she said. "They could do nothing but talk and talk and ask questions; and I had waffles, too, and they got stone-cold."

The babel of friendly outcry which broke out on his entry was made up of jokes, ejaculations, questions, and congratulatory outbursts from all sides.

"Good old T. T.!" "Give him a Harvard yell! Rah! Rah! Rah!" "Lend me fifty-five cents?" "Where's your tiara?" "Darned glad of it!" "Make us a speech!"

"Say, people," said Tembarom, "don't you get me rattled or I can't tell you anything. I'm rattled enough already."

"Well, is it true?" called out Mr. Striper.

"No," Tembarom answered back, sitting down. "It couldn't be; that's what I told Palford. I shall wake up in a minute or two and find myself in a hospital with a peacherino of a trained nurse smoothing 'me piller.' You can't fool ME with a pipe-dream like this. Palford's easier; he's not a New Yorker. He says it IS true, and I can't get out of it."

"Whew! Great Jakes!" A long breath was exhaled all round the table.

"What are you, anyhow?" cried Jim Bowles across the dishes.

Tembarom rested his elbow on the edge of the table and began to check off his points on his fingers.

"I'm this," he said: "I'm Temple Temple Barholm, Esquire, of Temple Barholm, Lancashire, England. At the time of the flood my folks knocked up a house just about where the ark landed, and I guess they've held on to it ever since. I don't know what business they went into, but they made money. Palford swears I've got three hundred and fifty thousand dollars a year. I wasn't going to call the man a liar; but I just missed it, by jings!"

He was trying to "bluff it out." Somehow he felt he had to. He felt it more than ever when a momentary silence fell upon those who sat about the table. It fell when he said "three hundred and fifty thousand dollars a year." No one could find voice to make any remark for a few seconds after that.

"Are you a lord—or a duke?" some one asked after breath had recovered itself.

"No, I'm not," he replied with relief. "I just got out from under that; but the Lord knows how I did it."

"What are you going to do first?" said Jim Bowles.

"I've got to go and 'take possession.' That's what Palford calls it. I've been a lost heir for nearly two years, and I've got to show myself."

Hutchinson had not joined the clamor of greeting, but had grunted disapproval more than once. He felt that, as an Englishman, he had a certain dignity to maintain. He knew something about big estates and their owners. He was not like these common New York chaps, who regarded them as Arabian Nights tales to make jokes about. He had grown up as a village boy in proper awe of Temple Barholm. They were ignorant fools, this lot. He had no patience with them. He had left the village and gone to work in Manchester when he was a boy of twelve, but as long as he had remained in his mother's cottage it had been only decent good manners for him to touch his forehead respectfully when a Temple Barholm, or a Temple Barholm guest or carriage or pony phaeton, passed him by. And this chap was Mr. Temple Temple Barholm himself! Lord save us!

Little Ann said nothing at all; but, then, she seldom said anything during meal-times. When the rest of the boarders laughed, she ate her dinner and smiled. Several times, despite her caution, Tembarom caught her eye, and somehow held it a second with his. She smiled at him when this happened; but there was something restless and eager in his look which made her wish to evade it. She knew what he felt, and she knew why he kept up his jokes and never once spoke seriously. She knew he was not comfortable, and did not enjoy talking about hundreds of thousands a year to people who worked hard for ten or twenty "per." To-morrow morning was very near, she kept thinking. To-morrow night she would be lying in her berth in the steerage, or more probably taking care of her father, who would be very uncomfortable.

"What will Galton do?" Mr. Striper asked.

"I don't know," Tembarom answered, and he looked troubled. Three hundred and fifty thousand dollars a year might not be able to give aid to a wounded society page.

"What are you going to do with your Freak?" called out Julius Steinberger.

Tembarom actually started. As things had surged over him, he had had too much to think over. He had not had time to give to his strange responsibility; it had become one nevertheless.

"Are you going to leave him behind when you go to England?"

He leaned forward and put his chin on his hand.

"Why, say," he said, as though he were thinking it out, "he's spoken about England two or three times. He's said he must go there. By jings! I'll take him with me, and see what'll happen."

When Little Ann got up to leave the room he followed her and her father into the hall.

"May I come up and talk it over with you?" he appealed. "I've got to talk to some one who knows something about it. I shall go dotty if I don't. It's too much like a dream."

"Come on up when you're ready," answered Hutchinson. "Ann and me can give you a tip or two."

"I'm going to be putting the last things in the trunks," said Ann, "but I dare say you won't mind that. The express'll be here by eight in the morning."

"O Lord!" groaned Tembarom.

When he went up to the fourth floor a little later, Hutchinson had fallen into a doze in his chair over his newspaper, and Ann was kneeling by a trunk in the hall, folding small articles tightly, and fitting them into corners. To Tembarom she looked even more than usual like a slight child thing one could snatch up in one's arms and carry about or set on one's knee without feeling her weight at all. An inferior gas-jet on the wall just above her was doing its best with the lot of soft, red hair, which would have been an untidy bundle if it had not been hers.

Tembarom sat down on the trunk next to her.

"O Little Ann!" he broke out under his breath, lest the sound of his voice might check Hutchinson's steady snoring. "O Little Ann!"

Ann leaned back, sitting upon her small heels, and looked up at him.

"You're all upset, and it's not to be wondered at, Mr. Temple Barholm," she said.

"Upset! You're going away to-morrow morning! And, for the Lord's sake, don't call me that!" he protested.

"You're going away yourself next Wednesday. And you ARE Mr. Temple Barholm. You'll never be called anything else in England."

"How am I going to stand it?" he protested again. "How could a fellow like me stand it! To be yanked out of good old New York, and set down in a place like a museum, with Central Park round it, and called Mr. Temple Temple Barholm instead of just 'Tem' or 'T. T.'! It's not natural."

"What you must do, Mr. Temple Barholm, is to keep your head clear, that's all," she replied maturely.

"Lord! if I'd got a head like yours!"

She seemed to take him in, with a benign appreciativeness, in his entirety.

"Well, you haven't," she admitted, though quite without disparagement, merely with slight reservation. "But you've got one like your own. And it's a good head—when you try to think steady. Yours is a man's head, and mine's only a woman's."

"It's Little Ann Hutchinson's, by gee!" said Tembarom, with feeling.

"Listen here, Mr. Tem—Temple Barholm," she went on, as nearly disturbed as he had ever seen her outwardly. "It's a wonderful thing that's happened to you. It's like a novel. That splendid place, that splendid name! It seems so queer to think I should ever have talked to a Mr. Temple Barholm as I've talked to you."

He leaned forward a little as though something drew him.

"But"—there was unsteady appeal in his voice—"you have liked me, haven't you, Little Ann?"

Her own voice seemed to drop into an extra quietness that made it remote. She looked down at her hands on her lap.

"Yes, I have liked you. I have told Father I liked you," she answered.

He got up, and made an impetuous rush at his goal.

"Then—say, I'm going in there to wake up Mr. Hutchinson and ask him not to sail to-morrow morning."

"You'd better not wake him up," she answered, smiling; but he saw that her face changed and flushed. "It's not a good time to ask Father anything when he's just been waked up. And we HAVE to go. The express is coming at eight."

"Send it away again; tell 'em you're not going. Tell 'em any old thing. Little Ann, what's the matter with you? Something's the matter. Have I made a break?"

He had felt the remoteness in her even before he had heard it in her dropped voice. It had been vaguely there even when he sat down on the trunk. Actually there was a touch of reserve about her, as though she was keeping her little place with the self-respecting propriety of a girl speaking to a man not of her own world.

"I dare say I've done some fool thing without knowing it. I don't know where I'm at, anyhow," he said woefully.

"Don't look at me like that, Mr. Temple Barholm," she said—"as if I was unkind. I—I'm NOT."

"But you're different," he implored. "I saw it the minute I came up. I ran upstairs just crazy to talk to you,—yes, crazy to talk to you—and you—well, you were different. Why are you, if you're not mad?"

Then she rose and stood holding one of her neatly rolled packages in her hand. Her eyes were soft and clear, and appealed maternally to his reason.

"Because everything's different. You just think a bit," she answered.

He stared at her a few seconds, and then understanding of her dawned upon him. He made a human young dash at her, and caught her arm.

"What!" he cried out. "You mean this Temple Barholm song and dance makes things different? Not on your life! You're not the girl to work that on me, as if it was my fault. You've got to hear me speak my piece. Ann—you've just got to!"

He had begun to tremble a little, and she herself was not steady; but she put a hand on his arm.

"Don't say anything you've not had time to think about," she said.

"I've been thinking of pretty near nothing else ever since I came here. Just as soon as I looked at you across the table that first day I saw my finish, and every day made me surer. I'd never had any comfort or taking care of,—I didn't know the first thing about it,—and it seemed as if all there was of it in the world was just in YOU."

"Did you think that?" she asked falteringly.

"Did I? That's how you looked to me, and it's how you look now. The way you go about taking care of everybody and just handing out solid little chunks of good sense to every darned fool that needs them, why—" There was a break in his voice—"why, it just knocked me out the first round." He held her a little away from him, so that he could yearn over her, though he did not know he was yearning. "See, I'd sworn I'd never ask a girl to marry me until I could keep her. Well, you know how it was, Ann. I couldn't have kept a goat, and I wasn't such a fool that I didn't know it. I've been pretty sick when I thought how it was; but I never worried you, did I?"

"No, you didn't."

"I just got busy. I worked like—well, I got busier than I ever was in my life. When I got the page SURE, I let myself go a bit, sort of hoping. And then this Temple Barholm thing hits me."

"That's the thing you've got to think of now," said Little Ann. "I'm going to talk sensible to you."

"Don't, Ann! Good Lord! DON'T!"

"I MUST." She put her last tight roll into the trunk and tried to shut the lid. "Please lock this for me."

He locked it, and then she seated herself on the top of it, though it was rather high for her, and her small feet dangled. Her eyes looked large and moist like a baby's, and she took out a handkerchief and lightly touched them.

"You've made me want to cry a bit," she said, "but I'm not going to."

"Are you going to tell me you don't want me?" he asked, with anxious eyes.

"No, I'm not."

"God bless you!" He was going to make a dash at her again, but pulled himself up because he must. "No, by jings!" he said. "I'm not going to till you let me."

"You see, it's true your head's not like mine," she said reasonably. "Men's heads are mostly not like women's. They're men, of course, and they're superior to women, but they're what I'd call more fluttery-like. Women must remind them of things."

"What—what kind of things?"

"This kind. You see, Grandmother lives near Temple Barholm, and I know what it's like, and you don't. And I've seen what seventy thousand pounds a year means, and you haven't. And you've got to go and find out for yourself."

"What's the matter with you coming along to help me?"

"I shouldn't help you; that's it. I should hold you back. I'm nothing but Ann Hutchinson, and I talk Manchester—and I drop my h's."

"I love to hear you drop your little h's all over the place," he burst forth impetuously. "I love it."

She shook her head.

"The girls that go to garden-parties at Temple Barholm look like those in the `Ladies' Pictorial', and they've got names and titles same as those in novels."

He answered her in genuine anguish. He had never made any mistake about her character, and she was beginning to make him feel afraid of her in the midst of his adoration.

"What do I want with a girl out of a magazine?" he cried. "Where should I hang her up?"

She was not unfeeling, but unshaken and she went on:

"I should look like a housemaid among them. How would you feel with a wife of that sort, when the other sort was about?"

"I should feel like a king, that's what I should feel like," he replied indignantly.

"I shouldn't feel like a queen. I should feel MISERABLE."

She sat with her little feet dangling, and her hands folded in her lap. Her infantile blue eyes held him as the Ancient Mariner had been held. He could not get away from the clear directness of them. He did not want to exactly, but she frightened him more and more.

"I should be ashamed," she proceeded. "I should feel as if I had taken an advantage. What you've got to do is to find out something no one else can find out for you, Mr. Temple Barholm."

"How can I find it out without you? It was you who put me on to the wedding-cake; you can put me on to other things."

"Because I've lived in the place," she answered unswervingly. "I know how funny it is for any one to think of me being Mrs. Temple Barholm. You don't."

"You bet I don't," he answered; "but I'll tell you what I do know, and that's how funny it is that I should be Mr. Temple Barholm. I've got on to that all right, all right. Have you?"

She looked at him with a reflection that said much. She took him in with a judicial summing up of which it must be owned an added respect was part. She had always believed he had more sense than most young men, and now she knew it.

"When a person's clever enough to see things for himself, he's generally clever enough to manage them," she replied.

He knelt down beside the trunk and took both her hands in his. He held them fast and rather hard.

"Are you throwing me down for good, Little Ann?" he said. "If you are, I can't stand it, I won't stand it."

"If you care about me like that, you'll do what I tell you," she interrupted, and she slipped down from the top of her trunk. "I know what Mother would say. She'd say, 'Ann, you give that young man a chance.' And I'm going to give you one. I've said all I'm going to, Mr. Temple Barholm."

He took both her elbows and looked at her closely, feeling a somewhat awed conviction.

"I—believe—you have," he said.

And here the sound of Mr. Hutchinson's loud and stertorous breathing ceased, and he waked up, and came to the door to find out what Ann was doing.

"What are you two talking about?" he asked. "People think when they whisper it's not going to disturb anybody, but it's worse than shouting in a man's ear."

Tembarom walked into the room.

"I've been asking Little Ann to marry me," he announced, "and she won't."

He sat down in a chair helplessly, and let his head fall into his hands.

"Eh!" exclaimed Hutchinson. He turned and looked at Ann disturbedly. "I thought a bit ago tha didn't deny but what tha'd took to him?"

"I didn't, Father," she answered. "I don't change my mind that quick. I—would have been willing to say 'Yes' when you wouldn't have been willing to let me. I didn't know he was Mr. Temple Barholm then."

Hutchinson rubbed the back of his head, reddening and rather bristling.

"Dost tha think th' Temple Barholms would look down on thee?"

"I should look down on myself if I took him up at his first words, when he's all upset with excitement, and hasn't had time to find out what things mean. I'm—well, I 'm too fond of him, Father."

Hutchinson gave her a long, steady look.

"You are?" he said.

"Yes, I am."

Tembarom lifted his head, and looked at her, too.

"Are you?" he asked.

She put her hands behind her back, and returned his look with the calm of ages.

"I'm not going to argue about it," she answered. "Arguing's silly."

His involuntary rising and standing before her was a sort of unconscious tribute of respect.

"I know that," he owned. "I know you. That's why I take it like this. But I want you to tell me one thing. If this hadn't happened, if I'd only had twenty dollars a week, would you have taken me?"

"If you'd had fifteen, and Father could have spared me, I'd have taken you. Fifteen dollars a week is three pounds two and sixpence, and I've known curates' wives that had to bring up families on less. It wouldn't go as far in New York as it would in the country in England, but we could have made it do—until you got more. I know you, too, Mr. Temple Barholm."

He turned to her father, and saw in his florid countenance that which spurred him to bold disclosure.

"Say," he put it to him, as man to man, "she stands there and says a thing like that, and she expects a fellow not to jerk her into his arms and squeeze the life out of her! I daren't do it, and I'm not going to try; but—well, you said her mother was like her, and I guess you know what I'm up against."

Hutchinson's grunting chuckle contained implications of exultant tenderness and gratified paternal pride.

"She's th' very spit and image of her mother," he said, "and she had th' sense of ten women rolled into one, and th' love of twenty. You let her be, and you're as safe as th' Rock of Ages."

"Do you think I don't know that?" answered Tembarom, his eyes shining almost to moisture. "But what hits me, by thunder! is that I've lost the chance of seeing her work out that fifteen-dollar-a-week proposition, and it drives me crazy."

"I should have downright liked to try it," said Little Ann, with speculative reflection, and while she knitted her brows in lovely consideration of the attractive problem, several previously unknown dimples declared themselves about her mouth.

"Ann," Tembarom ventured, "if I go to Temple Barholm and try it a year and learn all about it——"

"It would take more than a year," said Ann.

"Don't make it two," Tembarom pleaded. "I'll sit up at night with wet towels round my head to learn; I'll spend fourteen hours a day with girls that look like the pictures in the 'Ladies' Pictorial', or whatever it is in England; I'll give them every chance in life, if you'll let me off afterward. There must be another lost heir somewhere; let's dig him up and then come back to little old New

York and be happy. Gee! Ann,"—letting himself go and drawing nearer to her,—"how happy we could be in one of those little flats in Harlem!"

She was a warm little human thing, and a tender one, and when he came close to her, glowing with tempestuous boyish eagerness, her eyes grew bluer because they were suddenly wet, and she was obliged to move softly back.

"Yes," she said; "I know those little flats. Any one could——" She stopped herself, because she had been going to reveal what a home a woman could make in rooms like the compartments in a workbox. She knew and saw it all. She drew back a little again, but she put out a hand and laid it on his sleeve.

"When you've had quite time enough to find out, and know what the other thing means, I'll do whatever you want me to do," she said. "It won't matter what it is. I'll do it."

"She means that," Hutchinson mumbled unsteadily, turning aside. "Same as her mother would have meant it. And she means it in more ways than one."

And so she did. The promise included quite firmly the possibility of not unnatural changes in himself such as young ardor could not foresee, even the possibility of his new life withdrawing him entirely from the plane on which rapture could materialize on twenty dollars a week in a flat in Harlem.

CHAPTER IX

Type as exotic as Tembarom's was to his solicitor naturally suggested problems. Mr. Palford found his charge baffling because, according to ordinary rules, a young man so rudimentary should have presented no problems not perfectly easy to explain. It was herein that he was exotic. Mr. Palford, who was not given to subtle analysis of differences in character and temperament, argued privately that an English youth who had been brought up in the streets would have been one of two or three things. He would have been secretly terrified and resentful, roughly awkward and resentful, or boastfully delighted and given to a common youth's excitedly common swagger at finding himself suddenly a "swell."

This special kind of youth would most assuredly have constantly thought of himself as a "swell" and would have lost his head altogether, possibly with results in the matter of conduct in public which would have been either maddening or crushing to the spirit of a well-bred, mature-minded legal gentleman temporarily thrust into the position of bear-leader.

But Tembarom was none of these things. If he was terrified, he did not reveal his anguish. He was without doubt not resentful, but on the contrary interested and curious, though he could not be said to bear himself as one elated. He indulged in no frolics or extravagances. He saw the Hutchinsons off on their steamer, and supplied them with fruit and flowers and books with respectful moderation. He did not conduct himself as a benefactor bestowing unknown luxuries, but as a young man on whom unexpected luck had bestowed decent opportunities to express his friendship. In fact, Palford's taste approved of his attitude. He was evidently much under the spell of the slight girl with the Manchester accent and sober blue eyes, but she was neither flighty nor meretricious, and would have sense enough to give no trouble even when he naturally forgot her in the revelations of his new life. Her father also was plainly a respectable working-man, with a blunt Lancashire pride which would keep him from intruding.

"You can't butt in and get fresh with a man like that," Tembarom said. "Money wouldn't help you. He's too independent."

After the steamer had sailed away it was observable to his solicitor that Mr. Temple Barholm was apparently occupied every hour. He did not explain why he seemed to rush from one part of New York to another and why he seemed to be seeking interviews with persons it was plainly difficult to get at. He was evidently working hard to accomplish something or other before he left the United States, perhaps. He asked some astutely practical business questions; his intention seeming to be to gain a definite knowledge of what his future resources would be and of his freedom to use them as he chose.

Once or twice Mr. Palford was rather alarmed by the tendency of his questions. Had he actually some prodigious American scheme in view? He seemed too young and inexperienced in the handling of large sums for such a possibility. But youth and inexperience and suddenly inherited wealth not infrequently led to rash adventures. Something which Palford called "very handsome" was done for Mrs. Bowse and the boarding-house. Mrs. Bowse was evidently not proud enough to resent being made secure for a few years' rent. The extraordinary page was provided for after a large amount of effort and expenditure of energy.

"I couldn't leave Galton high and dry," Tembarom explained when he came in after rushing about. "I think I know a man he might try, but I've got to find him and put him on to things. Good Lord! nobody rushed about to find me and offer me the job. I hope this fellow wants it as bad as I did. He'll be up in the air." He discovered the whereabouts of the young man in question, and finding him, as the youngster almost tearfully declared, "about down and out," his proposition was met with the gratitude the relief from a prospect of something extremely like starvation would mentally produce. Tembarom took him to Galton after having talked him over in detail.

"He's had an education, and you know how much I'd had when I butted into the page," he said. "No one but you would have let me try it. You did it only because you saw—you saw—"

"Yes, I saw," answered Galton, who knew exactly what he had seen and who found his up-town social representative and his new situation as interesting as amusing and just touched with the pathetic element. Galton was a traveled man and knew England and several other countries well.

"You saw that a fellow wanted the job as much as I did would be likely to put up a good fight to hold it down. I was scared out of my life when I started out that morning of the blizzard, but I couldn't afford to be scared. I guess soldiers who are scared fight like that when they see bayonets coming at them. You have to."

"I wonder how often a man finds out that he does pretty big things when bayonets are coming at him," answered Galton, who was actually neglecting his work for a few minutes so that he might look at and talk to him, this New York descendant of Norman lords and Saxon kings.

"Joe Bennett had been trying to live off free-lunch counters for a week when I found him," Tembarom explained. "You don't know what that is. He'll go at the page all right. I'm going to take him up-town and introduce him to my friends there and get them to boost him along."

"You made friends," said Galton. "I knew you would."

"Some of the best ever. Good-natured and open-handed. Well, you bet! Only trouble was they wanted you to eat and drink everything in sight, and they didn't quite like it when you couldn't get outside all the champagne they'd offer you."

He broke into a big, pleased laugh.

"When I went in and told Munsberg he pretty near threw a fit. Of course he thought I was kidding. But when I made him believe it, he was as glad as if he'd had luck himself. It was just fine the way people took it. Tell you what, it takes good luck, or bad luck, to show you how good-natured a lot of folks are. They'll treat Bennett and the page all right; you'll see."

"They'll miss you," said Galton.

"I shall miss them," Tembarom answered in a voice with a rather depressed drop in it.

"I shall miss you," said Galton.

Tembarom's face reddened a little.

"I guess it'd seem rather fresh for me to tell you how I shall miss you," he said. "I said that first day that I didn't know how to tell you how I—well, how I felt about you giving a mutt like me that big chance. You never thought I didn't know how little I did know, did you?" he inquired almost anxiously.

"That was it—that you did know and that you had the backbone and the good spirits to go in and win," Galton replied. "I'm a tired man, and good spirits and good temper seem to me about the biggest assets a man can bring into a thing. I shouldn't have dared do it when I was your age. You deserved the Victoria Cross," he added, chuckling.

"What's the Victoria Cross?" asked Tembarom.

"You'll find out when you go to England."

"Well, I'm not supposing that you don't know about how many billion things I'll have to find out when I go to England."

"There will be several thousand," replied Galton moderately; "but you'll learn about them as you go on."

"Say," said Tembarom, reflectively, "doesn't it seem queer to think of a fellow having to keep up his spirits because he's fallen into three hundred and fifty thousand a year? You wouldn't think he'd have to, would you?"

"But you find he has?" queried Galton, interestedly.

Tembarom's lifted eyes were so honest that they were touching.

"I don't know where I'm at," he said. "I'm going to wake up in a new place—like people that die. If you knew what it was like, you wouldn't mind it so much; but you don't know a blamed thing. It's not having seen a sample that rattles you."

"You're fond of New York?"

"Good Lord! it's all the place I know on earth, and it's just about good enough for me, by gee! It's kept me alive when it might have starved me to death. My! I've had good times here," he added, flushing with emotion. "Good times—when I hadn't a whole meal a day!"

"You'd have good times anywhere," commented Galton, also with feeling. "You carry them over your shoulder, and you share them with a lot of other people."

He certainly shared some with Joe Bennett, whom he took up-town and introduced right and left to his friendly patrons, who, excited by the atmosphere of adventure and prosperity, received him with open arms. To have been the choice of T. Tembarom as a mere representative of the EARTH would have been a great thing for Bennett, but to be the choice of the hero of a romance of wildest opulence was a tremendous send-off. He was accepted at once, and when Tembarom actually "stood for" a big farewell supper of his own in "The Hall," and nearly had his hand shaken off by congratulating acquaintances, the fact that he kept the new aspirant by his side, so that the waves of high popularity flowed over him until he sometimes lost his joyful breath, established him as a sort of hero himself.

Mr. Palford did not know of this festivity, as he also found he was not told of several other things. This he counted as a feature of his client's exoticism. His extraordinary lack of concealment of things vanity forbids many from confessing combined itself with a quite cheerful power to keep his own counsel when he was, for reasons of his own, so inclined.

"He can keep his mouth shut, that chap," Hutchinson had said once, and Mr. Palford remembered it. "Most of us can't. I've got a notion I can; but I don't many's the time when I should. There's a lot more in him than you'd think for. He's naught but a lad, but he is na half such a fool as he looks."

He was neither hesitant nor timid, Mr. Palford observed. In an entirely unostentatious way he soon realized that his money gave things into his hands. He knew he could do most things he chose to do, and that the power to do them rested in these days with himself without the necessity of detailed explanation or appeal to others, as in the case, for instance, of this mysterious friend or protege whose name was Strangeways. Of the history of his acquaintance with him Palford knew nothing, and that he should choose to burden himself with a half-witted invalid—in these terms the solicitor described him—was simply in-explainable. If he had asked for advice or by his manner left an opening for the offering of it, he would have been most strongly counseled to take him to a public asylum and leave him there; but advice on the subject seemed the last thing he desired or anticipated, and talk about his friend was what he seemed least likely to indulge in. He made no secret of his intentions, but he frankly took charge of them as his own special business, and left the rest alone.

"Say nothing and saw wood," Palford had once been a trifle puzzled by hearing him remark casually, and he remembered it later, as he remembered the comments of Joseph Hutchinson. Tembarom had explained himself to Little Ann.

"You'll understand," he said. "It is like this. I guess I feel like you do when a dog or a cat in big trouble just looks at you as if you were all they had, and they know if you don't stick by them they'll be killed, and it just drives them crazy. It's the way they look at you that you can't stand. I believe something would burst in that fellow's brain if I left him. When he found out I was going to do it he'd just let out some awful kind of a yell I'd remember till I died. I dried right up almost as soon as I spoke of him to Palford. He couldn't see anything but that he was crazy and ought to be put in an asylum. Well, he's not. There're times when he talks to me almost sensible; only he's always so awful low down in his mind you're afraid to let him go on. And he's a little bit better than he was. It seems queer to get to like a man that's sort of dotty, but I tell you, Ann, because you'll understand—I've got to sort of like him, and want to see if I can work it out for him somehow. England seems to sort of stick in his mind. If I can't spend my money in living the way I want to live,—buying jewelry and clothes for the girl I'd like to see dressed like a queen—I'm going to do this just to please myself. I'm going to take him to England and keep him quiet and see what'll happen. Those big doctors ought to know about all there is to know, and I can pay them any old thing they want. By jings! isn't it the limit—to sit here and say that and know it's true!"

Beyond the explaining of necessary detail to him and piloting him to England, Mr. Palford did not hold himself many degrees responsible. His theory of correct conduct assumed no form of altruism. He had formulated it even before he reached middle age. One of his fixed rules was to avoid the error of allowing sympathy or sentiment to hamper him with any unnecessary burden. Natural tendency of temperament had placed no obstacles in the way of his keeping this rule. To burden himself with the instruction or modification of this unfortunately hopeless young New Yorker would be unnecessary. Palford's summing up of him was that he was of a type with which nothing palliative could be done. There he was. As unavoidable circumstances forced one to take him,—commonness, slanginess, appalling ignorance, and all,—one could not leave him. Fortunately, no respectable legal firm need hold itself sponsor for a "next of kin" provided by fate and the wilds of America.

The Temple Barholm estate had never, in Mr. Palford's generation, been specially agreeable to deal with. The late Mr. Temple Temple Barholm had been a client of eccentric and abominable temper. Interviews with him had been avoided as much as possible. His domineering insolence of bearing had at times been on the verge of precipitating unheard-of actions, because it was almost more than gentlemanly legal flesh and blood could bear. And now appeared this young man.

He rushed about New York strenuously attending to business concerning himself and his extraordinary acquaintances, and on the day of the steamer's sailing he presented himself at the last moment in an obviously just purchased suit of horribly cut clothes. At all events, their cut was horrible in the eyes of Mr. Palford, who accepted no cut but that of a West End tailor. They were badly made things enough, because they were unconsidered garments that Tembarom had barely found time to snatch from a "ready-made" counter at the last moment. He had been too much "rushed" by other things to remember that he must have them until almost too late to get them at all. He bought them merely because they were clothes, and warm enough to make a voyage in. He possessed a monster ulster, in which, to Mr. Palford's mind, he looked like a flashy black-leg. He did not know it was flashy. His opportunities for cultivating a refined taste in the matter of wardrobe had been limited, and he had wasted no time in fastidious consideration or regrets. Palford did him some injustice in taking it for granted that his choice of costume was the result of deliberate bad taste. It was really not choice at all. He neither liked his clothes nor disliked them. He had been told he needed warm garments, and he had accepted the advice of the first salesman who took charge of him when he dropped into the big department store he was most familiar with because it was the cheapest in town. Even when it was no longer necessary to be cheap, it was time-saving and easy to go into a place one knew.

The fact that he was as he was, and that they were the subjects of comment and objects of unabated interest through-out the voyage, that it was proper that they should be companions at table and on deck, filled Mr. Palford with annoyed unease.

Of course every one on board was familiar with the story of the discovery of the lost heir. The newspapers had reveled in it, and had woven romances about it which might well have caused the deceased Mr. Temple Barholm to turn in his grave. After the first day Tembarom had been picked out from among the less-exciting passengers, and when he walked the deck, books were lowered into laps or eyes followed him over their edges. His steamer-chair being placed in a prominent position next to that of a pretty, effusive Southern woman, the mother of three daughters whose eyes and eyelashes attracted attention at the distance of a deck's length, he was without undue delay provided with acquaintances who were prepared to fill his every moment with entertainment.

"The three Gazelles," as their mother playfully confided to Tembarom her daughters were called in Charleston, were destructively lovely. They were swaying reeds of grace, and being in radiant spirits at the prospect of "going to Europe," were companions to lure a man to any desperate lengths. They laughed incessantly, as though they were chimes of silver bells; they had magnolia-petal skins which neither wind nor sun blemished; they had nice young manners, and soft moods in which their gazelle eyes melted and glowed and their long lashes drooped. They could dance, they played on guitars, and they sang. They were as adorable as they were lovely and gay.

"If a fellow was going to fall in love," Tembarom said to Palford, "there'd be no way out of this for him unless he climbed the rigging and dragged his food up in a basket till he got to Liverpool. If he didn't go crazy about Irene, he'd wake up raving about Honora; and if he got away from Honora, Adelia Louise would have him `down on the mat.'" From which Mr. Palford argued that the impression made by the little Miss Hutchinson with the Manchester accent had not yet had time to obliterate itself.

The Gazelles were of generous Southern spirit, and did not surround their prize with any barrier of precautions against other young persons of charm. They introduced him to one girl after another, and in a day or two he was the center of animated circles whenever he appeard. The singular thing, however, was that he did not appear as often as the other men who were on board. He seemed to stay a great deal with Strangeways, who shared his suite of rooms and never came on deck. Sometimes the Gazelles prettily reproached him. Adelia Louise suggested to the others that his lack of advantages in the past had made him feel rather awkward and embarrassed; but Palford knew he was not embarrassed. He accepted his own limitations too simply to be disturbed by them. Palford would have been extremely bored by him if he had been of the type of young outsider who is anxiouus about himself and expansive in self-revelation and appeals for advice; but sometimes Tembarom's air of frankness, which was really the least expansive thing in the world and revealed nothing whatever, besides concealing everything it chose, made him feel himself almost irritatingly baffled. It would have been more natural if he had not been able to keep anything to himself and had really talked too much.

CHAPTER X

The necessary business in London having been transacted, Tembarom went north to take possession of the home of his forefathers. It had rained for two days before he left London, and it rained steadily all the way to Lancashire, and was raining steadily when he reached Temple Barholm. He had never seen such rain before. It was the quiet, unmoved persistence of it which amazed him. As he sat in the railroad carriage and watched the slanting lines of its unabating downpour, he felt that Mr. Palford must inevitably make some remark upon it. But Mr. Palford continued to read his newspapers undisturbedly, as though the condition of atmosphere surrounding him were entirely accustomed and natural. It was of course necessary and proper that he should accompany his client to his destination, but the circumstances of the case made the whole situation quite abnormal. Throughout the centuries each Temple Barholm had succeeded to his estate in a natural and conventional manner. He had either been welcomed or resented by his neighbors, his tenants, and his family, and proper and fitting ceremonies had been observed. But here was an heir whom nobody knew, whose very existence nobody had even suspected, a young man who had been an outcast in the streets of the huge American city of which lurid descriptions are given. Even in New York he could have produced no circle other than Mrs. Bowse's boarding-house and the objects of interest to the up-town page, so he brought no one with him; for Strangeways seemed to have been mysteriously disposed of after their arrival in London.

Never had Palford & Grimby on their hands a client who seemed so entirely alone. What, Mr. Palford asked himself, would he do in the enormity of Temple Barholm, which always struck one as being a place almost without limit. But that, after all, was neither here nor there. There he was. You cannot undertake to provide a man with relatives if he has none, or with acquaintances if people do not want to know him. His past having been so extraordinary, the neighborhood would naturally be rather shy of him. At first, through mere force of custom and respect for an old name, punctilious, if somewhat alarmed, politeness would be shown by most people; but after the first calls all would depend upon how much people could stand of the man himself.

The aspect of the country on a wet winter's day was not enlivening. The leafless and dripping hedges looked like bundles of sticks; the huge trees, which in June would be majestic bowers of greenery, now held out great skeleton arms, which seemed to menace both earth and sky. Heavy-faced laborers tramped along muddy lanes; cottages with soaked bits of dead gardens looked like hovels; big, melancholy cart-horses, dragging jolting carts along the country roads, hung their heads as they splashed through the mire.

As Tembarom had known few persons who had ever been out of America, he had not heard that England was beautiful, and he saw nothing which led him to suspect its charms. London had impressed him as gloomy, dirty, and behind the times despite its pretensions; the country struck him as "the limit." Hully gee! was he going to be expected to spend his life in this! Should he be obliged to spend his life in it. He'd find that out pretty quick, and then, if there was no hard-and-fast law against it, him for little old New York again, if he had to give up the whole thing and live on ten per. If he had been a certain kind of youth, his discontent would have got the better of him, and he might have talked a good deal to Mr. Palford and said many disparaging things.

"But the man was born here," he reflected. "I guess he doesn't know anything else, and thinks it's all right. I've heard of English fellows who didn't like New York. He looks like that kind."

He had supplied himself with newspapers and tried to read them. Their contents were as unexciting as the rain-sodden landscape. There were no head-lines likely to arrest any man's attention. There was a lot about Parliament and the Court, and one of them had a column or two about what lords and ladies were doing, a sort of English up-town or down-town page.

He knew the stuff, but there was no snap in it, and there were no photographs or descriptions of dresses. Galton would have turned it down. He could never have made good if he had done no better than that. He grinned to himself when he read that the king had taken a drive and that a baby prince had the measles.

"I wonder what they'd think of the Sunday Earth," he mentally inquired.

He would have been much at sea if he had discovered what they really would have thought of it. They passed through smoke-vomiting manufacturing towns, where he saw many legs seemingly bearing about umbrellas, but few entire people; they whizzed smoothly past drenched suburbs, wet woodlands, and endless-looking brown moors, covered with dead bracken and bare and prickly gorse. He thought these last great desolate stretches worse than all the rest.

But the railroad carriage was luxuriously upholstered and comfortable, though one could not walk about and stretch his legs. In the afternoon, Mr. Palford ordered in tea, and plainly expected him to drink two cups and eat thin bread and butter. He felt inclined to laugh, though the tea was all right, and so was the bread and butter, and he did not fail his companion in any respect. The inclination to laugh was aroused by the thought of what Jim Bowles and Julius would say if they could see old T. T. with nothing to do at

4:30 but put in cream and sugar, as though he were at a tea-party on Fifth Avenue.

But, gee! this rain did give him the Willies. If he was going to be sorry for himself, he might begin right now. But he wasn't. He was going to see this thing through.

The train had been continuing its smooth whir through fields, wooded lands, and queer, dead-and-alive little villages for some time before it drew up at last at a small station. Bereft by the season of its garden bloom and green creepers, it looked a bare and uninviting little place. On the two benches against the wall of the platform a number of women sat huddled together in the dampness. Several of them held children in their laps and all stared very hard, nudging one another as he descended from the train. A number of rustics stood about the platform, giving it a somewhat crowded air. It struck Tembarom that, for an out-of-the-way place, there seemed to be a good many travelers, and he wondered if they could all be going away. He did not know that they were the curious element among such as lived in the immediate neighborhood of the station and had come out merely to see him on his first appearance. Several of them touched their hats as he went by, and he supposed they knew Palford and were saluting him. Each of them was curious, but no one was in a particularly welcoming mood. There was, indeed, no reason for anticipating enthusiasm. It was, however, but human nature that the bucolic mind should bestir itself a little in the desire to obtain a view of a Temple Barholm who had earned his living by blacking boots and selling newspapers, unknowing that he was "one o' th' gentry."

When he stepped from his first-class carriage, Tembarom found himself confronted by a very straight, clean-faced, and well-built young man, who wore a long, fawn-colored livery coat with claret facings and silver buttons. He touched his cockaded hat, and at once took up the Gladstone bags. Tembarom knew that he was a footman because he had seen something like him outside restaurants, theaters, and shops in New York, but he was not sure whether he ought to touch his own hat or not. He slightly lifted it from his head to show there was no ill feeling, and then followed him and Mr. Palford to the carriage waiting for them. It was a severe but sumptuous equipage, and the coachman was as well dressed and well built as the footman. Tembarom took his place in it with many mental reservations.

"What are the illustrations on the doors?" he inquired.

"The Temple Barholm coat of arms," Mr. Palford answered. "The people at the station are your tenants. Members of the family of the stout man with the broad hat have lived as yeoman farmers on your land for three hundred years."

They went on their way, with more rain, more rain, more dripping hedges, more soaked fields, and more bare, huge-armed trees. CLOP, CLOP, CLOP, sounded the horses' hoofs along the road, and from his corner of the carriage Mr. Palford tried to make polite conversation. Faces peered out of the windows of the cottages, sometimes a whole family group of faces, all crowded together, eager to look, from the mother with a baby in her arms to the old man or woman, plainly grandfather or grandmother—sharp, childishly round, or bleared old eyes, all excited and anxious to catch glimpses.

"They are very curious to see you," said Mr. Palford. "Those two laborers are touching their hats to you. It will be as well to recognize their salute."

At a number of the cottage doors the group stood upon the threshold and touched foreheads or curtsied. Tembarom saluted again and again, and more than once his friendly grin showed itself. It made him feel queer to drive along, turning from side to side to acknowledge obeisances, as he had seen a well-known military hero acknowledge them as he drove down Broadway.

The chief street of the village of Temple Barholm wandered almost within hailing distance of the great entrance to the park. The gates were supported by massive pillars, on which crouched huge stone griffins. Tembarom felt that they stared savagely over his head as he was driven toward them as for inspection, and in disdainful silence allowed to pass between them as they stood on guard, apparently with the haughtiest mental reservations.

The park through which the long avenue rolled concealed its beauty to the unaccustomed eye, showing only more bare trees and sodden stretches of brown grass. The house itself, as it loomed up out of the thickening rain-mist, appalled Tembarom by its size and gloomily gray massiveness. Before it was spread a broad terrace of stone, guarded by more griffins of even more disdainful aspect than those watching over the gates. The stone noses held themselves rigidly in the air as the reporter of the up-town society page passed with Mr. Palford up a flight of steps broad enough to make him feel as though he were going to church. Footmen with powdered heads received him at the carriage door, seemed to assist him to move, to put one foot before the other for him, to stand in rows as though they were a military guard ready to take him into custody.

Then he was inside, standing in an enormous hall filled with furnishings such as he had never seen or heard of before. Carved oak, suits of armor, stone urns, portraits, another flight of church steps mounting upward to surrounding galleries, stained-glass windows, tigers' and lions' heads, horns of tremendous size, strange and beautiful weapons, suggested to him that the dream he had been living in for weeks had never before been so much a dream. He had walked about as in a vision, but among familiar surroundings.

Mrs. Bowse's boarders and his hall bedroom had helped him to retain some hold over actual existence. But here the reverently saluting villagers staring at him through windows as though he were General Grant, the huge, stone entrance, the drive of what seemed to be ten miles through the park, the gloomy mass of architecture looming up, the regiment of liveried men-servants, with respectfully lowered but excitedly curious eyes, the dark and solemn richness inclosing and claiming him—all this created an atmosphere wholly unreal. As he had not known books, its parallel had not been suggested to him by literature. He had literally not heard that such things existed. Selling newspapers and giving every moment to the struggle for life or living, one did not come within the range of splendors. He had indeed awakened in that other world of which he had spoken. And though he had heard that there was another world, he had had neither time nor opportunity to make mental pictures of it. His life so far had expressed itself in another language of figures. The fact that he had in his veins the blood of the Norman lords and Saxon kings may or may not have had something to do with the fact that he was not abashed, but bewildered. The same factor may or may not have aided him to preserve a certain stoic, outward composure. Who knows what remote influences express themselves in common acts of modern common life? As Cassivellaunus observed his surroundings as he followed in captive chains his conqueror's triumphal car through the streets of Rome, so the keen-eyed product of New York pavement life "took in" all about him. Existence had forced upon him the habit of sharp observance. The fundamental working law of things had expressed itself in the simple colloquialism, "Keep your eye skinned, and don't give yourself away." In what phrases the parallel of this concise advice formulated itself in 55 B.C. no classic has yet exactly informed us, but doubtless something like it was said in ancient Rome. Tembarom did not give himself away, and he took rapid, if uncertain, inventory of people and things. He remarked, for instance, that Palford's manner of speaking to a servant was totally different from the manner he used in addressing himself. It was courteous, but remote, as though he spoke across an accepted chasm to beings of another race. There was no hint of incivility in it, but also no hint of any possibility that it could occur to the person addressed to hesitate or resent. It was a subtle thing, and Tembarom wondered how he did it.

They were shown into a room the walls of which seemed built of books; the furniture was rich and grave and luxuriously comfortable. A fire blazed as well as glowed in a fine chimney, and a table near it was set with a glitter of splendid silver urn and equipage for tea.

"Mrs. Butterworth was afraid you might not have been able to get tea, sir," said the man-servant, who did not wear livery, but whose butler's air of established authority was more impressive than any fawn color and claret enriched with silver could have encompassed.

Tea again? Perhaps one was obliged to drink it at regular intervals. Tembarom for a moment did not awaken to the fact that the man was speaking to him, as the master from whom orders came. He glanced at Mr. Palford.

"Mr. Temple Barholm had tea after we left Crowly," Mr. Palford said. "He will no doubt wish to go to his room at once, Burrill."

"Yes, sir," said Burrill, with that note of entire absence of comment with which Tembarom later became familiar. "Pearson is waiting."

It was not unnatural to wonder who Pearson was and why he was waiting, but Tembarom knew he would find out. There was a slight relief on realizing that tea was not imperative. He and Mr. Palford were led through the hall again. The carriage had rolled away, and two footmen, who were talking confidentially together, at once stood at attention. The staircase was more imposing as one mounted it than it appeared as one looked at it from below. Its breadth made Tembarom wish to lay a hand on a balustrade, which seemed a mile away. He had never particularly wished to touch balustrades before. At the head of the first flight hung an enormous piece of tapestry, its forest and hunters and falconers awakening Tembarom's curiosity, as it looked wholly unlike any picture he had ever seen in a shop-window. There were pictures everywhere, and none of them looked like chromos. Most of the people in the portraits were in fancy dress. Rumors of a New York millionaire ball had given him some vague idea of fancy dress. A lot of them looked like freaks. He caught glimpses of corridors lighted by curious, high, deep windows with leaded panes. It struck him that there was no end to the place, and that there must be rooms enough in it for a hotel.

"The tapestry chamber, of course, Burrill," he heard Mr. Palford say in a low tone.

"Yes, sir. Mr. Temple Barholm always used it."

A few yards farther on a door stood open, revealing an immense room, rich and gloomy with tapestry-covered walls and dark oak furniture. A bed which looked to Tembarom incredibly big, with its carved oak canopy and massive posts, had a presiding personality of its own. It was mounted by steps, and its hangings and coverlid were of embossed velvet, time-softened to the perfection of purples and blues. A fire enriched the color of everything, and did its best to drive the shadows away. Deep windows opened either into the leafless boughs of close-growing trees or upon outspread spaces of heavily timbered park, where gaunt, though magnificent, bare branches menaced and defied. A slim, neat young man, with a rather pale face and a touch of anxiety in his expression, came forward at once.

"This is Pearson, who will valet you," exclaimed Mr. Palford.

"Thank you, sir," said Pearson in a low, respectful voice. His manner was correctness itself.

There seemed to Mr. Palford to be really nothing else to say. He wanted, in fact, to get to his own apartment and have a hot bath and a rest before dinner.

"Where am I, Burrill?" he inquired as he turned to go down the corridor.

"The crimson room, sir," answered Burrill, and he closed the door of the tapestry chamber and shut Tembarom in alone with Pearson.

CHAPTER XI

For a few moments the two young men looked at each other, Pearson's gaze being one of respectfulness which hoped to propitiate, if propitiation was necessary, though Pearson greatly trusted it was not. Tembarom's was the gaze of hasty investigation and inquiry. He suddenly thought that it would have been "all to the merry" if somebody had "put him on to" a sort of idea of what was done to a fellow when he was "valeted." A valet, he had of course gathered, waited on one somehow and looked after one's clothes. But were there by chance other things he expected to do,—manicure one's nails or cut one's hair,—and how often did he do it, and was this the day? He was evidently there to do something, or he wouldn't have been waiting behind the door to pounce out the minute he appeared, and when the other two went away, Burrill wouldn't have closed the door as solemnly as though he shut the pair of them in together to get through some sort of performance.

"Here's where T. T. begins to feel like a fool," he thought. "And here's where there's no way out of looking like one. I don't know a thing."

But personal vanity was not so strong in him as healthy and normal good temper. Despite the fact that the neat correctness of Pearson's style and the finished expression of his neat face suggested that he was of a class which knew with the most finished exactness all that custom and propriety demanded on any occasion on which "valeting" in its most occult branches might be done, he was only "another fellow," after all, and must be human. So Tembarom smiled at him.

"Hello, Pearson," he said. "How are you?"

Pearson slightly started. It was the tiniest possible start, quite involuntary, from which he recovered instantly, to reply in a tone of respectful gratefulness:

"Thank you, sir, very well; thank you, sir."

"That's all right," answered Tembarom, a sense of relief because he'd "got started" increasing the friendliness of his smile. "I see you got my trunk open," he said, glancing at some articles of clothing neatly arranged upon the bed.

Pearson was slightly alarmed. It occurred to him suddenly that perhaps it was not the custom in America to open a gentleman's box and lay out his clothes for him. For special reasons he was desperately anxious to keep his place, and above all things he felt he must avoid giving offense by doing things which, by being too English, might seem to cast shades of doubt on the entire correctness of the customs of America. He had known ill feeling to arise between "gentlemen's gentlemen" in the servants' hall in the case of slight differences in customs, contested with a bitterness of feeling which had made them almost an international question. There had naturally been a great deal of talk about the new Mr. Temple Barholm and what might be expected of him. When a gentleman was not a gentleman,—this was the form of expression in "the hall,"—the Lord only knew what would happen. And this one, who had, for all one knew, been born in a workhouse, and had been a boot-black kicked about in American streets,—they did not know Tembarom,—and nearly starved to death, and found at last in a low lodging-house, what could he know about decent living? And ten to one he'd be American enough to swagger and bluster and pretend he knew everything better than any one else, and lose his temper frightfully when he made mistakes, and try to make other people seem to blame. Set a beggar on horseback, and who didn't know what he was? There were chances enough and to spare that not one of them would be able to stand it, and that in a month's time they would all be looking for new places.

So while Tembarom was rather afraid of Pearson and moved about in an awful state of uncertainty, Pearson was horribly afraid of Tembarom, and was, in fact, in such a condition of nervous anxiety that he was obliged more than once furtively to apply to his damp, pale young forehead his exceedingly fresh and spotless pocket-handkerchief.

In the first place, there was the wardrobe. What COULD he do? How could he approach the subject with sufficient delicacy? Mr. Temple Barholm had brought with him only a steamer trunk and a Gladstone bag, the latter evidently bought in London, to be stuffed with hastily purchased handkerchiefs and shirts, worn as they came out of the shop, and as evidently bought without the slightest idea of the kind of linen a gentleman should own. What most terrified Pearson, who was of a timid and most delicate-minded nature, was that having the workhouse and the boot-blacking as a background, the new Mr. Temple Barholm COULDN'T know, as all this had come upon him so suddenly. And was it to be Pearson's calamitous duty to explain to him that he had NOTHING, that he apparently KNEW nothing, and that as he had no friends who knew, a mere common servant must educate him, if he did not wish to see him derided and looked down upon and actually "cut" by gentlemen that WERE gentlemen? All this to say nothing of Pearson's own well-earned reputation for knowledge of custom, intelligence, and deftness in turning out the objects of his care in such form as to be a reference in themselves when a new place was wanted. Of course sometimes there were even real gentlemen who were most careless and indifferent to appearance, and who, if left to themselves, would buy garments which made the blood run cold when one realized that his own character and hopes for the future often depended upon his latest employer's outward aspect. But the ulster in which Mr. Temple Barholm had presented himself was of a cut and material such as Pearson's most discouraged moments had never forced him to contemplate. The limited wardrobe in the steamer trunk was all new and all equally bad. There was no evening dress, no proper linen,—not what Pearson called "proper,"—no proper toilet appurtenances. What was Pearson called upon by duty to do? If he had only had the initiative to anticipate this, he might have asked permission to consult in darkest secrecy with Mr. Palford. But he had never dreamed of such a situation, and apparently he would be obliged to send his new charge down to his first dinner in the majestically decorous dining-room, "before all the servants," in a sort of speckled tweed cutaway, with a brown necktie.

Tembarom, realizing without delay that Pearson did not expect to be talked to and being cheered by the sight of the fire, sat down before it in an easy-chair the like of which for luxurious comfort he had never known. He was, in fact, waiting for developments. Pearson would say or do something shortly which would give him a chance to "catch on," or perhaps he'd go out of the room and leave him to himself, which would be a thing to thank God for. Then he could wash his face and hands, brush his hair, and wait till the dinner-bell rang. They'd be likely to have one. They'd have to in a place like this.

But Pearson did not go out of the room. He moved about behind him for a short time with footfall so almost entirely soundless that Tembarom became aware that, if it went on long, he should be nervous; in fact, he was nervous already. He wanted to know what he was doing. He could scarcely resist the temptation to turn his head and look; but he did not want to give himself away more entirely than was unavoidable, and, besides, instinct told him that he might frighten Pearson, who looked frightened enough, in a neat and well-mannered way, already. Hully gee! how he wished he would go out of the room!

But he did not. There were gently gliding footsteps of Pearson behind him, quiet movements which would have seemed stealthy if they had been a burglar's, soft removals of articles from one part of the room to another, delicate brushings, and almost noiseless foldings. Now Pearson was near the bed, now he had opened a wardrobe, now he was looking into the steamer trunk, now he had stopped somewhere behind him, within a few yards of his chair. Why had he ceased moving? What was he looking at? What kept him quiet?

Tembarom expected him to begin stirring mysteriously again; but he did not. Why did he not? There reigned in the room entire silence; no soft footfalls, no brushing, no folding. Was he doing nothing? Had he got hold of something which had given him a fit? There had been no sound of a fall; but perhaps even if an English valet had a fit, he'd have it so quietly and respectfully that one wouldn't hear it. Tembarom felt that he must be looking at the back of his head, and he wondered what was the matter with it. Was his hair cut in a way so un-English that it had paralyzed him? The back of his head began to creep under an investigation so prolonged. No sound at all, no movement. Tembarom stealthily took out his watch—good old Waterbury he wasn't going to part with—and began to watch the minute-hand. If nothing happened in three minutes he was going to turn round. One—two—three—and the silence made it seem fifteen. He returned his Waterbury to his pocket and turned round.

Pearson was not dead. He was standing quite still and resigned, waiting. It was his business to wait, not to intrude or disturb, and having put everything in order and done all he could do, he was waiting for further commands—in some suspense, it must be admitted.

"Hello!" exclaimed Tembarom, involuntarily.

"Shall I get your bath ready, sir?" inquired Pearson. "Do you like it hot or cold, sir?"

Tembarom drew a relieved breath. He hadn't dropped dead and he hadn't had a fit, and here was one of the things a man did when he valeted you—he got your bath ready. A hasty recollection of the much-used, paint-smeared tin bath on the fourth floor of Mrs. Bowse's boarding-house sprang up before him. Everybody had to use it in turn, and you waited hours for the chance to make a dash into it. No one stood still and waited fifteen minutes until you got good and ready to tell him he could go and turn on the water. Gee whizz!

Being relieved himself, he relieved Pearson by telling him he might "fix it" for him, and that he would have hot water.

"Very good, sir. Thank you, sir," said Pearson, and silently left the room.

Then Tembarom got up from his chair and began to walk about rather restlessly. A new alarm seized him. Did Pearson expect to WASH him or to stand round and hand him soap and towels and things while he washed himself?

If it was supposed that you hadn't the strength to turn the faucets yourself, it might be supposed you didn't have the energy to use a flesh-brush and towels. Did valeting include a kind of shampoo all over?

"I couldn't stand for that," he said. "I'd have to tell him there'd been no Turkish baths in mine, and I'm not trained up to them. When I've got on to this kind of thing a bit more, I'll make him understand what I'm NOT in for; but I don't want to scare the life out of him right off. He looks like a good little fellow."

But Pearson's duties as valet did not apparently include giving him his bath by sheer physical force. He was deft, calm, amenable. He led Tembarom down the corridor to the bath-room, revealed to him stores of sumptuous bath-robes and towels, hot-and cold-water faucets, sprays, and tonic essences. He forgot nothing and, having prepared all, mutely vanished, and returned to the bedroom to wait—and gaze in troubled wonder at the speckled tweed cutaway. There was an appalling possibility—he was aware that he was entirely ignorant of American customs—that tweed was the fashionable home evening wear in the States. Tembarom, returning from his bath much refreshed after a warm plunge and a cold shower, evidently felt that as a costume it was all that could be desired.

"Will you wear—these, sir,—this evening?" Pearson suggested.

It was suggestive of more than actual inquiry. If he had dared to hope that his manner might suggest a number of things! For instance, that in England gentlemen really didn't wear tweed in the evening even in private. That through some unforeseen circumstances his employer's evening-dress suit had been delayed, but would of course arrive to-morrow!

But Tembarom, physically stimulated by hot and cold water, and relief at being left alone, was beginning to recover his natural buoyancy.

"Yes, I'll wear 'em," he answered, snatching at his hairbrush and beginning to brush his damp hair. It was a wooden-backed brush that Pearson had found in his Gladstone bag and shudderingly laid in readiness on the dressing-table. "I guess they're all right, ain't they?"

"Oh, quite right, sir, quite," Pearson ventured—"for morning wear."

"Morning?" said Tembarom, brushing vigorously. "Not night?"

"Black, sir," most delicately hinted Pearson, "is—more usual—in the evening—in England." After which he added, "So to speak," with a vague hope that the mollifying phrase might counteract the effect of any apparently implied aspersion on colors preferred in America.

Tembarom ceased brushing his hair, and looked at him in good-natured desire for information.

"Frock-coats or claw-hammer?" he asked. Despite his natural anxiety, and in the midst of it, Pearson could not but admit that he had an uncondemnatory voice and a sort of young way with him which gave one courage. But he was not quite sure of "claw-hammer."

"Frock-coats for morning dress and afternoon wear, sir," he ventured. "The evening cut, as you know, is—"

"Claw-hammer. Swallow-tail, I guess you say here," Tembarom ended for him, quite without hint of rancor, he was rejoiced to see.

"Yes, sir," said Pearson.

The ceremony of dressing proved a fearsome thing as it went on. Pearson moved about deftly and essayed to do things for the new Mr. Temple Barholm which the new Mr. Temple Barholm had never heard of a man not doing for himself. He reached for things Pearson was about to hand to him or hold for him. He unceremoniously achieved services for himself which it was part of Pearson's manifest duty to perform. They got into each other's way; there was even danger sometimes of their seeming to snatch things from each other, to Pearson's unbounded horror. Mr. Temple Barholm did not express any irritation whatsoever misunderstandings took place, but he held his mouth rather close-shut, and Pearson, not aware that he did this as a precaution against open grinning or shouts of laughter as he found himself unable to adjust himself to his attendant's movements, thought it possible that he was secretly annoyed and regarded the whole matter with disfavor. But when the dressing was at an end and he stood ready to go down in all his innocent ignoring of speckled tweed and brown necktie, he looked neither flurried nor out of humor, and he asked a question in a voice which was actually friendly. It was a question dealing with an incident which had aroused much interest in the servants' hall as suggesting a touch of mystery.

"Mr. Strangeways came yesterday all right, didn't he?" he inquired.

"Yes, sir," Pearson answered. "Mr. Hutchinson and his daughter came with him. They call her `Little Ann Hutchinson.' She's a sensible little thing, sir, and she seemed to know exactly what you'd want done to make him comfortable. Mrs. Butterworth put him in the west room, sir, and I valeted him. He was not very well when he came, but he seems better to-day, sir, only he's very anxious to see you."

"That's all right," said Tembarom. "You show me his room. I'll go and see him now."

And being led by Pearson, he went without delay.

CHAPTER XII

The chief objection to Temple Barholm in Tembarom's mind was that it was too big for any human use. That at least was how it struck him. The entrance was too big, the stairs were too wide, the rooms too broad and too long and too high to allow of eyes accustomed to hall bedrooms adjusting their vision without discomfort. The dining-room in which the new owner took his first meal in company with Mr. Palford, and attended by the large, serious man who wore no livery and three tall footmen who did, was of a size and stateliness which made him feel homesick for Mrs. Bowse's dining-room, with its two hurried, incompetent, and often-changed waitresses and its prevailing friendly custom of pushing things across the table to save time. Meals were quickly disposed of at Mrs. Bowse's. Everybody was due up-town or down-town, and regarded food as an unavoidable, because necessary, interference with more urgent business. At Temple Barholm one sat half the night—this was the impression made upon Tembarom—watching things being brought in and taken out of the room, carved on a huge buffet, and passed from one man to another; and when they were brought solemnly to you, if you turned them down, it seemed that the whole ceremony had to be gone through with again. All sorts of silver knives, forks, and spoons were given to one and taken away, and half a dozen sorts of glasses stood by your plate; and if you made a move to do anything for yourself, the man out of livery stopped you as though you were too big a fool to be trusted. The food was all right, but when you knew what anything was, and were inclined to welcome it as an old friend, it was given to you in some way that made you get rattled. With all the swell dishes, you had no butter-plate, and ice seemed scarce, and the dead, still way the servants moved about gave you a sort of feeling that you were at a funeral and that it wasn't decent to talk so long as the remains were in the room. The head-man and the foot-men seemed to get on by signs, though Tembarom never saw them making any; and their faces never changed for a moment. Once or twice he tried a joke, addressing it to Mr. Palford, to see what would happen. But as Mr. Palford did not seem to see the humor of it, and gave him the "glassy eye," and neither the head-man nor the footmen seemed to hear it, he thought that perhaps they didn't know it was a joke; and if they didn't, and they thought anything at all, they must think he was dippy. The dinner was a deadly, though sumptuous, meal, and long drawn out, when measured by meals at Mrs. Bowse's. He did not know, as Mr. Palford did, that it was perfect, and served with a finished dexterity that was also perfection.

Mr. Palford, however, was himself relieved when it was at an end. He had sat at dinner with the late Mr. Temple Barholm in his day, and had seen him also served by the owners of impassive countenances; but he had been aware that whatsoever of secret dislike and resentment was concealed by them, there lay behind their immovability an acceptance of the fact that he represented, even in his most objectionable humors, centuries of accustomedness to respectful service and of knowledge of his right and power to claim it. The solicitor was keenly aware of the silent comments being made upon the tweed suit and brown necktie and on the manner in which their wearer boldly chose the wrong fork or erroneously made use of a knife or spoon. Later in the evening, in the servants' hall, the comment would not be silent, and there could be no doubt of what its character would be. There would be laughter and the relating of incidents. Housemaids and still-room maids would giggle, and kitchen-maids and boot-boys would grin and whisper in servile tribute to the witticisms of the superior servants.

After dinner the rest of the evening could at least be spent in talk about business matters. There still remained details to be enlarged upon before Palford himself returned to Lincoln's Inn and left Mr. Temple Barholm to the care of the steward of his estate. It was not difficult to talk to him when the sole subject of conversation was of a business nature.

Before they parted for the night the mystery of the arrangements made for Strangeways had been cleared. In fact, Mr. Temple Barholm made no mystery of them. He did not seem ignorant of the fact that what he had chosen to do was unusual, but he did not appear hampered or embarrassed by the knowledge. His remarks on the subject were entirely civil and were far from actually suggesting that his singular conduct was purely his own business and none of his solicitor's; but for a moment or so Mr. Palford was privately just a trifle annoyed. The Hutchinsons had traveled from London with Strangeways in their care the day before. He would have been unhappy and disturbed if he had been obliged to travel with Mr. Palford, who was a stranger to him, and Miss Hutchinson had a soothing effect on him. Strangeways was for the present comfortably installed as a guest of the house, Miss Hutchinson having talked to the housekeeper, Mrs. Butterworth, and to Pearson. What the future held for him Mr. Temple Barholm did not seem to feel the necessity of going into. He left him behind as a subject, and went on talking cheerfully of other things almost as if he had forgotten him.

They had their coffee in the library, and afterward sat at the writing-table and looked over documents and talked until Mr. Palford felt that he could quite decorously retire to his bedroom. He was glad to be relieved of his duties, and Tembarom was amiably resigned to parting with him.

Tembarom did not go up-stairs at once himself. He sat by the fire and smoked several pipes of tobacco and thought things over. There were a lot of things to think over, and several decisions to make, and he thought it would be a good idea to pass them in review. The quiet of the dead surrounded him. In a house the size of this the servants were probably half a mile away. They'd need trolleys to get to one, he thought, if you rang for them in a hurry. If an armed burglar made a quiet entry without your knowing it, he could get in some pretty rough work before any of the seventy-five footmen could come to lend a hand. He was not aware that there were two of them standing in waiting in the hall, their powdered heads close together, so that their whispers and chuckles could be heard. A sound of movement in the library would have brought them up standing to a decorous attitude of attention conveying to the uninitiated the impression that they had not moved for hours.

Sometimes as he sat in the big morocco chair, T. Tembarom looked grave enough; sometimes he looked as though he was confronting problems which needed puzzling out and with which he was not making much headway; sometimes he looked as though he was thinking of little Ann Hutchinson, and not infrequently he grinned. Here he was up to the neck in it, and he was darned if he knew what he was going to do. He didn't know a soul, and nobody knew him. He didn't know a thing he ought to know, and he didn't know any one who could tell him. Even the Hutchinsons had never been inside a place like Temple Barholm, and they were going back to Manchester after a few weeks' stay at the grandmother's cottage.

Before he had left New York he had seen Hadman and some other fellows and got things started, so that there was an even chance that the invention would be put on its feet. He had worked hard and used his own power to control money in the future as a lever which had proved to be exactly what was needed.

Hadman had been spurred and a little startled when he realized the magnitude of what really could be done, and saw also that this slangy, moneyed youth was not merely an enthusiastic fool, but saw into business schemes pretty sharply and was of a most determined readiness. With this power ranging itself on the side of Hutchinson and his invention, it was good business to begin to move, if one did not want to run a chance of being left out in the cold.

Hutchinson had gone to Manchester, and there had been barely time for a brief but characteristic interview between him and Tembarom, when he rushed back to London. Tembarom felt rather excited when he remembered it, recalling what he had felt in confronting the struggles against emotion in the blunt-featured, red face, the breaks in the rough voice, the charging up and down the room like a curiously elated bull in a china shop, and the big effort to restrain relief and gratitude the degree of which might seem to under-value the merits of the invention itself.

Once or twice when he looked serious, Tembarom was thinking this over, and also once or twice when he grinned. Relief and gratitude notwithstanding, Hutchinson had kept him in his place, and had not made unbounded efforts to conceal his sense of the incongruity of his position as the controller of fortunes and the lord of Temple Barholm, which was still vaguely flavored with indignation.

When he had finished his last pipe, Tembarom rose and knocked the ashes out of it.

"Now for Pearson," he said.

He had made up his mind to have a talk with Pearson, and there was no use wasting time. If things didn't suit you, the best thing was to see what you could do to fix them right away—if it wasn't against the law. He went out into the hall, and seeing the two footmen standing waiting, he spoke to them.

"Say, I didn't know you fellows were there," he said. "Are you waiting up for me? Well, you can go to bed, the sooner the quicker. Good night." And he went up-stairs whistling.

The glow and richness and ceremonial order of preparation in his bedroom struck him as soon as he opened the door. Everything which could possibly have been made ready for his most luxurious comfort had been made ready. He did not, it is true, care much for the huge bed with its carved oak canopy and massive pillars.

"But the lying-down part looks about all right," he said to himself.

The fine linen, the soft pillows, the downy blankets, would have allured even a man who was not tired. The covering had been neatly turned back and the snowy whiteness opened. That was English, he supposed. They hadn't got on to that at Mrs. Bowse's.

"But I guess a plain little old New York sleep will do," he said. "Temple Barholm or no Temple Barholm, I guess they can't change that."

Then there sounded a quiet knock at the door. He knew who it would turn out to be, and he was not mistaken. Pearson stood in the corridor, wearing his slightly anxious expression, but ready for orders.

Mr. Temple Barholm looked down at him with a friendly, if unusual, air.

"Say, Pearson," he announced, "if you've come to wash my face and put my hair up in crimping-pins, you needn't do it, because I'm not used to it. But come on in."

If he had told Pearson to enter and climb the chimney, it cannot be said that the order would have been obeyed upon the spot, but Pearson would certainly have hesitated and explained with respectful delicacy the fact that the task was not "his place." He came into the room.

"I came to see, if I could do anything further and—" making a courageous onslaught upon the situation for which he had been preparing himself for hours—"and also—if it is not too late—to venture to trouble you with regard to your wardrobe." He coughed a low, embarrassed cough. "In unpacking, sir, I found—I did not find—"

"You didn't find much, did you?" Tembarom assisted him.

"Of course, sir," Pearson apologized, "leaving New York so hurriedly, your—your man evidently had not time to—er—"

Tembarom looked at him a few seconds longer, as if making up his mind to something. Then he threw himself easily into the big chair by the fire, and leaned back in it with the frankest and best-natured smile possible.

"I hadn't any man," he said. "Say, Pearson," waving his hand to another chair near by, "suppose you take a seat."

Long and careful training came to Pearson's aid and supported him, but he was afraid that he looked nervous, and certainly there was a lack of entire calm in his voice.

"I—thank you, sir,—I think I'd better stand, sir."

"Why?" inquired Tembarom, taking his tobacco-pouch out of his pocket and preparing to fill another pipe.

"You're most kind, sir, but—but—" in impassioned embarrassment—"I should really PREFER to stand, sir, if you don't mind. I should feel more— more at 'ome, sir," he added, dropping an h in his agitation.

"Well, if you'd like it better, that's all right," yielded Mr. Temple Barholm, stuffing tobacco into the pipe. Pearson darted to a table, produced a match, struck it, and gave it to him.

"Thank you," said Tembarom, still good-naturedly. "But there are a few things I've GOT to say to you RIGHT now."

Pearson had really done his best, his very best, but he was terrified because of the certain circumstances once before referred to.

"I beg pardon, sir," he appealed, "but I am most anxious to give satisfaction in every respect." He WAS, poor young man, horribly anxious. "To-day being only the first day, I dare say I have not been all I should have been. I have never valeted an American gentleman before, but I'm sure I shall become accustomed to everything QUITE soon—almost immediately."

- 105 -

"Say," broke in Tembarom, "you're 'way off. I'm not complaining. You're all right."

The easy good temper of his manner was so singularly assuring that Pearson, unexplainable as he found him in every other respect, knew that this at least was to be depended upon, and he drew an almost palpable breath of relief. Something actually allured him into approaching what he had never felt it safe to approach before under like circumstances—a confidential disclosure.

"Thank you, sir: I am most grateful. The—fact is, I hoped especially to be able to settle in place just now. I—I'm hoping to save up enough to get married, sir."

"You are?" Tembarom exclaimed. "Good business! So was I before all this"—he glanced about him—"fell on top of me."

"I've been saving for three years, sir, and if I can know I'm a permanency—if I can keep this place—"

"You're going to keep it all right," Tembarom cheered him up with. "If you've got an idea you're going to be fired, just you forget it. Cut it right out."

"Is—I beg your pardon, sir," Pearson asked with timorous joy, "but is that the American for saying you'll be good enough to keep me on?"

Mr. Temple Barholm thought a second.

"Is 'keep me on' the English for 'let me stay'?"

"Yes, sir."

"Then we're all right. Let's start from there. I'm going to have a heart-to-heart talk with you, Pearson."

"Thank you, sir," said Pearson in a deferential murmur. But if he was not dissatisfied, what was going to happen?

"It'll save us both trouble, and me most. I'm not one of those clever Clarences that can keep up a bluff, making out I know things I don't know. I couldn't deceive a setting hen or a Berlin wool antimacassar."

Pearson swallowed something with effort.

"You see, I fell into this thing KERCHUNK, and I'm just RATTLED—I'm rattled." As Pearson slightly coughed again, he translated for him, "That's American for 'I don't know where I'm at'."

"Those American jokes, sir, are very funny indeed," answered Pearson, appreciatively.

"Funny!" the new Mr. Temple Barholm exclaimed even aggrievedly. "If you think this lay-out is an American joke to me, Pearson, there's where you're 'way off. Do you think it a merry jest for a fellow like me to sit up in a high chair in a dining-room like a cathedral and not know whether he ought to bite his own bread or not? And not dare to stir till things are handed to him by five husky footmen? I thought that plain-clothes man was going to cut up my meat, and slap me on the back if I choked."

Pearson's sense of humor was perhaps not inordinate, but unseemly mirth, which he had swallowed at the reference to the setting hen and the Berlin wool antimacassar, momentarily got the better of him, despite his efforts to cough it down, and broke forth in a hoarse, ill-repressed sound.

"I beg pardon, sir," he said with a laudable endeavor to recover his professional bearing. "It's your—American way of expressing it which makes me forget myself. I beg pardon."

Tembarom laughed outright boyishly.

"Oh, cut that out," he said. "Say, how old are you?"

"Twenty-five, sir."

"So am I. If you'd met me three months ago, beating the streets of New York for a living, with holes in my shoes and a celluloid collar on, you'd have looked down on me. I know you would."

"Oh, no, sir," most falsely insisted Pearson.

"Oh, yes, you would," protested Tembarom, cheerfully. "You'd have said I talked through my nose, and I should have laughed at you for dropping your h's. Now you're rattled because I'm Mr. Temple Temple Barholm; but you're not half as rattled as I am."

"You'll get over it, sir, almost immediately," Pearson assured him, hopefully.

"Of course I shall," said Tembarom, with much courage. "But to start right I've got to get over YOU."

"Me, sir?" Pearson breathed anxiously.

"Yes. That's what I want to get off my chest. Now, first off, you came in here to try to explain to me that, owing to my New York valet having left my New York wardrobe behind, I've not got anything to wear, and so I shall have to buy some clothes."

"I failed to find any dress-shirts, sir," began Pearson, hesitatingly.

Mr. Temple Barholm grinned.

"I always failed to find them myself. I never had a dress-shirt. I never owned a suit of glad rags in my life."

"Gl—glad rags, sir?" stammered Pearson, uncertainly.

"I knew you didn't catch on when I said that to you before dinner. I mean claw-hammer and dress-suit things. Don't you be frightened, Pearson. I never had six good shirts at once, or two pair of shoes, or more than four ten-cent handkerchiefs at a time since I was born. And when Mr. Palford yanked me away from New York, he didn't suspect a fellow could be in such a state. And I didn't know I was in a state, anyhow. I was too busy to hunt up people to tell me, because I was rushing something important right through, and I couldn't stop. I just bought the first things I set eyes on and crammed them into my trunk. There, I guess you know the most of this, but you didn't know I knew you knew it. Now you do, and you needn't be afraid to hurt my feelings by telling me I haven't a darned thing I ought to have. You can go straight ahead."

As he leaned back, puffing away at his pipe, he had thrown a leg over the arm of his chair for greater comfort, and it really struck his valet that he had never seen a gentleman more at his ease, even one who WAS one. His casual candidness produced such a relief from the sense of strain and uncertainty that Pearson felt the color returning to his face. An opening had been given him, and it was possible for him to do his duty.

"If you wish, sir, I will make a list," he ventured further, "and the proper firms will send persons to bring things down from London on appro."

"What's 'appro' the English for?"

"Approval, sir."

"Good business! Good old Pearson!"

"Thank you, sir. Shall I attend to it to-night, to be ready for the morning post?"

"In five minutes you shall. But you threw me off the track a bit. The thing I was really going to say was more important than the clothes business."

There was something else, then, thought Pearson, some other unexpected point of view.

"What have you to do for me, anyhow?"

"Valet you, sir."

"That's English for washing my face and combing my hair and putting my socks on, ain't it?"

"Well, sir, it means doing all you require, and being always in attendance when you change."

"How much do you get for it?"

"Thirty shillings a week, sir."

"Say, Pearson," said Tembarom, with honest feeling, "I'll give you sixty shillings a week NOT to do it."

Calmed though he had felt a few moments ago, it cannot be denied that Pearson was aghast. How could one be prepared for developments of such an order?

"Not to do it, sir!" he faltered. "But what would the servants think if you had no one to valet you?"

"That's so. What would they think?" But he evidently was not dismayed, for he smiled widely. "I guess the plainclothes man would throw a fit."

But Pearson's view was more serious and involved a knowledge of not improbable complications. He knew "the hall" and its points of view.

"I couldn't draw my wages, sir," he protested. "There'd be the greatest dissatisfaction among the other servants, sir, if I didn't do my duties. There's always a—a slight jealousy of valets and ladies'-maids. The general idea is that they do very little to earn their salaries. I've seen them fairly hated."

"Is that so? Well, I'll be darned!" remarked Mr. Temple Barholm. He gave a moment to reflection, and then cheered up immensely.

"I'll tell you how we'll fix it. You come up into my room and bring your tatting or read a newspaper while I dress." He openly chuckled. "Holy smoke! I've GOT to put on my shirt and swear at my collar-buttons myself. If I'm in for having a trained nurse do it for me, it'll give me the Willies. When you danced around me before dinner—"

Pearson's horror forced him to commit the indiscretion of interrupting.

"I hope I didn't DANCE, sir," he implored. "I tried to be extremely quiet."

"That was it," said Tembarom. "I shouldn't have said danced; I meant crept. I kept thinking I should tread on you, and I got so nervous toward the end I thought I should just break down and sob on your bosom and beg to be taken back to home and mother."

"I'm extremely sorry, sir, I am, indeed," apologized Pearson, doing his best not to give way to hysterical giggling. How was a man to keep a decently straight face, and if one didn't, where would it end? One thing after another.

"It was not your fault. It was mine. I haven't a thing against you. You're a first-rate little chap."

"I will try to be more satisfactory to-morrow."

There must be no laughing aloud, even if one burst a blood-vessel. It would not do. Pearson hastily confronted a vision of a young footman or Mr. Burrill himself passing through the corridors on some errand and hearing master and valet shouting together in unseemly and wholly incomprehensible mirth. And the next remark was worse than ever.

"No, you won't, Pearson," Mr. Temple Barholm asserted. "There's where you're wrong. I've got no more use for a valet than I have for a pair of straight-front corsets."

This contained a sobering suggestion.

"But you said, sir, that—"

"Oh, I'm not going to fire you," said Tembarom, genially. "I'll 'keep you on', but little Willie is going to put on his own socks. If the servants have to be pacified, you come up to my room and do anything you like. Lie on the bed if you want to; get a jew's-harp and play on it—any old thing to pass the time. And I'll raise your wages. What do you say? Is it fixed?"

"I'm here, sir, to do anything you require," Pearson answered distressedly; "but I'm afraid—"

Tembarom's face changed. A sudden thought had struck him.

"I'll tell you one thing you can do," he said; "you can valet that friend of mine."

"Mr. Strangeways, sir?"

"Yes. I've got a notion he wouldn't mind it." He was not joking now. He was in fact rather suddenly thoughtful.

"Say, Pearson, what do you think of him?"

"Well, sir, I've not seen much of him, and he says very little, but I should think he was a GENTLEMAN, sir."

Mr. Temple Barholm seemed to think it over.

"That's queer," he said as though to himself. "That's what Ann said." Then aloud, "Would you say he was an American?"

In his unavoidable interest in a matter much talked over below stairs and productive of great curiosity Pearson was betrayed. He could not explain to himself, after he had spoken, how he could have been such a fool as to forget; but forget himself and the birthplace of the new Mr. Temple Barholm he did.

"Oh, no, sir," he exclaimed hastily; "he's QUITE the gentleman, sir, even though he is queer in his mind." The next instant he caught himself and turned cold. An American or a Frenchman or an Italian, in fact, a native of any country on earth so slighted with an unconsciousness so natural, if he had been a man of hot temper, might have thrown something at him or kicked him out of the room; but Mr. Temple Barholm took his pipe out of his mouth and looked at him with a slow, broadening smile.

"Would you call me a gentleman, Pearson?" he asked.

Of course there was no retrieving such a blunder, Pearson felt, but—

"Certainly, sir," he stammered. "Most—most CERTAINLY, sir."

"Pearson," said Tembarom, shaking his head slowly, with a grin so good-natured that even the frankness of his words was friendly humor itself—"Pearson, you're a liar. But that doesn't jolt me a bit. I dare say I'm not one, anyhow. We might put an 'ad' in one of your papers and find out."

"I—I beg your pardon, sir," murmured Pearson in actual anguish of mind.

Mr. Temple Barholm laughed outright.

"Oh, I've not got it in for you. How could you help it?" he said. Then he stopped joking again. "If you want to please ME," he added with deliberation, "you look after Mr. Strangeways, and don't let anything disturb him. Don't bother him, but just find out what he wants. When he gets restless, come and tell me. If I'm out, tell him I'm coming back. Don't let him worry. You understand—don't let him worry."

"I'll do my best—my very best, sir," Pearson answered devoutly. "I've been nervous and excited this first day because I am so anxious to please—everything seems to depend on it just now," he added, daring another confidential outburst. "But you'll see I do know how to keep my wits about me in general, and I've got a good memory, and I have learned my duties, sir. I'll attend to Mr. Strangeways most particular."

As Tembarom listened, and watched his neat, blond countenance, and noted the undertone of quite desperate appeal in his low voice, he was thinking of a number of things. Chiefly he was thinking of little Ann Hutchinson and the Harlem flat which might have been "run" on fifteen dollars a week.

"I want to know I have some one in this museum of a place who'll UNDERSTAND," he said—"some one who'll do just exactly what I say and ask no fool questions and keep his mouth shut. I believe you could do it."

"I'll swear I could, sir. Trust me," was Pearson's astonishingly emotional and hasty answer.

"I'm going to," returned Mr. Temple Barholm. "I've set my mind on putting something through in my own way. It's a queer thing, and most people would say I was a fool for trying it. Mr. Hutchinson does, but Miss Hutchinson doesn't."

There was a note in his tone of saying "Miss Hutchinson doesn't" which opened up vistas to Pearson—strange vistas when one thought of old Mrs. Hutchinson's cottage and the estate of Temple Barholm.

"We're just about the same age," his employer continued, "and in a sort of way we're in just about the same fix."

Their eyes looked into each other's a second; but it was not for Pearson to presume to make any comment whatsoever upon the possible nature of "the fix." Two or three more puffs, and Mr. Temple Barholm spoke again.

"Say, Pearson, I don't want to butt in, but what about that little bunch of calico of yours—the one you're saving up for?"

"Calico, sir?" said Pearson, at sea, but hopeful. Whatsoever the new Mr. Temple Barholm meant, one began to realize that it was not likely to be unfriendly.

"That's American for HER, Pearson. 'Her' stands for the same thing both in English and American, I guess. What's her name and where is she? Don't you say a word if you don't want to."

Pearson drew a step nearer. There was an extraordinary human atmosphere in the room which caused things to begin to go on in his breast. He had had a harder life than Tembarom because he had been more timid and less buoyant and less unselfconscious. He had been beaten by a drunken mother and kicked by a drunken father. He had gone hungry and faint to the board school and had been punished as a dull boy. After he had struggled into a place as page, he had been bullied by footmen and had had his ears boxed by cooks and butlers. Ladies'-maids and smart housemaids had sneered at him, and made him feel himself a hopeless, vulgar little worm who never would "get on." But he had got on, in a measure, because he had worked like a slave and openly resented nothing. A place like this had been his fevered hope and dream from his page days, though of course his imagination had not encompassed attendance on a gentleman who had never owned a dress-shirt in his life. Yet gentleman or no gentleman, he was a Temple Barholm, and there was something about him, something human in his young voice and grin and queer, unheard-of New York jokes, which Pearson had never encountered, and which had the effect of making him feel somehow more of a man than his timorous nature had ever allowed of his feeling before. It suggested that they were both, valet and master, merely masculine human creatures of like kind. The way he had said "Miss Hutchinson" and the twinkle in his eye when he'd made that American joke about the "little bunch of calico"! The curious fact was that thin, neat, white-blooded-looking Pearson was passionately in love. So he took the step nearer and grew hot and spoke low.

"Her name is Rose Merrick, sir, and she's in place in London. She's lady's-maid to a lady of title, and it isn't an easy place. Her lady has a high temper, and she's economical with her servants. Her maid has to sew early and late, and turn out as much as if she was a whole dressmaking establishment. She's clever with her needle, and it would be easier if she felt it was appreciated. But she's treated haughty and severe, though she tries her very best. She has to wait up half the night after balls, and I'm afraid it's breaking her spirit and her health. That's why,—I beg your pardon, sir," he added, his voice shaking—"that's why I'd bear anything on earth if I could give her a little home of her own."

"Gee whizz!" ejaculated Mr. Temple Barholm, with feeling. "I guess you would!"

"And that's not all, sir," said Pearson. "She's a beautiful girl, sir, with a figure, and service is sometimes not easy for a young woman like that. His lordship—the master of the house, sir,—is much too attentive. He's a man with bad habits; the last lady's-maid was sent away in disgrace. Her ladyship wouldn't believe she hadn't been forward when she saw things she didn't like, though every one in the hall knew the girl hated his bold ways with her, and her mother nearly broke her heart. He's begun with Rose, and it just drives me mad, sir, it does!"

He choked, and wiped his forehead with his clean handkerchief. It was damp, and his young eyes had fire in them, as Mr. Temple Barholm did not fail to observe.

"I'm taking a liberty talking to you like this, sir," he said. "I'm behaving as if I didn't know my place, sir."

"Your place is behind that fellow, kicking him till he'll never sit down again except on eider-down cushions three deep," remarked Mr. Temple Barholm, with fire in his eyes also. "That's where your place is. It's where mine would be if I was in the same house with him and caught him making a goat of himself. I bet nine Englishmen out of ten would break his darned neck for him if they got on to his little ways, even if they were lordships themselves."

"The decent ones won't know," Pearson said. "That's not what happens, sir. He can laugh and chaff it off with her ladyship and coax her round. But a girl that's discharged like that, Rose says, that's the worst of it: she says she's got a character fastened on to her for life that no respectable man ought to marry her with."

Mr. Temple Barholm removed his leg from the arm of his chair and got up. Long-legged, sinewy, but somewhat slouchy in his badly made tweed suit, sharp New York face and awful American style notwithstanding, he still looked rather nice as he laid his hand on his valet's shoulder and gave him a friendly push.

"See here," he said. "What you've got to say to Rose is that she's just got to cut that sort of thing out—cut it right out. Talking to a man that's in love with her as if he was likely to throw her down because lies were told. Tell her to forget it—forget it quick. Why, what does she suppose a man's FOR, by jinks? What's he FOR?"

"I've told her that, sir, though of course not in American. I just swore it on my knees in Hyde Park one night when she got out for an hour. But she laid her poor head on the back of the bench and cried and wouldn't listen. She says she cares for me too much to—"

Tembarom's hand clutched his shoulder. His face lighted and glowed suddenly.

"Care for you too much," he asked. "Did she say that? God bless her!"

"That's what I said," broke in Pearson.

"I heard another girl say that—just before I left New York—a girl that's just a wonder," said his master. "A girl can be a wonder, can't she?"

"Rose is, sir," protested Pearson. "She is, indeed, sir. And her eyes are that blue—"

"Blue, are they?" interrupted Tembarom. "I know the kind. I'm on to the whole thing. And what's more, I'm going to fix it. You tell Rose—and tell her from me—that she's going to leave that place, and you're going to stay in this one, and—well, presently things'll begin to happen. They're going to be all right—ALL RIGHT," he went on, with immensely convincing emphasis. "She's going to have that little home of her own." He paused a moment for reflection, and then a sudden thought presented itself to him. "Why, darn it!" he exclaimed, "there must be a whole raft of little homes that belong to me in one place or another. Why couldn't I fix you both up in one of them?"

"Oh, sir!" Pearson broke forth in some slight alarm. He went so fast and so far all in a moment. And Pearson really possessed a neat, well-ordered conscience, and, moreover, "knew his place." "I hope I didn't seem to be expecting you to trouble yourself about me, sir. I mustn't presume on your kindness."

"It's not kindness; it's—well, it's just human. I'm going to think this thing over. You just keep your hair on, and let me do my own valeting, and you'll see I'll fix it for you somehow."

What he thought of doing, how he thought of doing it, and what Pearson was to expect, the agitated young man did not know. The situation was of course abnormal, judged by all respectable, long-established custom. A man's valet and his valet's "young woman" were not usually of intimate interest. Gentlemen were sometimes "kind" to you—gave you half a sovereign or even a sovereign, and perhaps asked after your mother if you were supporting one; but—

"I never dreamed of going so far, sir," he said. "I forgot myself, I'm afraid."

"Good thing you did. It's made me feel as if we were brothers." He laughed again, enjoying the thought of the little thing who cared for Pearson "too much" and had eyes that were "that blue." "Say, I've just thought of something else. Have you bought her an engagement-ring yet?"

"No, sir. In our class of life jewelry is beyond the means."

"I just wondered," Mr. Temple Barholm said. He seemed to be thinking of something that pleased him as he fumbled for his pocket-book and took a clean banknote out of it. "I'm not on to what the value of this thing is in real money, but you go and buy her a ring with it, and I bet she'll be so pleased you'll have the time of your life."

Pearson taking it; and recognizing its value in UNreal money, was embarrassed by feeling the necessity of explanation.

"This is a five-pound note, sir. It's too much, sir, it is indeed. This would FURNISH THE FRONT PARLOR." He said it almost solemnly.

Mr. Temple Barholm looked at the note interestedly.

"Would it? By jinks!" and his laugh had a certain softness of recollection. "I guess that's just what Ann would say. She'd know what it would furnish, you bet your life!"

"I'm most grateful, sir," protested Pearson, "but I oughtn't to take it. Being an American gentleman and not accustomed to English money, you don't realize that—"

"I'm not accustomed to any kind of money," said his master. "I'm scared to be left alone in the room with it. That's what's the matter. If I don't give some away, I shall never know I've got it. Cheer up, Pearson. You take that and buy the ring, and when you start furnishing, I'll see you don't get left."

"I don't know what to say, sir," Pearson faltered emotionally. "I don't, indeed."

"Don't say a darned thing," replied Mr. Temple Barholm. And just here his face changed as Mr. Palford had seen it change before, and as Pearson often saw it change later. His New York jocular irreverence dropped from him, and he looked mature and oddly serious.

"I've tried to sort of put you wise to the way I've lived and the things I HAVEN'T had ever since I was born," he said, "but I guess you don't really know a thing about it. I've got more money coming in every year than a thousand of me would ever expect to see in their lives, according to my calculation. And I don't know how to do any of the things a fellow who is what you call `a gentleman' would know how to do. I mean in the way of spending it. Now, I've got to get some fun out of it. I should be a mutt if I didn't, so I'm going to spend it my own way. I may make about seventy-five different kinds of a fool of myself, but I guess I sha'n't do any particular harm."

"You'll do good, sir,—to every one."

"Shall I?"—said Tembarom, speculatively. "Well, I'm not exactly setting out with that in my mind. I'm no Young Men's Christian Association, but I'm not in for doing harm, anyway. You take your five-pound note—come to think of it, Palford said it came to about twenty-five dollars, real money. Hully gee! I never thought I'd have twenty-five dollars to GIVE AWAY! It makes me feel like I was Morgan."

"Thank you, sir; thank you," said Pearson, putting the note into his pocket with rapt gratitude in his neat face. "You—you do not wish me to remain—to do anything for you?"

"Not a thing. But just go and find out if Mr. Strangeways is asleep. If he isn't and seems restless, I'll come and have a talk with him."

"Yes, sir," said Pearson, and went at once.

CHAPTER XIII

In the course of two days Mr. Palford, having given his client the benefit of his own exact professional knowledge of the estate of Temple Barholm and its workings and privileges as far as he found them transferable and likely to be understood, returned to London, breathing perhaps something like a sigh of relief when the train steamed out of the little station. Whatsoever happened in days to come, Palford & Grimby had done their most trying and awkward duty by the latest Temple Barholm. Bradford, who was the steward of the estate, would now take him over, and could be trusted to furnish practical information of any ordinary order.

It did not appear to Mr. Palford that the new inheritor was particularly interested in his possessions or exhilarated by the extraordinary turn in his fortunes. The enormity of Temple Barholm itself, regarded as a house to live in in an everyday manner, seemed somewhat to depress him. When he was taken over its hundred and fifty rooms, he wore a detached air as he looked about him, and such remarks as he made were of an extraordinary nature and expressed in terms peculiar to America. Neither Mr. Palford nor Burrill understood them, but a young footman who was said to have once paid a visit to New York, and who chanced to be in the picture-gallery when his new master was looking at the portraits of his ancestors, over-hearing one observation, was guilty of a convulsive snort, and immediately made his way into the corridor, coughing violently. From this Mr. Palford gathered that one of the transatlantic jokes had been made. That was the New York idea—to be jocular. Yet he had not looked jocular when he had made the remark which had upset the equilibrium of the young footman. He had, in fact, looked reflective before speaking as he stood and studied a portrait of one of his ancestors. But, then, he had a trick of saying things incomprehensibly ridiculous with an unmoved expression of gravity, which led Palford to feel that he was ridiculous through utter ignorance and was not aware that he was exposing the fact. Persons who thought that an air of seriousness added to a humorous remark were especially annoying to the solicitor, because they frequently betrayed one into the position of seeming to be dull in the matter of seeing a point. That, he had observed, was often part of the New York manner—to make a totally absurdly exaggerated or seemingly ignorance-revealing observation, and then leave one's hearer to decide for himself whether the speaker was an absolute ignoramus and fool or a humorist.

More than once he had somewhat suspected his client of meaning to "get a rise out of him," after the odious manner of the tourists described in "The Innocents Abroad," though at the same time he felt rather supportingly sure of the fact that generally, when he displayed ignorance, he displayed it because he was a positive encyclopedia of lack of knowledge.

He knew no more of social customs, literature, and art than any other street lad. He had not belonged to the aspiring self-taught, who meritoriously haunt the night schools and free libraries with a view to improving their minds. If this had been his method, he might in one sense have been more difficult to handle, as Palford had seen the thing result in a bumptiousness most objectionable. He was markedly not bumptious, at all events.

A certain degree of interest in or curiosity concerning his ancestors as represented in the picture-gallery Mr. Palford had observed. He had stared at them and had said queer things—sometimes things which perhaps indicated a kind of uneducated thought. The fact that some of them looked so thoroughly alive, and yet had lived centuries ago, seemed to set him reflecting oddly. His curiosity, however, seemed to connect itself with them more as human creatures than as historical figures.

"What did that one do?" he inquired more than once. "What did he start, or didn't he start anything?"

When he disturbed the young footman he had stopped before a dark man in armor.

"Who's this fellow in the tin overcoat?" he asked seriously, and Palford felt it was quite possible that he had no actual intent of being humorous.

"That is Miles Gaspard Nevil John, who fought in the Crusades with Richard Coeur de Lion," he explained. "He is wearing a suit of armor." By this time the footman was coughing in the corridor.

"That's English history, I guess," Tembarom replied. "I'll have to get a history-book and read up about the Crusades."

He went on farther, and paused with a slightly puzzled expression before a boy in a costume of the period of Charles II.

"Who's this Fauntleroy in the lace collar?" he inquired. "Queer!" he added, as though to himself. "I can't ever have seen him in New York." And he took a step backward to look again.

"That is Miles Hugo Charles James, who was a page at the court of Charles II. He died at nineteen, and was succeeded by his brother Denzel Maurice John."

"I feel as if I'd had a dream about him sometime or other," said Tembarom, and he stood still a few seconds before he passed on. "Perhaps I saw something like him getting out of a carriage to go into the Van Twillers' fancy-dress ball. Seems as if I'd got the whole show shut up in here. And you say they're all my own relations?" Then he laughed. "If they were alive now!" he said. "By jinks!"

His laughter suggested that he was entertained by mental visions. But he did not explain to his companion. His legal adviser was not in the least able to form any opinion of what he would do, how he would be likely to comport himself, when he was left entirely to his own devices. He would not know also, one might be sure, that the county would wait with repressed anxiety to find out. If he had been a minor, he might have been taken in hand, and trained and educated to some extent. But he was not a minor.

On the day of Mr. Palford's departure a thick fog had descended and seemed to enwrap the world in the white wool. Tembarom found it close to his windows when he got up, and he had dressed by the light of tall wax candles, the previous Mr. Temple Barholm having objected to more modern and vulgar methods of illumination.

"I guess this is what you call a London fog," he said to Pearson.

"No, not exactly the London sort, sir," Pearson answered. "A London fog is yellow—when it isn't brown or black. It settles on the hands and face. A fog in the country isn't dirty with smoke. It's much less trying, sir."

When Palford had departed and he was entirely alone, Tembarom found a country fog trying enough for a man without a companion. A degree of relief permeated his being with the knowledge that he need no longer endeavor to make suitable reply to his solicitor's efforts at conversation. He had made conversational efforts himself. You couldn't let a man feel that you wouldn't talk to him if you could when he was doing business for you, but what in thunder did you have to talk about that a man like that wouldn't be bored stiff by? He didn't like New York, he didn't know anything about it, and he didn't want to know, and Tembarom knew nothing about anything else, and was homesick for the very stones of the roaring city's streets. When he said anything, Palford either didn't understand what he was getting at or he didn't like it. And he always looked as if he was watching to see if you were trying to get a joke on him. Tembarom was frequently not nearly so much inclined to be humorous as Mr. Palford had irritably suspected him of being. His modes of expression might on numerous occasions have roused to mirth when his underlying idea was almost entirely serious. The mode of expression was merely a result of habit.

Mr. Palford left by an extremely early train, and after he was gone, Tembarom sat over his breakfast as long as possible, and then, going to the library, smoked long. The library was certainly comfortable, though the fire and the big wax candles were called upon to do their best to defy the chill, mysterious dimness produced by the heavy, white wool curtain folding itself more and more thickly outside the windows.

But one cannot smoke in solitary idleness for much more than an hour, and when he stood up and knocked the ashes out of his last pipe, Tembarom drew a long breath.

"There's a hundred and thirty-six hours in each of these days," he said. "That's nine hundred and fifty-two in a week, and four thousand and eighty in a month—when it's got only thirty days in it. I'm not going to calculate how many there'd be in a year. I'll have a look at the papers. There's Punch. That's their comic one."

He looked out the American news in the London papers, and sighed hugely. He took up Punch and read every joke two or three times over. He did not know that the number was a specially good one and that there were some extremely witty things in it. The jokes were about bishops in gaiters, about garden-parties, about curates or lovely young ladies or rectors' wives and rustics, about Royal Academicians or esthetic poets. Their humor appealed to him as little and seemed as obscure as his had seemed to Mr. Palford.

"I'm not laughing my head off much over these," he said. "I guess I'm not on to the point."

He got up and walked about. The "L" in New York was roaring to and fro loaded with men and women going to work or to do shopping. Some of them were devouring morning papers bearing no resemblance to those of London, some of them carried parcels, and all of them looked as though they were intent on something or other and hadn't a moment to waste. They were all going somewhere in a hurry and had to get back in time for something. When the train whizzed and slackened at a station, some started up, hastily caught their papers or bundles closer, and pushed or were pushed out on the platform, which was crowded with other people who rushed to get in, and if they found seats, dropped into them hastily with an air of relief. The street-cars were loaded and rang their bells loudly, trucks and carriages and motors filled the middle of the thoroughfares, and people crowded the pavements. The store windows were dressed up for Christmas, and most of the people crowded before them were calculating as to what they could get for the inadequate sums they had on hand.

The breakfast at Mrs. Bowse's boarding-house was over, and the boarders had gone on cars or elevated trains to their day's work. Mrs. Bowse was getting ready to go out and do some marketing. Julius and Jim were downtown deep in the work pertaining to their separate "jobs." They'd go home at night, and perhaps, if they were in luck, would go to a "show" somewhere, and afterward come and sit in their tilted chairs in the hall bedroom and smoke and talk it over. And he wouldn't be there, and the Hutchinsons' rooms would be empty, unless some new people were in them. Galton would be sitting among his papers, working like mad. And Bennett—well, Bennett would be either "getting out his page," or would be rushing about in the hundredth streets to find items and follow up weddings or receptions.

"Gee!" he said, "every one of them trying their best to put something over, and with so much to think of they've not got time to breathe! It'd be no trouble for THEM to put in a hundred and thirty-six hours. They'd be darned glad of them. And, believe me, they'd put something over, too, before they got through. And I'm here, with three hundred and fifty thousand dollars a year round my neck and not a thing to spend it on, unless I pay some one part of it to give me lessons in tatting. What is tatting, anyhow?"

He didn't really know. It was vaguely supposed to imply some intensely feminine fancy-work done by old ladies, and used as a figure of speech in jokes.

"If you could ride or shoot, you could amuse yourself in the country," Palford had said.

"I can ride in a street-car when I've got five cents," Tembarom had answered. "That's as far as I've gone in riding—and what in thunder should I shoot?"

"Game," replied Mr. Palford, with chill inward disgust. "Pheasants, partridges, woodcock, grouse—"

"I shouldn't shoot anything like that if I went at it," he responded shamelessly. "I should shoot my own head off, or the fellow's that stood next to me, unless he got the drop on me first."

He did not know that he was ignominious. Nobody could have made it clear to him. He did not know that there were men who had gained distinction, popularity, and fame by doing nothing in particular but hitting things animate and inanimate with magnificent precision of aim.

He stood still now and listened to the silence.

"There's not a sound within a thousand miles of the place. What do fellows with money DO to keep themselves alive?" he said piteously. "They've got to do SOMETHING. Shall I have to go out and take a walk, as Palford called it? Take a walk, by gee!"

He couldn't conceive it, a man "taking a walk" as though it were medicine—a walk nowhere, to reach nothing, just to go and turn back again.

"I'll begin and take in sewing," he said, "or I'll open a store in the village—a department store. I could spend something on that. I'll ask Pearson what he thinks of it—or Burrill. I'd like to see Burrill if I said that to him."

He decided at last that he would practise his "short" awhile; that would be doing something, at any rate. He sat down at the big writing-table and began to dash off mystic signs at furious speed. But the speed did not keep up. The silence of the great room, of the immense house, of all the scores of rooms and galleries and corridors, closed in about him. He had practised his "short" in the night school, with the "L" thundering past at intervals of five minutes; in the newspaper office, with all the babel of New York about him and the bang of steam-drills going on below in the next lot, where the foundation of a new building was being excavated; he had practised it in his hall bedroom at Mrs. Bowse's, to the tumultuous accompaniment of street sounds and the whizz and TING-A-LING of street-cars dashing past, and he had not been disturbed. He had never practised it in any place which was silent, and it was the silence which became more than he could stand. He actually jumped out of his chair when he heard mysterious footsteps outside the door, and a footman appeared and spoke in a low voice which startled him as though it had been a thunderclap.

"A young person with her father wants to see you, sir," he announced. "I don't think they are villagers, but of the working-class, I should say."

"Where are they?"

"I didn't know exactly what to do, sir, so I left them in the hall. The young person has a sort of quiet, determined way—"

"Little Ann, by gee!" exclaimed Tembarom with mad joy, and shot out of the room.

The footman—he had not seen Little Ann when she had brought Strangeways—looked after him and rubbed his chin.

"Wouldn't you call that a rummy sort for Temple Barholm?" he said to one of his fellows who had appeared in the hall near him.

"It's not my sort," was the answer. "I'm going to give notice to old Butterworth."

Hutchinson and Little Ann were waiting in the hall. Hutchinson was looking at the rich, shadowy spaces about him with a sort of proud satisfaction. Fine, dark corners with armored figures lurking in them, ancient portraits, carved oak settles, and massive chairs and cabinets—these were English, and he was an Englishman, and somehow felt them the outcome of certain sterling qualities of his own. He looked robustly well, and wore a new rough tweed suit such as one of the gentry might tramp about muddy roads and fields in. Little Ann was dressed in something warm and rough also, a brown thing, with a little close, cap-like, brown hat, from under which her red hair glowed. The walk in the cold, white fog had made her bloom fresh, soft-red and white-daisy color. She was smiling, and showing three distinct dimples, which deepened when Tembarom dashed out of the library.

"Hully gee!" he cried out, "but I'm glad to see you!"

He shook hands with both of them furiously, and two footmen stood and looked at the group with image-like calm of feature, but with curiously interested eyes. Hutchinson was aware of them, and endeavored to present to them a back which by its stolid composure should reveal that he knew more about such things than this chap did and wasn't a bit upset by grandeur.

"Hully gee!" cried Tembarom again, "how glad I am! Come on in and sit down and let's talk it over."

Burrill made a stately step forward, properly intent on his duty, and his master waved him back.

"Say," he said hastily, "don't bring in any tea. They don't want it. They're Americans."

Hutchinson snorted. He could not stand being consigned to ignominy before the footmen.

"Nowt o' th' sort," he broke forth. "We're noan American. Tha'rt losing tha head, lad."

"He's forgetting because he met us first in New York," said Little Ann, smiling still more.

"Shall I take your hat and cane, sir?" inquired Burrill, unmovedly, at Hutchinson's side.

"He wasn't going to say anything about tea," explained Little Ann as they went into the library. "They don't expect to serve tea in the middle of the morning, Mr. Temple Barholm."

"Don't they?" said Tembarom, reckless with relieved delight. "I thought they served it every time the clock struck. When we were in London it seemed like Palford had it when he was hot and when he was cold and when he was glad and when he was sorry and when he was going out and when he was coming in. It's brought up to me, by jinks! as soon as I wake, to brace me up to put on my clothes—and Pearson wants to put those on."

He stopped short when they reached the middle of the room and looked her over.

"O Little Ann!" he breathed tumultuously. "O Little Ann!"

Mr. Hutchinson was looking about the library as he had looked about the hall.

"Well, I never thought I'd get inside Temple Barlholm in my day," he exclaimed. "Eh, lad, tha must feel like bull in a china shop."

"I feel like a whole herd of 'em," answered Tembarom. Hutchinson nodded. He understood.

"Well, perhaps tha'll get over it in time," he conceded, "but it'll take thee a good bit." Then he gave him a warmly friendly look. "I'll lay you know what Ann came with me for to-day." The way Little Ann looked at him—the way she looked at him!

"I came to thank you, Mr. Temple Barholm," she said—"to thank you." And there was an odd, tender sound in her voice.

"Don't you do it, Ann," Tembarom answered. "Don't you do it."

"I don't know much about business, but the way you must have worked, the way you must have had to run after people, and find them, and make then listen, and use all your New York cleverness—because you ARE clever. The way you've forgotten all about yourself and thought of nothing but father and the invention! I do know enough to understand that, and it seems as if I can't think of enough to say. I just wish I could tell you what it means to me." Two round pearls of tears brimmed over and fell down her cheeks. "I promised mother FAITHFUL I'd take care of him and see he never lost hope about it," she added, "and sometimes I didn't know whatever I was going to do."

It was perilous when she looked at one like that, and she was so little and light that one could have snatched her up in his arms and carried her to the big arm-chair and sat down with her and rocked her backward and forward and poured forth the whole thing that was making him feel as though he might explode.

Hutchinson provided salvation.

"Tha pulled me out o' the water just when I was going under, lad. God bless thee!" he broke out, and shook his hand with rough vigor. "I signed with the North Electric yesterday."

"Good business!" said Tembarom. "Now I'm in on the ground floor with what's going to be the biggest money-maker in sight."

"The way tha talked New York to them chaps took my fancy," chuckled Hutchinson. "None o' them chaps wants to be the first to jump over the hedge."

"We've got 'em started now," exulted Tembarom.

"Tha started 'em," said Hutchinson, "and it's thee I've got to thank."

"Say, Little Ann," said Tembarom, with sudden thought, "who's come into money now? You'll have it to burn."

"We've not got it yet, Mr. Temple Barholm," she replied, shaking her head. "Even when inventions get started, they don't go off like sky-rockets."

"She knows everything, doesn't she?" Tembarom said to Hutchinson. "Here, come and sit down. I've not seen you for 'steen years."

She took her seat in the big arm-chair and looked at him with softly examining eyes, as though she wanted to understand him sufficiently to be able to find out something she ought to do if he needed help.

He saw it and half laughed, not quite unwaveringly.

"You'll make me cry in a minute," he said. "You don't know what it's like to have some one from home and mother come and be kind to you."

"How is Mr. Strangeways?" she inquired.

"He's well taken care of, at any rate. That's where he's got to thank you. Those rooms you and the housekeeper chose were the very things for him. They're big and comfortable, and 'way off in a place where no one's likely to come near. The fellow that's been hired to valet me valets him instead, and I believe he likes it. It seems to come quite natural to him, any how. I go in and see him every now and then and try to get him to talk. I sort of invent things to see if I can start him thinking straight. He's quieted down some and he looks better. After a while I'm going to look up some big doctors in London and find out which of 'em's got the most plain horse sense. If a real big one would just get interested and come and see him on the quiet and not get him excited, he might do him good. I'm dead stuck on this stunt I've set myself—getting him right. It's something to work on."

"You'll have plenty to work on soon," said Little Ann. "There's a lot of everyday things you've got to think about. They may seem of no consequence to you, but they ARE, Mr. Temple Barholm."

"If you say they are, I guess they are," he answered. "I'll do anything you say, Ann."

"I came partly to tell you about some of them to-day," she went on, keeping the yearningly thoughtful eyes on him. It was rather hard for her, too, to be firm enough when there was so much she wanted to say and do. And he did not look half as twinkling and light-heartedly grinning as he had looked in New York.

He couldn't help dropping his voice a little coaxingly, though Mr. Hutchinson was quite sufficiently absorbed in examination of his surroundings.

"Didn't you come to save my life by letting me have a look at you, Little Ann—didn't you?" he pleaded.

She shook her wonderful, red head.

"No, I didn't, Mr. Temple Barholm," she answered with Manchester downrightness. "When I said what I did in New York, I meant it. I didn't intend to hang about here and let you—say things to me. You mustn't say them. Father and me are going back to Manchester in a few days, and very soon we have to go to America again because of the business."

"America!" he said. "Oh, Lord!" he groaned. "Do you want me to drop down dead here with a dull, sickening thud, Ann?"

"You're not going to drop down dead," she replied convincedly. "You're going to stay here and do whatever it's your duty to do, now you've come into Temple Barholm."

"Am I?" he answered. "Well, we'll see what I'm going to do when I've had time to make up my mind. It may be something different from what you'd think, and it mayn't. Just now I'm going to do what you tell me. Go ahead, Little Ann."

She thought the matter over with her most destructive little air of sensible intentness.

"Well, it may seem like meddling, but it isn't," she began rather concernedly. "It's just that I'm used to looking after people. I wanted to talk to you about your clothes."

"My clothes?" he replied, bewildered a moment; but the next he understood and grinned. "I haven't got any. My valet—think of T. T. with a valet!—told me so last night."

"That's what I thought," she said maternally. "I got Mrs. Bowse to write to me, and she told me you were so hurried and excited you hadn't time for anything."

"I just rushed into Cohen's the last day and yanked a few things off the ready-made counter."

She looked him over with impersonal criticism.

"I thought so. Those you've got on won't do at all."

Tembarom glanced at them.

"That's what Pearson says."

"They're not the right shape," she explained. "I know what a gentleman's clothes mean in England, and—" her face flushed, and sudden, warm spirit made her speak rather fast—"I couldn't ABIDE to think of you coming here and—being made fun of—just because you hadn't the right clothes."

She said it, the little thing, as though he were hers—her very own, and defend him against disrespect she WOULD. Tembarom, being but young flesh and blood, made an impetuous dart toward her, and checked himself, catching his breath.

"Ann," he said, "has your grandmother got a dog?"

"Y-e-s," she said, faltering because she was puzzled.

"How big is he?"

"He's a big one. He's a brindled bulldog. Why?"

"Well," he said, half pathetic, half defiant, "if you're going to come and talk to me like that, and look like that, you've got to bring that bull along and set him on me when I make a break; for there's nothing but a dog can keep me where you want me to stay—and a big one at that."

He sat down on an ottoman near her and dropped his head on his hands. It was not half such a joke as it sounded.

Little Ann saw it wasn't and she watched him tenderly, catching her breath once quickly. Men had ways of taking some things hard and feeling them a good bit more than one would think. It made trouble many a time if one couldn't help them to think reasonable.

"Father," she said to Hutchinson.

"Aye," he answered, turning round.

"Will you tell Mr. Temple Barholm that you think I'm right about giving him his chance?"

"Of course I think she's right," Hutchinson blustered, "and it isn't the first time either. I'm not going to have my lass married into any family where she'd be looked down upon."

But that was not what Little Ann wanted; it was not, in fact, her argument. She was not thinking of that side of the situation.

"It's not me that matters so much, Father," she said; "it's him."

"Oh, is it?" disagreed Hutchinson, dictatorially. "That's not th' road I look at it. I'm looking after you, not him. Let him take care of himself. No chap shall put you where you won't be looked up to, even if I AM grateful to him. So there you have it."

"He can't take care of himself when he feels like this," she answered. "That's WHY I'm taking care of him. He'll think steadier when he's himself again." She put out her hand and softly touched his shoulder.

"Don't do that," she said. "You make me want to be silly." There was a quiver in her voice, but she tried to change it. "If you don't lift your head," she added with a great effort at disciplinarian firmness, "I shall have to go away without telling you the other things."

He lifted his head, but his attempt at a smile was not hilarious.

"Well, Ann," he submitted, "I've warned you. Bring along your dog."

She took a sheet of paper out of one of the neat pockets in her rough, brown coat.

"I just wrote down some of the very best tailors' addresses—the very best," she explained. "Don't you go to any but the very best, and be a bit sharp with them if they're not attentive. They'll think all the better of you. If your valet's a smart one, take him with you."

"Yes, Ann," he said rather weakly. "He's going to make a list of things himself, anyhow."

"That sounds as if he'd got some sense." She handed him the list of addresses. "You give him this, and tell him he must go to the very best ones."

"What do I want to put on style for?" he asked desperately. "I don't know a soul on this side of the Atlantic Ocean."

"You soon will," she replied, with calm perspicacity. "You've got too much money not to."

A gruff chuckle made itself heard from Hutchinson's side of the room.

"Aye, seventy thousand a year'll bring th' vultures about thee, lad."

"We needn't call them vultures exactly," was Little Ann's tolerant comment; "but a lot of people will come here to see you. That was one of the things I thought I might tell you about."

"Say, you're a wonder!"

"I'm nothing of the sort. I'm just a girl with a bit of common sense—and grandmother's one that's looked on a long time, and she sees things. The country gentlemen will begin to call on you soon, and then you'll be invited to their houses to meet their wives and daughters, and then you'll be kept pretty busy."

Hutchinson's bluff chuckle broke out again.

"You will that, my lad, when th' match-making mothers get after you. There's plenty on 'em."

"Father's joking," she said. Her tone was judicially unprejudiced. "There are young ladies that—that'd be very suitable. Pretty ones and clever ones. You'll see them all."

"I don't want to see them."

"You can't help it," she said, with mild decision. "When there are daughters and a new gentleman comes into a big property in the neighborhood, it's nothing but natural that the mothers should be a bit anxious."

"Aye, they'll be anxious enough. Mak' sure o' that," laughed Hutchinson.

"Is that what you want me to put on style for, Little Ann?" Tembarom asked reproachfully.

"I want you to put it on for yourself. I don't want you to look different from other men. Everybody's curious about you. They're ready to LAUGH because you came from America and once sold newspapers."

"It's the men he'll have to look out for," Hutchinson put in, with an experienced air. "There's them that'll want to borrow money, and them that'll want to drink and play cards and bet high. A green American lad'll be a fine pigeon for them to pluck. You may as well tell him, Ann; you know you came here to do it."

"Yes, I did," she admitted. "I don't want you to seem not to know what people are up to and what they expect."

That little note of involuntary defense was a dangerous thing for Tembarom. He drew nearer.

"You don't want them to take me for a fool, Little Ann. You're standing up for me; that's it."

"You can stand up for yourself, Mr. Temple Barholm, if you're not taken by surprise," she said confidently. "If you understand things a bit, you won't be."

His feelings almost overpowered him.

"God bless your dear little soul!" he broke out. "Say, if this goes on, that dog of your grandmother's wouldn't have a show, Ann. I should bite him before he could bite me."

"I won't go on if you can't be sensible, Mr. Temple Barholm. I shall just go away and not come back again. That's what I shall do." Her tone was that of a young mother.

He gave in incontinently.

"Good Lord! no!" he exclaimed. "I'll do anything if you'll stay. I'll lie down on the mat and not open my mouth. Just sit here and tell me things. I know you won't let me hold your hand, but just let me hold a bit of your dress and look at you while you talk." He took a bit of her brown frock between his fingers and held it, gazing at her with all his crude young soul in his eyes. "Now tell me," he added.

"There's only one or two things about the people who'll come to Temple Barholm. Grandmother's talked it over with me. She knew all about those that came in the late Mr. Temple Barholm's time. He used to hate most of them."

"Then why in thunder did he ask them to come?"

"He didn't. They've got clever, polite ways of asking themselves sometimes. He couldn't bear the Countess of Mallowe. She'll come. Grandmother says you may be sure of that."

"What'll she come for?"

Little Ann's pause and contemplation of him were fraught with thoughtfulness.

"She'll come for you," at last she said.

"She's got a daughter she thinks ought to have been married eight years ago," announced Hutchinson.

Tembarom pulled at the bit of brown tweed he held as though it were a drowning man's straw.

"Don't you drive me to drink, Ann," he said. "I'm frightened. Your grandmother will have to lend ME the dog."

This was a flightiness which Little Ann did not encourage.

"Lady Joan—that's her daughter—is very grand and haughty. She's a great beauty. You'll look at her, but perhaps she won't look at you. But it's not her I'm troubled about. I'm thinking of Captain Palliser and men like him."

"Who's he?"

"He's one of those smooth, clever ones that's always getting up some company or other and selling the stock. He'll want you to know his friends and he'll try to lead you his way."

As Tembarom held to his bit of her dress, his eyes were adoring ones, which was really not to be wondered at. She WAS adorable as her soft, kind, wonderfully maternal girl face tried to control itself so that it should express only just enough to help and nothing to disturb.

"I don't want him to spoil you. I don't want anything to make you—different. I couldn't bear it."

He pulled the bit of dress pleadingly.

"Why, Little Ann?" he implored quite low.

"Because," she said, feeling that perhaps she was rash—"because if you were different, you wouldn't be T. Tembarom; and it was T. Tembarom that—that was T. Tembarom," she finished hastily.

He bent his head down to the bit of tweed and kissed it.

"You just keep looking after me like that," he said, "and there's not one of them can get away with me."

She got up, and he rose with her. There was a touch of fire in the forget-me-not blue of her eyes.

"Just you let them see—just you let them see that you're not one they can hold light and make use of." But there she stopped short, looking up at him. He was looking down at her with a kind of matureness in his expression. "I needn't be afraid," she said. "You can take care of yourself; I ought to have known that."

"You did," he said, smiling; "but you wanted to sort of help me. And you've done it, by gee! just by saying that thing about T. Tembarom. You set me right on my feet. That's YOU."

Before they went away they paid a visit to Strangeways in his remote, undisturbed, and beautiful rooms. They were in a wing of the house untouched by any ordinary passing to and fro, and the deep windows looked out upon gardens which spring and summer would crowd with loveliness from which clouds of perfume would float up to him on days when the sun warmed and the soft airs stirred the flowers, shaking the fragrance from their full incense-cups. But the white fog shut out to-day even their winter bareness. There were light and warmth inside, and every added charm of rich harmony of deep color and comfort made beautiful. There were books and papers waiting to be looked over, but they lay untouched on the writing-table, and Strangeways was sitting close to the biggest window, staring into the fog. His eyes looked hungry and hollow and dark. Ann knew he was "trying to remember" something.

When the sound of footsteps reached his ear, he turned to look at them, and rose mechanically at sight of Ann. But his expression was that of a man aroused from a dream of far-off places.

"I remember you," he said, but hesitated as though making an effort to recall something.

"Of course you do," said Little Ann. "You know me quite well. I brought you here. Think a bit. Little—Little—"

"Yes," he broke forth. "Of course, Little Ann! Thank God I've not forgotten." He took her hand in both his and held it tenderly. "You have a sweet little face. It's such a wise little face!" His voice sounded dreamy.

Ann drew him to his chair with a coaxing laugh and sat down by him.

"You're flattering me. You make me feel quite shy," she said. "You know HIM, too," nodding toward Tembarom.

"Oh, yes," he replied, and he looked up with a smile. "He is the one who remembers. You said you did." He had turned to Tembarom.

"You bet your life I do," Tembarom answered. "And you will, too, before long."

"If I did not try so hard," said Strangeways, thoughtfully. "It seems as if I were shut up in a room, and so many things were knocking at the doors—hundreds of them—knocking because they want to be let in. I am damnably unhappy—damnably." He hung his head and stared at the floor. Tembarom put a hand on his shoulder and gave him a friendly shake.

"Don't you worry a bit," he said. "You take my word for it. It'll all come back. I'm working at it myself." Strangeways lifted his head.

"You are the one I know best. I trust you." But there was the beginning of a slight drag in his voice. "I don't always—quite recollect—your name. Not quite. Good heavens! I mustn't forget that."

Little Ann was quite ready.

"You won't," she said, "because it's different from other names. It begins with a letter—just a letter, and then there is the name. Think."

"Yes, yes," he said anxiously.

Little Ann bent forward and fixed her eyes on his with concentrated suggestion. They had never risked confusing him by any mention of the new name. She began to repeat letters of the alphabet slowly and distinctly until she reached the letter T.

"T," she ended with much emphasis—"R. S. T."

His expression cleared itself.

"T," he repeated. "T—Tembarom. R, S, T. How clever you are!"

Little Ann's gaze concentrated itself still more intently.

"Now you'll never forget it again," she said, "because of the T. You'll say the other letters until you come to it. R, S, T."

"T. Tembarom," he ended relievedly. "How you help me!" He took her hand and kissed it very gently.

"We are all going to help you," Ann soothed him, "T. Tembarom most of all."

"Say," Tembarom broke out in an aside to her, "I'm going to come here and try things on him every day. When it seems like he gets on to something, however little a thing it is, I'm going to follow it up and see if it won't get somewhere."

Ann nodded.

"There'll be something some day," she said. "Are you quite comfortable here?" she asked aloud to Strangeways.

"Very comfortable, thank you," he answered courteously. "They are beautiful rooms. They are furnished with such fine old things. This is entirely Jacobean. It's quite perfect." He glanced about him. "And so quiet. No one comes in here but my man, and he is a very nice chap. I never had a man who knew his duties better."

Little Ann and Tembarom looked at each other.

"I shouldn't be a bit surprised," she said after they had left the room, "if it wouldn't be a good thing to get Pearson to try to talk to him now and then. He's been used to a man-servant."

"Yes," answered Tembarom. "Pearson didn't rattle HIM, you bet your life."

CHAPTER XIV

He could not persuade them to remain to take lunch with him. The firmness of Hutchinson's declination was not unconnected with a private feeling that "them footmen chaps 'u'd be on the lookout to see the way you handled every bite you put in your mouth." He couldn't have stood it, dang their impudence! Little Ann, on her part, frankly and calmly said, "It wouldn't DO." That was all, and evidently covered everything.

After they had gone, the fog lifted somewhat, but though it withdrew from the windows, it remained floating about in masses, like huge ghosts, among the trees of the park. When Tembarom sat down alone to prolong his lunch with the aid of Burrill and the footmen, he was confronted by these unearthly shapes every time he lifted his eyes to the window he faced from his place at the table. It was an outlook which did not inspire to cheerfulness, and the fact that Ann and her father were going back to Manchester and later to America left him without even the simple consolation of a healthy appetite. Things were bound to get better after a while; they were BOUND to. A fellow would be a fool if he couldn't fix it somehow so that he could enjoy himself, with money to burn. If you made up your mind you couldn't stand the way things were, you didn't have to lie down under them, with a thousand or so "per" coming in. You could fix it so that it would be different. By jinks! there wasn't any law against your giving it all to the church but just enough to buy a flat in Harlem out-right, if you wanted to. But you weren't going to run crazy and do a lot of fool things in a minute, and be sorry the rest of your life. Money was money. And first and foremost there was Ann, with her round cheeks flushed and her voice all sweet and queer, saying, "You wouldn't be T. Tembarom; and it was T. Tembarom that—that was T. Tembarom."

He couldn't help knowing what she had begun to say, and his own face flushed as he thought of it. He was at that time of life when there generally happens to be one center about which the world revolves. The creature who passes through this period of existence without watching it revolve about such a center has missed an extraordinary and singularly developing experience. It is sometimes happy, often disastrous, but always more or less developing. Speaking calmly, detachedly, but not cynically, it is a phase. During its existence it is the blood in the veins, the sight of the eyes, the beat of the pulse, the throb of the heart. It is also the day and the night, the sun, the moon, and the stars, heaven and hell, the entire universe. And it doesn't matter in the least to any one but the creatures living through it. T. Tembarom was in the midst of it. There was Ann. There was this new crazy thing which had happened to him—"this fool thing," as he called it. There was this monstrous, magnificent house,—he knew it was magnificent, though it wasn't his kind,—there was old Palford and his solemn talk about ancestors and the name of Temple Barholm. It always reminded him of how ashamed he had been in Brooklyn of the "Temple Temple" and how he had told lies to prevent the fellows finding out about it. And there was seventy thousand pounds a year, and there was Ann, who looked as soft as a baby,— Good Lord! how soft she'd feel if you got her in your arms and squeezed her!—and yet was somehow strong enough to keep him just where she wanted him to stay and believed he ought to stay until "he had found out." That was it. She wasn't doing it for any fool little idea of making herself seem more important: she just believed it. She was doing it because she wanted to let him "have his chance," just as if she were his mother instead of the girl he was clean crazy about. His chance! He laughed outright—a short, confident laugh which startled Burrill exceedingly.

When he went back to the library and lighted his pipe he began to stride up and down as he continued to think it over.

"I wish she was as sure as I am," he said. "I wish she was as sure of me as I am of myself—and as I am of her." He laughed the short, confident laugh again. "I wish she was as sure as I am of us both. We're all right. I've got to get through this, and find out what it's best to do, and I've got to show her. When I've had my chance good and plenty, us two for little old New York! Gee! won't it be fine!" he exclaimed imaginatively. "Her going over her bills, looking like a peach of a baby that's trying to knit its brows, and adding up, and thinking she ought to economize. She'd do it if we had ten million." He laughed outright joyfully. "Good Lord! I should kiss her to death!"

The simplest process of ratiocination would lead to a realization of the fact that though he was lonely and uncomfortable, he was not in the least pathetic or sorry for himself. His normal mental and physical structure kept him steady on his feet, and his practical and unsentimental training, combining itself with a touch of iron which centuries ago had expressed itself through some fighting Temple Barholm and a medium of battle-axes, crossbows, and spears, did the rest.

"It'd take more than this to get me where I'd be down and out. I'm feeling fine," he said. "I believe I'll go and 'take a walk,' as Palford says."

The fog-wreaths in the park were floating away, and he went out grinning and whistling, giving Burrill and the footman a nod as he passed them with a springing young stride. He got the door open so quickly that he left them behind him frustrated and staring at each other.

"It wasn't our fault," said Burrill, gloomily. "He's never had a door opened for him in his life. This won't do for me."

He was away for about an hour, and came back in the best of spirits. He had found out that there was something in "taking a walk" if a fellow had nothing else to do. The park was "fine," and he had never seen anything like it. When there were leaves on the trees and the grass and things were green, it would be better than Central Park itself. You could have base-ball matches in it. What a cinch it would be if you charged gate-money! But he supposed you couldn't if it belonged to you and you had three hundred and fifty thousand a year. You had to get used to that. But it did seem a fool business to have all that land and not make a cent out of it. If it was just outside New York and you cut it up into lots, you'd just pile it up. He was quite innocent—calamitously innocent and commercial and awful in his views. Thoughts such as these had been crammed into his brain by life ever since he had gone down the staircase of the Brooklyn tenement with his twenty-five cents in his ten-year-old hand.

The stillness of the house seemed to have accentuated itself when he returned to it. His sense of it let him down a little as he entered. The library was like a tomb—a comfortable luxurious tomb with a bright fire in it. A new Punch and the morning papers had been laid upon a table earlier in the day, and he sat down to look at them.

"I guess about fifty-seven or eight of the hundred and thirty-six hours have gone by," he said. "But, gee! ain't it lonesome!"

He sat so still trying to interest himself in "London Day by Day" in the morning paper that the combination of his exercise in the fresh air and the warmth of the fire made him drowsy. He leaned back in his chair and closed his eyes without being aware that he did so. He was on the verge of a doze.

He remained upon the verge for a few minutes, and then a soft, rustling sound made him open his eyes.

An elderly little lady had timidly entered the room. She was neatly dressed in an old-fashioned and far-from-new black silk dress, with a darned lace collar and miniature brooch at her neck. She had also thin, gray side-ringlets dangling against her cheeks from beneath a small, black lace cap with pale-purple ribbons on it. She had most evidently not expected to find any one in the room, and, having seen Tembarom, gave a half-frightened cough.

"I—I beg your pardon," she faltered. "I really did not mean to intrude—really."

Tembarom jumped up, awkward, but good-natured. Was she a kind of servant who was a lady?

"Oh, that's all right," he said.

But she evidently did not feel that it was all right. She looked as though she felt that she had been caught doing something wrong, and must properly propitiate by apology.

"I'm so sorry. I thought you had gone out—Mr. Temple Barholm."

"I did go out—to take a walk; but I came in."

Having been discovered in her overt act, she evidently felt that duty demanded some further ceremony from her. She approached him very timidly, but with an exquisite, little elderly early-Victorian manner. She was of the most astonishingly perfect type, though Tembarom was not aware of the fact. The manner, a century earlier, would have expressed itself in a curtsy.

"It is Mr. Temple Barholm, isn't it?" she inquired.

"Yes; it has been for the last few weeks," he answered, wondering why she seemed so in awe of him and wishing she didn't.

"I ought to apologize for being here," she began.

"Say, don't, please!" he interrupted. "What I feel is, that it ought to be up to me to apologize for being here."

She was really quite flurried and distressed.

"Oh, please, Mr. Temple Barholm!" she fluttered, proceeding to explain hurriedly, as though he without doubt understood the situation. "I should of course have gone away at once after the late Mr. Temple Barholm died, but—but I really had nowhere to go—and was kindly allowed to remain until about two months ago, when I went to make a visit. I fully intended to remove my little belongings before you arrived, but I was detained by illness and could not return until this morning to pack up. I understood you were in the park, and I remembered I had left my knitting-bag here." She glanced nervously about the room, and seemed to catch sight of something on a remote corner table. "Oh, there it is. May I take it?" she said, looking at him appealingly. "It was a kind present from a dear lost friend, and—and—" She paused, seeing his puzzled and totally non-comprehending air. It was plainly the first moment it had dawned upon her that he did not know what she was talking about. She took a small, alarmed step toward him.

"Oh, I BEG your pardon," she exclaimed in delicate anguish. "I'm afraid you don't know who I am. Perhaps Mr. Palford forgot to mention me. Indeed, why should he mention me? There were so many more important things. I am a sort of distant—VERY distant relation of yours. My name is Alicia Temple Barholm."

Tembarom was relieved. But she actually hadn't made a move toward the knitting-bag. She seemed afraid to do it until he gave her permission. He walked over to the corner table and brought it to her, smiling broadly.

"Here it is," he said. "I'm glad you left it. I'm very happy to be acquainted with you, Miss Alicia."

He was glad just to see her looking up at him with her timid, refined, intensely feminine appeal. Why she vaguely brought back something that reminded him of Ann he could not have told. He knew nothing whatever of types early-Victorian or late.

He took her hand, evidently to her greatest possible amazement, and shook it heartily. She knew nothing whatever of the New York street type, and it made her gasp for breath, but naturally with an allayed terror.

"Gee!" he exclaimed whole-heartedly, "I'm glad to find out I've got a relation. I thought I hadn't one in the world. Won't you sit down?" He was drawing her toward his own easy-chair. But he really didn't know, she was agitatedly thinking. She really must tell him. He seemed so good tempered and—and DIFFERENT. She herself was not aware of the enormous significance which lay in that word "different." There must be no risk of her seeming to presume upon his lack of knowledge.

"It is MOST kind of you," she said with grateful emphasis, "but I mustn't sit down and detain you. I can explain in a few words—if I may."

He positively still held her hand in the oddest, natural, boyish way, and before she knew what she was doing he had made her take the chair—quite MADE her.

"Well, just sit down and explain," he said. "I wish to thunder you would detain me. Take all the time you like. I want to hear all about it—honest Injun."

There was a cushion in the chair, and as he talked, he pulled it out and began to arrange it behind her, still in the most natural and matter-of-fact way—so natural and matter-of-fact, indeed, that its very natural matter-of-factedness took her breath away.

"Is that fixed all right?" he asked.

Being a little lady, she could only accept his extraordinary friendliness with grateful appreciation, though she could not help fluttering a little in her bewilderment.

"Oh, thank you, thank you, Mr. Temple Barholm," she said.

He sat down on the square ottoman facing her, and leaned forward with an air of making a frank confession.

"Guess what I was thinking to myself two minutes before you came in? I was thinking, 'Lord, I'm lonesome—just sick lonesome!' And then I opened my eyes and looked—and there was a relation! Hully gee! I call that luck!"

"Dear me!" she said, shyly delighted. "DO you, Mr. Temple Barholm—REALLY?"

Her formal little way of saying his name was like Ann's.

"Do I? I'm tickled to death. My mother died when I was ten, and I've never had any women kin-folks."

"Poor bo—" She had nearly said "Poor boy!" and only checked the familiarity just in time—"Poor Mr. Temple Barholm!"

"Say, what are we two to each other, anyhow?" He put it to her with great interest.

"It is a very distant relationship, if it is one at all," she answered. "You see, I was only a second cousin to the late Mr. Temple Barholm, and I had not really the SLIGHTEST claim upon him." She placed pathetic emphasis on the fact. "It was most generous of him to be so kind to me. When my poor father died and I was left quite penniless, he gave me a—a sort of home here."

"A sort of home?" Tembarom repeated.

"My father was a clergyman in VERY straitened circumstances. We had barely enough to live upon—barely. He could leave me nothing. It actually seemed as if I should have to starve—it did, indeed." There was a delicate quiver in her voice. "And though the late Mr. Temple Barholm had a great antipathy to ladies, he was so—so noble as to send word to me that there were a hundred and fifty rooms in his house, and that if I would keep out of his way I might live in one of them."

"That was noble," commented her distant relative.

"Oh, yes, indeed, especially when one considers how he disliked the opposite sex and what a recluse he was. He could not endure ladies. I scarcely ever saw him. My room was in quite a remote wing of the house, and I never went out if I knew he was in the park. I was most careful. And when he died of course I knew I must go away."

Tembarom was watching her almost tenderly.

"Where did you go?"

"To a kind clergyman in Shropshire who thought he might help me."

"How was he going to do it?"

She answered with an effort to steady a somewhat lowered and hesitating voice.

"There was near his parish a very nice—charity,"—her breath caught itself pathetically,—"some most comfortable almshouses for decayed gentlewomen. He thought he might be able to use his influence to get me into one." She paused and smiled, but her small, wrinkled hands held each other closely.

Tembarom looked away. He spoke as though to himself, and without knowing that he was thinking aloud.

"Almshouses!" he said. "Wouldn't that jolt you!" He turned on her again with a change to cheerful concern. "Say, that cushion of yours ain't comfortable. I'm going to get you another one." He jumped up and, taking one from a sofa, began to arrange it behind her dexterously.

"But I mustn't trouble you any longer. I must go, really," she said, half rising nervously. He put a hand on her shoulder and made her sit again.

"Go where?" he said. "Just lean back on that cushion, Miss Alicia. For the next few minutes this is going to be MY funeral."

She was at once startled and uncomprehending. What an extraordinary expression! What COULD it mean?

"F—funeral?" she stammered.

Suddenly he seemed somehow to have changed. He looked as serious as though he was beginning to think out something all at once. What was he going to say?

"That's New York slang," he answered. "It means that I want to explain myself to you and ask a few questions."

"Certainly, certainly, Mr. Temple Barholm."

He leaned his back against the mantel, and went into the matter practically.

"First off, haven't you ANY folks?" Then, answering her puzzled look, added, "I mean relations."

Miss Alicia gently shook her head.

"No sisters or brothers or uncles or aunts or cousins?"

She shook her head again.

He hesitated a moment, putting his hands in his pockets and taking them out again awkwardly as he looked down at her.

"Now here's where I'm up against it," he went on. "I don't want to be too fresh or to butt in, but—didn't old Temple Barholm leave you ANY money?"

"Oh, no!" she exclaimed. "Dear me! no! I couldn't possibly EXPECT such a thing."

He gazed at her as though considering the situation. "Couldn't you?" he said.

There was an odd reflection in his eyes, and he seemed to consider her and the situation again.

"Well," he began after his pause, "what I want to know is what you expect ME to do."

There was no unkindness in his manner, in fact, quite the contrary, even when he uttered what seemed to Miss Alicia these awful, unwarranted words. As though she had forced herself into his presence to make demands upon his charity! They made her tremble and turn pale as she got up quickly, shocked and alarmed.

"Oh, nothing! nothing! nothing WHATEVER, Mr. Temple Barholm!" she exclaimed, her agitation doing its best to hide itself behind a fine little dignity. He saw in an instant that his style of putting it had been "'way off," that his ignorance had betrayed him, that she had misunderstood him altogether. He almost jumped at her.

"Oh, say, I didn't mean THAT!" he cried out. "For the Lord's sake! don't think I'm such a Tenderloin tough as to make a break like that! Not on your life!"

Never since her birth had a male creature looked at Miss Alicia with the appeal which showed itself in his eyes as he actually put his arm half around her shoulders, like a boy begging a favor from his mother or his aunt.

"What I meant was—" He broke off and began again quite anxiously, "say, just as a favor, will you sit down again and let me tell you what I did mean?"

It was that natural, warm, boyish way which overcame her utterly. It reminded her of the only boy she had ever really known, the one male creature who had allowed her to be fond of him. There was moisture in her eyes as she let him put her back into her chair. When he had done it, he sat down on the ottoman again and poured himself forth.

"You know what kind of a chap I am. No, you don't, either. You mayn't know a thing about me; and I want to tell you. I'm so different from everything you've ever known that I scare you. And no wonder. It's the way

I've lived. If you knew, you'd understand what I was thinking of when I spoke just now. I've been cold, I've been hungry, I've walked the wet streets on my uppers. I know all about GOING WITHOUT. And do you expect that I am going to let a—a little thing like you—go away from here without friends and without money on the chance of getting into an almshouse that isn't vacant? Do you expect that of me? Not on your life! That was what I meant."

Miss Alicia quivered; the pale-purple ribbons on her little lace cap quivered.

"I haven't," she said, and the fine little dignity was piteous, "a SHADOW of a claim upon you." It was necessary for her to produce a pocket-handkerchief. He took it from her, and touched her eyes as softly as though she were a baby.

"Claim nothing!" he said. "I've got a claim on YOU. I'm going to stake one out right now." He got up and gesticulated, taking in the big room and its big furniture. "Look at all this! It fell on me like a thunderbolt. It's nearly knocked the life out of me. I'm like a lost cat on Broadway. You can't go away and leave me, Miss Alicia; it's your duty to stay. You've just GOT to stay to take care of me." He came over to her with a wheedling smile. "I never was taken care of in my life. Just be as noble to me as old Temple Barholm was to you: give me a sort of home."

If a little gentlewoman could stare, it might be said that Miss Alicia stared at him. She trembled with amazed emotion.

"Do you mean—" Despite all he had said, she scarcely dared to utter the words lest, after all, she might be taking for granted more than it was credible could be true. "Can you mean that if I stayed here with you it would make Temple Barholm seem more like HOME? Is it possible you—you mean THAT?"

"I mean just that very thing."

It was too much for her. Finely restrained little elderly gentlewoman as she was, she openly broke down under it.

"It can't be true!" she ejaculated shakily. "It isn't possible. It is too—too beautiful and kind. Do forgive me! I c-a-n't help it." She burst into tears.

She knew it was most stupidly wrong. She knew gentlemen did not like tears. Her father had told her that men never really forgave women who cried at them. And here, when her fate hung in the balance, she was not able to behave herself with feminine decorum.

Yet the new Mr. Temple Barholm took it in as matter-of-fact a manner as he seemed to take everything. He stood by her chair and soothed her in his dear New York voice.

"That's all right, Miss Alicia," he commented. "You cry as much as you want to, just so that you don't say no. You've been worried and you're tired. I'll tell you there's been two or three times lately when I should like to have cried myself if I'd known how. Say," he added with a sudden outburst of imagination, "I bet anything it's about time you had tea."

The suggestion was so entirely within the normal order of things that it made her feel steadier, and she was able to glance at the clock.

"A cup of tea would be refreshing," she said. "They will bring it in very soon, but before the servants come I must try to express—"

But before she could express anything further the tea appeared. Burrill and a footman brought it on splendid salvers, in massive urn and tea-pot, with chaste, sacrificial flame flickering, and wonderful, hot buttered and toasted things and wafers of bread and butter attendant. As they crossed the threshold, the sight of Miss Alicia's small form enthroned in their employer's chair was one so obviously unanticipated that Burrill made a step backward and the footman almost lost the firmness of his hold on the smaller tray. Each recovered himself in time, however, and not until the tea was arranged upon the table near the fire was any outward recognition of Miss Alicia's presence made. Then Burrill, pausing, made an announcement entirely without prejudice:

"I beg pardon, sir, but Higgins's cart has come for Miss Temple Barholm's box; he is asking when she wants the trap."

"She doesn't want it at all," answered Tembarom. "Carry her trunk up-stairs again. She's not going away."

The lack of proper knowledge contained in the suggestion that Burrill should carry trunks upstairs caused Miss Alicia to quail in secret, but she spoke with outward calm.

"No, Burrill," she said. "I am not going away."

"Very good, Miss," Burrill replied, and with impressive civility he prepared to leave the room. Tembarom glanced at the tea-things.

"There's only one cup here," he said. "Bring one for me."

Burrill's expression might perhaps have been said to start slightly.

"Very good, sir," he said, and made his exit. Miss Alicia was fluttering again.

"That cup was really for you, Mr. Temple Barholm," she ventured.

"Well, now it's for you, and I've let him know it," replied Tembarom.

"Oh, PLEASE," she said in an outburst of feeling—"PLEASE let me tell you how GRATEFUL—how grateful I am!"

But he would not let her.

"If you do," he said, "I'll tell you how grateful *I* am, and that'll be worse. No, that's all fixed up between us. It goes. We won't say any more about it."

He took the whole situation in that way, as though he was assuming no responsibility which was not the simple, inevitable result of their drifting across each other—as though it was only what any man would have done, even as though she was a sort of delightful, unexpected happening. He turned to the tray.

"Say, that looks all right, doesn't it?" he said. "Now you are here, I like the way it looks. I didn't yesterday."

Burrill himself brought the extra cup and saucer and plate. He wished to make sure that his senses had not deceived him. But there she sat who through years had existed discreetly in the most unconsidered rooms in an uninhabited wing, knowing better than to presume upon her privileges—there she sat with an awed and rapt face gazing up at this new outbreak into Temple Barholm's and "him joking and grinning as though he was as pleased as Punch."

CHAPTER XV

To employ the figure of Burrill, Tembarom was indeed "as pleased as Punch." He was one of the large number of men who, apart from all sentimental relations, are made particularly happy by the kindly society of women; who expand with quite unconscious rejoicing when a woman begins to take care of them in one way or another. The unconsciousness is a touching part of the condition. The feminine nearness supplies a primeval human need. The most complete of men, as well as the weaklings, feel it. It is a survival of days when warm arms held and protected, warm hands served, and affectionate voices soothed. An accomplished male servant may perform every domestic service perfectly, but the fact that he cannot be a woman leaves a sense of lack. An accustomed feminine warmth in the surrounding daily atmosphere has caused many a man to marry his housekeeper or even his cook, as circumstances prompted.

Tembarom had known no woman well until he had met Little Ann. His feeling for Mrs. Bowse herself had verged on affection, because he would have been fond of any woman of decent temper and kindliness, especially if she gave him opportunities to do friendly service. Little Ann had seemed the apotheosis of the feminine, the warmly helpful, the subtly supporting, the kind. She had been to him an amazement and a revelation. She had continually surprised him by revealing new characteristics which seemed to him nicer things than he had ever known before, but which, if he had been aware of it, were not really surprising at all. They were only the characteristics of a very nice young feminine creature.

The presence of Miss Alicia, with the long-belated fashion of her ringlets and her little cap, was delightful to him. He felt as though he would like to take her in his arms and hug her. He thought perhaps it was partly because she was a little like Ann, and kept repeating his name in Ann's formal little way. Her delicate terror of presuming or intruding he felt in its every shade. Mentally she touched him enormously. He wanted to make her feel that she need not be afraid of him in the least, that he liked her, that in his opinion she had more right in the house than he had. He was a little frightened lest through ignorance he should say things the wrong way, as he had said that thing about wanting to know what she expected him to do. What he ought to have said was, "You're not expecting me to let that sort of thing go on." It had made him sick when he saw what a break he'd made and that she thought he was sort of insulting her. The room seemed all right now that she was in it. Small and unassuming as she was, she seemed to make it less over-sized. He didn't so much mind the loftiness of the ceiling, the depth and size of the windows, and the walls covered with thousands of books he knew nothing whatever about. The innumerable books had been an oppressing feature. If he had been one of those "college guys" who never could get enough of books, what a "cinch" the place would have been for him—good as the Astor Library! He hadn't a word to say against books,—good Lord! no;—but even if he'd had the education and the time to read, he didn't believe he was naturally that kind, anyhow. You had to be "that kind" to know about books. He didn't suppose she—meaning Miss Alicia—was learned enough to make you throw a fit. She didn't look that way, and he was mighty glad of it, because perhaps she wouldn't like him much if she was. It would worry her when she tried to talk to him and found out he didn't know a darned thing he ought to.

They'd get on together easier if they could just chin about common sort of every-day things. But though she didn't look like the Vassar sort, he guessed that she was not like himself: she had lived in libraries before, and books didn't frighten her. She'd been born among people who read lots of them and maybe could talk about them. That was why she somehow seemed to fit into the room. He was aware that, timid as she was and shabby as her neat dress looked, she fitted into the whole place, as he did not. She'd been a poor relative and had been afraid to death of old Temple Barholm, but she'd not been afraid of him because she wasn't his sort. She was a lady; that was what was the matter with her. It was what made things harder for her, too. It was what made her voice tremble when she'd tried to seem so contented and polite when she'd talked about going into one of those "decayed almshouses." As if the old ladies were vegetables that had gone wrong, by gee! he thought.

He liked her little, modest, delicate old face and her curls and her little cap with the ribbons so much that he smiled with a twinkling eye every time he looked at her. He wanted to suggest something he thought would be mighty comfortable, but he was half afraid he might be asking her to do something which wasn't "her job," and it might hurt her feelings. But he ventured to hint at it.

"Has Burrill got to come back and pour that out?" he asked, with an awkward gesture toward the tea-tray. "Has he just GOT to?"

"Oh, no, unless you wish it," she answered. "Shall—may I give it to you?"

"Will you?" he exclaimed delightedly. "That would be fine. I shall feel like a regular Clarence."

She was going to sit at the table in a straight-backed chair, but he sprang at her.

"This big one is more comfortable," he said, and he dragged it forward and made her sit in it. "You ought to have a footstool," he added, and he got one and put it under her feet. "There, that's all right."

A footstool, as though she were a royal personage and he were a gentleman in waiting, only probably gentlemen in waiting did not jump about and look so pleased. The cheerful content of his boyish face when he himself sat down near the table was delightful.

"Now," he said, "we can ring up for the first act."

She filled the tea-pot and held it for a moment, and then set it down as though her feelings were too much for her.

"I feel as if I were in a dream," she quavered happily. "I do indeed."

"But it's a nice one, ain't it?" he answered. "I feel as if I was in two. Sitting here in this big room with all these fine things about me, and having afternoon tea with a relation! It just about suits me. It didn't feel like this yesterday, you bet your life!"

"Does it seem—nicer than yesterday?" she ventured. "Really, Mr. Temple Barholm?"

"Nicer!" he ejaculated. "It's got yesterday beaten to a frazzle."

It was beyond all belief. He was speaking as though the advantage, the relief, the happiness, were all on his side. She longed to enlighten him.

"But you can't realize what it is to me," she said gratefully, "to sit here, not terrified and homeless and—a beggar any more, with your kind face before me. Do forgive me for saying it. You have such a kind young face, Mr. Temple Barholm. And to have an easy-chair and cushions, and actually a buffet brought for my feet!" She suddenly recollected herself. "Oh, I mustn't let your tea get cold," she added, taking up the tea-pot apologetically. "Do you take cream and sugar, and is it to be one lump or two?"

"I take everything in sight," he replied joyously, "and two lumps, please."

She prepared the cup of tea with as delicate a care as though it had been a sacramental chalice, and when she handed it to him she smiled wistfully.

"No one but you ever thought of such a thing as bringing a buffet for my feet—no one except poor little Jem," she said, and her voice was wistful as well as her smile.

She was obviously unaware that she was introducing an entirely new acquaintance to him. Poor little Jem was supposed to be some one whose whole history he knew.

"Jem?" he repeated, carefully transferring a piece of hot buttered crumpet to his plate.

"Jem Temple Barholm," she answered. "I say little Jem because I remember him only as a child. I never saw him after he was eleven years old."

"Who was he?" he asked. The tone of her voice, and her manner of speaking made him feel that he wanted to hear something more.

She looked rather startled by his ignorance. "Have you—have you never heard of him?" she inquired.

"No. Is he another distant relation?"

Her hesitation caused him to neglect his crumpet, to look up at her. He saw at once that she wore the air of a sensitive and beautifully mannered elderly lady who was afraid she had made a mistake and said something awkward.

"I am so sorry," she apologized. "Perhaps I ought not to have mentioned him."

"Why shouldn't he be mentioned?"

She was embarrassed. She evidently wished she had not spoken, but breeding demanded that she should ignore the awkwardness of the situation, if awkwardness existed.

"Of course—I hope your tea is quite as you like it—of course there is no real reason. But—shall I give you some more cream? No? You see, if he hadn't died, he—he would have inherited Temple Barholm."

Now he was interested. This was the other chap.

"Instead of me?" he asked, to make sure. She endeavored not to show embarrassment and told herself it didn't really matter—to a thoroughly nice person. But—

"He was the next of kin—before you. I'm so sorry I didn't know you hadn't heard of him. It seemed natural that Mr. Palford should have mentioned him."

"He did say that there was a young fellow who had died, but he didn't tell me about him. I guess I didn't ask. There were such a lot of other things. I'd like to hear about him. You say you knew him?"

"Only when he was a little fellow. Never after he grew up. Something happened which displeased my father. I'm afraid papa was very easily displeased. Mr. Temple Barholm disliked him, too. He would not have him at Temple Barholm."

"He hadn't much luck with his folks, had he?" remarked Tembarom.

"He had no luck with any one. I seemed to be the only person who was fond of him, and of course I didn't count."

"I bet you counted with him," said Tembarom.

"I do think I did. Both his parents died quite soon after he was born, and people who ought to have cared for him were rather jealous because he stood so near to Temple Barholm. If Mr. Temple Barholm had not been so eccentric and bitter, everything would have been done for him; but as it was, he seemed to belong to no one. When he came to the vicarage it used to make me so happy. He used to call me Aunt Alicia, and he had such pretty ways." She hesitated and looked quite tenderly at the tea-pot, a sort of shyness in her face. "I am sure," she burst forth, "I feel quite sure that you will understand and won't think it indelicate; but I had thought so often that I should like to have a little boy—if I had married," she added in hasty tribute to propriety.

Tembarom's eyes rested on her in a thoughtfulness openly touched with affection. He put out his hand and patted hers two or three times in encouraging sympathy.

"Say," he said frankly, "I just believe every woman that's the real thing'd like to have a little boy—or a little girl—or a little something or other. That's why pet cats and dogs have such a cinch of it. And there's men that's the same way. It's sort of nature."

"He had such a high spirit and such pretty ways," she said again. "One of his pretty ways was remembering to do little things to make one comfortable, like thinking of giving one a cushion or a buffet for one's feet. I noticed it so much because I had never seen boys or men wait upon women. My own dear papa was used to having women wait upon him—bring his slippers, you know, and give him the best chair. He didn't like Jem's ways. He said he liked a boy who was a boy and not an affected nincompoop. He wasn't really quite just." She paused regretfully and sighed as she looked back into a past doubtlessly enriched with many similar memories of "dear papa." "Poor Jem! Poor Jem!" she breathed softly.

Tembarom thought that she must have felt the boy's loss very much, almost as much as though she had really been his mother; perhaps more pathetically because she had not been his mother or anybody's mother. He could see what a good little mother she would have made, looking after her children and doing everything on earth to make them happy and comfortable, just the kind of mother Ann would make, though she had not Ann's steady wonder of a little head or her shrewd farsightedness. Jem would have been in luck if he had been her son. It was a darned pity he hadn't been. If he had, perhaps he would not have died young.

"Yes," he answered sympathetically, "it's hard for a young fellow to die. How old was he, anyhow? I don't know."

"Not much older than you are now. It was seven years ago. And if he had only died, poor dear! There are things so much worse than death."

"Worse!"

"Awful disgrace is worse," she faltered. She was plainly trying to keep moisture out of her eyes.

"Did he get into some bad mix-up, poor fellow?" If there had been anything like that, no wonder it broke her up to think of him.

It surely did break her up. She flushed emotionally.

"The cruel thing was that he didn't really do what he was accused of," she said.

"He didn't?"

"No; but he was a ruined man, and he went away to the Klondike because he could not stay in England. And he was killed—killed, poor boy! And afterward it was found out that he was innocent—too late."

"Gee!" Tembarom gasped, feeling hot and cold. "Could you beat that for rotten luck! What was he accused of?"

Miss Alicia leaned forward and spoke in a whisper. It was too dreadful to speak of aloud.

"Cheating at cards—a gentleman playing with gentlemen. You know what that means."

Tembarom grew hotter and colder. No wonder she looked that way, poor little thing!

"But,"—he hesitated before he spoke,—"but he wasn't that kind, was he? Of course he wasn't."

"No, no. But, you see,"—she hesitated herself here,—"everything looked so much against him. He had been rather wild." She dropped her voice even lower in making the admission.

Tembarom wondered how much she meant by that.

"He was so much in debt. He knew he was to be rich in the future, and he was poor just in those reckless young days when it seemed unfair. And he had played a great deal and had been very lucky. He was so lucky that sometimes his luck seemed uncanny. Men who had played with him were horrible about it afterward."

"They would be," put in Tembarom. "They'd be sore about it, and bring it up."

They both forgot their tea. Miss Alicia forgot everything as she poured forth her story in the manner of a woman who had been forced to keep silent and was glad to put her case into words. It was her case. To tell the truth of this forgotten wrong was again to offer justification of poor handsome Jem whom everybody seemed to have dropped talk of, and even preferred not to hear mentioned.

"There were such piteously cruel things about it," she went on. "He had fallen very much in love, and he meant to marry and settle down. Though we had not seen each other for years, he actually wrote to me and told me about it. His letter made me cry. He said I would understand and care about the thing which seemed to have changed everything and made him a new man. He was so sorry that he had not been better and more careful. He was going to try all over again. He was not going to play at all after this one evening when he was obliged to keep an engagement he had made months before to give his revenge to a man he had won a great deal of money from. The very night the awful thing happened he had told Lady Joan, before he went into the card-room, that this was to be his last game."

Tembarom had looked deeply interested from the first, but at her last words a new alertness added itself.

"Did you say Lady Joan?" he asked. "Who was Lady Joan?"

"She was the girl he was so much in love with. Her name was Lady Joan Fayre."

"Was she the daughter of the Countess of Mallowe?"

"Yes. Have you heard of her?"

He recalled Ann's reflective consideration of him before she had said, "She'll come after you." He replied now: "Some one spoke of her to me this morning. They say she's a beauty and as proud as Lucifer."

"She was, and she is yet, I believe. Poor Lady Joan—as well as poor Jem!"

"She didn't believe it, did she?" he put in hastily. "She didn't throw him down?"

"No one knew what happened between them afterward. She was in the card-room, looking on, when the awful thing took place."

She stopped, as though to go on was almost unbearable. She had been so overwhelmed by the past shame of it that even after the passing of years the anguish was a living thing. Her small hands clung hard together as they rested on the edge of the table. Tembarom waited in thrilled suspense. She spoke in a whisper again:

"He won a great deal of money—a great deal. He had that uncanny luck again, and of course people in the other rooms heard what was going on, and a number drifted in to look on. The man he had promised to give his revenge to almost showed signs of having to make an effort to conceal his irritation and disappointment. Of course, as he was a gentleman, he was as cool as possible; but just at the most exciting moment, the height of the game, Jem made a quick movement, and—and something fell out of his sleeve."

"Something," gasped Tembarom, "fell out of his sleeve!"

Miss Alicia's eyes overflowed as she nodded her beribboned little cap.

"It"—her voice was a sob of woe—"it was a marked card. The man he was playing against snatched it and held it up. And he laughed out loud."

"Holy cats!" burst from Tembarom; but the remarkable exclamation was one of genuine horror, and he turned pale, got up from his seat, and took two or three strides across the room, as though he could not sit still.

"Yes, he laughed—quite loudly," repeated Miss Alicia, "as if he had guessed it all the time. Papa heard the whole story from some one who was present."

Tembarom came back to her rather breathless.

"What in thunder did he do—Jem?" he asked.

She actually wrung her poor little hands.

"What could he do? There was a dead silence. People moved just a little nearer to the table and stood and stared, merely waiting. They say it was awful to see his face—awful. He sprang up and stood still, and slowly became as white as if he were dying before their eyes. Some one thought Lady Joan Fayre took a step toward him, but no one was quite sure. He never uttered one word, but walked out of the room and down the stairs and out of the house."

"But didn't he speak to the girl?"

"He didn't even look at her. He passed her by as if she were stone."

"What happened next?"

"He disappeared. No one knew where at first, and then there was a rumor that he had gone to the Klondike and had been killed there. And a year later—only a year! Oh, if he had only waited in England!—a worthless villain of a valet he had discharged for stealing met with an accident, and because he thought he was going to die, got horribly frightened, and confessed to the clergyman that he had tucked the card in poor Jem's sleeve himself just to pay him off. He said he did it on the chance that it would drop out where some one would see it, and a marked card dropping out of a man's sleeve anywhere would look black enough, whether he was playing or not. But poor Jem was in his grave, and no one seemed to care, though every one had been interested enough in the scandal. People talked about that for weeks."

Tembarom pulled at his collar excitedly.

"It makes me sort of strangle," he said. "You've got to stand your own bad luck, but to hear of a chap that's had to lie down and take the worst that could come to him and know it wasn't his—just KNOW it! And die before he's cleared! That knocks me out."

Almost every sentence he uttered had a mystical sound to Miss Alicia, but she knew how he was taking it, with what hot, young human sympathy and indignation. She loved the way he took it, and she loved the feeling in his next words,

"And the girl—good Lord!—the girl?"

"I never met her, and I know very little of her; but she has never married."

"I'm glad of that," he said. "I'm darned glad of it. How could she?" Ann wouldn't, he knew. Ann would have gone to her grave unmarried. But she would have done things first to clear her man's name. Somehow she would have cleared him, if she'd had to fight tooth and nail till she was eighty.

"They say she has grown very bitter and haughty in her manner. I'm afraid Lady Mallowe is a very worldly woman. One hears they don't get on together, and that she is bitterly disappointed because her daughter has not made a good match. It appears that she might have made several, but she is so hard and cynical that men are afraid of her. I wish I had known her a little—if she really loved Jem."

Tembarom had thrust his hands into his pockets, and was standing deep in thought, looking at the huge bank of red coals in the fire-grate. Miss Alicia hastily wiped her eyes.

"Do excuse me," she said.

"I'll excuse you all right," he replied, still looking into the coals. "I guess I shouldn't excuse you as much if you didn't." He let her cry in her gentle way while he stared, lost in reflection.

"And if he hadn't fired that valet chap, he would be here with you now—instead of me. Instead of me," he repeated.

And Miss Alicia did not know what to say in reply. There seemed to be nothing which, with propriety and natural feeling, one could say.

"It makes me feel just fine to know I'm not going to have my dinner all by myself," he said to her before she left the library.

She had a way of blushing about things he noticed, when she was shy or moved or didn't know exactly what to say. Though she must have been sixty, she did it as though she were sixteen. And she did it when he said this, and looked as though suddenly she was in some sort of trouble.

"You are going to have dinner with me," he said, seeing that she hesitated—"dinner and breakfast and lunch and tea and supper and every old thing that goes. You can't turn me down after me staking out that claim."

"I'm afraid—" she said. "You see, I have lived such a secluded life. I scarcely ever left my rooms except to take a walk. I'm sure you understand. It would not have been necessary even if I could have afforded it, which I really couldn't—I'm afraid I have nothing—quite suitable—for evening wear."

"You haven't!" he exclaimed gleefully. "I don't know what is suitable for evening wear, but I haven't got it either. Pearson told me so with tears in his eyes. It never was necessary for me either. I've got to get some things to quiet Pearson down, but until I do I've got to eat my dinner in a tweed cutaway; and what I've caught on to is that it's unsuitable enough to throw a man into jail. That little black dress you've got on and that little cap are just 'way out of sight, they're so becoming. Come down just like you are."

She felt a little as Pearson had felt when confronting his new employer's entire cheerfulness in face of a situation as exotically hopeless as the tweed cutaway, and nothing else by way of resource. But there was something so nice about him, something which was almost as though he was actually a gentleman, something which absolutely, if one could go so far, stood in the place of his being a gentleman. It was impossible to help liking him more and more at every queer speech he made. Still, there were of course things he did not realize, and perhaps one ought in kindness to give him a delicate hint.

"I'm afraid," she began quite apologetically. "I'm afraid that the servants, Burrill and the footmen, you know, will be—will think—"

"Say," he took her up, "let's give Burrill and the footmen the Willies out and out. If they can't stand it, they can write home to their mothers and tell 'em they've got to take 'em away. Burrill and the footmen needn't worry. They're suitable enough, and it's none of their funeral, anyhow."

He wasn't upset in the least. Miss Alicia, who, as a timid dependent either upon "poor dear papa" or Mr. Temple Barholm, had been secretly, in her sensitive, ladylike little way, afraid of superior servants all her life, knowing that they realized her utterly insignificant helplessness, and resented giving her attention because she was not able to show her appreciation of their services in the proper manner—Miss Alicia saw that it had not occurred to him to endeavor to propitiate them in the least, because somehow it all seemed a joke to him, and he didn't care. After the first moment of being startled, she regarded him with a novel feeling, almost a kind of admiration. Tentatively she dared to wonder if there was not something even rather— rather ARISTOCRATIC in his utter indifference.

If he had been a duke, he would not have regarded the servants' point of view; it wouldn't have mattered what they thought. Perhaps, she hastily decided, he was like this because, though he was not a duke, boot-blacking in New York notwithstanding he was a Temple Barholm. There were few dukes as old of blood as a Temple Barholm. That must be it. She was relieved.

Whatsoever lay at the root of his being what he was and as he was, he somehow changed the aspect of things for her, and without doing anything but be himself, cleared the atmosphere of her dread of the surprise and mental reservations of the footmen and Burrill when she came down to dinner in her high-necked, much-cleaned, and much-repaired black silk, and with no more distinguishing change in her toilet than a white lace cap instead of a black one, and with "poor dear mamma's" hair bracelet with the gold clasp on her wrist, and a weeping-willow made of "poor dear papa's" hair in a brooch at her collar.

It was so curious, though still "nice," but he did not offer her his arm when they were going into the dining-room, and he took hold of hers with his hand and affectionately half led, half pushed, her along with him as they went. And he himself drew back her chair for her at the end of the table opposite his own. He did not let a footman do it, and he stood behind it, talking in his cheerful way all the time, and he moved it to exactly the right place, and then actually bent down and looked under the table.

"Here," he said to the nearest man-servant, "where's there a footstool? Get one, please," in that odd, simple, almost aristocratic way. It was not a rude dictatorial way, but a casual way, as though he knew the man was there to do things, and he didn't expect any time to be wasted.

And it was he himself who arranged the footstool, making it comfortable for her, and then he went to his own chair at the head of the table and sat down, smiling at her joyfully across the glass and silver and flowers.

"Push that thing in the middle on one side, Burrill," he said. "It's too high. I can't see Miss Alicia."

Burrill found it difficult to believe the evidence of his hearing.

"The epergne, sir?" he inquired.

"Is that what it's called, an apern? That's a new one on me. Yes, that's what I mean. Push the apern over."

"Shall I remove it from the table, sir?" Burrill steeled himself to exact civility. Of what use to behave otherwise? There always remained the liberty to give notice if the worst came to the worst, though what the worst might eventually prove to be it required a lurid imagination to depict. The epergne was a beautiful thing of crystal and gold, a celebrated work of art, regarded as an exquisite possession. It was almost remarkable that Mr. Temple Barholm had not said, "Shove it on one side," but Burrill had been spared the poignant indignity of being required to "shove."

"Yes, suppose you do. It's a fine enough thing when it isn't in the way, but I've got to see you while I talk, Miss Alicia," said Mr. Temple Barholm. The episode of the epergne—Burrill's expression, and the rigidly restrained mouths of Henry and James as the decoration was removed, leaving a painfully blank space of table-cloth until Burrill silently filled it with flowers in a low bowl—these things temporarily flurried Miss Alicia somewhat, but the pleased smile at the head of the table calmed even that trying moment.

Then what a delightful meal it was, to be sure! How entertaining and cheerful and full of interesting conversation! Miss Alicia had always admired what she reverently termed "conversation." She had read of the houses of brilliant people where they had it at table, at dinner and supper parties, and in drawing-rooms. The French, especially the French ladies, were brilliant conversationalists. They held "salons" in which the conversation was wonderful—Mme. de Stael and Mme. Roland, for instance; and in England, Lady Mary Wortley Montague, Sydney Smith, and Horace Walpole, and surely Miss Fanny Burney, and no doubt L. E. L., whose real name was Miss Letitia Elizabeth Landon—what conversation they must have delighted their friends with and how instructive it must have been even to sit in the most obscure corner and listen!

Such gifted persons seemed to have been chosen by Providence to delight and inspire every one privileged to hear them. Such privileges had been omitted from the scheme of Miss Alicia's existence. She did not know, she would have felt it sacrilegious to admit it even if the fact had dawned upon her, that "dear papa" had been a heartlessly arrogant, utterly selfish, and tyrannical old blackguard of the most pronounced type. He had been of an absolute morality as far as social laws were concerned. He had written and delivered a denunciatory sermon a week, and had made unbearable by his ministrations the suffering hours and the last moments of his parishioners during the long years of his pastorate. When Miss Alicia, in reading records of the helpful relationship of the male progenitors of the Brontes, Jane Austen, Fanny Burney, and Mrs. Browning, was frequently reminded of him, she revealed a perception of which she was not aware. He had combined the virile qualities of all of them. Consequently, brilliancy of conversation at table had not been the attractive habit of the household; "poor dear papa" had confined himself to scathing criticism of the incompetence of females who could not teach their menials to "cook a dinner which was not a disgrace to any decent household." When not virulently aspersing the mutton, he was expressing his opinion of muddle-headed weakness which would permit household bills to mount in a manner which could only bring ruin and disaster upon a minister of the gospel who throughout a protracted career of usefulness had sapped his intellectual manhood in the useless effort to support in silly idleness a family of brainless and maddening fools. Miss Alicia had heard her character, her unsuccessful physical appearance, her mind, and her pitiful efforts at table-talk, described in detail with a choice of adjective and adverb which had broken into terrified fragments every atom of courage and will with which she had been sparsely dowered.

So, not having herself been gifted with conversational powers to begin with, and never having enjoyed the exhibition of such powers in others, her ideals had been high. She was not sure that Mr. Temple Barholm's fluent and cheerful talk could be with exactness termed "conversation." It was perhaps not sufficiently lofty and intellectual, and did not confine itself rigorously to one exalted subject. But how it did raise one's spirits and open up curious vistas! And how good tempered and humorous it was, even though sometimes the humor was a little bewildering! During the whole dinner there never occurred even one of those dreadful pauses in which dead silence fell, and one tried, like a frightened hen flying from side to side of a coop, to think of something to say which would not sound silly, but perhaps might divert attention from dangerous topics. She had often thought it would be so interesting to hear a Spaniard or a native Hindu talk about himself and his own country in English. Tembarom talked about New York and its people and atmosphere, and he did not know how foreign it all was. He described the streets—Fifth Avenue and Broadway and Sixth Avenue—and the street-cars and the elevated railroad, and the way "fellows" had to "hustle" "to put it over." He spoke of a boarding-house kept by a certain Mrs. Bowse, and a presidential campaign, and the election of a mayor, and a quick-lunch counter, and when President Garfield had been assassinated, and a department store; and the electric lights, and the way he had of making a sort of picture of everything was really instructive and, well, fascinating. She felt as though she had been taken about the city in one of the vehicles the conductor of which described things through a megaphone.

Not that Mr. Temple Barholm suggested a megaphone, whatsoever that might be, but he merely made you feel as if you had seen things. Never had she been so entertained and enlightened. If she had been a beautiful girl, he could not have seemed more as though in amusing her he was also really pleasing himself. He was so very funny sometimes that she could not help laughing in a way which was almost unladylike, because she could not stop, and was obliged to put her handkerchief up to her face and wipe away actual tears of mirth.

Fancy laughing until you cried, and the servants looking on!

Once Burrill himself was obliged to turn hastily away, and twice she heard him severely reprove an overpowered young footman in a rapid undertone.

Tembarom at least felt that the unlifting heaviness of atmosphere which had surrounded him while enjoying the companionship of Mr. Palford was a thing of the past.

The thrilled interest, the surprise and delight of Miss Alicia would have stimulated a man in a comatose condition, it seemed to him. The little thing just loved every bit of it—she just "eat it up." She asked question after question, sometimes questions which would have made him shout with laughter if he had not been afraid of hurting her feelings. She knew as little of New York as he knew of Temple Barholm, and was, it made him grin to see, allured by it as by some illicit fascination. She did not know what to make of it, and sometimes she was obliged hastily to conceal a fear that it was a sort of Sodom and Gomorrah; but she wanted to hear more about it, and still more.

And she brightened up until she actually did not look frightened, and ate her dinner with an excellent appetite.

"I really never enjoyed a dinner so much in my life," she said when they went into the drawing-room to have their coffee. "It was the conversation which made it so delightful. Conversation is such a stimulating thing!"

She had almost decided that it was "conversation," or at least a wonderful substitute.

When she said good night to him and went beaming to bed, looking forward immensely to breakfast next morning, he watched her go up the staircase, feeling wonderfully normal and happy.

"Some of these nights, when she's used to me," he said as he stuffed tobacco into his last pipe in the library—"some of these nights I'm darned if I sha'n't catch hold of the sweet, little old thing and hug her in spite of myself. I sha'n't be able to help it." He lit his pipe, and puffed it even excitedly. "Lord!" he said, "there's some blame' fool going about the world right now that might have married her. And he'll never know what a break he made when he didn't."

CHAPTER XVI

A fugitive fine day which had strayed into the month from the approaching spring appeared the next morning, and Miss Alicia was uplifted by the enrapturing suggestion that she should join her new relative in taking a walk, in fact that it should be she who took him to walk and showed him some of his possessions. This, it had revealed itself to him, she could do in a special way of her own, because during her life at Temple Barholm she had felt it her duty to "try to do a little good" among the villagers. She and her long-dead mother and sister had of course been working adjuncts of the vicarage, and had numerous somewhat trying tasks to perform in the way of improving upon "dear papa's" harrying them into attending church, chivying the mothers into sending their children to Sunday-school, and being unsparing in severity of any conduct which might be construed into implying lack of appreciation of the vicar or respect for his eloquence.

It had been necessary for them as members of the vicar's family—always, of course, without adding a sixpence to the household bills—to supply bowls of nourishing broth and arrowroot to invalids and to bestow the aid and encouragement which result in a man of God's being regarded with affection and gratitude by his parishioners. Many a man's career in the church, "dear papa" had frequently observed, had been ruined by lack of intelligence and effort on the part of the female members of his family.

"No man could achieve proper results," he had said, "if he was hampered by the selfish influence and foolishness of his womenkind. Success in the church depends in one sense very much upon the conduct of a man's female relatives."

After the deaths of her mother and sister, Miss Alicia had toiled on patiently, fading day by day from a slim, plain, sweet-faced girl to a slim, even plainer and sweeter-faced middle-aged and at last elderly woman. She had by that time read aloud by bedsides a great many chapters in the Bible, had given a good many tracts, and bestowed as much arrowroot, barley-water, and beef-tea as she could possibly encompass without domestic disaster. She had given a large amount of conscientious, if not too intelligent, advice, and had never failed to preside over her Sunday-school class or at mothers' meetings. But her timid unimpressiveness had not aroused enthusiasm or awakened comprehension. "Miss Alicia," the cottage women said, "she's well meanin', but she's not one with a head." "She reminds me," one of them had summed her up, "of a hen that lays a' egg every day, but it's too small for a meal, and 'u'd never hatch into anythin'."

During her stay at Temple Barholm she had tentatively tried to do a little "parish work," but she had had nothing to give, and she was always afraid that if Mr. Temple Barholm found her out, he would be angry, because he would think she was presuming. She was aware that the villagers knew that she was an object of charity herself, and a person who was "a lady" and yet an object of charity was, so to speak, poaching upon their own legitimate preserves. The rector and his wife were rather grand people, and condescended to her greatly on the few occasions of their accidental meetings. She was neither smart nor influential enough to be considered as an asset.

It was she who "conversed" during their walk, and while she trotted by Tembarom's side looking more early-Victorian than ever in a neat, fringed mantle and a small black bonnet of a fashion long decently interred by a changing world, Tembarom had never seen anything resembling it in New York; but he liked it and her increasingly at every moment.

It was he who made her converse. He led her on by asking her questions and being greatly interested in every response she made. In fact, though he was quite unaware of the situation, she was creating for him such an atmosphere as he might have found in a book, if he had had the habit of books. Everything she told him was new and quaint and very often rather touching. She related anecdotes about herself and her poor little past without knowing she was doing it. Before they had talked an hour he had an astonishing clear idea of "poor dear papa" and "dearest Emily" and "poor darling mama" and existence at Rowcroft Vicarage. He "caught on to" the fact that though she was very much given to the word "dear,"—people were "dear," and so were things and places,—she never even by chance slipped into saying "dear Rowcroft," which she would certainly have done if she had ever spent a happy moment in it.

As she talked to him he realized that her simple accustomedness to English village life and all its accompaniments of county surroundings would teach him anything and everything he might want to know. Her obscurity had been surrounded by stately magnificence, with which she had become familiar without touching the merest outskirts of its privileges. She knew names and customs and families and things to be cultivated or avoided, and though she would be a little startled and much mystified by his total ignorance of all she had breathed in since her birth, he felt sure that she would not regard him either with private contempt or with a lessened liking because he was a vandal pure and simple.

And she had such a nice, little, old polite way of saying things. When, in passing a group of children, he failed to understand that their hasty bobbing up and down meant that they were doing obeisance to him as lord of the manor, she spoke with the prettiest apologetic courtesy.

"I'm sure you won't mind touching your hat when they make their little curtsies, or when a villager touches his forehead," she said.

"Good Lord! no," he said, starting. "Ought I? I didn't know they were doing it at me." And he turned round and made a handsome bow and grinned almost affectionately at the small, amazed party, first puzzling, and then delighting, them, because he looked so extraordinarily friendly. A gentleman who laughed at you like that ought to be equal to a miscellaneous distribution of pennies in the future, if not on the spot. They themselves grinned and chuckled and nudged one another, with stares and giggles.

"I am sorry to say that in a great many places the villagers are not nearly so respectful as they used to be," Miss Alicia explained. "In Rowcroft the children were very remiss about curtseying. It's quite sad. But Mr. Temple Barholm was very strict indeed in the matter of demanding proper respectfulness. He has turned men off their farms for incivility. The villagers of Temple Barholm have much better manners than some even a few miles away."

"Must I tip my hat to all of them?" he asked.

"If you please. It really seems kinder. You—you needn't quite lift it, as you did to the children just now. If you just touch the brim lightly with your hand in a sort of military salute—that is what they are accustomed to."

After they had passed through the village street she paused at the end of a short lane and looked up at him doubtfully.

"Would you—I wonder if you would like to go into a cottage," she said.

"Go into a cottage?" he asked. "What cottage? What for?"

He had not the remotest idea of any reason why he should go into a cottage inhabited by people who were entire strangers to him, and Miss Alicia felt a trifle awkward at having to explain anything so wholly natural.

"You see, they are your cottages, and the people are your tenants, and—"

"But perhaps they mightn't like it. It might make 'em mad," he argued. "If their water-pipes had busted, and they'd asked me to come and look at them or anything; but they don't know me yet. They might think I was Mr. Buttinski."

"I don't quite—" she began. "Buttinski is a foreign name; it sounds Russian or Polish. I'm afraid I don't quite understand why they should mistake you for him."

Then he laughed—a boyish shout of laughter which brought a cottager to the nearest window to peep over the pots of fuchsias and geraniums blooming profusely against the diamond panes.

"Say," he apologized, "don't be mad because I laughed. I'm laughing at myself as much as at anything. It's a way of saying that they might think I was 'butting in' too much—pushing in where I wasn't asked. See? I said they might think I was Mr. Butt-in-ski! It's just a bit of fool slang. You're not mad, are you?"

"Oh, no!" she said. "Dear me! no. It is very funny, of course. I'm afraid I'm extremely ignorant about—about foreign humor" It seemed more delicate to say "foreign" than merely "American." But her gentle little countenance for a few seconds wore a baffled expression, and she said softly to herself, "Mr. Buttinski, Butt-in—to intrude. It sounds quite Polish; I think even more Polish than Russian."

He was afraid he would yell with glee, but he did not. Herculean effort enabled him to restrain his feelings, and present to her only an ordinary-sized smile.

"I shouldn't know one from the other," he said; "but if you say it sounds more Polish, I bet it does."

"Would you like to go into a cottage?" she inquired. "I think it might be as well. They will like the attention."

"Will they? Of course I'll go if you think that. What shall I say?" he asked somewhat anxiously.

"If you think the cottage looks clean, you might tell them so, and ask a few questions about things. And you must be sure to inquire about Susan Hibblethwaite's legs."

"What?" ejaculated Tembarom.

"Susan Hibblethwaite's legs," she replied in mild explanation. "Susan is Mr. Hibblethwaite's unmarried sister, and she has very bad legs. It is a thing one notices continually among village people, more especially the women, that they complain of what they call 'bad legs.' I never quite know what they mean, whether it is rheumatism or something different, but the trouble is always spoken of as 'bad legs' And they like you to inquire about them, so that they can tell you their symptoms."

"Why don't they get them cured?"

"I don't know, I'm sure. They take a good deal of medicine when they can afford it. I think they like to take it. They're very pleased when the doctor gives them `a bottle o' summat,' as they call it. Oh, I mustn't forget to tell you that most of them speak rather broad Lancashire."

"Shall I understand them?" Tembarom asked, anxious again. "Is it a sort of Dago talk?"

"It is the English the working-classes speak in Lancashire. 'Summat' means 'something.' 'Whoam' means 'home.' But I should think you would be very clever at understanding things."

"I'm scared stiff," said Tembarom, not in the least uncourageously; "but I want to go into a cottage and hear some of it. Which one shall we go into?"

There were several whitewashed cottages in the lane, each in its own bit of garden and behind its own hawthorn hedge, now bare and wholly unsuggestive of white blossoms and almond scent to the uninitiated. Miss Alicia hesitated a moment.

"We will go into this one, where the Hibblethwaites live," she decided. "They are quite clean, civil people. They have a naughty, queer, little crippled boy, but I suppose they can't keep him in order because he is an invalid. He's rather rude, I'm sorry to say, but he's rather sharp and clever, too. He seems to lie on his sofa and collect all the gossip of the village."

They went together up the bricked path, and Miss Alicia knocked at the low door with her knuckles. A stout, apple-faced woman opened it, looking a shade nervous.

"Good morning, Mrs. Hibblethwaite," said Miss Alicia in a kind but remote manner. "The new Mr. Temple Barholm has been kind enough to come to see you. It's very good of him to come so soon, isn't it?"

"It is that," Mrs. Hibblethwaite answered respectfully, looking him over. "Wilt tha coom in, sir?"

Tembarom accepted the invitation, feeling extremely awkward because Miss Alicia's initiatory comment upon his goodness in showing himself had "rattled" him. It had made him feel that he must appear condescending, and he had never condescended to any one in the whole course of his existence. He had, indeed, not even been condescended to. He had met with slanging and bullying, indifference and brutality of manner, but he had not met with condescension.

"I hope you're well, Mrs. Hibblethwaite," he answered. "You look it."

"I deceive ma looks a good bit, sir," she answered. "Mony a day ma legs is nigh as bad as Susan's."

"Tha 'rt jealous o' Susan's legs," barked out a sharp voice from a corner by the fire.

The room had a flagged floor, clean with recent scrubbing with sandstone; the whitewashed walls were decorated with pictures cut from illustrated papers; there was a big fireplace, and by it was a hard-looking sofa covered with blue-and-white checked cotton stuff. A boy of about ten was lying on it, propped up with a pillow. He had a big head and a keen, ferret-eyed face, and just now was looking round the end of his sofa at the visitors. "Howd tha tongue, Tummas!" said his mother. "I wunnot howd it," Tummas answered. "Ma tongue's th' on'y thing about me as works right, an' I'm noan goin' to stop it."

"He's a young nowt," his mother explained; "but, he's a cripple, an' we conna do owt wi' him."

"Do not be rude, Thomas," said Miss Alicia, with dignity.

"Dunnot be rude thysen," replied Tummas. "I'm noan o' thy lad."

Tembarom walked over to the sofa.

"Say," he began with jocular intent, "you've got a grouch on, ain't you?"

Tummas turned on him eyes which bored. An analytical observer or a painter might have seen that he had a burning curiousness of look, a sort of investigatory fever of expression.

"I dunnot know what tha means," he said. "Happen tha'rt talkin' 'Merican?"

"That's just what it is," admitted Tembarom. "What are you talking?"

"Lancashire," said Tummas. "Theer's some sense i' that."

Tembarom sat down near him. The boy turned over against his pillow and put his chin in the hollow of his palm and stared.

"I've wanted to see thee," he remarked. "I've made mother an' Aunt Susan an' feyther tell me every bit they've heared about thee in the village. Theer was a lot of it. Tha coom fro' 'Meriker?"

"Yes." Tembarom began vaguely to feel the demand in the burning curiosity.

"Gi' me that theer book," the boy said, pointing to a small table heaped with a miscellaneous jumble of things and standing not far from him. "It's a' atlas," he added as Tembarom gave it to him. "Yo' con find places in it." He turned the leaves until he found a map of the world. "Theer's 'Meriker," he said, pointing to the United States. "That theer's north and that theer's south. All th' real 'Merikens comes from the North, wheer New York is."

"I come from New York," said Tembarom.

"Tha wert born i' th' workhouse, tha run about th' streets i' rags, tha pretty nigh clemmed to death, tha blacked boots, tha sold newspapers, tha feyther was a common workin'-mon—and now tha's coom into Temple Barholm an' sixty thousand a year."

"The last part's true all right," Tembarom owned, "but there's some mistakes in the first part. I wasn't born in the workhouse, and though I've been hungry enough, I never starved to death—if that's what `clemmed' means."

Tummas looked at once disappointed and somewhat incredulous.

"That's th' road they tell it i' th' village," he argued.

"Well, let them tell it that way if they like it best. That's not going to worry me," Tembarom replied uncombatively.

Tummas's eyes bored deeper into him.

"Does na tha care?" he demanded.

"What should I care for? Let every fellow enjoy himself his own way."

"Tha'rt not a bit like one o' th' gentry," said Tummas. "Tha'rt quite a common chap. Tha'rt as common as me, for aw tha foine clothes."

"People are common enough, anyhow," said Tembarom. "There's nothing much commoner, is there? There's millions of 'em everywhere—billions of 'em. None of us need put on airs."

"Tha'rt as common as me," said Tummas, reflectively. "An' yet tha owns Temple Barholm an' aw that brass. I conna mak' out how th' loike happens."

"Neither can I; but it does all samee."

"It does na happen i' 'Meriker," exulted Tummas. "Everybody's equal theer."

"Rats!" ejaculated Tembarom. "What about multimillionaires?"

He forgot that the age of Tummas was ten. It was impossible not to forget it. He was, in fact, ten hundred, if those of his generation had been aware of the truth. But there he sat, having spent only a decade of his most recent incarnation in a whitewashed cottage, deprived of the use of his legs.

Miss Alicia, seeing that Tembarom was interested in the boy, entered into domestic conversation with Mrs. Hibblethwaite at the other side of the room. Mrs. Hibblethwaite was soon explaining the uncertainty of Susan's temper on wash-days, when it was necessary to depend on her legs.

"Can't you walk at all?" Tembarom asked. Tummas shook his head. "How long have you been lame?"

"Ever since I wur born. It's summat like rickets. I've been lyin' here aw my days. I look on at foak an' think 'em over. I've got to do summat. That's why I loike th' atlas. Little Ann Hutchinson gave it to me onct when she come to see her grandmother."

Tembarom sat upright.

"Do you know her?" he exclaimed.

"I know her best o' onybody in th' world. An' I loike her best."

"So do I," rashly admitted Tembarom.

"Tha does?" Tummas asked suspiciously. "Does she loike thee?"

"She says she does." He tried to say it with proper modesty.

"Well, if she says she does, she does. An' if she does, then yo an' me'll be friends." He stopped a moment, and seemed to be taking Tembarom in with thoroughness. "I could get a lot out o' thee," he said after the inspection.

"A lot of what?" Tembarom felt as though he would really like to hear.

"A lot o' things I want to know about. I wish I'd lived th' life tha's lived, clemmin' or no clemmin'. Tha's seen things goin' on every day o' thy loife."

"Well, yes, there's been plenty going on, plenty," Tembarom admitted.

"I've been lying here for ten year'," said Tummas, savagely. "An' I've had nowt i' th' world to do an' nowt to think on but what I could mak' foak tell me about th' village. But nowt happens but this chap gettin' drunk an' that chap deein' or losin' his place, or wenches gettin' married or havin' childer. I know everything that happens, but it's nowt but a lot o' women clackin'. If I'd not been a cripple, I'd ha' been at work for mony a year by now, 'arnin' money to save by an' go to 'Meriker."

"You seem to be sort of stuck on America. How's that?"

"What dost mean?"

"I mean you seem to like it."

"I dunnot loike it nor yet not loike it, but I've heard a bit more about it than I have about th' other places on th' map. Foak goes there to seek their fortune, an' it seems loike there's a good bit doin'."

"Do you like to read newspapers?" said Tembarom, inspired to his query by a recollection of the vision of things "doin'" in the Sunday Earth.

"Wheer'd I get papers from?" the boy asked testily. "Foak like us hasn't got th' brass for 'em."

"I'll bring you some New York papers," promised Tembarom, grinning a little in anticipation. "And we'll talk about the news that's in them. The Sunday Earth is full of pictures. I used to work on that paper myself."

"Tha did?" Tummas cried excitedly. "Did tha help to print it, or was it th' one tha sold i' th' streets?"

"I wrote some of the stuff in it."

"Wrote some of th' stuff in it? Wrote it thaself? How could tha, a common chap like thee?" he asked, more excited still, his ferret eyes snapping.

"I don't know how I did it," Tembarom answered, with increased cheer and interest in the situation. "It wasn't high-brow sort of work."

Tummas leaned forward in his incredulous eagerness.

"Does tha mean that they paid thee for writin' it—paid thee?"

"I guess they wouldn't have done it if they'd been Lancashire," Tembarom answered. "But they hadn't much more sense than I had. They paid me twenty-five dollars a week—that's five pounds."

"I dunnot believe thee," said Tummas, and leaned back on his pillow short of breath.

"I didn't believe it myself till I'd paid my board two weeks and bought a suit of clothes with it," was Tembarom's answer, and he chuckled as he made it.

But Tummas did believe it. This, after he had recovered from the shock, became evident. The curiosity in his face intensified itself; his eagerness was even vaguely tinged with something remotely resembling respect. It was not, however, respect for the money which had been earned, but for the store of things "doin'" which must have been required. It was impossible that this chap knew things undreamed of.

"Has tha ever been to th' Klondike?" he asked after a long pause.

"No. I've never been out of New York."

Tummas seemed fretted and depressed.

"Eh, I'm sorry for that. I wished tha'd been to th' Klondike. I want to be towd about it," he sighed. He pulled the atlas toward him and found a place in it.

"That theer's Dawson," he announced. Tembarom saw that the region of the Klondike had been much studied. It was even rather faded with the frequent passage of searching fingers, as though it had been pored over with special curiosity.

"There's gowd-moines theer," revealed Tummas. "An' theer's welly newt else but snow an' ice. A young chap as set out fro' here to get theer froze to death on th' way."

"How did you get to hear about it?"

"Ann she browt me a paper onet." He dug under his pillow, and brought out a piece of newspaper, worn and frayed and cut with age and usage. "This heer's what's left of it." Tembarom saw that it was a fragment from an old American sheet and that a column was headed "The Rush for the Klondike."

"Why didna tha go theer?" demanded Tummas. He looked up from his fragment and asked his question with a sudden reflectiveness, as though a new and interesting aspect of things had presented itself to him.

"I had too much to do in New York," said Tembarom. "There's always something doing in New York, you know."

Tummas silently regarded him a moment or so.

"It's a pity tha didn't go," he said. "Happen tha'd never ha' coom back."

Tembarom laughed the outright laugh.

"Thank you," he answered.

Tummas was still thinking the matter over and was not disturbed.

"I was na thinkin' o' thee," he said in an impersonal tone. "I was thinkin' o' t' other chap. If tha'd gon i'stead o' him, he'd ha' been here i'stead o' thee. Eh, but it's funny." And he drew a deep breath like a sigh having its birth in profundity of baffled thought.

Both he and his evident point of view were "funny" in the Lancashire sense, which does not imply humor, but strangeness and the unexplainable. Singular as the phrasing was, Tembarom knew what he meant, and that he was thinking of the oddity of chance. Tummas had obviously heard of "poor Jem" and had felt an interest in him.

"You're talking about Jem Temple Barholm I guess," he said. Perhaps the interest he himself had felt in the tragic story gave his voice a tone somewhat responsive to Tummas's own mood, for Tummas, after one more boring glance, let himself go. His interest in this special subject was, it revealed itself, a sort of obsession. The history of Jem Temple Barholm had been the one drama of his short life.

"Aye, I was thinkin' o' him," he said. "I should na ha' cared for th' Klondike so much but for him."

"But he went away from England when you were a baby."

"Th' last toime he coom to Temple Barholm wur when I wur just born. Foak said he coom to ax owd Temple Barholm if he'd help him to pay his debts, an' th' owd chap awmost kicked him out o' doors. Mother had just had me, an' she was weak an' poorly an' sittin' at th' door wi' me in her arms, an' he passed by an' saw her. He stopped an' axed her how she was doin'. An' when he was goin' away, he gave her a gold sovereign, an' he says, `Put it in th' savin's-bank for him, an' keep it theer till he's a big lad an' wants it.' It's been in th' savin's-bank ever sin'. I've got a whole pound o' ma own out at interest. There's not many lads ha' got that."

"He must have been a good-natured fellow," commented Tembarom. "It was darned bad luck him going to the Klondike."

"It was good luck for thee," said Tummas, with resentment.

"Was it?" was Tembarom's unbiased reply. "Well, I guess it was, one way or the other. I'm not kicking, anyhow."

Tummas naturally did not know half he meant. He went on talking about Jem Temple Barholm, and as he talked his cheeks flushed and his eyes lighted.

"I would na spend that sovereign if I was starvin'. I'm going to leave it to Ann Hutchinson in ma will when I dee. I've axed questions about him reet and left ever sin' I can remember, but theer's nobody knows much. Mother says he was fine an' handsome, an' gentry through an' through. If he'd coom into th' property, he'd ha' coom to see me again I'll lay a shillin', because I'm a cripple an' I canna spend his sovereign. If he'd coom back from th' Klondike, happen he'd ha' towd me about it." He pulled the atlas toward him, and laid his thin finger on the rubbed spot. "He mun ha' been killed somewheer about here," he sighed. "Somewheer here. Eh, it's funny."

Tembarom watched him. There was something that rather gave you the "Willies" in the way this little cripple seemed to have taken to the dead man and worried along all these years thinking him over and asking questions and studying up the Klondike because he was killed there. It was because he'd made a kind of story of it. He'd enjoyed it in the way people enjoy stories in a newspaper. You always had to give 'em a kind of story; you had to make a story even if you were telling about a milk-wagon running away. In newspaper offices you heard that was the secret of making good with what you wrote. Dish it up as if it was a sort of story.

He not infrequently arrived at astute enough conclusions concerning things. He had arrived at one now. Shut out even from the tame drama of village life, Tummas, born with an abnormal desire for action and a feverish curiosity, had hungered and thirsted for the story in any form whatsoever. He caught at fragments of happenings, and colored and dissected them for the satisfying of unfed cravings. The vanished man had been the one touch of pictorial form and color in his ten years of existence. Young and handsome and of the gentry, unfavored by the owner of the wealth which some day would be his own possession, stopping "gentry-way" at a cottage door to speak good-naturedly to a pale young mother, handing over the magnificence of a whole sovereign to be saved for a new-born child, going away to vaguely understood disgrace, leaving his own country to hide himself in distant lands, meeting death amid snow and ice and surrounded by gold-mines, leaving his empty place to be filled by a boot-black newsboy—true there was enough to lie and think over and to try to follow with the help of maps and excited questions.

"I wish I could ha' seen him," said Tummas. "I'd awmost gi' my sovereign to get a look at that picture in th' gallery at Temple Barholm."

"What picture?" Tembarom asked. "Is there a picture of him there?"

"There is na one o' him, but there's one o' a lad as deed two hundred year' ago as they say wur th' spit an' image on him when he wur a lad hissen. One o' th' owd servants towd mother it wur theer."

This was a natural stimulus to interest and curiosity.

"Which one is it? Jinks! I'd like to see it myself. Do you know which one it is? There's hundreds of them."

"No, I dunnot know," was Tummas's dispirited answer, "an' neither does mother. Th' woman as knew left when owd Temple Barholm deed."

"Tummas," broke in Mrs. Hibblethwaite from the other end of the room, to which she had returned after taking Miss Alicia out to complain about the copper in the "wash-'us'—" "Tummas, tha'st been talkin' like a magpie. Tha'rt a lot too bold an' ready wi' tha tongue. Th' gentry's noan comin' to see thee if tha clacks th' heads off theer showthers."

"I'm afraid he always does talk more than is good for him," said Miss Alicia. "He looks quite feverish."

"He has been talking to me about Jem Temple Barholm," explained Tembarom. "We've had a regular chin together. He thinks a heap of poor Jem."

Miss Alicia looked startled, and Mrs. Hibblethwaite was plainly flustered tremendously. She quite lost her temper.

"Eh," she exclaimed, "tha wants tha young yed knocked off, Tummas Hibblethwaite. He's fair daft about th' young gentleman as—as was killed. He axes questions mony a day till I'd give him th' stick if he wasna a cripple. He moithers me to death."

"I'll bring you some of those New York papers to look at," Tembarom said to the boy as he went away.

He walked back through the village to Temple Barholm, holding Miss Alicia's elbow in light, affectionate guidance and support, a little to her embarrassment and also a little to her delight. Until he had taken her into the dining-room the night before she had never seen such a thing done. There was no over-familiarity in the action. It merely seemed somehow to suggest liking and a wish to take care of her.

"That little fellow in the village," he said after a silence in which it occurred to her that he seemed thoughtful, "what a little freak he is! He's got an idea that there's a picture in the gallery that's said to look like Jem Temple Barholm when he was a boy. Have you ever heard anything about it? He says a servant told his mother it was there."

"Yes, there is one," Miss Alicia answered. "I sometimes go and look at it. But it makes me feel very sad. It is the handsome boy who was a page in the court of Charles II. He died in his teens. His name was Miles Hugo Charles James. Jem could see the likeness himself. Sometimes for a little joke I used to call him Miles Hugo."

"I believe I remember him," said Tembarom. "I believe I asked Palford his name. I must go and have a look at him again. He hadn't much better luck than the fellow that looked like him, dying as young as that."

CHAPTER XVII

Form, color, drama, and divers other advantages are necessary to the creation of an object of interest. Presenting to the world none of these assets, Miss Alicia had slipped through life a scarcely remarked unit. No little ghost of prettiness had attracted the wandering eye, no suggestion of agreeable or disagreeable power of self-assertion had arrested attention. There had been no hour in her life when she had expected to count as being of the slightest consequence. When she had knocked at the door of the study at Rowcroft Vicarage, and "dear papa" had exclaimed irritably: "Who is that? Who is that?" she had always replied, "It is only Alicia."

This being the case, her gradual awakening to the singularity of her new situation was mentally a process full of doubts and sometimes of alarmed bewilderments. If in her girlhood a curate, even a curate with prominent eyes and a receding chin, had proposed to her that she should face with him a future enriched by the prospect of being called upon to bring up a probable family of twelve on one hundred and fifty pounds a year, with both parish and rectory barking and snapping at her worn-down heels, she would have been sure to assert tenderly that she was afraid she was "not worthy." This was the natural habit of her mind, and in the weeks which followed the foggy afternoon when Tembarom "staked out his claim" she dwelt often upon her unworthiness of the benefits bestowed upon her.

First the world below-stairs, then the village, and then the county itself awoke to the fact that the new Temple Temple Barholm had "taken her up." The first tendency of the world below-stairs was to resent the unwarranted uplifting of a person whom there had been a certain luxury in regarding with disdain and treating with scarcely veiled lack of consideration. To be able to do this with a person who, after all was said and done, was not one of the servant class, but a sort of lady of birth, was not unstimulating. And below-stairs the sense of personal rancor against "a 'anger-on" is strong. The meals served in Miss Alicia's remote sitting-room had been served at leisure, her tea had rarely been hot, and her modestly tinkled bell irregularly answered. Often her far from liberally supplied fire had gone out on chilly days, and she had been afraid to insist on its being relighted. Her sole defense against inattention would have been to complain to Mr. Temple Barholm, and when on one occasion a too obvious neglect had obliged her to gather her quaking being together in mere self-respect and say, "If this continues to occur, William, I shall be obliged to speak to Mr. Temple Barholm," William had so looked at her and so ill hid a secret smile that it had been almost tantamount to his saying, "I'd jolly well like to see you."

And now! Sitting at the end of the table opposite him, if you please! Walking here and walking there with him! Sitting in the library or wherever he was, with him talking and laughing and making as much of her as though she were an aunt with a fortune to leave, and with her making as free in talk as though at liberty to say anything that came into her head! Well, the beggar that had found himself on horseback was setting another one galloping alongside of him. In the midst of this natural resentment it was "a bit upsetting," as Burrill said, to find it dawning upon one that absolute exactness of ceremony was as much to be required for "her" as for "him." Miss Alicia had long felt secretly sure that she was spoken of as "her" in the servants' hall. That businesslike sharpness which Palford had observed in his client aided Tembarom always to see things without illusions. He knew that There was no particular reason why his army of servants should regard him for the present as much more than an intruder; but he also knew that if men and women had employment which was not made hard for them, and were well paid for doing, they were not anxious to lose it, and the man who paid their wages might give orders with some certainty of finding them obeyed. He was "sharp" in more ways than one. He observed shades he might have been expected to overlook. He observed a certain shade in the demeanor of the domestics when attending Miss Alicia, and it was a shade which marked a difference between service done for her and service done for himself. This was only at the outset, of course, when the secret resentment was felt; but he observed it, mere shade though it was.

He walked out into the hall after Burrill one morning. Not having yet adjusted himself to the rule that when one wished to speak to a man one rang a bell and called him back, fifty times if necessary, he walked after Burrill and stopped him.

"This is a pretty good place for servants, ain't it?" he said.

"Yes, sir."

"Good pay, good food, not too much to do?"

"Certainly, sir," Burrill replied, somewhat disturbed by a casualness which yet suggested a method of getting at something or other.

"You and the rest of them don't want to change, do you?"

"No, sir. There is no complaint whatever as far as I have heard."

"That's all right." Mr. Temple Barholm had put his hands into his pockets, and stood looking non-committal in a steady sort of way. "There's something I want the lot of you to get on to—right away. Miss Temple Barholm is going to stay here. She's got to have everything just as she wants it. She's got to be pleased. She's the lady of the house. See?"

"I hope, sir," Burrill said with professional dignity, "that Miss Temple Barholm has not had reason to express any dissatisfaction."

"I'm the one that would express it—quick," said Tembarom. "She wouldn't have time to get in first. I just wanted to make sure I shouldn't have to do it. The other fellows are under you. You've got a head on your shoulders, I guess. It's up to you to put 'em on to it. That's all."

"Thank you, sir," said Burrill.

His master went back into the library smiling genially, and Burrill stood still a moment or so gazing at the door he closed behind him.

Be sure the village, and finally circles not made up of cottagers, heard of this, howsoever mysteriously. Miss Alicia was not aware that the incident had occurred. She could not help observing, however, that the manners of the servants of the household curiously improved; also, when she passed through the village, that foreheads were touched without omission and the curtseys of playing children were prompt. When she dropped into a cottage, housewives polished off the seats of chairs vigorously before offering them, and symptoms and needs were explained with a respectful fluency which at times almost suggested that she might be relied on to use influence.

"I'm afraid I have done the village people injustice," she said leniently to Tembarom. "I used to think them so disrespectful and unappreciative. I dare say it was because I was so troubled myself. I'm afraid one's own troubles do sometimes make one unfair."

"Well, yours are over," said Tembarom. "And so are mine as long as you stay by me."

Never had Miss Alicia been to London. She had remained, as was demanded of her by her duty to dear papa, at Rowcroft, which was in Somersetshire. She had only dreamed of London, and had had fifty-five years of dreaming. She had read of great functions, and seen pictures of some of them in the illustrated papers. She had loyally endeavored to follow at a distance the doings of her Majesty,—she always spoke of Queen Victoria reverentially as "her Majesty,"—she rejoiced when a prince or a princess was born or christened or married, and believed that a "drawing-room" was the most awe-inspiring, brilliant, and important function in the civilized world, scarcely second to Parliament. London—no one but herself or an elderly gentlewoman of her type could have told any one the nature of her thoughts of London.

Let, therefore, those of vivid imagination make an effort to depict to themselves the effect produced upon her mind by Tembarom's casually suggesting at breakfast one morning that he thought it might be rather a good "stunt" for them to run up to London. By mere good fortune she escaped dropping the egg she had just taken from the egg-stand.

"London!" she said. "Oh!"

"Pearson thinks it would be a first-rate idea," he explained. "I guess he thinks that if he can get me into the swell clothing stores he can fix me up as I ought to be fixed, if I'm not going to disgrace him. I should hate to disgrace Pearson. Then he can see his girl, too, and I want him to see his girl."

"Is—Pearson—engaged?" she asked; but the thought which was repeating itself aloud to her was "London! London!"

"He calls it 'keeping company,' or 'walking out,'" Tembarom answered. "She's a nice girl, and he's dead stuck on her. Will you go with me, Miss Alicia?"

"Dear Mr. Temple Barholm," she fluttered, "to visit London would be a privilege I never dreamed it would be my great fortune to enjoy—never."

"Good business!" he ejaculated delightedly. "That's luck for me. It gave me the blues—what I saw of it. But if you are with me, I'll bet it'll be as different as afternoon tea was after I got hold of you. When shall we start? To-morrow?"

Her sixteen-year-old blush repeated itself.

"I feel so sorry. It seems almost undignified to mention it, but—I fear I should not look smart enough for London. My wardrobe is so very limited. I mustn't," she added with a sweet effort at humor, "do the new Mr. Temple Barholm discredit by looking unfashionable."

He was more delighted than before.

"Say," he broke out, "I'll tell you what we'll do: we'll go together and buy everything 'suitable' in sight. The pair of us'll come back here as suitable as Burrill and Pearson. We'll paint the town red."

He actually meant it. He was like a boy with a new game. His sense of the dreariness of London had disappeared. He knew what it would be like with Miss Alicia as a companion. He had really seen nothing of the place himself, and he would find out every darned thing worth looking at, and take her to see it—theaters, shops, every show in town. When they left the breakfast-table it was agreed upon that they would make the journey the following day.

He did not openly refer to the fact that among the plans for their round of festivities he had laid out for himself the attending to one or two practical points. He was going to see Palford, and he had made an appointment with a celebrated nerve specialist. He did not discuss this for several reasons. One of them was that his summing up of Miss Alicia was that she had had trouble enough to think over all her little life, and the thing for a fellow to do for her, if he liked her, was to give her a good time and make her feel as if she was at a picnic right straight along—not let her even hear of a darned thing that might worry her. He had said comparatively little to her about Strangeways. His first mention of his condition had obviously made her somewhat nervous, though she had been full of kindly interest. She was in private not sorry that it was felt better that she should not disturb the patient by a visit to his room. The abnormality of his condition seemed just slightly alarming to her.

"But, oh, how good, how charitable, you are!" she had murmured.

"Good," he answered, the devout admiration of her tone rather puzzling him. "It ain't that. I just want to see the thing through. I dropped into it by accident, and then I dropped into this by accident, and that made it as easy as falling off a log. I believe he's going to get well sometime. I guess I kind of like him because he holds on to me so and believes I'm just It. Maybe it's because I'm stuck on myself."

His visit to Strangeways was longer than usual that afternoon. He explained the situation to him so that he understood it sufficiently not to seem alarmed by it. This was one of the advances Tembarom had noticed recently, that he was less easily terrified, and seemed occasionally to see facts in their proper relation to one another. Sometimes the experiments tried on him were successful, sometimes they were not, but he never resented them.

"You are trying to help me to remember," he said once. "I think you will sometime."

"Sure I will," said Tembarom. "You're better every day."

Pearson was to remain in charge of him until toward the end of the London visit. Then he was to run up for a couple of days, leaving in his place a young footman to whom the invalid had become accustomed.

The visit to London was to Miss Alicia a period of enraptured delirium. The beautiful hotel in which she was established, the afternoons at the Tower, the National Gallery, the British Museum, the evenings at the play, during which one saw the most brilliant and distinguished actors, the mornings in the shops, attended as though one were a person of fortune, what could be said of them? And the sacred day on which she saw her Majesty drive slowly by, glittering helmets, splendid uniforms, waving plumes, and clanking swords accompanying and guarding her, and gentlemen standing still with their hats off, and everybody looking after her with that natural touch of awe which royalty properly inspires! Miss Alicia's heart beat rapidly in her breast, and she involuntarily made a curtsey as the great lady in mourning drove by. She lost no shade of any flavor of ecstatic pleasure in anything, and was to Tembarom, who knew nothing about shades and flavors, indeed a touching and endearing thing.

He had never got so much out of anything. If Ann had just been there, well, that would have been the limit. Ann was on her way to America now, and she wouldn't write to him or let him write to her. He had to make a fair trial of it. He could find out only in that way, she said. It was not to be denied that the youth and longing in him gave him some half-hours to face which made him shut himself up in his room and stare hard at the wall, folding his arms tightly as he tilted his chair.

There arrived a day when one of the most exalted shops in Bond Street was invaded by an American young man of a bearing the peculiarities of which were subtly combined with a remotely suggested air of knowing that if he could find what he wanted, there was no doubt as to his power to get it. What he wanted was not usual, and was explained with a frankness which might have seemed unsophisticated, but, singularly, did not. He wanted to have a private talk with some feminine power in charge, and she must be some one who knew exactly what ladies ought to have.

Being shown into a room, such a feminine power was brought to him and placed at his service. She was a middle-aged person, wearing beautifully fitted garments and having an observant eye and a dignified suavity of manner. She looked the young American over with a swift inclusion of all possibilities. He was by this time wearing extremely well-fitting garments himself, but she was at once aware that his tailored perfection was a new thing to him.

He went to his point without apologetic explanation.

"You know all the things any kind of a lady ought to have," he said—"all the things that would make any one feel comfortable and as if they'd got plenty? Useful things as well as ornamental ones?"

"Yes, sir," she replied, with rising interest. "I have been in the establishment thirty years."

"Good business," Tembarom replied. Already he felt relieved. "I've got a relation, a little old lady, and I want her to fix herself out just as she ought to be fixed. Now, what I'm afraid of is that she won't get everything she ought to unless I manage it for her somehow beforehand. She's got into a habit of—well, economizing. Now the time's past for that, and I want her to get everything a woman like you would know she really wants, so that she could look her best, living in a big country house, with a relation that thinks a lot of her."

He paused a second or so, and then went further, fixing a clear and astonishingly shrewd eye upon the head of the department listening to him.

"I found out this was a high-class place," he explained. "I made sure of that before I came in. In a place that was second or third class there might be people who'd think they'd caught a 'sucker' that would take anything that was unloaded on to him, because he didn't know. The things are for Miss Temple Barholm, and she DOES know. I shall ask her to come here herself tomorrow morning, and I want you to take care of her, and show her the best you've got that's suitable." He seemed to like the word; he repeated it—"Suitable," and quickly restrained a sudden, unexplainable, wide smile.

The attending lady's name was Mrs. Mellish. Thirty years' experience had taught her many lessons. She was a hard woman and a sharp one, but beneath her sharp hardness lay a suppressed sense of the perfect in taste. To have a customer with unchecked resources put into her hands to do her best by was an inspiring incident. A quiver of enlightenment had crossed her countenance when she had heard the name of Temple Barholm. She had a newspaper knowledge of the odd Temple Barholm story. This was the next of kin who had blacked boots in New York, and the obvious probability that he was a fool, if it had taken the form of a hope, had been promptly nipped in the bud. The type from which he was furthest removed was that of the fortune-intoxicated young man who could be obsequiously flattered into buying anything which cost money enough.

"Not a thing's to be unloaded on her that she doesn't like," he added, "and she's not a girl that goes to pink teas. She's a—a—lady—and not young—and used to quiet ways."

The evidently New York word "unload" revealed him to his hearer as by a flash, though she had never heard it before.

"We have exactly the things which will be suitable, sir," she said. "I think I quite understand." Tembarom smiled again, and, thanking her, went away still smiling, because he knew Miss Alicia was safe.

There were of course difficulties in the way of persuading Miss Alicia that her duty lay in the direction of spending mornings in the most sumptuous of Bond Street shops, ordering for herself an entire wardrobe on a basis of unlimited resources. Tembarom was called upon to employ the most adroitly subtle reasoning, entirely founded on his "claim" and her affectionate willingness to give him pleasure.

He really made love to her in the way a joyful young fellow can make love to his mother or his nicest aunt. He made her feel that she counted for so much in his scheme of enjoyment that to do as he asked would be to add a glow to it.

"And they won't spoil you," he said. "The Mellish woman that's the boss has promised that. I wouldn't have you spoiled for a farm," he added heartily.

And he spoke the truth. If he had been told that he was cherishing her type as though it were a priceless bit of old Saxe, he would have stared blankly and made a jocular remark. But it was exactly this which he actually clung to and adored. He even had a second private interview with Mrs. Mellish, and asked her to "keep her as much like she was" as was possible.

Stimulated by the suppressed touch of artistic fervor, Mrs. Mellish guessed at something even before her client arrived; but the moment she entered the showroom all was revealed to her at once. The very hint of flush and tremor in Miss Alicia's manner was an assistance. Surrounded by a small and extremely select court composed of Mrs. Mellish and two low-voiced, deft-handed assistants, it was with a fine little effort that Miss Alicia restrained herself from exterior suggestion of her feeling that there was something almost impious in thinking of possessing the exquisite stuffs and shades displayed to her in flowing beauty on every side. Such linens and batistes and laces, such delicate, faint grays and lavenders and soft-falling blacks! If she had been capable of approaching the thought, such luxury might even have hinted at guilty splendor.

Mrs. Mellish became possessed of an "idea" To create the costume of an exquisite, early-Victorian old lady in a play done for the most fashionable and popular actor manager of the most "drawing-room" of West End theaters, where one saw royalty in the royal box, with bouquets on every side, the orchestra breaking off in the middle of a strain to play "God Save the Queen," and the audience standing up as the royal party came in—that was her idea. She carried it out, steering Miss Alicia with finished tact through the shoals and rapids of her timidities. And the result was wonderful; color,—or, rather, shades,—textures, and forms were made subservient by real genius. Miss Alicia—as she was turned out when the wardrobe was complete—might have been an elderly little duchess of sweet and modest good taste in the dress of forty years earlier. It took time, but some of the things were prepared as though by magic, and the night the first boxes were delivered at the hotel Miss Alicia, on going to bed, in kneeling down to her devotions prayed fervently that she might not be "led astray by fleshly desires," and that her gratitude might be acceptable, and not stained by a too great joy "in the things which corrupt."

The very next day occurred Rose. She was the young person to whom Pearson was engaged, and it appeared that if Miss Alicia would make up her mind to oblige Mr. Temple Barholm by allowing the girl to come to her as lady's-maid, even if only temporarily, she would be doing a most kind and charitable thing. She was a very nice, well-behaved girl, and unfortunately she had felt herself forced to leave her place because her mistress's husband was not at all a nice man. He had shown himself so far from nice that Pearson had been most unhappy, and Rose had been compelled to give notice, though she had no other situation in prospect and her mother was dependent on her. This was without doubt not Mr. Temple Barholm's exact phrasing of the story, but it was what Miss Alicia gathered, and what moved her deeply. It was so cruel and so sad! That wicked man! That poor girl! She had never had a lady's-maid, and might be rather at a loss at first, but it was only like Mr. Temple Barholm's kind heart to suggest such a way of helping the girl and poor Pearson.

So occurred Rose, a pretty creature whose blue eyes suppressed grateful tears as she took Miss Alicia's instructions during their first interview. And Pearson arrived the same night, and, waiting upon Tembarom, stood before him, and with perfect respect, choked.

"Might I thank you, if you please, sir," he began, recovering himself—"might I thank you and say how grateful—Rose and me, sir—" and choked again.

"I told you it would be all right," answered Tembarom. "It is all right. I wish I was fixed like you are, Pearson."

When the Countess of Mallowe called, Rose had just dressed Miss Alicia for the afternoon in one of the most perfect of the evolutions of Mrs. Mellish's idea. It was a definite creation, as even Lady Mallowe detected the moment her eyes fell upon it. Its hue was dull, soft gray, and how it managed to concede points and elude suggestions of modes interred, and yet remain what it did remain, and accord perfectly with the side ringlets and the lace cap of Mechlin, only dressmaking genius could have explained. The mere wearing of it gave Miss Alicia a support and courage which she could scarcely believe to be her own. When the cards of Lady Mallowe and Lady Joan Fayre were brought up to her, she was absolutely not really frightened; a little nervous for a moment, perhaps, but frightened, no. A few weeks of relief and ease, of cheery consideration, of perfectly good treatment and good food and good clothes, had begun a rebuilding of the actual cells of her.

Lady Mallowe entered alone. She was a handsome person, and astonishingly young when considered as the mother of a daughter of twenty-seven. She wore a white veil, and looked pink through it. She swept into the room, and shook hands with Miss Alicia with delicate warmth.

"We do not really know each other at all," she said. "It is disgraceful how little relatives see of one another."

The disgrace, if measured by the extent of the relationship, was not immense. Perhaps this thought flickered across Miss Alicia's mind among a number of other things. She had heard "dear papa" on Lady Mallowe, and, howsoever lacking in graces, the vicar of Rowcroft had not lacked an acrid shrewdness. Miss Alicia's sensitively self-accusing soul shrank before a hasty realization of the fact that if he had been present when the cards were brought up, he would, on glancing over them through his spectacles, have jerked out immediately: "What does the woman want? She's come to get something." Miss Alicia wished she had not been so immediately beset by this mental vision.

Lady Mallowe had come for something. She had come to be amiable to Miss Temple Barholm and to establish relations with her.

"Joan should have been here to meet me," she explained. "Her dressmaker is keeping her, of course. She will be so annoyed. She wanted very much to come with me."

It was further revealed that she might arrive at any moment, which gave Miss Alicia an opportunity to express, with pretty grace, the hope that she would, and her trust that she was quite well.

"She is always well," Lady Mallowe returned. "And she is of course as interested as we all are in this romantic thing. It is perfectly delicious, like a three-volumed novel."

"It is romantic," said Miss Alicia, wondering how much her visitor knew or thought she knew, and what circumstances would present themselves to her as delicious.

"Of course one has heard only the usual talk one always hears when everybody is chattering about a thing," Lady Mallowe replied, with a propitiating smile. "No one really knows what is true and what isn't. But it is nice to notice that all the gossip speaks so well of him. No one seems to pretend that he is anything but extremely nice himself, notwithstanding his disadvantages."

She kept a fine hazel eye, surrounded by a line which artistically represented itself as black lashes, steadily resting on Miss Alicia as she said the last words.

"He is," said Miss Alicia, with gentle firmness, "nicer than I had ever imagined any young man could be—far nicer."

Lady Mallowe's glance round the luxurious private sitting-room and over the perfect "idea" of Mrs. Mellish was so swift as to be almost imperceptible.

"How delightful!" she said. "He must be unusually agreeable, or you would not have consented to stay and take care of him."

"I cannot tell you how HAPPY I am to have been asked to stay with him, Lady Mallowe," Miss Alicia replied, the gentle firmness becoming a soft dignity.

"Which of course shows all the more how attractive he must be. And in view of the past lack of advantages, what a help you can be to him! It is quite wonderful for him to have a relative at hand who is an Englishwoman and familiar with things he will feel he must learn."

A perhaps singular truth is that but for the unmistakable nature of the surroundings she quickly took in the significance of, and but for the perfection of the carrying out of Mrs. Mellish's delightful idea, it is more than probable that her lady-ship's manner of approaching Miss Alicia and certain subjects on which she desired enlightenment would have been much more direct and much less propitiatory. Extraordinary as it was, "the creature"— she thought of Tembarom as "the creature"—had plainly been so pleased with the chance of being properly coached that he had put everything, so to speak, in the little old woman's hands. She had got a hold upon him. It was quite likely that to regard her as a definite factor would only be the part of the merest discretion. She was evidently quite in love with him in her early-Victorian, spinster way. One had to be prudent with women like that who had got hold of a male creature for the first time in their lives, and were almost unaware of their own power. Their very unconsciousness made them a dangerous influence.

With a masterly review of these facts in her mind Lady Mallowe went on with a fluent and pleasant talk, through the medium of which she managed to convey a large number of things Miss Alicia was far from being clever enough to realize she was talking about. She lightly waved wings of suggestion across the scene, she dropped infinitesimal seeds in passing, she left faint echoes behind her—the kind of echoes one would find oneself listening to and trying to hear as definitely formed sounds. She had been balancing herself on a precarious platform of rank and title, unsupported by any sordid foundation of a solid nature, through a lifetime spent in London. She had learned to catch fiercely at straws of chance, and bitterly to regret the floating past of the slightest, which had made of her a finished product of her kind. She talked lightly, and was sometimes almost witty. To her hearer she seemed to know every brilliant personage and to be familiar with every dazzling thing. She knew well what social habits and customs meant, what their value, or lack of value, was. There were customs, she implied skilfully, so established by time that it was impossible to ignore them. Relationships, for instance, stood for so much that was fine in England that one was sometimes quite touched by the far-reachingness of family loyalty. The head of the house of a great estate represented a certain power in the matter of upholding the dignity of his possessions, of caring for his tenantry, of standing for proper hospitality and friendly family feeling. It was quite beautiful as one often saw it. Throughout the talk there were several references to Joan, who really must come in shortly, which were very interesting to Miss Alicia. Lady Joan, Miss

Alicia heard casually, was a great beauty. Her perfection and her extreme cleverness had made her perhaps a trifle difficile. She had not done—Lady Mallowe put it with a lightness of phrasing which was delicacy itself—what she might have done, with every exalted advantage, so many times. She had a profound nature. Here Lady Mallowe waved away, as it were, a ghost of a sigh. Since Miss Temple Barholm was a relative, she had no doubt heard of the unfortunate, the very sad incident which her mother sometimes feared prejudiced the girl even yet.

"You mean—poor Jem!" broke forth involuntarily from Miss Alicia's lips. Lady Mallowe stared a little.

"Do you call him that?" she asked. "Did you know him, then?"

"I loved him," answered Miss Alicia, winking her eyes to keep back the moisture in them, "though it was only when he was a little boy."

"Oh," said Lady Mallowe, with a sudden, singular softness, "I must tell Joan that."

Lady Joan had not appeared even after they had had tea and her mother went away, but somehow Miss Alicia had reached a vaguely yearning feeling for her and wished very much the dressmaker had released her. She was quite stirred when it revealed itself almost at the last moment that in a few weeks both she and Lady Mallowe were to pay a visit at no great distance from Temple Barholm itself, and that her ladyship would certainly arrange to drive over to continue her delightful acquaintance and to see the beautiful old place again.

"In any case one must, even if he lived in lonely state, pay one's respects to the head of the house. The truth is, of course, one is extremely anxious to meet him, and it is charming to know that one is not merely invading the privacy of a bachelor," Lady Mallowe put it.

"She'll come for YOU," Little Ann had soberly remarked.

Tembarom remembered the look in her quiet, unresentful blue eyes when he came in to dinner and Miss Alicia related to him the events of the afternoon.

CHAPTER XVIII

The spring, when they traveled back to the north, was so perceptibly nearer that the fugitive soft days strayed in advance at intervals that were briefer. They chose one for their journey, and its clear sunshine and hints at faint greenness were so exhilarating to Miss Alicia that she was a companion to make any journey an affair to rank with holidays and adventures. The strange luxury of traveling in a reserved first-class carriage, of being made timid by no sense of unfitness of dress or luggage, would have filled her with grateful rapture; but Rose, journeying with Pearson a few coaches behind, appeared at the carriage window at every important station to say, "Is there anything I may do for you, ma'am?" And there really never was anything she could do, because Mr. Temple Barholm remembered everything which could make her comfort perfect. In the moods of one who searches the prospect for suggestions as to pleasure he can give to himself by delighting a dear child, he had found and bought for her a most elegant little dressing-bag, with the neatest of plain-gold fittings beautifully initialed. It reposed upon the cushioned seat near her, and made her heart beat every time she caught sight of it anew. How wonderful it would be if poor dear, darling mama could look down and see everything and really know what happiness had been vouchsafed to her unworthy child!

Having a vivid recollection of the journey made with Mr. Palford, Tembarom felt that his whole world had changed for him. The landscape had altered its aspect. Miss Alicia pointed out bits of freshening grass, was sure of the breaking of brown leaf-buds, and more than once breathlessly suspected a primrose in a sheltered hedge corner. A country-bred woman, with country-bred keenness of eye and a country-bred sense of the seasons' change, she saw so much that he had never known that she began to make him see also. Bare trees would be thick-leaved nesting-places, hedges would be white with hawthorn, and hold blue eggs and chirps and songs. Skylarks would spring out of the fields and soar into the sky, dropping crystal chains of joyous trills. The cottage gardens would be full of flowers, there would be poppies gleaming scarlet in the corn, and in buttercup-time all the green grass would be a sheet of shining gold.

"When it all happens I shall be like a little East-Sider taken for a day in the country. I shall be asking questions at every step," Tembarom said. "Temple Barholm must be pretty fine then."

"It is so lovely," said Miss Alicia, turning to him almost solemnly, "that sometimes it makes one really lose one's breath."

He looked out of the window with sudden wistfulness.

"I wish Ann—" he began and then, seeing the repressed question in her eyes, made up his mind.

He told her about Little Ann. He did not use very many words, but she knew a great deal when he had finished. And her spinster soul was thrilled. Neither she nor poor Emily had ever had an admirer, and it was not considered refined for unsought females to discuss "such subjects." Domestic delirium over the joy of an engagement in families in which daughters were a drug she had seen. It was indeed inevitable that there should be more rejoicing over one Miss Timson who had strayed from the fold into the haven of marriage than over the ninety-nine Misses Timson who remained behind. But she had never known intimately any one who was in love—really in love. Mr. Temple Barholm must be. When he spoke of Little Ann he flushed shyly and his eyes looked so touching and nice. His voice sounded different, and though of course his odd New York expressions were always rather puzzling, she felt as though she saw things she had had no previous knowledge of—things which thrilled her.

"She must be a very—very nice girl," she ventured at length. "I am afraid I have never been into old Mrs. Hutchinson's cottage. She is quite comfortably off in her way, and does not need parish care. I wish I had seen Miss Hutchinson."

"I wish she had seen you," was Tembarom's answer.

Miss Alicia reflected.

"She must be very clever to have such—sensible views," she remarked.

If he had remained in New York, and there had been no question of his inheriting Temple Barholm, the marriage would have been most suitable. But however "superior" she might be, a vision of old Mrs. Hutchinson's granddaughter as the wife of Mr. Temple Barholm, and of noisy old Mr. Hutchinson as his father-in-law was a staggering thing.

"You think they were sensible?" asked Tembarom. "Well, she never did anything that wasn't. So I guess they were. And what she says GOES. I wanted you to know, anyhow. I wouldn't like you not to know. I'm too fond of you, Miss Alicia." And he put his hand round her neat glove and squeezed it. The tears of course came into her tender eyes. Emotion of any sort always expressed itself in her in this early-Victorian manner.

"This Lady Joan girl," he said suddenly not long afterward, "isn't she the kind that I'm to get used to—the kind in the pictorial magazine Ann talked about? I bought one at the news-stand at the depot before we started. I wanted to get on to the pictures and see what they did to me."

He found the paper among his belongings and regarded it with the expression of a serious explorer. It opened at a page of illustrations of slim goddesses in court dresses. By actual measurement, if regarded according to scale, each was about ten feet high; but their long lines, combining themselves with court trains, waving plumes, and falling veils, produced an awe-inspiring effect. Tembarom gazed at them in absorbed silence.

"Is she something like any of these?" he inquired finally.

Miss Alicia looked through her glasses.

"Far more beautiful, I believe," she answered. "These are only fashion-plates, and I have heard that she is a most striking girl."

"A beaut' from Beautsville!" he said. "So that's what I'm up against! I wonder how much use that kind of a girl would have for me."

He gave a good deal of attention to the paper before he laid it aside. As she watched him, Miss Alicia became gradually aware of the existence of a certain hint of determined squareness in his boyish jaw. It was perhaps not much more than a hint, but it really was there, though she had not noticed it before. In fact, it usually hid itself behind his slangy youthfulness and his readiness for any good cheer.

One may as well admit that it sustained him during his novitiate and aided him to pass through it without ignominy or disaster. He was strengthened also by a private resolve to bear himself in such a manner as would at least do decent credit to Little Ann and her superior knowledge. With the curious eyes of servants, villagers, and secretly outraged neighborhood upon him, he was shrewd enough to know that he might easily become a perennial fount of grotesque anecdote, to be used as a legitimate source of entertainment in cottages over the consumption of beans and bacon, as well as at great houses when dinner-table talk threatened to become dull if not enlivened by some spice. He would not have thought of this or been disturbed by it but for Ann. She knew, and he was not going to let her be met on her return from America with what he called "a lot of funny dope" about him.

"No girl would like it," he said to himself. "And the way she said she 'cared too much' just put it up to me to see that the fellow she cares for doesn't let himself get laughed at."

Though he still continued to be jocular on subjects which to his valet seemed almost sacred, Pearson was relieved to find that his employer gradually gave himself into his hands in a manner quite amenable. In the touching way in which nine out of ten nice, domesticated American males obey the behests of the women they are fond of, he had followed Ann's directions to the letter. Guided by the adept Pearson, he had gone to the best places in London and purchased the correct things, returning to Temple Barholm with a wardrobe to which any gentleman might turn at any moment without a question.

"He's got good shoulders, though he does slouch a bit," Pearson said to Rose. "And a gentleman's shoulders are more than half the battle."

What Tembarom himself felt cheered by was the certainty that if Ann saw him walking about the park or the village, or driving out with Miss Alicia in the big landau, or taking her in to dinner every evening, or even going to church with her, she would not have occasion to flush at sight of him.

The going to church was one of the duties of his position he found out. Miss Alicia "put him on" to that. It seemed that he had to present himself to the villagers "as an example." If the Temple Barholm pews were empty, the villagers, not being incited to devotional exercise by his exalted presence, would feel at liberty to remain at home, and in the irreligious undress of shirt-sleeves sit and smoke their pipes, or, worse still, gather at "the Hare and Hounds" and drink beer. Also, it would not be "at all proper" not to go to church.

Pearson produced a special cut of costume for this ceremony, and Tembarom walked with Miss Alicia across the park to the square-towered Norman church.

In a position of dignity the Temple Barholm pews over-looked the congregation. There was the great square pew for the family, with two others for servants. Footmen and house-maids gazed reverentially at prayer-books. Pearson, making every preparation respectfully to declare himself a "miserable sinner" when the proper moment arrived, could scarcely re-strain a rapid side glance as the correctly cut and fitted and entirely "suitable" work of his hands opened the pew-door for Miss Alicia, followed her in, and took his place.

Let not the fact that he had never been to church before be counted against him. There was nothing very extraordinary in the fact. He had felt no antipathy to church-going, but he had not by chance fallen under proselyting influence, and it had certainly never occurred to him that he had any place among the well-dressed, comfortable-looking people he had seen flocking into places of worship in New York. As far as religious observances were concerned, he was an unadulterated heathen, and was all the more to be congratulated on being a heathen of genial tendencies.

The very large pew, under the stone floor of which his ancestors had slept undisturbedly for centuries, interested him greatly. A recumbent marble crusader in armor, with feet crossed in the customary manner, fitted into a sort of niche in one side of the wall. There were carved tablets and many inscriptions in Latin wheresoever one glanced. The place was like a room. A heavy, round table, on which lay prayer-books, Bibles, and hymn-books, occupied the middle. About it were arranged beautiful old chairs, with hassocks to kneel on. Toward a specially imposing chair with arms Miss Alicia directed, him with a glance. It was apparently his place. He was going to sit down when he saw Miss Alicia gently push forward a hassock with her foot, and kneel on it, covering her face with her hands as she bent her head. He hastily drew forth his hassock and followed her example.

That was it, was it? It wasn't only a matter of listening to a sermon; you had to do things. He had better watch out and see that he didn't miss anything. She didn't know it was his first time, and it might worry her to the limit if he didn't put it over all right. One of the things he had noticed in her was her fear of attracting attention by failing to do exactly the "proper thing." If he made a fool of himself by kneeling down when he ought to stand up, or lying down when he ought to sit, she'd get hot all over, thinking what the villagers or the other people would say. Well, Ann hadn't wanted him to look different from other fellows or to make breaks. He'd look out from start to finish. He directed a watchful eye at Miss Alicia through his fingers. She remained kneeling a few moments, and then very quietly got up. He rose with her, and took his big chair when she sat down. He breathed more freely when they had got that far. That was the first round.

It was not a large church, but a gray and solemn impression of dignity brooded over it. It was dim with light, which fell through stained-glass memorial windows set deep in the thick stone walls. The silence which reigned throughout its spaces seemed to Tembarom of a new kind, different from the silence of the big house. The occasional subdued rustle of turned prayer-book leaves seemed to accentuate it; the most careful movement could not conceal itself; a slight cough was a startling thing. The way, Tembarom thought, they could get things dead-still in English places!

The chimes, which had been ringing their last summons to the tardy, slackened their final warning notes, became still slower, stopped. There was a slight stir in the benches occupied by the infant school. It suggested that something new was going to happen. From some unseen place came the sound of singing voices—boyish voices and the voices of men. Tembarom involuntarily turned his head. Out of the unseen place came a procession in white robes. Great Scott! every one was standing up! He must stand up, too. The boys and men in white garments filed into their seats. An elderly man, also in white robes, separated himself from them, and, going into his special place, kneeled down. Then he rose and began to read:

"When the wicked man turneth away from his wickedness—"

Tembarom took the open book which Miss Alicia had very delicately pushed toward him. He read the first words,—that was plain sailing,—then he seemed to lose his place. Miss Alicia turned a leaf. He turned one also.

"Dearly beloved brethren—"

There you were. This was once more plain sailing. He could follow it. What was the matter with Miss Alicia? She was kneeling again, everybody was kneeling. Where was the hassock? He went down upon his knees, hoping Miss Alicia had not seen that he wasn't going to kneel at all. Then when the minister said "Amen," the congregation said it, too, and he came in too late, so that his voice sounded out alone. He must watch that. Then the minister knelt, and all the people prayed aloud with him. With the book before him he managed to get in after the first few words; but he was not ready with the responses, and in the middle of them everybody stood up again. And then the organ played, and every one sang. He couldn't sing, anyhow, and he knew he couldn't catch on to the kind of thing they were doing. He hoped Miss Alicia wouldn't mind his standing up and holding his book and doing nothing. He could not help seeing that eyes continually turned toward him. They'd notice every darned break he made, and Miss Alicia would know they did. He felt quite hot more than once. He watched Miss Alicia like a hawk; he sat down and listened to reading, he stood up and listened to singing; he kneeled, he tried to chime in with "Amens" and to keep up with Miss Alicia's bending of head and knee. But the creed, with its sudden turn toward the altar, caught him unawares, he lost himself wholly in the psalms, the collects left him in deep water, hopeless of ever finding his place again, and the litany baffled him, when he was beginning to feel safe, by changing from "miserable sinners" to "Spare us Good Lord" and "We beseech thee to hear us." If he could just have found the place he would have been all right, but an honest anxiety to be right excited him, and the fear of embarrassing Miss Alicia by going wrong made the morning a strenuous thing. He was so relieved to find he might sit still when the sermon began that he gave the minister an attention which might have marked him, to the chance beholder, as a religious enthusiast.

By the time the service had come to an end the stately peace of the place had seemed to sink into his being and become part of himself. The voice of the minister bestowing his blessing, the voices of the white-clothed choir floating up into the vaulted roof, stirred him to a remote pleasure. He liked it, or he knew he would like it when he knew what to do. The filing out of the choristers, the silent final prayer, the soft rustle of people rising gently from their knees, somehow actually moved him by its suggestion of something before unknown. He was a heathen still, but a heathen vaguely stirred.

He was very quiet as he walked home across the park with Miss Alicia.

"How did you enjoy the sermon?" she asked with much sweetness.

"I'm not used to sermons, but it seemed all right to me," he answered. "What I've got to get on to is knowing when to stand up and when to sit down. I wasn't much of a winner at it this morning. I guess you noticed that."

But his outward bearing had been much more composed than his inward anxiety had allowed him to believe. His hesitations had not produced the noticeable effect he had feared.

"Do you mean you are not quite familiar with the service?" she said. Poor dear boy! he had perhaps not been able to go to church regularly at all.

"I'm not familiar with any service," he answered without prejudice. "I never went to church before."

She slightly started and then smiled.

"Oh, you mean you have never been to the Church of England," she said.

Then he saw that, if he told her the exact truth, she would be frightened and shocked. She would not know what to say or what to think. To her unsophisticated mind only murderers and thieves and criminals NEVER went to church. She just didn't know. Why should she? So he smiled also.

"No, I've never been to the Church of England," he said.

CHAPTER XIX

The country was discreetly conservative in its social attitude. The gulf between it and the new owner of Temple Barholm was too wide and deep to be crossed without effort combined with immense mental agility. It was on the whole, much easier not to begin a thing at all than to begin it and find one must hastily search about for not too noticeable methods of ending it. A few unimportant, tentative calls were made, and several ladies who had remained unaware of Miss Alicia during her first benefactor's time drove over to see what she was like and perhaps by chance hear something of interest. One or two of them who saw Tembarom went away puzzled and amazed. He did not drop his h's, which they had of course expected, and he was well dressed, and not bad-looking; but it was frequently impossible to understand what he was talking about, he used such odd phrases. He seemed good natured enough, and his way with little old Miss Temple Barholm was really quite nice, queer as it was. It was queer because he was attentive to her in a manner in which young men were not usually attentive to totally insignificant, elderly dependents.

Tembarom derived an extremely diluted pleasure from the visits. The few persons he saw reminded him in varying degrees of Mr. Palford. They had not before seen anything like his species, and they did not know what to do with him. He also did not know what to do with them. A certain inelasticity frustrated him at the outset. When, in obedience to Miss Alicia's instructions, he had returned the visits, he felt he had not gone far.

Serious application enabled him to find his way through the church service, and he accompanied Miss Alicia to church with great regularity. He began to take down the books from the library shelves and look them over gravely. The days gradually ceased to appear so long, but he had a great deal of time on his hands, and he tried to find ways of filling it. He wondered if Ann would be pleased if he learned things out of books.

When he tentatively approached the subject of literature with Miss Alicia, she glowed at the delightful prospect of his reading aloud to her in the evenings—"reading improving things like history and the poets."

"Let's take a hack at it some night," he said pleasantly.

The more a fellow knew, the better it was for him, he supposed; but he wondered, if anything happened and he went back to New York, how much "improving things" and poetry would help a man in doing business.

The first evening they began with Gray's "Elegy," and Miss Alicia felt that it did not exhilarate him; she was also obliged to admit that he did not read it very well. But she felt sure he would improve. Personally she was touchingly happy. The sweetly domestic picture of the situation, she sitting by the fire with her knitting and he reading aloud, moved and delighted her. The next evening she suggested Tennyson's "Maud." He was not as much stirred by it as she had hoped. He took a somewhat humorous view of it.

"He had it pretty bad, hadn't he?" he said of the desperate lover.

"Oh, if only you could once have heard Sims Reeves sing 'Come into the Garden, Maud'!" she sighed. "A kind friend once took me to hear him, and I have never, never forgotten it."

But Mr. Temple Barholm notably did not belong to the atmosphere of impassioned tenors.

On still another evening they tried Shakspere. Miss Alicia felt that a foundation of Shakspere would be "improving" indeed. They began with "Hamlet."

He found play-reading difficult and Shaksperian language baffling, but he made his way with determination until he reached a point where he suddenly grew quite red and stopped.

"Say, have you read this?" he inquired after his hesitation.

"The plays of Shakspere are a part of every young lady's education," she answered; "but I am afraid I am not at all a Shaksperian scholar."

"A young lady's education?" he repeated. "Gee whizz!" he added softly after a pause.

He glanced over a page or so hastily, and then laid the book down.

"Say," he suggested, with an evasive air, "let's go over that 'Maud' one again. It's—well, it's easier to read aloud."

The crude awkwardness of his manner suddenly made Miss Alicia herself flush and drop a stitch in her knitting. How dreadful of her not to have thought of that!

"The Elizabethan age was, I fear, a rather coarse one in some respects. Even history acknowledges that Queen Elizabeth herself used profane language." She faltered and coughed a little apologetic cough as she picked up her stitch again.

"I bet Ann's never seen inside Shakspere," said Tembarom. Before reading aloud in the future he gave some previous personal attention to the poem or subject decided upon. It may be at once frankly admitted that when he read aloud it was more for Miss Alicia's delectation than for his own. He saw how much she enjoyed the situation.

His effect of frankness and constant boyish talk was so inseparable from her idea of him that she found it a puzzling thing to realize that she gradually began to feel aware of a certain remote reserve in him, or what might perhaps be better described as a habit of silence upon certain subjects. She felt it marked in the case of Strangeways. She surmised that he saw Strangeways often and spent a good deal of time with him, but he spoke of him rarely, and she never knew exactly what hours were given to him. Sometimes she imagined he found him a greater responsibility than he had expected. Several times when she believed that he had spent part of a morning or afternoon in his room, he was more silent than usual and looked puzzled and thoughtful. She observed, as Mr. Palford had, that the picture-gallery, with its portraits of his ancestors, had an attraction. A certain rainy day he asked her to go with him and look them over. It was inevitable that she should soon wander to the portrait of Miles Hugo and remain standing before it. Tembarom followed, and stood by her side in silence until her sadness broke its bounds with a pathetic sigh.

"Was he very like him?" he asked.

She made an unconscious, startled movement. For the moment she had forgotten his presence, and she had not really expected him to remember.

"I mean Jem," he answered her surprised look. "How was he like him? Was there—" he hesitated and looked really interested—"was he like him in any particular thing?"

"Yes," she said, turning to the portrait of Miles Hugo again. "They both had those handsome, drooping eyes, with the lashes coming together at the corners. There is something very fascinating about them, isn't there? I used to notice it so much in dear little Jem. You see how marked they are in Miles Hugo."

"Yes," Tembarom answered. "A fellow who looked that way at a girl when he made love to her would get a strangle-holt. She wouldn't forget him soon."

"It strikes you in that way, too?" said Miss Alicia, shyly. "I used to wonder if it was—not quite nice of me to think of it. But it did seem that if any one did look at one like that—" Maidenly shyness overcame her. "Poor Lady Joan!" she sighed.

"There's a sort of cleft in his chin, though it's a good, square chin," he suggested. "And that smile of his—Were Jem's—?"

"Yes, they were. The likeness was quite odd sometimes—quite."

"Those are things that wouldn't be likely to change much when he grew up," Tembarom said, drawing a little closer to the picture. "Poor Jem! He was up against it hard and plenty. He had it hardest. This chap only died."

There was no mistaking his sympathy. He asked so many questions that they sat down and talked instead of going through the gallery. He was interested in the detail of all that had occurred after the ghastly moment when Jem had risen from the card-table and stood looking around, like some baited dying animal, at the circle of cruel faces drawing in about him. How soon had he left London? Where had he gone first? How had he been killed? He had been buried with others beneath a fall of earth and stones. Having heard this much, Tembarom saw he could not ask more questions. Miss Alicia became pale, and her hands trembled. She could not bear to discuss details so harrowing.

"Say, I oughtn't to let you talk about that," he broke out, and he patted her hand and made her get up and finish their walk about the gallery. He held her elbow in his own odd, nice way as he guided her, and the things he said, and the things he pretended to think or not to understand, were so amusing that in a short time he had made her laugh. She knew him well enough by this time to be aware that he was intentionally obliging her to forget what it only did her harm to remember. That was his practical way of looking at it.

"Getting a grouch on or being sorry for what you can't help cuts no ice," he sometimes said. "When it does, me for getting up at daybreak and keeping at it! But it doesn't, you bet your life on that."

She could see that he had really wanted to hear about Jem, but he knew it was bad for her to recall things, and he would not allow her to dwell on them, just as she knew he would not allow himself to dwell on little Miss Hutchinson, remotely placed among the joys of his beloved New York.

Two other incidents besides the visit to Miles Hugo afterward marked that day when Miss Alicia looked back on it. The first was his unfolding to her his plans for the house-party, which was characteristic of his habit of thinking things over and deciding them before he talked about them.

"If I'm going to try the thing out, as Ann says I must," he began when they had gone back to the library after lunch, "I've got to get going. I'm not seeing any of those Pictorial girls, and I guess I've got to see some."

"You will be invited to dine at places," said Miss Alicia,—"presently," she added bravely, in fact, with an air of greater conviction than she felt.

"If it's not the law that they've got to invite me or go to jail," said Tembarom, "I don't blame 'em for not doing it if they're not stuck on me. And they're not; and it's natural. But I've got to get in my fine work, or my year'll be over before I've 'found out for myself,' as Ann called it. There's where I'm at, Miss Alicia—and I've been thinking of Lady Joan and her mother. You said you thought they'd come and stay here if they were properly asked."

"I think they would," answered Miss Alicia with her usual delicacy. "I thought I gathered from Lady Mallowe that, as she was to be in the neighborhood, she would like to see you and Temple Barholm, which she greatly admires."

"If you'll tell me what to do, I'll get her here to stay awhile," he said, "and Lady Joan with her. You'd have to show me how to write to ask them; but perhaps you'd write yourself."

"They will be at Asshawe Holt next week," said Miss Alicia, "and we could go and call on them together. We might write to them in London before they leave."

"We'll do it," answered Tembarom. His manner was that of a practical young man attacking matter-of-fact detail. "From what I hear, Lady Joan would satisfy even Ann. They say she's the best-looker on the slate. If I see her every day I shall have seen the blue-ribbon winner. Then if she's here, perhaps others of her sort'll come, too; and they'll have to see me whether they like it or not—and I shall see them. Good Lord!" he added seriously, "I'd let 'em swarm all over me and bite me all summer if it would fix Ann."

He stood up, with his hands thrust deep in his pockets, and looked down at the floor.

"I wish she knew T. T. like T. T. knows himself," he said. It was quite wistful.

It was so wistful and so boyish that Miss Alicia was thrilled as he often thrilled her.

"She ought to be a very happy girl," she exclaimed.

"She's going to be," he answered, "sure as you're alive. But whatever she does, is right, and this is as right as everything else. So it just goes."

They wrote their letters at once, and sent them off by the afternoon post. The letter Miss Alicia composed, and which Tembarom copied, he read and reread, with visions of Jim Bowles and Julius looking over his shoulder. If they picked it up on Broadway, with his name signed to it, and read it, they'd throw a fit over it, laughing. But he supposed she knew what you ought to write.

It had not, indeed, the masculine touch. When Lady Mallowe read it, she laughed several times. She knew quite well that he had not known what to say, and, allowing Miss Alicia to instruct him, had followed her instructions to the letter. But she did not show the letter to Joan, who was difficult enough to manage without being given such material to comment upon.

The letters had just been sent to the post when a visitor was announced—Captain Palliser. Tembarom remembered the name, and recalled also certain points connected with him. He was the one who was a promoter of schemes—"One of the smooth, clever ones that get up companies," Little Ann had said.

That in a well-bred and not too pronounced way he looked smooth and clever might be admitted. His effect was that of height, finished slenderness of build, and extremely well-cut garments. He was no longer young, and he had smooth, thin hair and a languidly observant gray eye.

"I have been staying at Detchworth Grange," he explained when he had shaken hands with the new Temple Barholm and Miss Alicia. "It gave me an excellent opportunity to come and pay my respects."

There was a hint of uncertainty in the observant gray eye. The fact was that he realized in the space of five minutes that he knew his ground even less than he had supposed he did. He had not spent his week at Detchworth Grange without making many quiet investigations, but he had found out nothing whatever. The new man was an ignoramus, but no one had yet seemed to think him exactly a fool. He was not excited by the new grandeurs of his position and he was not ashamed of himself. Captain Palliser wondered if he was perhaps sharp—one of those New Yorkers shrewd even to light-fingeredness in clever scheming. Stories of a newly created method of business dealing involving an air of candor and almost primitive good nature—an American method—had attracted Captain Palliser's attention for some time. A certain Yankee rawness of manner played a part as a factor, a crudity which would throw a man off guard if he did not recognize it. The person who employed the method was of philosophical non-combativeness. The New York phrase was that "He jollied a man along." Immense schemes had been carried through in that way. Men in London, in England, were not sufficiently light of touch in their jocularity. He wondered if perhaps this young fellow, with his ready laugh and rather loose-jointed, casual way of carrying himself, was of this dangerous new school.

What, however, could he scheme for, being the owner of Temple Barholm's money? It may be mentioned at once that Captain Palliser's past had been such as had fixed him in the belief that every one was scheming for something. People with money wanted more or were privately arranging schemes to prevent other schemers from getting any shade the better of them. Debutantes with shy eyes and slim figures had their little plans to engineer delicately. Sometimes they were larger plans than the uninitiated would have suspected as existing in the brains of creatures in their 'teens, sometimes they were mere fantastic little ideas connected with dashing young men or innocent dances which must be secured or lovely young rivals who must be evaded. Young men had also deft things to do—people to see or not to see, reasons for themselves being seen or avoiding observation. As years increased, reasons for schemes became more numerous and amazingly more varied. Women with daughters, with sons, with husbands, found in each relationship a necessity for active, if quiet, manoeuvering. Women like Lady Mallowe—good heaven! by what schemes did not that woman live and have her being—and her daughter's—from day to day! Without money, without a friend who was an atom more to be relied on than she would have been herself if an acquaintance had needed her aid, her outwardly well-to-do and fashionable existence was a hand-to-hand fight. No wonder she had turned a still rather brilliant eye upon Sir Moses Monaldini, the great Israelite financier. All of these types passed rapidly before his mental vision as he talked to the American Temple Barholm. What could he want, by chance? He must want something, and it would be discreet to find out what it chanced to be.

If it was social success, he would be better off in London, where in these days you could get a good run for your money and could swing yourself up from one rung of the ladder to another if you paid some one to show you how. He himself could show him how. A youngster who had lived the beastly hard life he had lived would be likely to find exhilaration in many things not difficult to purchase. It was an odd thing, by the way, the fancy he had taken to the little early-Victorian spinster. It was not quite natural. It perhaps denoted tendencies—or lack of tendencies—it would also be well to consider. Palliser was a sufficiently finished product himself to be struck greatly by the artistic perfection of Miss Alicia, and to wonder how much the new man understood it.

He did not talk to him about schemes. He talked to him of New York, which he had never seen and hoped sometime shortly to visit. The information he gained was not of the kind he most desired, but it edified him. Tembarom's knowledge of high finance was a street lad's knowledge of it, and he himself knew its limitations and probable unreliability. Such of his facts as rested upon the foundation of experience did not include multimillionaires and their resources.

Captain Palliser passed lightly to Temple Barholm and its neighborhood. He knew places and names, and had been to Detchworth more than once. He had never visited Temple Barholm, and his interest suggested that he would like to walk through the gardens. Tembarom took him out, and they strolled about for some time. Even an alert observer would not have suspected the fact that as they strolled, Tembarom slouching a trifle and with his hands in his pockets, Captain Palliser bearing himself with languid distinction, each man was summing up the other and considering seriously how far and in what manner he could be counted as an asset.

"You haven't been to Detchworth yet?" Palliser inquired.

"No, not yet," answered Tembarom. The Granthams were of those who had not yet called.

"It's an agreeable house. The Granthams are agreeable people."

"Are there any young people in the family?" Tembarom asked.

"Young people? Male or female?" Palliser smilingly put it. Suddenly it occurred to him that this might give him a sort of lead.

"Girls," said Tembarom, crudely—"just plain girls."

Palliser laughed. Here it was, perhaps.

"They are not exactly 'plain' girls, though they are not beauties. There are four Misses Grantham. Lucy is the prettiest. Amabel is quite tremendous at tennis."

"Are they ladies?" inquired Tembarom.

Captain Palliser turned and involuntarily stared at him. What was the fellow getting at?

"I'm afraid I don't quite understand," he said.

The new Temple Barholm looked quite serious. He did not, amazing to relate, look like a fool even when he gave forth his extraordinary question. It was his almost business-like seriousness which saved him.

"I mean, do you call them Lady Lucy and Lady Amabel?" he answered.

If he had been younger, less hardened, or less finished, Captain Palliser would have laughed outright. But he answered without self-revelation.

"Oh, I see. You were asking whether the family is a titled one. No; it is a good old name, quite old, in fact, but no title goes with the estate."

"Who are the titled people about here?" Tembarom asked, quite unabashed.

"The Earl of Pevensy at Pevensy Park, the Duke of Stone at Stone Hover, Lord Hambrough at Doone. Doone is in the next county, just over the border."

"Have they all got daughters?"

Captain Palliser found it expedient to clear his throat before speaking.

"Lord Pevensy has daughters, so has the duke. Lord Hambrough has three sons."

"How many daughters are there—in a bunch?" Mr. Temple Barholm suggested liberally.

There Captain Palliser felt it safe to allow himself to smile, as though taking it with a sense of humor.

"'In a bunch' is an awfully good way of putting it," he said. "It happens to apply perhaps rather unfortunately well; both families are much poorer than they should be, and daughters must be provided for. Each has four. 'In a bunch' there are eight: Lady Alice, Lady Edith, Lady Ethel, and Lady Celia at Stone Hover; Lady Beatrice, Lady Gwynedd, Lady Honora, and Lady Gwendolen at Pevensy Park. And not a fortune among them, poor girls!"

"It's not the money that matters so much," said the astounding foreigner, "it's the titles."

Captain Palliser stopped short in the garden path for a moment. He could scarcely believe his ears. The crude grotesqueness of it so far got the better of him that if he had not coughed he would have betrayed himself.

"I've had a confounded cold lately," he said. "Excuse me; I must get it over."

He turned a little aside and coughed energetically.

After watching him a few seconds Tembarom slipped two fingers into his waistcoat pocket and produced a small tube of tablets.

"Take two of these," he said as soon as the cough stopped. "I always carry it about with me. It's a New York thing called 'G. Destroyer.' G stands for grippe."

Palliser took it.

"Thanks. With water? No? Just dissolve in the mouth. Thanks awfully." And he took two, with tears still standing in his eyes.

"Don't taste bad, do they?" Mr. Temple Barholm remarked encouragingly.

"Not at all. I think I shall be all right now. I just needed the relief. I have been trying to restrain it."

"That's a mistake," said Tembarom. They strolled on a pace or so, and he began again, as though he did not mean to let the subject drop. "It's the titles," he said, "and the kind. How many of them are good-lookers?"

Palliser reflected a moment, as though making mental choice.

"Lady Alice and Lady Celia are rather plain," he said, "and both of them are invalidish. Lady Ethel is tall and has handsome eyes, but Lady Edith is really the beauty of the family. She rides and dances well and has a charming color."

"And the other ones," Tembaron suggested as he paused—"Lady Beatrice and Lady Gwynedd and Lady Honora and Lady Gwendolen."

"You remember their names well," Palliser remarked with a half-laugh.

"Oh, I shall remember them all right," Tembarom answered. "I earned twenty-five per in New York by getting names down fine."

"The Talchesters are really all rather taking. Talchester is Lord Pevensy's family name," Palliser explained. "They are girls who have pretty little noses and bright complexions and eyes. Lady Gwynedd and Lady Honora both have quite fascinating dimples."

"Dimples!" exclaimed his companion. "Good business."

"Do you like dimples particularly?" Palliser inquired with an impartial air.

"I'd always make a bee-line for a dimple," replied Mr. Temple Barholm. "Clear the way when I start."

This was New York phrasing, and was plainly humorous; but there was something more than humor in his eye and smile—something hinting distantly at recollection.

"You'll find them at Pevensy Park," said Palliser.

"What about Lady Joan Fayre?" was the next inquiry.

Palliser's side glance at him was observant indeed. He asked himself how much the man could know. Taking the past into consideration, Lady Joan might turn out to be a subject requiring delicate handling. It was not the easiest thing in the world to talk at all freely to a person with whom one desired to keep on good terms, about a young woman supposed still to cherish a tragic passion for the dead man who ought to stand at the present moment in the person's, figuratively speaking, extremely ill-fitting shoes.

"Lady Joan has been from her first season an undeniable beauty," he replied.

"She and the old lady are going to stay at a place called Asshawe Holt. I think they're going next week," Tembarom said.

"The old lady?" repeated Captain Palliser.

"I mean her mother. The one that's the Countess of Mallowe."

"Have you met Lady Mallowe?" Palliser inquired with a not wholly repressed smile. A vision of Lady Mallowe over-hearing their conversation arose before him.

"No, I haven't. What's she like?"

"She is not the early-or mid-Victorian old lady," was Palliser's reply. "She wears Gainsborough hats, and looks a quite possible eight and thirty. She is a handsome person herself."

He was not aware that the term "old lady" was, among Americans of the class of Mrs. Bowse's boarders, a sort of generic term signifying almost anything maternal which had passed thirty.

Tembarom proceeded.

"After they get through at the Asshawe Holt place, I've asked them to come here."

"Indeed," said Palliser, with an inward start. The man evidently did not know what other people did. After all, why should he? He had been selling something or other in the streets of New York when the thing happened, and he knew nothing of London.

"The countess called on Miss Alicia when we were in London," he heard next. "She said we were relations."

"You are—as we are. The connection is rather distant, but it is near enough to form a sort of link."

"I've wanted to see Lady Joan," explained Tembarom. "From what I've heard, I should say she was one of the 'Lady's Pictorial' kind."

"I am afraid—" Palliser's voice was slightly unsteady for the moment—"I have not studied the type sufficiently to know. The 'Pictorial' is so exclusively a women's periodical."

His companion laughed.

"Well, I've only looked through it once myself just to find out. Some way I always think of Lady Joan as if she was like one of those Beaut's from Beautsville, with trains as long as parlor-cars and feathers in their heads—dressed to go to see the queen. I guess she's been presented at court," he added.

"Yes, she has been presented."

"Do they let 'em go more than once?" he asked with casual curiosity.

"Confound this cough!" exclaimed Captain Palliser, and he broke forth again.

"Take another G," said Tembarom, producing his tube. "Say, just take the bottle and keep it in your pocket."

When the brief paroxysm was over and they moved on again, Palliser was looking an odd thing or so in the face. "I always think of Lady Joan" was one of them. "Always" seemed to go rather far. How often and why had he "always thought"? The fellow was incredible. Did his sharp, boyish face and his slouch conceal a colossal, vulgar, young ambition? There was not much concealment about it, Heaven knew. And as he so evidently was not aware of the facts, how would they affect him when he discovered them? And though Lady Mallowe was a woman not in the least distressed or hampered by shades of delicacy and scruple, she surely was astute enough to realize that even this bounder's dullness might be awakened to realize that there was more than a touch of obvious indecency in bringing the girl to the house of the man she had tragically loved, and manoeuvering to work her into it as the wife of the man who, monstrously unfit as he was, had taken his place. Captain Palliser knew well that the pressing of the relationship had meant only one thing. And how, in the name of the Furies! had she dragged Lady Joan into the scheme with her?

It was as unbelievable as was the new Temple Barholm himself. And how unconcerned the fellow looked! Perhaps the man he had supplanted was no more to him than a scarcely remembered name, if he was as much as that. Then Tembarom, pacing slowly by his side, hands in pockets, eyes on the walk, spoke:

"Did you ever see Jem Temple Barholm?" he asked.

It was like a thunderbolt. He said it as though he were merely carrying his previous remarks on to their natural conclusion; but Palliser felt himself so suddenly unadjusted, so to speak, that he palpably hesitated.

"Did you?" his companion repeated.

"I knew him well," was the answer made as soon as readjustment was possible.

"Remember just how he looked?"

"Perfectly. He was a striking fellow. Women always said he had fascinating eyes."

"Sort of slant downward on the outside corners—and black eyelashes sorter sweeping together?"

Palliser turned with a movement of surprise.

"How did you know? It was just that odd sort of thing."

"Miss Alicia told me. And there's a picture in the gallery that's like him."

Captain Palliser felt as embarrassed as Miss Alicia had felt, but it was for a different reason. She had felt awkward because she had feared she had touched on a delicate subject. Palliser was embarrassed because he was entirely thrown out of all his calculations. He felt for the moment that there was no calculating at all, no security in preparing paths. You never know where they would lead. Here had he been actually alarmed in secret! And the oaf stood before him undisturbedly opening up the subject himself.

"For a fellow like that to lose a girl as he lost Lady Joan was pretty tough," the oaf said. "By gee! it was tough!"

He knew it all—the whole thing, scandal, tragically broken marriage, everything. And knowing it, he was laying his Yankee plans for getting the girl to Temple Barholm to look her over. It was of a grossness one sometimes heard of in men of his kind, and yet it seemed in its casualness to out-leap any little scheme of the sort he had so far looked on at.

"Lady Joan felt it immensely," he said.

A footman was to be seen moving toward them, evidently bearing a message. Tea was served in the drawing-room, and he had come to announce the fact.

They went back to the house, and Miss Alicia filled cups for them and presided over the splendid tray with a persuasive suggestion in the matter of hot or cold things which made it easy to lead up to any subject. She was the best of unobtrusive hostesses.

Palliser talked of his visit at Detchworth, which had been shortened because he had gone to "fit in" and remain until a large but uncertain party turned up. It had turned up earlier than had been anticipated, and of course he could only delicately slip away.

"I am sorry it has happened, however," he said, "not only because one does not wish to leave Detchworth, but because I shall miss Lady Mallowe and Lady Joan, who are to be at Asshawe Holt next week. I particularly wanted to see them."

Miss Alicia glanced at Tembarom to see what he would do. He spoke before he could catch her glance.

"Say," he suggested, "why don't you bring your grip over here and stay? I wish you would."

"A grip means a Gladstone bag," Miss Alicia murmured in a rapid undertone.

Palliser replied with appreciative courtesy. Things were going extremely well.

"That's awfully kind of you," he answered. "I should like it tremendously. Nothing better. You are giving me a delightful opportunity. Thank you, thank you. If I may turn up on Thursday I shall be delighted."

There was satisfaction in this at least in the observant gray eye when he went away.

CHAPTER XX

Dinner at Detchworth Grange was most amusing that evening. One of the chief reasons—in fact, it would not be too venturesome to say THE chief reason—for Captain Palliser's frequent presence in very good country houses was that he had a way of making things amusing. His relation of anecdotes, of people and things, was distinguished by a manner which subtly declined to range itself on the side of vulgar gossip. Quietly and with a fine casualness he conveyed the whole picture of the new order at Temple Barholm. He did it with wonderfully light touches, and yet the whole thing was to be seen— the little old maid in her exquisite clothes, her unmistakable stamp of timid good breeding, her protecting adoration combined with bewilderment; the long, lean, not altogether ill-looking New York bounder, with his slight slouch, his dangerously unsophisticated-looking face, and his American jocularity of slang phrase.

"He's of a class I know nothing about. I own he puzzled me a trifle at first," Palliser said with his cool smile. "I'm not sure that I've 'got on to him' altogether yet. That's an expressive New York phrase of his own. But when we were strolling about together, he made revelations apparently without being in the least aware that they were revelations. He was unbelievable. My fear was that he would not go on."

"But he did go on?" asked Amabel. "One must hear something of the revelations."

Then was given in the best possible form the little drama of the talk in the garden. No shade of Mr. Temple Barholm's characteristics was lost. Palliser gave occasionally an English attempt at the reproduction of his nasal twang, but it was only a touch and not sufficiently persisted in to become undignified.

"I can't do it," he said. "None of us can really do it. When English actors try it on the stage, it is not in the least the real thing. They only drawl through their noses, and it is more than that."

The people of Detchworth Grange were not noisy people, but their laughter was unrestrained before the recital was finished. Nobody had gone so far as either to fear or to hope for anything as undiluted in its nature as this was.

"Then he won't give us a chance, the least chance," cried Lucy and Amabel almost in unison. "We are out of the running."

"You won't get even a look in—because you are not 'ladies,'" said their brother.

"Poor Jem Temple Barholm! What a different thing it would have been if we had had him for a neighbor!" Mr. Grantham fretted.

"We should have had Lady Joan Fayre as well," said his wife.

"At least she's a gentlewoman as well as a 'lady,'" Mr. Grantham said. "She would not have become so bitter if that hideous thing had not occurred."

They wondered if the new man knew anything about Jem. Palliser had not reached that part of his revelation when the laughter had broken into it. He told it forthwith, and the laughter was overcome by a sort of dismayed disgust. This did not accord with the rumors of an almost "nice" good nature.

"There's a vulgar horridness about it," said Lucy.

"What price Lady Mallowe!" said the son. "I'll bet a sovereign she began it."

"She did," remarked Palliser; "but I think one may leave Mr. Temple Barholm safely to Lady Joan." Mr. Grantham laughed as one who knew something of Lady Joan.

"There's an Americanism which I didn't learn from him," Palliser added, "and I remembered it when he was talking her over. It's this: when you dispose of a person finally and forever, you 'wipe up the earth with him.' Lady Joan will 'wipe up the earth' with your new neighbor."

There was a little shout of laughter. "Wipe up the earth" was entirely new to everybody, though even the country in England was at this time by no means wholly ignorant of American slang.

This led to so many other things both mirth-provoking and serious, even sometimes very serious indeed, that the entire evening at Detchworth was filled with talk of Temple Barholm. Very naturally the talk did not end by confining itself to one household. In due time Captain Palliser's little sketches were known in divers places, and it became a habit to discuss what had happened, and what might possibly happen in the future. There were those who went to the length of calling on the new man because they wanted to see him face to face. People heard new things every few days, but no one realized that it was vaguely through Palliser that there developed a general idea that, crude and self-revealing as he was, there lurked behind the outward candor of the intruder a hint of over-sharpness of the American kind. There seemed no necessity for him to lay schemes beyond those he had betrayed in his inquiries about "ladies," but somehow it became a fixed idea that he was capable of doing shady things if at any time the temptation arose. That was really what his boyish casualness meant. That in truth was Palliser's final secret conclusion. And he wanted very much to find out why exactly little old Miss Temple Barholm had been taken up. If the man wanted introductions, he could have contrived to pick up a smart and enterprising unprofessional chaperon in London who would have done for him what Miss Temple Barholm would never presume to attempt. And yet he seemed to have chosen her deliberately. He had set her literally at the head of his house. And Palliser, having heard a vague rumor that he had actually settled a decent income upon her, had made adroit inquiries and found it was true.

It was. To arrange the matter had been one of his reasons for going to see Mr. Palford during their stay in London.

"I wanted to fix you—fix you safe," he said when he told Miss Alicia about it. "I guess no one can take it away from you, whatever old thing happens."

"What could happen, dear Mr. Temple Barholm?" said Miss Alicia in the midst of tears of gratitude and tremulous joy. "You are so young and strong and—everything! Don't even speak of such a thing in jest. What could happen?"

"Anything can happen," he answered, "just anything. Happening's the one thing you can't bet on. If I was betting, I'd put my money on the thing I was sure couldn't happen. Look at this Temple Barholm song and dance! Look at T. T. as he was half strangling in the blizzard up at Harlem and thanking his stars little Munsberg didn't kick him out of his confectionery store less than a year ago! So long as I'm all right, you're all right. But I wanted you fixed, anyhow."

He paused and looked at her questioningly for a moment. He wanted to say something and he was not sure he ought. His reverence for her little finenesses and reserves increased instead of wearing away. He was always finding out new things about her.

"Say," he broke forth almost impetuously after his hesitation, "I wish you wouldn't call me Mr. Temple Barholm."

"D-do you?" she fluttered. "But what could I call you?"

"Well," he answered, reddening a shade or so, "I'd give a house and lot if you could just call me Tem."

"But it would sound so unbecoming, so familiar," she protested.

"That's just what I'm asking for," he said—"some one to be familiar with. I'm the familiar kind. That's what's the matter with me. I'd be familiar with Pearson, but he wouldn't let me. I'd frighten him half to death. He'd think that he wasn't doing his duty and earning his wages, and that somehow he'd get fired some day without a character."

He drew nearer to her and coaxed.

"Couldn't you do it?" he asked almost as though he were asking a favor of a girl. "Just Tem? I believe that would come easier to you than T. T. I get fonder and fonder of you every day, Miss Alicia, honest Injun. And I'd be so grateful to you if you'd just be that unbecomingly familiar."

He looked honestly in earnest; and if he grew fonder and fonder of her, she without doubt had, in the face of everything, given her whole heart to him.

"Might I call you Temple—to begin with?" she asked. "It touches me so to think of your asking me. I will begin at once. Thank you—Temple," with a faint gasp. "I might try the other a little later."

It was only a few evenings later that he told her about the flats in Harlem. He had sent to New York for a large bundle of newspapers, and when he opened them he read aloud an advertisement, and showed her a picture of a large building given up entirely to "flats."

He had realized from the first that New York life had a singular attraction for her. The unrelieved dullness of her life—those few years of youth in which she had stifled vague longings for the joys experienced by other girls; the years of middle age spent in the dreary effort to be "submissive to the will of God," which, honestly translated, signified submission to the exactions and domestic tyrannies of "dear papa" and others like him—had left her with her capacities for pleasure as freshly sensitive as a child's. The smallest change in the routine of existence thrilled her with excitement. Tembarom's casual references to his strenuous boyhood caused her eyes to widen with eagerness to hear more. Having seen this, he found keen delight in telling her stories of New York life—stories of himself or of other lads who had been his companions. She would drop her work and gaze at him almost with bated breath. He was an excellent raconteur when he talked of the things he knew well. He had an unconscious habit of springing from his seat and acting his scenes as he depicted them, laughing and using street-boy phrasing:

"It's just like a tale," Miss Alicia would breathe, enraptured as he jumped from one story to another. "It's exactly like a wonderful tale."

She learned to know the New York streets when they blazed with heat, when they were hard with frozen snow, when they were sloppy with melting slush or bright with springtime sunshine and spring winds blowing, with pretty women hurrying about in beflowered spring hats and dresses and the exhilaration of the world-old springtime joy. She found herself hurrying with them. She sometimes hung with him and his companions on the railing outside dazzling restaurants where scores of gay people ate rich food in the sight of their boyish ravenousness. She darted in and out among horses and vehicles to find carriages after the theater or opera, where everybody was dressed dazzlingly and diamonds glittered.

"Oh, how rich everybody must have seemed to you—how cruelly rich, poor little boy!"

"They looked rich, right enough," he answered when she said it. "And there seemed a lot of good things to eat all corralled in a few places. And you wished you could be let loose inside. But I don't know as it seemed cruel. That was the way it was, you know, and you couldn't help it. And there were places where they'd give away some of what was left. I tell you, we were in luck then."

There was some spirit in his telling it all—a spirit which had surely been with him through his hardest days, a spirit of young mirth in rags—which made her feel subconsciously that the whole experience had, after all, been somehow of the nature of life's high adventure. He had never been ill or heart-sick, and he laughed when he talked of it, as though the remembrance was not a recalling of disaster.

"Clemmin' or no clemmin'. I wish I'd lived the loife tha's lived," Tummas Hibblethwaite had said.

Her amazement would indeed have been great if she had been told that she secretly shared his feeling.

"It seems as if somehow you had never been dull," was her method of expressing it.

"Dull! Holy cats! no," he grinned. "There wasn't any time for being anything. You just had to keep going."

She became in time familiar with Mrs. Bowse's boarding-house and boarders. She knew Mrs. Peck and Mr. Jakes and the young lady from the notion counter (those wonderful shops!). Julius and Jem and the hall bedroom and the tilted chairs and cloud of smoke she saw so often that she felt at home with them.

"Poor Mrs. Bowse," she said, "must have been a most respectable, motherly, hard-working creature. Really a nice person of her class." She could not quite visualize the "parlor," but it must have been warm and comfortable. And the pianola—a piano which you could play without even knowing your notes—What a clever invention! America seemed full of the most wonderfully clever things.

Tembarom was actually uplifted in soul when he discovered that she laid transparent little plans for leading him into talk about New York. She wanted him to talk about it, and the Lord knows he wanted to talk about himself. He had been afraid at first. She might have hated it, as Palford did, and it would have hurt him somehow if she hadn't understood. But she did. Without quite realizing the fact, she was beginning to love it, to wish she had seen it. Her Somerset vicarage imagination did not allow of such leaps as would be implied by the daring wish that sometime she might see it.

But Tembarom's imagination was more athletic.

"Jinks! wouldn't it be fine to take her there! The lark in London wouldn't be ace high to it."

The Hutchinsons were not New Yorkers, but they had been part of the atmosphere of Mrs. Bowse's. Mr. Hutchinson would of course be rather a forward and pushing man to be obliged to meet, but Little Ann! She did so like Little Ann! And the dear boy did so want, in his heart of hearts, to talk about her at times. She did not know whether, in the circumstances, she ought to encourage him; but he was so dear, and looked so much dearer when he even said "Little Ann," that she could not help occasionally leading him gently toward the subject.

When he opened the newspapers and found the advertisements of the flats, she saw the engaging, half-awkward humorousness come into his eyes.

"Here's one that would do all right," he said—"four rooms and a bath, eleventh floor, thirty-five dollars a month."

He spread the newspaper on the table and rested on his elbow, gazing at it for a few minutes wholly absorbed. Then he looked up at her and smiled.

"There's a plan of the rooms," he said. "Would you like to look at it? Shall I bring your chair up to the table while we go over it together?"

He brought the chair, and side by side they went over it thoroughly. To Miss Alicia it had all the interest of a new kind of puzzle. He explained it in every detail. One of his secrets had been that on several days when Galton's manner had made him hopeful he had visited certain flat buildings and gone into their intricacies. He could therefore describe with color their resources—the janitor; the elevator; the dumb-waiters to carry up domestic supplies and carry down ashes and refuse; the refrigerator; the unlimited supply of hot and cold water, the heating plan; the astonishing little kitchen, with stationary wash-tubs; the telephone, if you could afford it,—all the conveniences which to Miss Alicia, accustomed to the habits of Rowcroft Vicarage, where you lugged cans of water up-stairs and down if you took a bath or even washed your face; seemed luxuries appertaining only to the rich and great.

"How convenient! How wonderful! Dear me! Dear me!" she said again and again, quite flushed with excitement. "It is like a fairy-story. And it's not big at all, is it?"

"You could get most of it into this," he answered, exulting. "You could get all of it into that big white-and gold parlor."

"The white saloon?"

He showed his teeth.

"I guess I ought to remember to call it that," he said, "but it always makes me think of Kid MacMurphy's on Fourth Avenue. He kept what was called a saloon, and he'd had it painted white."

"Did you know him?" Miss Alicia asked.

"Know him! Gee! no! I didn't fly as high as that. He'd have thought me pretty fresh if I'd acted like I knew him. He thought he was one of the Four Hundred. He'd been a prize-fighter. He was the fellow that knocked out Kid Wilkens in four rounds." He broke off and laughed at himself. "Hear me talk to you about a tough like that!" he ended, and he gave her hand the little apologetic, protective pat which always made her heart beat because it was so "nice."

He drew her back to the advertisements, and drew such interesting pictures of what the lives of two people—mother and son or father and daughter or a young married couple who didn't want to put on style—might be in the tiny compartments, that their excitement mounted again.

This could be a bedroom, that could be a bedroom, that could be the living-room, and if you put a bit of bright carpet on the hallway and hung up a picture or so, it would look first-rate. He even went into the matter of measurements, which made it more like putting a puzzle together than ever, and their relief when they found they could fit a piece of furniture he called "a lounge" into a certain corner was a thing of flushing delight. The "lounge," she found, was a sort of cot with springs. You could buy them for three dollars, and when you put on a mattress and covered it with a "spread," you could sit on it in the daytime and sleep on it at night, if you had to.

From measurements he went into calculations about the cost of things. He had seen unpainted wooden tables you could put mahogany stain on, and they'd look all you'd want. He'd seen a splendid little rocking-chair in Second Avenue for five dollars, one of the padded kind that ladies like. He had seen an arm-chair for a man that was only seven; but there mightn't be room for both, and you'd have to have the rocking-chair. He had once asked the price of a lot of plates and cups and saucers with roses on them, and you could get them for six; and you didn't need a stove because there was the range.

He had once heard Little Ann talking to Mrs. Bowse about the price of frying-pans and kettles, and they seemed to cost next to nothing. He'd looked into store windows and noticed the prices of groceries and vegetables and things like that—sugar, for instance; two people wouldn't use much sugar in a week—and they wouldn't need a ton of tea or flour or coffee. If a fellow had a mother or sister or wife who had a head and knew about things, you could "put it over" on mighty little, and have a splendid time together, too. You'd even be able to work in a cheap seat in a theater every now and then. He laughed and flushed as he thought of it.

Miss Alicia had never had a doll's house. Rowcroft Vicarage did not run to dolls and their belongings. Her thwarted longing for a doll's house had a sort of parallel in her similarly thwarted longing for "a little boy."

And here was her doll's house so long, so long unpossessed! It was like that, this absorbed contriving and fitting of furniture into corners. She also flushed and laughed. Her eyes were so brightly eager and her cheeks so pink that she looked quite girlish under her lace cap.

"How pretty and cozy it might be made, how dear!" she exclaimed. "And one would be so high up on the eleventh floor, that one would feel like a bird in a nest."

His face lighted. He seemed to like the idea tremendously.

"Why, that's so," he laughed. "That idea suits me down to the ground. A bird in a nest. But there'd have to be two. One would be lonely. Say, Miss Alicia, how would you like to live in a place like that?"

"I am sure any one would like it—if they had some dear relative with them."

He loved her "dear relative," loved it. He knew how much it meant of what had lain hidden unacknowledged, even unknown to her, through a lifetime in her early-Victorian spinster breast.

"Let's go to New York and rent one and live in it together. Would you come?" he said, and though he laughed, he was not jocular in the usual way. "Would you, if we waked up and found this Temple Barholm thing was a dream?"

Something in his manner, she did not know what, puzzled her a little.

"But if it were a dream, you would be quite poor again," she said, smiling.

"No, I wouldn't. I'd get Galton to give me back the page. He'd do it quick—quick," he said, still with a laugh. "Being poor's nothing, anyhow. We'd have the time of our lives. We'd be two birds in a nest. You can look out those eleventh-story windows 'way over to the Bronx, and get bits of the river. And perhaps after a while Ann would do like she said, and we'd be three birds."

"Oh!" she sighed ecstatically. "How beautiful it would be! We should be a little family!"

"So we should," he exulted. "Think of T. T. with a family!" He drew his paper of calculations toward him again. "Let's make believe we're going to do it, and work out what it would cost—for three. You know about housekeeping, don't you? Let's write down a list."

If he had warmed to his work before, he warmed still more after this. Miss Alicia was drawn into it again, and followed his fanciful plans with a new fervor. They were like two children who had played at make-believe until they had lost sight of commonplace realities.

Miss Alicia had lived among small economies and could be of great assistance to him. They made lists and added up lines of figures until the fine, huge room and its thousands of volumes melted away. In the great hall, guarded by warriors in armor, the powdered heads of the waiting footmen drooped and nodded while the prices of pounds of butter and sugar and the value of potatoes and flour and nutmegs were balanced with a hectic joy, and the relative significance of dollars and cents and shillings and half-crowns and five-cent pieces caused Miss Alicia a mild delirium.

By the time that she had established the facts that a shilling was something like twenty-five cents, a dollar was four and twopence, and twenty-five dollars was something over five pounds, it was past midnight.

They heard the clock strike the half-hour, and stopped to stare at each other.

Tembarom got up with yet another laugh.

"Say, I mustn't keep you up all night," he said. "But haven't we had a fine time—haven't we? I feel as if I'd been there."

They had been there so entirely that Miss Alicia brought herself back with difficulty.

"I can scarcely believe that we have not," she said. "I feel as if I didn't like to leave it. It was so delightful." She glanced about her. "The room looks huge," she said—"almost too huge to live in."

"Doesn't it?" he answered. "Now you know how I feel." He gathered his scraps of paper together with a feeling touch. "I didn't want to come back myself. When I get a bit of a grouch I shall jerk these out and go back there again."

"Oh, do let me go with you!" she said. "I have so enjoyed it."

"You shall go whenever you like," he said. "We'll keep it up for a sort of game on rainy days. How much is a dollar, Miss Alicia?"

"Four and twopence. And sugar is six cents a pound."

"Go to the head," he answered. "Right again."

The opened roll of newspapers was lying on the table near her. They were copies of The Earth, and the date of one of them by merest chance caught her eye.

"How odd!" she said. "Those are old papers. Did you notice? Is it a mistake? This one is dated" She leaned forward, and her eye caught a word in a headline.

"The Klondike," she read. "There's something in it about the Klondike." He put his hand out and drew the papers away.

"Don't you read that," he said. "I don't want you to go to bed and dream about the Klondike. You've got to dream about the flat in Harlem."

"Yes," she answered. "I mustn't think about sad things. The flat in Harlem is quite happy. But it startled me to see that word."

"I only sent for them—because I happened to want to look something up," he explained. "How much is a pound, Miss Alicia?"

"Four dollars and eighty-six cents," she replied, recovering herself.

"Go up head again. You're going to stay there."

When she gave him her hand on their parting for the night he held it a moment. A subtle combination of things made him do it. The calculations, the measurements, the nest from which one could look out over the Bronx, were prevailing elements in its make-up. Ann had been in each room of the Harlem flat, and she always vaguely reminded him of Ann.

"We are relations, ain't we?" he asked.

"I am sure we often seem quite near relations—Temple." She added the name with very pretty kindness.

"We're not distant ones any more, anyhow," he said. "Are we near enough—would you let me kiss you good night, Miss Alicia?"

An emotional flush ran up to her cap ribbons.

"Indeed, my dear boy—indeed, yes."

Holding her hand with a chivalric, if slightly awkward, courtesy, he bent, and kissed her cheek. It was a hearty, affectionately grateful young kiss, which, while it was for herself, remotely included Ann.

"It's the first time I've ever said good night to any one like that," he said. "Thank you for letting me."

He patted her hand again before releasing it. She went up-stairs blushing and feeling rather as though she had been proposed to, and yet, spinster though she was, somehow quite understanding about the nest and Ann.

CHAPTER XXI

Lady Mallowe and her daughter did not pay their visit to Asshawe Holt, the absolute, though not openly referred to, fact being that they had not been invited. The visit in question had merely floated in the air as a delicate suggestion made by her ladyship in her letter to Mrs. Asshe Shaw, to the effect that she and Joan were going to stay at Temple Barholm, the visit to Asshawe they had partly arranged some time ago might now be fitted in.

The partial arrangement itself, Mrs. Asshe Shaw remarked to her eldest daughter when she received the suggesting note, was so partial as to require slight consideration, since it had been made "by the woman herself, who would push herself and her daughter into any house in England if a back door were left open." In the civilly phrased letter she received in answer to her own, Lady Mallowe read between the lines the point of view taken, and writhed secretly, as she had been made to writhe scores of times in the course of her career. It had happened so often, indeed, that it might have been imagined that she had become used to it; but the woman who acted as maid to herself and Joan always knew when "she had tried to get in somewhere" and failed.

The note of explanation sent immediately to Miss Alicia was at once adroit and amiable. They had unfortunately been detained in London a day or two past the date fixed for their visit to Asshawe, and Lady Mallowe would not allow Mrs. Asshe Shawe, who had so many guests, to be inconvenienced by their arriving late and perhaps disarranging her plans. So if it was quite convenient, they would come to Temple Barholm a week earlier; but not, of course, if that would be the least upsetting.

When they arrived, Tembarom himself was in London. He had suddenly found he was obliged to go. The business which called him was something which could not be put off. He expected to return at once. It was made very easy for him when he made his excuses to Palliser, who suggested that he might even find himself returning by the same train with his guests, which would give him opportunities. If he was detained, Miss Alicia could take charge of the situation. They would quite understand when she explained. Captain Palliser foresaw for himself some quiet entertainment in his own meeting with the visitors. Lady Mallowe always provided a certain order of amusement for him, and no man alive objected to finding interest and even a certain excitement in the society of Lady Joan. It was her chief characteristic that she inspired in a man a vague, even if slightly irritated, desire to please her in some degree. To lead her on to talk in her sometimes brilliant, always heartlessly unsparing, fashion, perhaps to smile her shade of a bitter smile, gave a man something to do, especially if he was bored. Palliser anticipated a possible chance of repeating the dialogue of "the ladies," not, however, going into the Jem Temple Barholm part of it. When one finds a man whose idle life has generated in him the curiosity which is usually called feminine, it frequently occupies him more actively than he is aware or will admit.

A fashionable male gossip is a curious development. Palliser was, upon the whole, not aware that he had an intense interest in finding out the exact reason why Lady Mallowe had not failed utterly in any attempt to drag her daughter to this particular place, to be flung headlong, so to speak, at this special man. Lady Mallowe one could run and read, but Lady Joan was in this instance unexplainable. And as she never deigned the slightest concealment, the story of the dialogue would no doubt cause her to show her hand. She must have a hand, and it must be one worth seeing.

It was not he, however, who could either guess or understand. The following would have been his summing up of her: "Flaringly handsome girl, brought up by her mother to one end. Bad temper to begin with. Girl who might, if she lost her head, get into some frightful mess. Meets a fascinating devil in the first season. A regular Romeo and Juliet passion blazes up—all for love and the world well lost. All London looking on. Lady Mallowe frantic and furious. Suddenly the fascinating devil ruined for life, done for. Bolts, gets killed. Lady Mallowe triumphant. Girl dragged about afterward like a beautiful young demon in chains. Refuses all sorts of things. Behaves infernally. Nobody knows anything else."

Nobody did know; Lady Mallowe herself did not. From the first year in which Joan had looked at her with child consciousness she had felt that there was antagonism in the deeps of her eyes. No mother likes to recognize such a thing, and Lady Mallowe was a particularly vain woman. The child was going to be an undeniable beauty, and she ought to adore the mother who was to arrange her future. Instead of which, she plainly disliked her. By the time she was three years old, the antagonism had become defiance and rebellion. Lady Mallowe could not even indulge herself in the satisfaction of showing her embryo beauty off, and thus preparing a reputation for her. She was not cross or tearful, but she had the temper of a little devil. She would not be shown off. She hated it, and her bearing dangerously suggested that she hated her handsome young mother. No effects could be produced with her.

Before she was four the antagonism was mutual, and it increased with years. The child was of a passionate nature, and had been born intensely all her mother was not, and intensely not all her mother was. A throw-back to some high-spirited and fiercely honest ancestor created in her a fury at the sight of mean falsities and dishonors. Before she was old enough to know the exact cause of her rage she was shaken by it. She thought she had a bad temper, and was bad enough to hate her own mother without being able to help it. As she grew older she found out that she was not really so bad as she had thought, though she was obliged to concede that nothing palliative could be said about the temper. It had been violent from the first, and she had lived in an atmosphere which infuriated it. She did not suppose such a thing could be controlled. It sometimes frightened her. Had not the old Marquis of Norborough been celebrated through his entire life for his furies? Was there not a hushed-up rumor that he had once thrown a decanter at his wife, and so nearly killed her that people had been asking one another in whispers if a peer of the realm could be hanged. He had been born that way, so had she. Her school-room days had been a horror to her, and also a terror, because she had often almost flung ink-bottles and heavy rulers at her silly, lying governesses, and once had dug a pair of scissors into one sneaking old maid fool's arm when she had made her "see red" by her ignoble trickeries. Perhaps she would be hanged some day herself. She once prayed for a week that she might be made better tempered,—not that she believed in prayer,—and of course nothing came of it.

Every year she lived she raged more furiously at the tricks she saw played by her mother and every one who surrounded her; the very servants were greater liars and pilferers than any other servants. Her mother was always trying to get things from people which they did not want to give her. She would carry off slights and snubs as though they were actual tributes, if she could gain her end. The girl knew what the meaning of her own future would be. Since she definitely disliked her daughter, Lady Mallowe did not mince matters when they were alone. She had no money, she was extremely good looking, she had a certain number of years in which to fight for her own hand among the new debutantes who were presented every season. Her first season over, the next season other girls would be fresher than she was, and newer to the men who were worth marrying. Men like novelty. After her second season the debutantes would seem fresher still by contrast. Then people would begin to say, "She was presented four or five years ago." After that it would be all struggle,—every season it would be worse. It would become awful. Unmarried women over thirty-five would speak of her as though they had been in the nursery together. Married girls with a child or so would treat her as though she were a maiden aunt. She knew what was before her. Beggary stared them both in the face if she did not make the most of her looks and waste no time. And Joan knew it was all true, and that worse, far worse things were true also. She would be obliged to spend a long life with her mother in cheap lodgings, a faded, penniless, unmarried woman, railed at, taunted, sneered at, forced to be part of humiliating tricks played to enable them to get into debt and then to avoid paying what they owed. Had she not seen one horrible old woman of their own rank who was an example of what poverty might bring one to, an old harpy who tried to queen it over her landlady in an actual back street, and was by turns fawned upon and disgustingly "your ladyshiped" or outrageously insulted by her landlady?

Then that first season! Dear, dear God! that first season when she met Jem! She was not nineteen, and the facile world pretended to be at her feet, and the sun shone as though London were in Italy, and the park was marvelous with flowers, and there were such dances and such laughter!

And it was all so young—and she met Jem! It was at a garden-party at a lovely old house on the river, a place with celebrated gardens which would always come back to her memory as a riot of roses. The frocks of the people on the lawn looked as though they were made of the petals of flowers, and a mad little haunting waltz was being played by the band, and there under a great copper birch on the green velvet turf near her stood Jem, looking at her with dark, liquid, slanting eyes! They were only a few feet from each other,—and he looked, and she looked, and the haunting, mad little waltz played on, and it was as though they had been standing there since the world began, and nothing else was true.

Afterward nothing mattered to either of them. Lady Mallowe herself ceased to count. Now and then the world stops for two people in this unearthly fashion. At such times, as far as such a pair are concerned, causes and effects cease. Her bad temper fled, and she knew she would never feel its furious lash again.

With Jem looking at her with his glowing, drooping eyes, there would be no reason for rage and shame. She confessed the temper to him and told of her terror of it; he confessed to her his fondness for high play, and they held each other's hands, not with sentimental youthful lightness, but with the strong clasp of sworn comrades, and promised on honor that they would stand by each other every hour of their lives against their worst selves.

They would have kept the pact. Neither was a slight or dishonest creature. The phase of life through which they passed is not a new one, but it is not often so nearly an omnipotent power as was their three-months' dream.

It lasted only that length of time. Then came the end of the world. Joan did not look fresh in her second season, and before it was over men were rather afraid of her. Because she was so young the freshness returned to her cheek, but it never came back to her eyes.

What exactly had happened, or what she thought, it was impossible to know. She had delicate, black brows, and between them appeared two delicate, fierce lines. Her eyes were of a purplish-gray, "the color of thunder," a snubbed admirer had once said. Between their black lashes they were more deeply thunder-colored. Her life with her mother was a thing not to be spoken of. To the desperate girl's agony of rebellion against the horror of fate Lady Mallowe's taunts and beratings were devilish. There was a certain boudoir in the house in Hill Street which was to Joan like the question chamber of the Inquisition. Shut up in it together, the two went through scenes which in their cruelty would have done credit to the Middle Ages. Lady Mallowe always locked the door to prevent the unexpected entrance of a servant, but servants managed to hover about it, because her ladyship frequently forgot caution so far as to raise her voice at times, as ladies are not supposed to do.

"We fight," Joan said with a short, horrible laugh one morning—"we fight like cats and dogs. No, like two cats. A cat-and-dog fight is more quickly over. Some day we shall scratch each other's eyes out."

"Have you no shame?" her mother cried.

"I am burning with it. I am like St. Lawrence on his gridiron. 'Turn me over on the other side,'" she quoted.

This was when she had behaved so abominably to the Duke of Merthshire that he had actually withdrawn his more than half-finished proposal. That which she hated more than all else was the God she had prayed to when she asked she might be helped to control her temper.

She had not believed in Him at the time, but because she was frightened after she had stuck the scissors into Fraulein she had tried the appeal as an experiment. The night after she met Jem, when she went to her room in Hill Street for the night, she knelt down and prayed because she suddenly did believe. Since there was Jem in the world, there must be the other somewhere.

As day followed day, her faith grew with her love. She told Jem about it, and they agreed to say a prayer together at the same hour every night. The big young man thought her piety beautiful, and, his voice was unsteady as they talked. But she told him that she was not pious, but impious.

"I want to be made good," she said. "I have been bad all my life. I was a bad child, I have been a bad girl; but now I must be good."

On the night after the tragic card-party she went to her room and kneeled down in a new spirit. She knelt, but not to cover her face, she knelt with throat strained and her fierce young face thrown back and upward.

Her hands were clenched to fists and flung out and shaken at the ceiling. She said things so awful that her own blood shuddered as she uttered them. But she could not—in her mad helplessness—make them awful enough. She flung herself on the carpet at last, her arms outstretched like a creature crucified face downward on the cross.

"I believed in You!" she gasped. "The first moment you gave me a reason I believed. I did! I did! We both said our prayer to You every night, like children. And you've done this—this—this!" And she beat with her fists upon the floor.

Several years had passed since that night, and no living being knew what she carried in her soul. If she had a soul, she said to herself, it was black—black. But she had none. Neither had Jem had one; when the earth and stones had fallen upon him it had been the end, as it would have been if he had been a beetle.

This was the guest who was coming to the house where Miles Hugo smiled from his frame in the picture-gallery—the house which would to-day have been Jem's if T. Tembarom had not inherited it.

Tembarom returned some twenty-four hours after Miss Alicia had received his visitors for him. He had been "going into" absorbing things in London. His thoughts during his northward journey were puzzled and discouraged ones. He sat in the corner of the railway carriage and stared out of the window without seeing the springtime changes in the flying landscape.

The price he would have given for a talk with Ann would not have been easy to compute. Her head, her level little head, and her way of seeing into things and picking out facts without being rattled by what didn't really count, would have been worth anything. The day itself was a discouraging one, with heavy threatenings of rain which did not fall.

The low clouds were piles of dark-purple gray, and when the sun tried to send lances of ominous yellow light through them, strange and lurid effects were produced, and the heavy purple-gray masses rolled together again. He wondered why he did not hear low rumblings of thunder.

He went to his room at once when he reached home. He was late, and Pearson told him that the ladies were dressing for dinner. Pearson was in waiting with everything in readiness for the rapid performance of his duties. Tembarom had learned to allow himself to be waited upon. He had, in fact, done this for the satisfying of Pearson, whose respectful unhappiness would otherwise have been manifest despite his efforts to conceal it. He dressed quickly and asked some questions about Strangeways. Otherwise Pearson thought he seemed preoccupied. He only made one slight joke.

"You'd be a first-rate dresser for a quick-change artist, Pearson," he remarked.

On his way to the drawing-room he deflected from the direct path, turning aside for a moment to the picture-gallery because for a reason of his own he wanted to take a look at Miles Hugo. He took a look at Miles Hugo oftener than Miss Alicia knew.

The gallery was dim and gloomy enough, now closing in in the purple-gray twilight. He walked through it without glancing at the pictures until he came to the tall boy in the satin and lace of Charles II period. He paused there only for a short time, but he stood quite near the portrait, and looked hard at the handsome face.

"Gee!" he exclaimed under his breath, "it's queer, gee!"

Then he turned suddenly round toward one of the big windows. He turned because he had been startled by a sound, a movement. Some one was standing before the window. For a second's space the figure seemed as though it was almost one with the purple-gray clouds that were its background. It was a tall young woman, and her dress was of a thin material of exactly their color—dark-gray and purple at once. The wearer held her head high and haughtily. She had a beautiful, stormy face, and the slender, black brows were drawn together by a frown. Tembarom had never seen a girl as handsome and disdainful. He had, indeed, never been looked at as she looked at him when she moved slightly forward.

He knew who it was. It was the Lady Joan girl, and the sudden sight of her momentarily "rattled" him.

"You quite gave me a jolt," he said awkwardly, and knowing that he said it like a "mutt." "I didn't know any one was in the gallery."

"What are you doing here?" she asked. She spoke to him as though she were addressing an intruding servant. There was emphasis on the word "you."

Her intention was so evident that it increased his feeling of being "rattled." To find himself confronting deliberate ill nature of a superior and finished kind was like being spoken to in a foreign language.

"I—I'm T. Tembarom." he answered, not able to keep himself from staring because she was such a "winner" as to looks.

"T. Tembarom?" she repeated slowly, and her tone made him at once see what a fool he had been to say it.

"I forgot," he half laughed. "I ought to have said I'm Temple Barholm."

"Oh!" was her sole comment. She actually stood still and looked him up and down.

She knew perfectly well who he was, and she knew perfectly well that no palliative view could possibly be taken by any well-bred person of her bearing toward him. He was her host. She had come, a guest, to his house to eat his bread and salt, and the commonest decency demanded that she should conduct herself with civility. But she cared nothing for the commonest, or the most uncommon, decency. She was thinking of other things. As she had stood before the window she had felt that her soul had never been so black as it was when she turned away from Miles Hugo's portrait—never, never. She wanted to hurt people. Perhaps Nero had felt as she did and was not so hideous as he seemed.

The man's tailor had put him into proper clothes, and his features were respectable enough, but nothing on earth could make him anything but what he so palpably was. She had seen that much across the gallery as she had watched him staring at Miles Hugo.

"I should think," she said, dropping the words slowly again, "that you would often forget that you are Temple Barholm."

"You're right there," he answered. "I can't nail myself down to it. It seems like a sort of joke."

She looked him over again.

"It is a joke," she said.

It was as though she had slapped him in the face, though she said it so quietly. He knew he had received the slap, and that, as it was a woman, he could not slap back. It was a sort of surprise to her that he did not giggle nervously and turn red and shuffle his feet in impotent misery. He kept quite still a moment or so and looked at her, though not as she had looked at him. She wondered if he was so thick-skinned that he did not feel anything at all.

"That's so," he admitted. "That's so." Then he actually smiled at her. "I don't know how to behave myself, you see," he said. "You're Lady Joan Fayre, ain't you? I'm mighty glad to see you. Happy to make your acquaintance, Lady Joan."

He took her hand and shook it with friendly vigor before she knew what he was going to do.

"I'll bet a dollar dinner's ready," he added, "and Burrill's waiting. It scares me to death to keep Burrill waiting. He's got no use for me, anyhow. Let's go and pacify him."

He did not lead the way or drag her by the arm, as it seemed to her quite probable that he might, as costermongers do on Hampstead Heath. He knew enough to let her pass first through the door; and when Lady Mallowe looked up to see her enter the drawing-room, he was behind her. To her ladyship's amazement and relief, they came in, so to speak, together. She had been spared the trying moment of assisting at the ceremony of their presentation to each other.

CHAPTER XXII

In a certain sense she had been dragged to the place by her mother. Lady Mallowe had many resources, and above all she knew how to weary her into resistlessness which was almost indifference. There had been several shameless little scenes in the locked boudoir. But though she had been dragged, she had come with an intention. She knew what she would find herself being forced to submit to if the intruder were not disposed of at the outset, and if the manoeuvering began which would bring him to London. He would appear at her elbow here and there and at every corner, probably unaware that he was being made an offensive puppet by the astute cleverness against which she could not defend herself, unless she made actual scenes in drawing-rooms, at dinner-tables, in the very streets themselves. Gifted as Lady Mallowe was in fine and light-handed dealing of her cards in any game, her stakes at this special juncture were seriously high. Joan knew what they were, and that she was in a mood touched with desperation. The defenselessly new and ignorant Temple Barholm was to her mind a direct intervention of Providence, and it was only Joan herself who could rob her of the benefits and reliefs he could provide. With regard to Lady Joan, though Palliser's quoted New Yorkism, "wipe up the earth," was unknown to her, the process she had in mind when she left London for Lancashire would have been well covered by it. As in feudal days she might have ordered the right hand of a creature such as this to be struck off, forgetting that he was a man, so was she capable to-day of inflicting upon him any hurt which might sweep him out of her way. She had not been a tender-hearted girl, and in these years she was absolutely callous. The fellow being what he was, she had not the resources she might have called upon if he had been a gentleman. He would not understand the chills and slights of good manners. In the country he would be easier to manage than in town, especially if attacked in his first timidity before his new grandeurs. His big house no doubt frightened him, his servants, the people who were of a class of which he knew nothing. When Palliser told his story she saw new openings. He would stand in servile awe of her and of others like her. He would be afraid of her, to begin with, and she could make him more so.

But though she had come to alarm him so that he would be put to absolute flight, she had also come for another reason. She had never seen Temple Barholm, and she had discovered before they had known each other a week that it was Jem's secret passion. He had loved it with a slighted and lonely child's romantic longing; he had dreamed of it as boy and man, knowing that it must some time be his own, his home, and yet prevented by his uncle's attitude toward him from daring to act as though he remembered the fact.

Old Mr. Temple Barholm's special humor had been that of a man guarding against presumption.

Jem had not intended to presume, but he had been snubbed with relentless cruelty even for boyish expressions of admiration. And he had hid his feeling in his heart until he poured it out to Joan. To-day it would have been his. Together, together, they would have lived in it and loved every stone of it, every leaf on every great tree, every wild daffodil nodding in the green grass. Most people, God be thanked! can forget. The wise ones train themselves beyond all else to forgetting.

Joan had been a luckless, ill-brought-up, passionate child and girl. In her Mayfair nursery she had been as little trained as a young savage. Since her black hour she had forgotten nothing, allowed herself no palliating moments. Her brief dream of young joy had been the one real thing in her life. She absolutely had lain awake at night and reconstructed the horror of Jem's death, had lived it over again, writhing in agony on her bed, and madly feeling that by so doing she was holding her love close to her life.

And the man who stood in the place Jem had longed for, the man who sat at the head of his table, was this "thing!" That was what she felt him to be, and every hurt she could do him, every humiliation which should write large before him his presumption and grotesque unfitness, would be a blow struck for Jem, who could never strike a blow for himself again. It was all senseless, but she had not want to reason. Fate had not reasoned in her behalf. She watched Tembarom under her lids at the dinner-table.

He had not wriggled or shuffled when she spoke to him in the gallery; he did neither now, and made no obvious efforts to seem unembarrassed. He used his knife and fork in odd ways, and he was plainly not used to being waited upon. More than once she saw the servants restrain smiles. She addressed no remarks to him herself, and answered with chill indifference such things as he said to her. If conversation had flagged between him and Mr. Palford because the solicitor did not know how to talk to him, it did not even reach the point of flagging with her, because she would not talk and did not allow it to begin. Lady Mallowe, sick with annoyance, was quite brilliant. She drew out Miss Alicia by detailed reminiscences of a visit paid to Rowlton Hall years before. The vicar had dined at the hall while she had been there. She remembered perfectly his charm of manner and powerful originality of mind, she said sweetly. He had spoken with such affection of his "little Alicia," who was such a help to him in his parish work.

"I thought he was speaking of a little girl at first," she said smilingly, "but it soon revealed itself that 'little Alicia' was only his caressing diminutive."

A certain widening of Miss Alicia's fascinated eye, which could not remove itself from her face, caused her to quail slightly.

"He was of course a man of great force of character and—and expression," she added. "I remember thinking at the time that his eloquent frankness of phrase might perhaps seem even severe to frivolous creatures like myself. A really remarkable personality."

"His sermons," faltered Miss Alicia, as a refuge, "were indeed remarkable. I am sure he must greatly have enjoyed his conversations with you. I am afraid there were very few clever women in the neighborhood of Rowlton."

Casting a bitter side glance on her silent daughter, Lady Mallowe lightly seized upon New York as a subject. She knew so much of it from delightful New Yorkers. London was full of delightful New Yorkers. She would like beyond everything to spend a winter in New York. She understood that the season there was in the winter and that it was most brilliant. Mr. Temple Barholm must tell them about it.

"Yes," said Lady Joan, looking at him through narrowed lids, "Mr. Temple Barholm ought to tell us about it."

She wanted to hear what he would say, to see how he would try to get out of the difficulty or flounder staggeringly through it. Her mother knew in an instant that her own speech had been a stupid blunder. She had put the man into exactly the position Joan would enjoy seeing him in. But he wasn't in a position, it appeared.

"What is the season, anyhow?" he said. "You've got one on me when you talk about seasons."

"In London," Miss Alicia explained courageously, "it is the time when her Majesty is at Buckingham Palace, and when the drawing-rooms are held, and Parliament sits, and people come up to town and give balls."

She wished that Lady Mallowe had not made her remark just at this time. She knew that the quietly moving servants were listening, and that their civilly averted eyes had seen Captain Palliser smile and Lady Joan's curious look, and that the whole incident would form entertainment for their supper-table.

"I guess they have it in the winter in New York, then, if that's it," he said. "There's no Buckingham Palace there, and no drawing-rooms, and Congress sits in Washington. But New York takes it out in suppers at Sherry's and Delmonico's and theaters and receptions. Miss Alicia knows how I used to go to them when I was a little fellow, don't you, Miss Alicia?" he added, smiling at her across the table.

"You have told me," she answered. She noticed that Burrill and the footmen stood at attention in their places.

"I used to stand outside in the snow and look in through the windows at the people having a good time," he said. "Us kids that were selling newspapers used to try to fill ourselves up with choosing whose plate we'd take if we could get at it. Beefsteak and French fried potatoes were the favorites, and hot oyster stews. We were so all-fired hungry!"

"How pathetic!" exclaimed Lady Mallowe. "And how interesting, now that it is all over!"

She knew that her manner was gushing, and Joan's slight side glance of subtle appreciation of the fact exasperated her almost beyond endurance. What could one do, what could one talk about, without involving oneself in difficulties out of which one's hasty retreat could be effected only by gushing? Taking into consideration the awkwardness of the whole situation and seeing Joan's temper and attitude, if there had not been so much at stake she would have received a summoning telegram from London the next day and taken flight. But she had been forced to hold her ground before in places she detested or where she was not wanted, and she must hold it again until she had found out the worst or the best. And, great heaven! how Joan was conducting herself, with that slow, quiet insultingness of tone and look, the wicked, silent insolence of bearing which no man was able to stand, however admiringly he began! The Duke of Merthshire had turned his back upon it even after all the world had known his intentions, even after the newspapers had prematurely announced the engagement and she herself had been convinced that he could not possibly retreat. She had worked desperately that season, she had fawned on and petted newspaper people, and stooped to little things no one but herself could have invented and which no one but herself knew of. And never had Joan been so superb; her beauty had seemed at its most brilliant height. The match would have been magnificent; but he could not stand her, and would not. Why, indeed, should any man? She glanced at her across the table. A beauty, of course; but she was thinner, and her eyes had a hungry fierceness in them, and the two delicate, straight lines between her black brows were deepening.

And there were no dukes on the horizon. Merthshire had married almost at once, and all the others were too young or had wives already. If this man would take her, she might feel herself lucky. Temple Barholm and seventy thousand a year were not to be trifled with by a girl who had made herself unpopular and who was twenty-six. And for her own luck the moment had come just before it was too late—a second marriage, wealth, the end of the hideous struggle. Joan was the obstacle in her path, and she must be forced out of it. She glanced quickly at Tembarom. He was trying to talk to Joan now. He was trying to please her. She evidently had a fascination for him. He looked at her in a curious way when she was not looking at him. It was a way different from that of other men whom she had watched as they furtively stared. It had struck her that he could not take his eyes away. That was because he had never before been on speaking terms with a woman of beauty and rank.

Joan herself knew that he was trying to please her, and she was asking herself how long he would have the courage and presumption to keep it up. He could scarcely be enjoying it.

He was not enjoying it, but he kept it up. He wanted to be friends with her for more reasons than one. No one had ever remained long at enmity with him. He had "got over" a good many people in the course of his career, as he had "got over" Joseph Hutchinson. This had always been accomplished because he presented no surface at which arrows could be thrown. She was the hardest proposition he had ever come up against, he was thinking; but if he didn't let himself be fool enough to break loose and get mad, she'd not hate him so much after a while. She would begin to understand that it wasn't his fault; then perhaps he could get her to make friends. In fact, if she had been able to read his thoughts, there is no certainty as to how far her temper might have carried her. But she could see him only as a sharp-faced, common American of the shop-boy class, sitting at the head of Jem Temple Barholm's table, in his chair.

As they passed through the hall to go to the drawing-room after the meal was over, she saw a neat, pale young man speaking to Burrill and heard a few of his rather anxiously uttered words.

"The orders were that he was always to be told when Mr. Strangeways was like this, under all circumstances. I can't quiet him, Mr. Burrill. He says he must see him at once."

Burrill walked back stiffly to the dining-room.

"It won't trouble HIM much to be disturbed at his wine," he muttered before going. "He doesn't know hock from port."

When the message was delivered to him, Tembarom excused himself with simple lack of ceremony.

"I 'll be back directly," he said to Palliser. "Those are good cigars." And he left the room without going into the matter further.

Palliser took one of the good cigars, and in taking it exchanged a glance with Burrill which distantly conveyed the suggestion that perhaps he had better remain for a moment or so. Captain Palliser's knowledge of interesting detail was obtained "by chance here and there," he sometimes explained, but it was always obtained with a light and casual air.

"I am not sure," he remarked as he took the light Burrill held for him and touched the end of his cigar—"I am not quite sure that I know exactly who Mr. Strangeways is."

"He's the gentleman, sir, that Mr. Temple Barholm brought over from New York," replied Burrill with a stolidity clearly expressive of distaste.

"Indeed, from New York! Why doesn't one see him?"

"He's not in a condition to see people, sir," said Burrill, and Palliser's slightly lifted eyebrow seeming to express a good deal, he added a sentence, "He's not all there, sir."

"From New York, and not all there. What seems to be the matter?" Palliser asked quietly. "Odd idea to bring a lunatic all the way from America. There must be asylums there."

"Us servants have orders to keep out of the way," Burrill said with sterner stolidity. "He's so nervous that the sight of strangers does him harm. I may say that questions are not encouraged."

"Then I must not ask any more," said Captain Palliser. "I did not know I was edging on to a mystery."

"I wasn't aware that I was myself, sir," Burrill remarked, "until I asked something quite ordinary of Pearson, who is Mr. Temple Barholm's valet, and it was not what he said, but what he didn't, that showed me where I stood."

"A mystery is an interesting thing to have in a house," said Captain Palliser without enthusiasm. He smoked his cigar as though he was enjoying its aroma, and even from his first remark he had managed not to seem to be really quite addressing himself to Burrill. He was certainly not talking to him in the ordinary way; his air was rather that of a gentleman overhearing casual remarks in which he was only vaguely interested. Before Burrill left the room, however, and he left it under the impression that he had said no more than civility demanded, Captain Palliser had reached the point of being able to deduce a number of things from what he, like Pearson, had not said.

CHAPTER XXIII

The man who in all England was most deeply submerged in deadly boredom was, the old Duke of Stone said with wearied finality, himself. He had been a sinful young man of finished taste in 1820; he had cultivated these tastes, which were for literature and art and divers other things, in the most richly alluring foreign capitals until finding himself becoming an equally sinful and finished elderly man, he had decided to marry. After the birth of her four daughters, his wife had died and left them on his hands. Developing at that time a tendency to rheumatic gout and a daily increasing realization of the fact that the resources of a poor dukedom may be hopelessly depleted by an expensive youth passed brilliantly in Vienna, Paris, Berlin, and London, when it was endurable, he found it expedient to give up what he considered the necessities of life and to face existence in the country in England. It is not imperative that one should enter into detail. There was much, and it covered years during which his four daughters grew up and he "grew down," as he called it. If his temper had originally been a bad one, it would doubtless have become unbearable; as he had been born an amiable person, he merely sank into the boredom which threatens extinction. His girls bored him, his neighbors bored him, Stone Hover bored him, Lancashire bored him, England had always bored him except at abnormal moments.

"I read a great deal, I walk when I can," this he wrote once to a friend in Rome. "When I am too stiff with rheumatic gout, I drive myself about in a pony chaise and feel like an aunt in a Bath chair. I have so far escaped the actual chair itself. It perpetually rains here, I may mention, so I don't get out often. You who gallop on white roads in the sunshine and hear Italian voices and vowels, figure to yourself your friend trundling through damp, lead-colored Lancashire lanes and being addressed in the Lancashire dialect. But so am I driven by necessity that I listen to it gratefully. I want to hear village news from villagers. I have become a gossip. It is a wonderful thing to be a gossip. It assists one to get through one's declining years. Do not wait so long as I did before becoming one. Begin in your roseate middle age."

An attack of gout more severe than usual had confined him to his room for some time after the arrival of the new owner of Temple Barholm. He had, in fact, been so far indisposed that a week or two had passed before he had heard of him. His favorite nurse had been chosen by him, because she was a comfortable village woman whom he had taught to lay aside her proper awe and talk to him about her own affairs and her neighbors when he was in the mood to listen. She spoke the broadest possible dialect,—he liked dialect, having learned much in his youth from mellow-eyed Neapolitan and Tuscan girls,—and she had never been near a hospital, but had been trained by the bedsides of her children and neighbors.

"If I were a writing person, she would become literature, impinging upon Miss Mitford's tales of 'Our Village,' Miss Austen's varieties, and the young Bronte woman's 'Wuthering Heights.' Mon Dieu! what a resource it would be to be a writing person!" he wrote to the Roman friend.

To his daughters he said:

"She brings back my tenderest youth. When she pokes the fire in the twilight and lumbers about the room, making me comfortable, I lie in my bed and watch the flames dancing on the ceiling and feel as if I were six and had the measles. She tucks me in, my dears—she tucks me in, I assure you. Sometimes I feel it quite possible that she will bend over and kiss me."

She had tucked him in luxuriously in his arm-chair by the fire on the first day of his convalescence, and as she gave him his tray, with his beef tea and toast, he saw that she contained anecdotal information of interest which tactful encouragement would cause to flow.

"Now that I am well enough to be entertained, Braddle," he said, "tell me what has been happening."

"A graidely lot, yore Grace," she answered; "but not so much i' Stone Hover as i' Temple Barholm. He's coom!"

Then the duke vaguely recalled rumors he had heard sometime before his indisposition.

"The new Mr. Temple Barholm? He's an American, isn't he? The lost heir who had to be sought for high and low—principally low, I understand."

The beef tea was excellently savory, the fire was warm, and relief from two weeks of pain left a sort of Nirvana of peace. Rarely had the duke passed a more delightfully entertaining morning. There was a richness in the Temple Barholm situation, as described in detail by Mrs. Braddle, which filled him with delight. His regret that he was not a writing person intensified itself. Americans had not appeared upon the horizon in Miss Mitford's time, or in Miss Austen's, or in the Brontes' the type not having entirely detached itself from that of the red Indian. It struck him, however, that Miss Austen might have done the best work with this affair if she had survived beyond her period. Her finely demure and sly sense of humor would have seen and seized upon its opportunities. Stark moorland life had not encouraged humor in the Brontes, and village patronage had not roused in Miss Mitford a sense of ironic contrasts. Yes, Jane Austen would have done it best.

That the story should be related by Mrs. Braddle gave it extraordinary flavor. No man or woman of his own class could have given such a recounting, or revealed so many facets of this jewel of entertainment. He and those like him could have seen the thing only from their own amused, outraged, bewildered, or cynically disgusted point of view. Mrs. Braddle saw it as the villagers saw it—excited, curious, secretly hopeful of undue lavishness from "a chap as had nivver had brass before an' wants to chuck it away for brag's sake," or somewhat alarmed at the possible neglecting of customs and privileges by a person ignorant of memorial benefactions. She saw it as the servants saw it—secretly disdainful, outwardly respectful, waiting to discover whether the sacrifice of professional distinction would be balanced by liberties permitted and lavishness of remuneration and largess. She saw it also from her own point of view—that of a respectable cottage dweller whose great-great-grandfather had been born in a black-and-white timbered house in a green lane, and who knew what were "gentry ways" and what nature of being could never even remotely approach the assumption of them. She had seen Tembarom more than once, and summed him up by no means ill-naturedly.

"He's not such a bad-lookin' chap. He is na short-legged or turn-up-nosed, an' that's summat. He con stride along, an' he looks healthy enow for aw he's thin. A thin chap nivver looks as common as a fat un. If he wur pudgy, it ud be a lot more agen him."

"I think, perhaps," amiably remarked the duke, sipping his beef tea, "that you had better not call him a `chap,' Braddle. The late Mr. Temple Barholm was never referred to as a `chap' exactly, was he?"

Mrs. Braddle gave vent to a sort of internal-sounding chuckle. She had not meant to be impertinent, and she knew her charge was aware that she had not, and that he was neither being lofty or severe with her.

"Eh, I'd 'a'loiked to ha' heard somebody do it when he was nigh," she said. "Happen I'd better be moindin' ma P's an' Q's a bit more. But that's what this un is, yore Grace. He's a `chap' out an' out. An' theer's some as is sayin' he's not a bad sort of a chap either. There's lots o' funny stories about him i' Temple Barholm village. He goes in to th' cottages now an' then, an' though a fool could see he does na know his place, nor other people's, he's downreet open-handed. An' he maks foak laugh. He took a lot o' New York papers wi' big pictures in 'em to little Tummas Hibblethwaite. An' wot does tha think he did one rainy day? He walks in to the owd Dibdens' cottage, an' sits down betwixt 'em as they sit one each side o' th' f're, an' he tells 'em they've got to cheer him up a bit becos he's got nought to do. An' he shows 'em th' picter-papers, too, an' tells 'em about New York, an' he ends up wi' singin' 'em a comic song. They was frightened out o' their wits at first, but somehow he got over 'em, an' made 'em laugh their owd heads nigh off."

Her charge laid his spoon down, and his shrewd, lined face assumed a new expression of interest.

"Did he! Did he, indeed!" he exclaimed. "Good Lord! what an exhilarating person! I must go and see him. Perhaps he'd make me laugh my `owd head nigh off.' What a sensation!"

There was really immense color in the anecdotes and in the side views accompanying them; the routing out of her obscurity of the isolated, dependent spinster relative, for instance. Delicious! The man was either desperate with loneliness or he was one of the rough-diamond benefactors favored by novelists, in which latter case he would not be so entertaining. Pure self-interest caused the Duke of Stone quite unreservedly to hope that he was anguished by the unaccustomedness of his surroundings, and was ready to pour himself forth to any one who would listen. There would be originality in such a situation, and one could draw forth revelations worth forming an audience to. He himself had thought that the volte-face such circumstances demanded would surely leave a man staring at things foreign enough to bore him. This, indeed, had been one of his cherished theories; but the only man he had ever encountered who had become a sort of millionaire between one day and another had been an appalling Yorkshire man, who had had some extraordinary luck with diamond-mines in South Africa, and he had been simply drunk with exhilaration and the delight of spending money with both hands, while he figuratively slapped on the back persons who six weeks before would have kicked him for doing it.

This man did not appear to be excited. The duke mentally rocked with gleeful appreciation of certain things Mrs. Braddle detailed. She gave, of course, Burrill's version of the brief interview outside the dining-room door when Miss Alicia's status in the household bad been made clear to him. But the duke, being a man endowed with a subtle sense of shades, was wholly enlightened as to the inner meaning of Burrill's master.

"Now, that was good," he said to himself, almost chuckling. "By the Lord! the man might have been a gentleman."

When to all this was added the story of the friend or poor relative, or what not, who was supposed to be "not quoite reet i' th' yed," and was taken care of like a prince, in complete isolation, attended by a valet, visited and cheered up by his benefactor, he felt that a boon had indeed been bestowed upon him. It was a nineteenth century "Mysteries of Udolpho" in embryo, though too greatly diluted by the fact that though the stranger was seen by no one, the new Temple Barholm made no secret of him.

If he had only made a secret of him, the whole thing would have been complete. There was of course in the situation a discouraging suggestion that Temple Barholm MIGHT turn out to be merely the ordinary noble character bestowing boons.

"I will burn a little candle to the Virgin and offer up prayers that he may NOT. That sort of thing would have no cachet whatever, and would only depress me," thought his still sufficiently sinful Grace.

"When, Braddle, do you think I shall be able to take a drive again?" he asked his nurse.

Braddle was not prepared to say upon her own responsibility, but the doctor would tell him when he came in that afternoon.

"I feel astonishingly well, considering the sharpness of the attack," her patient said. "Our little talk has quite stimulated me. When I go out,"—there was a gleam in the eye he raised to hers,—"I am going to call at Temple Barholm."

"I knowed tha would," she commented with maternal familiarity. "I dunnot believe tha could keep away."

And through the rest of the morning, as he sat and gazed into the fire, she observed that he several times chuckled gently and rubbed his delicate, chill, swollen knuckled hands together.

A few weeks later there were some warm days, and his Grace chose to go out in his pony carriage. Much as he detested the suggestion of "the aunt in the Bath chair," he had decided that he found the low, informal vehicle more entertaining than a more imposing one, and the desperation of his desire to be entertained can be comprehended only by those who have known its parallel. If he was not in some way amused, he found himself whirling, with rheumatic gout and seventy years, among recollections of vivid pictures better hung in galleries with closed doors. It was always possible to stop the pony carriage to look at views—bits of landscape caught at by vision through trees or under their spreading branches, or at the end of little green-hedged lanes apparently adorned with cottages, or farm-houses with ricks and barn-yards and pig-pens designed for the benefit of Morland and other painters of rusticity. He could also slacken the pony's pace and draw up by roadsides where solitary men sat by piles of stone, which they broke at leisure with hammers as though they were cracking nuts. He had spent many an agreeable half-hour in talk with a road-mender who could be led into conversation and was left elated by an extra shilling. As in years long past he had sat under chestnut-trees in the Apennines and shared the black bread and sour wine of a peasant, so in these days he frequently would have been glad to sit under a hedge and eat bread and cheese with a good fellow who did not know him and whose summing up of the domestic habits and needs of "th' workin' mon" or the amiabilities or degeneracies of the gentry would be expressed, figuratively speaking, in thoughts and words of one syllable. The pony, however, could not take him very far afield, and one could not lunch on the grass with a stone-breaker well within reach of one's own castle without an air of eccentricity which he no more chose to assume than he would have chosen to wear long hair and a flowing necktie. Also, rheumatic gout had not hovered about the days in the Apennines. He did not, it might be remarked, desire to enter into conversation with his humble fellow-man from altruistic motives. He did it because there was always a chance more or less that he would be amused. He might hear of little tragedies or comedies,—he much preferred the comedies,—and he often learned new words or phrases of dialect interestingly allied to pure Anglo-Saxon. When this last occurred, he entered them in a notebook he kept in his library. He sometimes pretended to himself that he was going to write a book on dialects; but he knew that he was a dilettante sort of creature and would really never do it. The pretense, however, was a sort of asset. In dire moments during rains or foggy weather when he felt twinges and had read till his head ached, he had wished that he had not eaten all his cake at the first course of life's feast, that he had formed a habit or so which might have survived and helped him to eke out even an easy-chair existence through the last courses. He did not find consolation in the use of the palliative adjective as applied to himself. A neatly cynical sense of humor prevented it. He knew he had always been an entirely selfish man and that he was entirely selfish still, and was not revoltingly fretful and domineering only because he was constitutionally unirritable.

He was, however, amiably obstinate, and was accustomed to getting his own way in most things. On this day of his outing he insisted on driving himself in the face of arguments to the contrary. He was so fixed in his intention that his daughters and Mrs. Braddle were obliged to admit themselves overpowered.

"Nonsense! Nonsense!" he protested when they besought him to allow himself to be driven by a groom. "The pony is a fat thing only suited to a Bath chair. He does not need driving. He doesn't go when he is driven. He frequently lies down and puts his cheek on his hand and goes to sleep, and I am obliged to wait until he wakes up."

"But, papa, dear," Lady Edith said, "your poor hands are not very strong. And he might run away and kill you. Please do be reasonable!"

"My dear girl," he answered, "if he runs, I shall run after him and kill him when I catch him. George," he called to the groom holding the plump pony's head, "tell her ladyship what this little beast's name is."

"The Indolent Apprentice, your Grace," the groom answered, touching his hat and suppressing a grin.

"I called him that a month ago," said the duke. "Hogarth would have depicted all sorts of evil ends for him. Three weeks since, when I was in bed being fed by Braddle with a spoon, I could have outrun him myself. Let George follow me on a horse if you like, but he must keep out of my sight. Half a mile behind will do."

He got into the phaeton, concealing his twinges with determination, and drove down the avenue with a fine air, sitting erect and smiling. Indoor existence had become unendurable, and the spring was filling the woods.

"I love the spring," he murmured to himself. "I am sentimental about it. I love sentimentality, in myself, when I am quite alone. If I had been a writing person, I should have made verses every year in April and sent them to magazines—and they would have been returned to me."

The Indolent Apprentice was, it is true, fat, though comely, and he was also entirely deserving of his name. Like his Grace of Stone, however, he had seen other and livelier days, and now and then he was beset by recollections. He was still a rather high, though slow, stepper—the latter from fixed preference. He had once stepped fast, as well as with a spirited gait. During his master's indisposition he had stood in his loose box and professed such harmlessness that he had not been annoyed by being taken out for exercise as regularly as he might have been. He had champed his oats and listened to the repartee of the stable-boys, and he had, perhaps, felt the coming of the spring when the cuckoo insisted upon it with thrilling mellowness across the green sweeps of the park land. Sometimes it made him sentimental, as it made his master, sometimes it made him stamp his small hoofs restlessly in his straw and want to go out. He did not intend, when he was taken out, to emulate the Industrious Apprentice by hastening his pace unduly and raising false hopes for the future, but he sniffed in the air the moist green of leafage and damp moss, massed with yellow primroses cuddling in it as though for warmth, and he thought of other fresh scents and the feel of the road under a pony's feet.

Therefore, when he found himself out in the world again, he shook his head now and then and even tossed it with the recurring sensations of a pony who was a mere boy and still slight in the waist.

"You feel it too, do you?" said the duke. "I won't remind you of your years."

The drive from Stone Hover to the village of Temple Barholm was an easy one, of many charms of leaf-arched lanes and green-edged road. The duke had always had a partiality for it, and he took it this morning. He would probably have taken it in any case, but Mrs. Braddle's anecdotes had been floating through his mind when he set forth and perhaps inclined him in its direction.

The groom was a young man of three and twenty, and he felt the spring also. The horse he rode was a handsome animal, and he himself was not devoid of a healthy young man's good looks. He knew his belted livery was becoming to him, and when on horseback he prided himself on what he considered an almost military bearing. Sarah Hibson, farmer Hibson's dimple-chinned and saucy-eyed daughter, had been "carryin' on a good bit" with a soldier who was a smart, well-set-up, impudent fellow, and it was the manifest duty of any other young fellow who had considered himself to be "walking out with her" to look after his charges. His Grace had been most particular about George's keeping far enough behind him; and as half a mile had been mentioned as near enough, certainly one was absolved from the necessity of keeping in sight. Why should not one turn into the lane which ended at Hibson's farm-yard, and drop into the dairy, and "have it out wi' Sarah?"

Dimpled chins and saucy eyes, and bare, dimpled arms and hands patting butter while heads are tossed in coquettishly alluring defiance, made even "having it out" an attractive and memory-obscuring process. Sarah was a plump and sparkling imp of prettiness, and knew the power of every sly glance and every dimple and every golden freckle she possessed. George did not know it so well, and in ten minutes had lost his head and entirely forgotten even the half-mile behind.

He was lover-like, he was masterful, he brought the spring with him; he "carried on," as Sarah put it, until he had actually out-distanced the soldier, and had her in his arms, kissing her as she laughed and prettily struggled.

"Shame o' tha face! Shame o' tha face, George!" she scolded and dimpled and blushed. "Wilt tha be done now? Wilt tha be done? I'll call mother."

And at that very moment mother came without being called, running, red of face, heavy-footed, and panting, with her cap all on one side.

"Th' duke's run away! Th' duke's run away!" she shouted. "Jo seed him. Pony got freetened at summat—an' what art doin' here, George Bind? Get o' thy horse an' gallop. If he's killed, tha 'rt a ruined man."

There was an odd turn of chance in it, the duke thought afterward. Though friskier than usual, the Indolent Apprentice had behaved perfectly well until they neared the gates of Temple Barholm, which chanced to be open because a cart had just passed through. And it was not the cart's fault, for the Indolent Apprentice regarded it with friendly interest. It happened, however, that perhaps being absorbed in the cart, which might have been drawn by a friend or even a distant relative, the Indolent Apprentice was horribly startled by a large rabbit which leaped out of the hedge almost under his nose, and, worse still, was followed the next instant by another rabbit even larger and more sudden and unexpected in its movements. The Indolent Apprentice snorted, pawed, whirled, dashed through the open gateway,—the duke's hands were even less strong than his daughter had thought,—and galloped, head in air and bit between teeth, up the avenue, the low carriage rocking from side to side.

"Damn! Damn!" cried the duke, rocking also. "Oh, damn! I shall be killed in a runaway perambulator!"

And ridiculous as it was, things surged through his brain, and once, though he laughed at himself bitterly afterward, he gasped "Ah, Heloise;" as he almost whirled over a jagged tree-stump; gallop and gallop and gallop, off the road and through trees, and back again on to the sward, and gallop and gallop and jerk and jolt and jerk, and he was nearing the house, and a long-legged young man ran down the steps, pushing aside footmen, and was ahead of the drunken little beast of a pony, and caught him just as the phaeton overturned and shot his grace safely though not comfortably in a heap upon the grass.

It was of course no trifle of a shock, but its victim's sensations gave him strong reason to hope, as he rolled over, that no bones were broken. The following servants were on the spot almost at once, and took the pony's head.

The young man helped the duke to his feet and dusted him with masterly dexterity. He did not know he was dusting a duke, and he would not have cared if he had.

"Hello," he said, "you're not hurt. I can see that. Thank the Lord! I don't believe you've got a scratch."

His grace felt a shade shaky, and he was slightly pale, but he smiled in a way which had been celebrated forty years earlier, and the charm of which had survived even rheumatic gout.

"Thank you. I'm not hurt in the least. I am the Duke of Stone. This isn't really a call. It isn't my custom to arrive in this way. May I address you as my preserver, Mr. Temple Barholm?"

CHAPTER XXIV

Upon the terrace, when he was led up the steps, stood a most perfect little elderly lady in a state of agitation much greater than his own or his rescuer's. It was an agitation as perfect in its femininity as she herself was. It expressed its kind tremors in the fashion which belonged to the puce silk dress and fine bits of collar and undersleeve the belated gracefulness of which caused her to present herself to him rather as a figure cut neatly from a book of the styles he had admired in his young manhood. It was of course Miss Alicia, who having, with Tembarom, seen the galloping pony from a window, had followed him when he darted from the room. She came forward, looking pale with charming solicitude.

"I do so hope you are not hurt," she exclaimed. "It really seemed that only divine Providence could prevent a terrible accident."

"I am afraid that it was more grotesque than terrible," he answered a shade breathlessly.

"Let me make you acquainted with the Duke of Stone, Miss Alicia," Tembarom said in the formula of Mrs. Bowse's boarders on state occasions of introduction. "Duke, let me make you acquainted, sir, with my— relation—Miss Alicia Temple Barholm."

The duke's bow had a remote suggestion of almost including a kissed hand in its gallant courtesy. Not, however, that Early Victorian ladies had been accustomed to the kissing of hands; but at the period when he had best known the type he had daily bent over white fingers in Continental capitals.

"A glass of wine," Miss Alicia implored. "Pray let me give you a glass of wine. I am sure you need it very much."

He was taken into the library and made to sit in a most comfortable easy-chair. Miss Alicia fluttered about him with sympathy still delicately tinged with alarm. How long, how long, it had been since he had been fluttered over! Nearly forty years. Ladies did not flutter now, and he remembered that it was no longer the fashion to call them "ladies." Only the lower-middle classes spoke of "ladies." But he found himself mentally using the word again as he watched Miss Alicia.

It had been "ladies" who had fluttered and been anxious about a man in this quite pretty way.

He could scarcely remove his eyes from her as he sipped his wine. She felt his escape "providential," and murmured such devout little phrases concerning it that he was almost consoled for the grotesque inward vision of himself as an aged peer of the realm tumbling out of a baby-carriage and rolled over on the grass at the feet of a man on whom later he had meant to make, in proper state, a formal call. She put her hand to her side, smiling half apologetically.

"My heart beats quite fast yet," she said. Whereupon a quaintly novel thing took place, at the sight of which the duke barely escaped opening his eyes very wide indeed. The American Temple Barholm put his arm about her in the most casual and informally accustomed way, and led her to a chair, and put her in it, so to speak.

"Say," he announced with affectionate authority, "you sit down right away. It's you that needs a glass of wine, and I'm going to give it to you."

The relations between the two were evidently on a basis not common in England even among people who were attached to one another. There was a spontaneous, every-day air of natural, protective petting about it, as though the fellow was fond of her in his crude fashion, and meant to take care of her. He was fond of her, and the duke perceived it with elation, and also understood. He might be the ordinary bestower of boons, but the protective curve of his arm included other things. In the blank dullness of his unaccustomed splendors he had somehow encountered this fine, delicately preserved little relic of other days, and had seized on her and made her his own.

"I have not seen anything as delightful as Miss Temple Barholm for many a year," the duke said when Miss Alicia was called from the room and left them together.

"Ain't she great?" was Tembarom's reply. "She's just great."

"It's an exquisite survival of type," said the duke. "She belongs to my time, not yours," he added, realizing that "survival of type" might not clearly convey itself.

"Well, she belongs to mine now," answered Tembarom. "I wouldn't lose her for a farm."

"The voice, the phrases, the carriage might survive,—they do in remote neighborhoods, I suppose—but the dress is quite delightfully incredible. It is a work of art," the duke went on. She had seemed too good to be true. Her clothes, however, had certainly not been dug out of a wardrobe of forty years ago.

"When I went to talk to the head woman in the shop in Bond Street I fixed it with 'em hard and fast that she was not to spoil her. They were to keep her like she was. She's like her little cap, you know, and her little mantles and tippets. She's like them," exclaimed Tembarom.

Did he see that? What an odd feature in a man of his sort! And how thoroughly New Yorkish it was that he should march into a fashionable shop and see that he got what he wanted and the worth of his money! There had been no rashness in the hope that the unexplored treasure might be a rich one. The man's simplicity was an actual complexity. He had a boyish eye and a grin, but there was a business-like line about his mouth which was strong enough to have been hard if it had not been good-natured.

"That was confoundedly clever of you," his grace commented heartily—"confoundedly. I should never have had the wit to think of it myself, or the courage to do it if I had. Shop-women make me shy."

"Oh, well, I just put it up to them," Tembarom answered easily.

"I believe," cautiously translated the duke, "that you mean that you made them feel that they alone were responsible."

"Yes, I do," assented Tembarom, the grin slightly in evidence. "Put it up to them's the short way of saying it."

"Would you mind my writing that down?" said the duke. "I have a fad for dialects and new phrases." He hastily scribbled the words in a tablet that he took from his pocket. "Do you like living in England?" he asked in course of time.

"I should like it if I'd been born here," was the answer.

"I see, I see."

"If it had not been for finding Miss Alicia, and that I made a promise I'd stay for a year, anyhow, I'd have broken loose at the end of the first week and worked my passage back if I hadn't had enough in my clothes to pay for it." He laughed, but it was not real laughter. There was a thing behind it. The situation was more edifying than one could have hoped. "I made a promise, and I'm going to stick it out," he said.

He was going to stick it out because he had promised to endure for a year Temple Barholm and an income of seventy thousand pounds! The duke gazed at him as at a fond dream realized.

"I've nothing to do," Tembarom added.

"Neither have I," replied the Duke of Stone.

"But you're used to it, and I'm not. I'm used to working 'steen hours a day, and dropping into bed as tired as a dog, but ready to sleep like one and get up rested."

"I used to play twenty hours a day once," answered the duke, "but I didn't get up rested. That's probably why I have gout and rheumatism combined. Tell me how you worked, and I will tell you how I played."

It was worth while taking this tone with him. It had been worth while taking it with the chestnut-gathering peasants in the Apennines, sometimes even with a stone-breaker by an English roadside. And this one was of a type more unique and distinctive than any other—a fellow who, with the blood of Saxon kings and Norman nobles in his veins, had known nothing but the street life of the crudest city in the world, who spoke a sort of argot, who knew no parallels of the things which surrounded him in the ancient home he had inherited and in which he stood apart, a sort of semi-sophisticated savage. The duke applied himself with grace and finished ability to drawing him out. The questions he asked were all seemingly those of a man of the world charmingly interested in the superior knowledge of a foreigner of varied experience. His method was one which engaged the interest of Tembarom himself. He did not know that he was not only questioned, but, so to speak, delicately cross-examined and that before the end of the interview the Duke of Stone knew more of him, his past existence and present sentiments, than even Miss Alicia knew after their long and intimate evening talks. The duke, however, had the advantage of being a man and of cherishing vivid recollections of the days of his youth, which, unlike as it had been to that of Tembarom, furnished a degree of solid foundation upon which go to build conjecture.

"A young man of his age," his grace reflected astutely, "has always just fallen out of love, is falling into it, or desires vaguely to do so. Ten years later there would perhaps be blank spaces, lean years during which he was not in love at all; but at his particular period there must be a young woman somewhere. I wonder if she is employed in one of the department stores he spoke of, and how soon he hopes to present her to us. His conversation has revealed so far, to use his own rich simile, 'neither hide nor hair' of her."

On his own part, he was as ready to answer questions as to ask them. In fact, he led Tembarom on to asking.

"I will tell you how I played" had been meant. He made a human document of the history he enlarged, he brilliantly diverged, he included, he made pictures, and found Tembarom's point of view or lack of it gave spice and humor to relations he had thought himself tired of. To tell familiar anecdotes of courts and kings to a man who had never quite believed that such things were realities, who almost found them humorous when they were casually spoken of, was edification indeed. The novel charm lay in the fact that his class in his country did not include them as possibilities. Peasants in other countries, plowmen, shopkeepers, laborers in England—all these at least they knew of, and counted them in as factors in the lives of the rich and great; but this dear young man—!

"What's a crown like? I'd like to see one. How much do you guess such a thing would cost—in dollars?"

"Did not Miss Temple Barholm take you to see the regalia in the Tower of London? I am quite shocked," said the duke. He was, in fact, a trifle disappointed. With the puce dress and undersleeves and little fringes she ought certainly to have rushed with her pupil to that seat of historical instruction on their first morning in London, immediately after breakfasting on toast and bacon and marmalade and eggs.

"She meant me to go, but somehow it was put off. She almost cried on our journey home when she suddenly remembered that we'd forgotten it, after all."

"I am sure she said it was a wasted opportunity," suggested his grace.

"Yes, that was what hit her so hard. She'd never been to London before, and you couldn't make her believe she could ever get there again, and she said it was ungrateful to Providence to waste an opportunity. She's always mighty anxious to be grateful to Providence, bless her!"

"She regards you as Providence," remarked the duke, enraptured. With a touch here and there, the touch of a master, he had gathered the whole little story of Miss Alicia, and had found it of a whimsical exquisiteness and humor.

"She's a lot too good to me," answered Tembarom. "I guess women as nice as her are always a lot too good to men. She's a kind of little old angel. What makes me mad is to think of the fellows that didn't get busy and marry her thirty-five years ago."

"Were there—er—many of 'em?" the duke inquired.

"Thousands of 'em, though most of 'em never saw her. I suppose you never saw her then. If you had, you might have done it."

The duke, sitting with an elbow on each arm of his chair, put the tips of his fine, gouty fingers together and smiled with a far-reaching inclusion of possibilities.

"So I might," he said; "so I might. My loss entirely—my abominable loss."

They had reached this point of the argument when the carriage from Stone Hover arrived. It was a stately barouche the coachman and footman of which equally with its big horses seemed to have hastened to an extent which suggested almost panting breathlessness. It contained Lady Edith and Lady

Celia, both pale, and greatly agitated by the news which had brought them horrified from Stone Hover without a moment's delay.

They both ascended in haste and swept in such alarmed anxiety up the terrace steps and through the hall to their father's side that they had barely a polite gasp for Miss Alicia and scarcely saw Tembarom at all.

"Dear Papa!" they cried when he revealed himself in his chair in the library intact and smiling. "How wicked of you, dear! How you have frightened us!"

"I begged you to be good, dearest," said Lady Edith, almost in tears. "Where was George? You must dismiss him at once. Really—really—"

"He was half a mile away, obeying my orders," said the duke. "A groom cannot be dismissed for obeying orders. It is the pony who must be dismissed, to my great regret; or else we must overfeed him until he is even fatter than he is and cannot run away."

Were his arms and legs and his ribs and collar-bones and head quite right? Was he sure that he had not received any internal injury when he fell out of the pony-carriage? They could scarcely be convinced, and as they hung over and stroked and patted him, Tembarom stood aside and watched them with interest. They were the girls he had to please Ann by "getting next to," giving himself a chance to fall in love with them, so that she'd know whether they were his kind or not. They were nice-looking, and had a way of speaking that sounded rather swell, but they weren't ace high to a little slim, redheaded thing that looked at you like a baby and pulled your heart up into your throat.

"Don't poke me any more, dear children. I am quite, quite sound," he heard the duke say. "In Mr. Temple Barholm you behold the preserver of your parent. Filial piety is making you behave with shocking ingratitude."

They turned to Tembarom at once with a pretty outburst of apologies and thanks. Lady Celia wasn't, it is true, "a looker," with her narrow shoulders and rather long nose, but she had an air of breeding, and the charming color of which Palliser had spoken, returning to Lady Edith's cheeks, illuminated her greatly.

They both were very polite and made many agreeably grateful speeches, but in the eyes of both there lurked a shade of anxiety which they hoped to be able to conceal. Their father watched them with a wicked pleasure. He realized clearly their well-behaved desire to do and say exactly the right thing and bear themselves in exactly the right manner, and also their awful uncertainty before an entirely unknown quantity. Almost any other kind of young man suddenly uplifted by strange fortune they might have known some parallel for, but a newsboy of New York! All the New Yorkers they had met or heard of had been so rich and grand as to make them feel themselves, by contrast, mere country paupers, quite shivering with poverty and huddling for protection in their barely clean rags, so what was there to go on? But how dreadful not to be quite right, precisely right, in one's approach—quite familiar enough, and yet not a shade too familiar, which of course would appear condescending! And be it said the delicacy of the situation was added to by the fact that they had heard something of Captain Palliser's extraordinary little story about his determination to know "ladies." Really, if Willocks the butcher's boy had inherited Temple Barholm, it would have been easier to know where one stood in the matter of being civil and agreeable to him. First Lady Edith, made perhaps bold by the suggestion of physical advantage bestowed by the color, talked to him to the very best of her ability; and when she felt herself fearfully flagging, Lady Celia took him up and did her very well-conducted best. Neither she nor her sister were brilliant talkers at any time, and limited by the absence of any common familiar topic, effort was necessary. The neighborhood he did not know; London he was barely aware of; social functions it would be an impertinence to bring in; games he did not play; sport he had scarcely heard of. You were confined to America, and if you knew next to nothing of American life, there you were.

Tembarom saw it all,—he was sharp enough for that,—and his habit of being jocular and wholly unashamed saved him from the misery of awkwardness that Willocks would have been sure to have writhed under. His casual frankness, however, for a moment embarrassed Lady Edith to the bitterest extremity. When you are trying your utmost to make a queer person oblivious to the fact that his world is one unknown to you, it is difficult to know where do you stand when he says.

"It's mighty hard to talk to a man who doesn't know a thing that belongs to the kind of world you've spent your life in, ain't it? But don't you mind me a minute. I'm glad to be talked to anyhow by people like you. When I don't catch on, I'll just ask. No man was ever electrocuted for not knowing, and that's just where I am. I don't know, and I'm glad to be told. Now, there's one thing. Burrill said 'Your Ladyship' to you, I heard him. Ought I to say it, er oughtn't I?"

"Oh, no," she answered, but somehow without distaste in the momentary stare he had startled her into; "Burrill is—"

"He's a servant," he aided encouragingly. "Well, I've never been a butler, but I've been somebody's servant all my life, and mighty glad of the chance. This is the first time I've been out of a job."

What nice teeth he had! What a queer, candid, unresentful creature! What a good sort of smile! And how odd that it was he who was putting her more at her ease by the mere way in which he was saying this almost alarming thing!

By the time he had ended, it was not alarming at all, and she had caught her breath again.

She was actually sorry when the door opened and Lady Joan Fayre came in, followed almost immediately by Lady Mallowe and Captain Palliser, who appeared to have just returned from a walk and heard the news.

Lady Mallowe was most sympathetic. Why not, indeed? The Duke of Stone was a delightful, cynical creature, and Stone Hover was, despite its ducal poverty, a desirable place to be invited to, if you could manage it. Her ladyship's method of fluttering was not like Miss Alicia's, its character being wholly modern; but she fluttered, nevertheless. The duke, who knew all about her, received her amiabilities with appreciative smiles, but it was the splendidly handsome, hungry-eyed young woman with the line between her black brows who engaged his attention. On the alert, as he always was, for a situation, he detected one at once when he saw his American address her. She did not address him, and scarcely deigned a reply when he spoke to her. When he spoke to others, she conducted herself as though he were not in the room, so obviously did she choose to ignore his existence. Such a bearing toward one's host had indeed the charm of being an interesting novelty. And what a beauty she was, with her lovely, ferocious eyes and the small, black head poised on the exquisite long throat, which was on the verge of becoming a trifle too thin! Then as in a flash he recalled between one breath and another the quite fiendish episode of poor Jem Temple Barholm—and she was the girl!

Then he became almost excited in his interest. He saw it all. As he had himself argued must be the case, this poor fellow was in love. But it was not with a lady in the New York department stores; it was with a young woman who would evidently disdain to wipe her feet upon him. How thrilling! As Lady Mallowe and Palliser and the others chattered, he watched him, observing his manner. He stood the handsome creature's steadily persistent rudeness very well; he made no effort to push into the talk when she coolly held him out of it. He waited without external uneasiness or spasmodic smiles. If he could do that despite the inevitable fact that he must feel his position uncomfortable, he was possessed of fiber. That alone would make him worth cultivating. And if there were persons who were to be made uncomfortable, why not cut in and circumvent the beauty somewhat and give her a trifle of unease? It was with the light and adroit touch of accustomedness to all orders of little situations that his grace took the matter in hand, with a shade, also, of amiable malice. He drew Tembarom adroitly into the center of things; he knew how to lead him to make easily the odd, frank remarks which were sufficiently novel to suggest that he was actually entertaining. He beautifully edged Lady Joan out of her position. She could not behave ill to him, he was far too old, he said to himself, leaving out the fact that a Duke of Stone is a too respectable personage to be quite waved aside.

Tembarom began to enjoy himself a little more. Lady Celia and Lady Edith began to enjoy themselves a little more also. Lady Mallowe was filled with admiring delight. Captain Palliser took in the situation, and asked himself questions about it. On her part, Miss Alicia was restored to the happiness any lack of appreciation of her "dear boy" touchingly disturbed. In circumstances such as these he appeared to the advantage which in a brief period would surely reveal his wonderful qualities. She clung so to his "wonderful qualities" because in all the three-volumed novels of her youth the hero, debarred from early advantages and raised by the turn of fortune's wheel to splendor, was transformed at once into a being of the highest accomplishments and the most polished breeding, and ended in the third volume a creature before whom emperors paled. And how more than charmingly cordial his grace's manner was when he left them!

"To-morrow," he said, "if my daughters do not discover that I have injured some more than vital organ, I shall call to proffer my thanks with the most immense formality. I shall get out of the carriage in the manner customary in respectable neighborhoods, not roll out at your feet. Afterward you will, I hope, come and dine with us. I am devoured by a desire to become more familiar with The Earth."

CHAPTER XXV

It was Lady Mallowe who perceived the moment when he became the fashion. The Duke of Stone called with the immense formality he had described, and his visit was neither brief nor dull. A little later Tembarom with his guests dined at Stone Hover, and the dinner was further removed from dullness than any one of numerous past dinners always noted for being the most agreeable the neighborhood afforded. The duke managed his guest as an impresario might have managed his tenor, though this was done with subtly concealed methods. He had indeed a novelty to offer which had been discussed with much uncertainty of point of view. He presented it to an only languidly entertained neighborhood as a trouvaille of his own choice. Here was drama, here was atmosphere, here was charm verging in its character upon the occult. You would not see it if you were not a collector of such values.

"Nobody will be likely to see him as he is unless he is pointed out to them," was what he said to his daughters. "But being bored to death,—we are all bored,—once adroitly assisted to suspect him of being alluring, most of them will spring upon him and clasp him to their wearied breasts. I haven't the least idea what will happen afterward. I shall in fact await the result with interest."

Being told Palliser's story of the "Ladies," he listened, holding the tips of his fingers together, and wearing an expression of deep interest slightly baffled in its nature. It was Lady Edith who related the anecdote to him.

"Now," he said, "it would be very curious and complicating if that were true; but I don't believe it is. Palliser, of course, likes to tell a good story. I shall be able to discover in time whether it is true or not; but at present I don't believe it."

Following the dinner party at Stone Hover came many others. All the well-known carriages began to roll up the avenue to Temple Barholm. The Temple Barholm carriages also began to roll down the avenue and between the stone griffins on their way to festive gatherings of varied order. Burrill and the footmen ventured to reconsider their early plans for giving warning. It wasn't so bad if the country was going to take him up.

"Do you see what is happening?" Lady Mallowe said to Joan. "The man is becoming actually popular."

"He is popular as a turn at a music hall is," answered Joan. "He will be dropped as he was taken up."

"There's something about him they like, and he represents what everybody most wants. For God's sake! Joan, don't behave like a fool this time. The case is more desperate. There is nothing else—nothing."

"There never was," said Joan, "and I know the desperateness of the case. How long are you going to stay here?"

"I am going to stay for some time. They are not conventional people. It can be managed very well. We are relatives."

"Will you stay," inquired Joan in a low voice, "until they ask you to remove yourself?"

Lady Mallowe smiled an agreeably subtle smile.

"Not quite that," she answered. "Miss Alicia would never have the courage to suggest it. It takes courage and sophistication to do that sort of thing. Mr. Temple Barholm evidently wants us to remain. He will be willing to make as much of the relationship as we choose to let him."

"Do you choose to let him make as much of it as will establish us here for weeks—or months?" Joan asked, her low voice shaking a little.

"That will depend entirely upon circumstances. It will, in fact, depend entirely upon you," said Lady Mallowe, her lips setting themselves into a straight, thin line.

For an appreciable moment Joan was silent; but after it she lost her head and whirled about.

"I shall go away," she cried.

"Where?" asked Lady Mallowe.

"Back to London."

"How much money have you?" asked her mother. She knew she had none. She was always sufficiently shrewd to see that she had none. If the girl had had a pound a week of her own, her mother had always realized that she would have been unmanageable. After the Jem Temple Barholm affair she would have been capable of going to live alone in slums. As it was, she knew enough to be aware that she was too handsome to walk out into Piccadilly without a penny in her pocket; so it had been just possible to keep her indoors.

"How much money have you?" she repeated quietly. This was the way in which their unbearable scenes began—the scenes which the servants passing the doors paused to listen to in the hope that her ladyship would forget that raised voices may be heard by the discreet outsider.

"How much money have you?" she said again.

Joan looked at her; this time it was for about five seconds. She turned her back on her and walked out of the room. Shortly afterward Lady Mallowe saw her walking down the avenue in the rain, which was beginning to fall.

She had left the house because she dared not stay in it. Once out in the park, she folded her long purple cloak about her and pulled her soft purple felt hat down over her brows, walking swiftly under the big trees without knowing where she intended to go before she returned. She liked the rain, she liked the heavy clouds; she wore her dark purples because she felt a fantastic, secret comfort in calling them her mourning—her mourning which she would wear forevermore.

No one could know so well as herself how desperate from her own point of view the case was. She had long known that her mother would not hesitate for a moment before any chance of a second marriage which would totally exclude her daughter from her existence. Why should she, after all, Joan thought? They had always been antagonists. The moment of chance had been looming on the horizon for months. Sir Moses Monaldini had hovered about fitfully and evidently doubtfully at first, more certainly and frequently of late, but always with a clearly objecting eye cast askance upon herself. With determination and desire to establish a social certainty, astute enough not to care specially for young beauty and exactions he did not purpose to submit to, and keen enough to see the advantage of a handsome woman with bitter reason to value what was offered to her in the form of a luxurious future, Sir Moses was moving toward action, though with proper caution. He would have no penniless daughters hanging about scowling and sneering. None of that for him. And the ripest apple upon the topmost bow in the highest wind would not drop more readily to his feet than her mother would, Joan knew with sharp and shamed burnings.

As the rain fell, she walked in her purple cloak, unpaid for, and her purple hat, for which they had been dunned with threatening insults, and knew that she did not own and could not earn a penny. She could not dig, and to beg she was ashamed, and all the more horribly because she had been a beggar of the meaner order all her life. It made her sick to think of the perpetual visits they had made where they were not wanted, of the times when they had been politely bundled out of places, of the methods which had been used to induce shop-keepers to let them run up bills. For years her mother and she had been walking advertisements of smart shops because both were handsome, wore clothes well, and carried them where they would be seen and talked about. Now this would be all over, since it had been Lady Mallowe who had managed all details. Thrown upon her own resources, Joan would have none of them, even though she must walk in rags. Her education had prepared her for only one thing—to marry well, if luck were on her side. It had never been on her side. If she had never met Jem, she would have married somebody, since that would have been better than the inevitable last slide into an aging life spent in cheap lodgings with her mother. But Jem had been the beginning and the end.

She bit her lips as she walked, and suddenly tears swept down her cheeks and dripped on to the purple cloth folded over her breast.

"And he sits in Jem's place! And every day that common, foolish stare will follow me!" she said.

He sat, it was true, in the place Jem Temple Barholm would have occupied if he had been a living man, and he looked at her a good deal. Perhaps he sometimes unconsciously stared because she made him think of many things. But if she had been in a state of mind admitting of judicial fairness, she would have been obliged to own that it was not quite a foolish stare. Absorbed, abstracted, perhaps, but it was not foolish. Sometimes, on the contrary, it was searching and keen.

Of course he was doing his best to please her. Of all the "Ladies," it seemed evident that he was most attracted by her. He tried to talk to her despite her unending rebuffs, he followed her about and endeavored to interest her, he presented a hide-bound unsensitiveness when she did her worst. Perhaps he did not even know that she was being icily rude. He was plainly "making up to her" after the manner of his class. He was perhaps playing the part of the patient adorer who melted by noble long-suffering in novels distinguished by heroes of humble origin.

She had reached the village when the rain changed its mind, and without warning began to pour down as if the black cloud passing overhead had suddenly opened. She was wondering if she would not turn in somewhere for shelter until the worst was over when a door opened and Tembarom ran out with an umbrella.

"Come in to the Hibblethwaites cottage, Lady Joan," he said. "This will be over directly."

He did not affectionately hustle her in by the arm as he would have hustled in Miss Alicia, but he closely guarded her with the umbrella until he guided her inside.

"Thank you," she said.

The first object she became aware of was a thin face with pointed chin and ferret eyes peering at her round the end of a sofa, then a sharp voice.

"Tak' off her cloak an' shake th' rain off it in th' wash 'us'," it said. "Mother an' Aunt Susan's out. Let him unbutton it fer thee."

"I can unbutton it myself, thank you," said Lady Joan. Tembarom took it when she had unbuttoned it. He took it from her shoulders before she had time to stop him. Then he walked into the tiny "wash 'us" and shook it thoroughly. He came back and hung it on a chair before the fire.

Tummas was leaning back in his pillows and gazing at her.

"I know tha name," he said. "He towd me," with a jerk of the head toward Tembarom.

"Did he?" replied Lady Joan without interest.

A flaringly illustrated New York paper was spread out upon his sofa. He pushed it aside and pulled the shabby atlas toward him. It fell open at a map of North America as if through long habit.

"Sit thee down," he ordered.

Tembarom had stood watching them both.

"I guess you'd better not do that," he suggested to Tummas.

"Why not?" said the boy, sharply. "She's th' wench he was goin' to marry. It's th' same as if he'd married her. If she wur his widder, she'd want to talk about him. Widders allus wants to talk. Why shouldn't she? Women's women. He'd ha' wanted to talk about her."

"Who is 'he'?" asked Joan with stiff lips.

"The Temple Barholm as' 'd be here if he was na."

Joan turned to Tembarom.

"Do you come here to talk to this boy about HIM?" she said. "How dare you!"

Tummas's eyes snapped; his voice snapped also.

"He knew next to nowt about him till I towd him," he said. "Then he came to ax me things an' foind out more. He knows as much as I do now. Us sits here an' talks him over."

Lady Joan still addressed Tembarom.

"What interest can you have in the man who ought to be in your place?" she asked. "What possible interest?"

"Well," he answered awkwardly, "because he ought to be, I suppose. Ain't that reason enough?"

He had never had to deal with women who hated him and who were angry and he did not know exactly what to say. He had known very few women, and he had always been good-natured with them and won their liking in some measure. Also, there was in his attitude toward this particular woman a baffled feeling that he could not make her understand him. She would always think of him as an enemy and believe he meant things he did not mean. If he had been born and educated in her world, he could have used her own language; but he could use only his own, and there were so many things he must not say for a time at least.

"Do you not realize," she said, "that you are presuming upon your position—that you and this boy are taking liberties?"

Tummas broke in wholly without compunction.

"I've taken liberties aw my loife," he stated, "an' I'm goin' to tak' 'em till I dee. They're th' on'y things I can tak', lyin' here crippled, an' I'm goin' to tak' 'em."

"Stop that, Tummas!" said Tembarom with friendly authority. "She doesn't catch on, and you don't catch on, either. You're both of you 'way off. Stop it!"

"I thought happen she could tell me things I didn't know," protested Tummas, throwing himself back on his pillows. "If she conna, she conna, an' if she wunnot, she wunnot. Get out wi' thee!" he said to Joan. "I dunnot want thee about th' place."

"Say," said Tembarom, "shut up!"

"I am going," said Lady Joan and turned to open the door.

The rain was descending in torrents, but she passed swiftly out into its deluge walking as rapidly as she could. She thought she cared nothing about the rain, but it dashed in her face and eyes, taking her breath away, and she had need of breath when her heart was beating with such fierceness.

"If she wur his widder," the boy had said.

Even chance could not let her alone at one of her worst moments. She walked faster and faster because she was afraid Tembarom would follow her, and in a few minutes she heard him splashing behind her, and then he was at her side, holding the umbrella over her head.

"You're a good walker," he said, "but I'm a sprinter. I trained running after street cars and catching the 'L' in New York."

She had so restrained her miserable hysteric impulse to break down and utterly humiliate herself under the unexpected blow of the episode in the cottage that she had had no breath to spare when she left the room, and her hurried effort to escape had left her so much less that she did not speak.

"I'll tell you something," he went on. "He's a little freak, but you can't blame him much. Don't be mad at him. He's never moved from that corner since he was born, I guess, and he's got nothing to do or to think of but just hearing what's happening outside. He's sort of crazy curious, and when he gets hold of a thing that suits him he just holds on to it till the last bell rings."

She said nothing whatever, and he paused a moment because he wanted to think over the best way to say the next thing.

"Mr. James Temple Barholm "—he ventured it with more delicacy of desire not to seem to "take liberties" than she would have credited him with—"saw his mother sitting with him in her arms at the cottage door a week or so after he was born. He stopped at the gate and talked to her about him, and he left him a sovereign. He's got it now. It seems a fortune to him. He's made a sort of idol of him. That's why he talks like he does. I wouldn't let it make me mad if I were you."

He did not know that she could not have answered him if she would, that she felt that if he did not stop she might fling herself down upon the wet heather and wail aloud.

"You don't like me," he began after they had walked a few steps farther. "You don't like me."

This was actually better. It choked back the sobs rising in her throat. The stupid shock of it, his tasteless foolishness, helped her by its very folly to a sort of defense against the disastrous wave of emotion she might not have been able to control. She gathered herself together.

"It must be an unusual experience," she answered.

"Well, it is—sort of," he said, but in a manner curiously free from fatuous swagger. "I've had luck that way. I guess it's been because I'd GOT to make friends so as I could earn a living. It seems sort of queer to know that some one's got a grouch against me that—that I can't get away with."

She looked up the avenue to see how much farther they must walk together, since she was not "a sprinter" and could not get away from him. She thought she caught a glimpse through the trees of a dog-cart driven by a groom, and hoped she had not mistaken and that it was driving in their direction.

"It must, indeed," she said, "though I am not sure I quite understand what a grouch is."

"When you've got a grouch against a fellow," he explained impersonally, "you want to get at him. You want to make him feel like a mutt; and a mutt's the worst kind of a fool. You've got one against me."

She looked before her between narrowed lids and faintly smiled—the most disagreeable smile she was capable of. And yet for some too extraordinary reason he went on. But she had seen men go on before this when all the odds were against them. Sometimes their madness took them this way.

"I knew there was a lot against me when I came here," he persisted. "I should have been a fool if I hadn't. I knew when you came that I was up against a pretty hard proposition; but I thought perhaps if I got busy and SHOWED you—you've got to SHOW a person—"

"Showed me what?" she asked contemptuously.

"Showed you—well—me," he tried to explain.

"You!"

"And that I wanted to be friends," he added candidly.

Was the man mad? Did he realize nothing? Was he too thick of skin even to see?

"Friends! You and I?" The words ought to have scorched him, pachyderm though he was.

"I thought you'd give me a chance—a sort of chance—"

She stopped short on the avenue.

"You did?"

She had not been mistaken. The dog-cart had rounded the far-off curve and was coming toward them. And the man went on talking.

"You've felt every minute that I was in a place that didn't belong to me. You know that if the man that it did belong to was here, you'd be here with him. You felt as if I'd robbed him of it—and I'd robbed you. It was your home—yours. You hated me too much to think of anything else. Suppose—suppose there was a way I could give it back to you—make it your home again."

His voice dropped and was rather unsteady. The fool, the gross, brutal, vulgar, hopeless fool! He thought this was the way to approach her, to lead her to listen to his proposal of marriage! Not for a second did she guess that they were talking at cross purposes. She did not know that as he kept himself steady under her contemptuousness he was thinking that Ann would have to own that he had been up against it hard and plenty while the thing was going on.

"I'm always up against it when I'm talking to you," he said. "You get me rattled. There's things I want to talk about and ask you. Suppose you give me a chance, and let us start out by being sort of friends."

"I am staying in your house," she answered in a deadly voice, "and I cannot go away because my mother will not let me. You can force yourself upon me, if you choose, because I cannot help it; but understand once for all that I will not give you your ridiculous chance. And I will not utter one word to you when I can avoid it."

He was silent for a moment and seemed to be thinking rather deeply. She realized now that he saw the nearing dog-cart.

"You won't. Then it's up to me," he said. Then with a change of tone, he added, "I'll stop the cart and tell the man to drive you to the house. I'm not going to force myself on you, as you call it. It'd be no use. Perhaps it'll come all right in the end."

He made a sign to the groom, who hastened his horse's pace and drew up when he reached them.

"Take this lady back to the house," he said.

The groom, who was a new arrival, began to prepare to get down and give up his place.

"You needn't do that," said Tembarom.

"Won't you get up and take the reins, sir?" the man asked uncertainly.

"No. I can't drive. You'll have to do it. I'll walk."

And to the groom's amazement, they left him standing under the trees looking after them.

"It's up to me," he was saying. "The whole durned thing's up to me."

CHAPTER XXVI

The neighborhood of Temple Barholm was not, upon the whole, a brilliant one. Indeed, it had been frankly designated by the casual guest as dull. The country was beautiful enough, and several rather large estates lay within reach of one another, but their owners were neither very rich nor especially notable personages. They were of extremely good old blood, and were of established respectability. None of them, however, was given to entertaining house parties made up of the smart and dazzlingly sinful world of fashion said by moralists to be composed entirely of young and mature beauties, male and female, capable of supplying at any moment enlivening detail for the divorce court—glittering beings whose wardrobes were astonishing and whose conversations were composed wholly of brilliant paradox and sparkling repartee.

Most of the residents took their sober season in London, the men of the family returning gladly to their pheasants, the women not regretfully to their gardens and tennis, because their successes in town had not been particularly delirious. The guests who came to them were generally as respectable and law-abiding as themselves, and introduced no iconoclastic diversions. For the greater portion of the year, in fact, diners out were of the neighborhood and met the neighborhood, and were reduced to discussing neighborhood topics, which was not, on the whole, a fevered joy. The Duke of Stone was, perhaps, the one man who might have furnished topics. Privately it was believed, and in part known, that he at least had had a brilliant, if not wholly unreprehensible, past. He might have introduced enlivening elements from London, even from Paris, Vienna, Berlin, and Rome; but the sobering influence of years of rheumatic gout and a not entirely sufficing income prevented activities, and his opinions of his social surroundings were vaguely guessed to be those of a not too lenient critic.

"I do not know anything technical or scientific about ditch-water," he had expressed himself in the bosom of his family. "I never analyzed it, but analyzers, I gather, consider it dull. If anything could be duller than ditch-water, I should say it was Stone Hover and its surrounding neighborhood." He had also remarked at another time: "If our society could be enriched by some of the characters who form the house parties and seem, in fact, integral parts of all country society in modern problem or even unproblem novels, how happy one might be, how edified and amused! A wicked lady or so of high, or extremely low, rank, of immense beauty and corruscating brilliancy; a lovely creature, male or female, whom she is bent upon undoing—"

"Dear papa!" protested Lady Celia.

"Reproach me, dearest. Reproach me as severely as you please. It inspires me. It makes me feel like a wicked, dangerous man, and I have not felt like one for many years. Such persons as I describe form the charm of existence, I assure you. A ruthless adventuress with any kind of good looks would be the making of us. Several of them, of different types, a handsome villain, and a few victims unknowing of their fate, would cause life to flow by like a peaceful stream."

Lady Edith laughed an unseemly little laugh—unseemly, since filial regret at paternal obliquity should have restrained it.

"Papa, you are quite horrible," she said. "You ought not to make your few daughters laugh at improper things."

"I would make my daughters laugh at anything so long as I must doom them to Stone Hover—and Lady Pevensy and Mrs. Stoughton and the rector, if one may mention names," he answered. "To see you laugh revives me by reminding me that once I was considered a witty person—quite so. Some centuries ago, however; about the time when things were being rebuilt after the flood."

In such circumstances it cannot be found amazing that a situation such as Temple Barholm presented should provide rich food for conversation, supposition, argument, and humorous comment.

T. Tembarom himself, after the duke had established him, furnished an unlimited source of interest. His household became a perennial fount of quiet discussion. Lady Mallowe and her daughter were the members of it who met with the most attention. They appeared to have become members of it rather than visitors. Her ladyship had plainly elected to extend her stay even beyond the period to which a fond relative might feel entitled to hospitality. She had been known to extend visits before with great cleverness, but this one assumed an established aspect. She was not going away, the neighborhood decided, until she had achieved that which she had come to accomplish. The present unconventional atmosphere of the place naturally supported her. And how probable it seemed, taking into consideration Captain Palliser's story, that Mr. Temple Barholm wished her to stay. Lady Joan would be obliged to stay also, if her mother intended that she should. But the poor American—there were some expressions of sympathy, though the situation was greatly added to by the feature—the poor American was being treated by Lady Joan as only she could treat a man. It was worth inviting the whole party to dinner or tea or lunch merely to see the two together. The manner in which she managed to ignore him and be scathing to him without apparently infringing a law of civility, and the number of laws she sometimes chose to sweep aside when it was her mood to do so, were extraordinary. If she had not been a beauty, with a sort of mystic charm for the male creature, surely he would have broken his chains. But he did not. What was he going to do in the end? What was she going to do? What was Lady Mallowe going to do if there was no end at all? He was not as unhappy-looking a lover as one might have expected, they said. He kept up his spirits wonderfully. Perhaps she was not always as icily indifferent to him as she chose to appear in public. Temple Barholm was a great estate, and Sir Moses Monaldini had been mentioned by rumor. Of course there would be something rather strange and tragic in it if she came to Temple Barholm as its mistress in such singular circumstances. But he certainly did not look depressed or discouraged. So they talked it over as they looked on.

"How they gossip! How delightfully they gossip!" said the duke. "But it is such a perfect subject. They have never been so enthralled before. Dear young man! how grateful we ought to be for him!"

One of the most discussed features of the case was the duke's own cultivation of the central figure. There was an actual oddity about it. He drove from Stone Hover to Temple Barholm repeatedly. He invited Tembarom to the castle and had long talks with him—long, comfortable talks in secluded, delightful rooms or under great trees on a lawn. He wanted to hear anecdotes of his past, to draw him on to giving his points of view. When he spoke of him to his daughters, he called him "T. Tembarom," but the slight derision of his earlier tone modified itself.

"That delightful young man will shortly become my closest intimate," he said. "He not only keeps up my spirits, but he opens up vistas. Vistas after a man's seventy-second birthday! At times I could clasp him to my breast."

"I like him first rate," Tembarom said to Miss Alicia. "I liked him the minute he got up laughing like an old sport when he fell out of the pony carriage."

As he became more intimate with him, he liked him still better. Obscured though it was by airy, elderly persiflage, he began to come upon a background of stability and points of view wholly to be relied on in his new acquaintance. It had evolved itself out of long and varied experience, with the aid of brilliant mentality. The old peer's reasons were always logical. He laughed at most things, but at a few he did not laugh at all. After several of the long conversations Tembarom began to say to himself that this seemed like a man you need not be afraid to talk things over with—things you didn't want to speak of to everybody.

"Seems to me," he said thoughtfully to Miss Alicia, "he's an old fellow you could tie to. I've got on to one thing when I've listened to him: he talks all he wants to and laughs a lot, but he never gives himself away. He wouldn't give another fellow away either if he said he wouldn't. He knows how not to."

There was an afternoon on which during a drive they took together the duke was enlightened as to several points which had given him cause for reflection, among others the story beloved of Captain Palliser and his audiences.

"I guess you've known a good many women," T. Tembarom remarked on this occasion after a few minutes of thought. "Living all over the world as you've done, you'd be likely to come across a whole raft of them one time and another."

"A whole raft of them, one time and another," agreed the duke. "Yes."

"You've liked them, haven't you?"

"Immensely. Sometimes a trifle disastrously. Find me a more absolutely interesting object in the universe than a woman—any woman—and I will devote the remainder of my declining years to the study of it," answered his grace.

He said it with a decision which made T. Tembarom turn to look at him, and after his look decide to proceed.

"Have you ever known a bit of a slim thing"—he made an odd embracing gesture with his arm—"the size that you could pick up with one hand and set on your knee as if she was a child"—the duke remained still, knowing this was only the beginning and pricking up his ears as he took a rapid kaleidoscopic view of all the "Ladies" in the neighborhood, and as hastily waved them aside—"a bit of a thing that some way seems to mean it all to you—and moves the world?" The conclusion was one which brought the incongruous touch of maturity into his face.

"Not one of the 'Ladies,'" the duke was mentally summing the matter up. "Certainly not Lady Joan, after all. Not, I think, even the young person in the department store."

He leaned back in his corner the better to inspect his companion directly.

"You have, I see," he replied quietly. "Once I myself did." (He had cried out, "Ah! Heloise!" though he had laughed at himself when he seemed facing his ridiculous tragedy.)

"Yes," confessed T. Tembarom. "I met her at the boarding-house where I lived. Her father was a Lancashire man and an inventor. I guess you've heard of him; his name is Joseph Hutchinson."

The whole country had heard of him; more countries, indeed, than one had heard. He was the man who was going to make his fortune in America because T. Tembarom had stood by him in his extremity. He would make a fortune in America and another in England and possibly several others on the Continent. He had learned to read in the village school, and the girl was his daughter.

"Yes," replied the duke.

"I don't know whether the one you knew had that quiet little way of seeing right straight into a thing, and making you see it, too," said Tembarom.

"She had," answered the duke, and an odd expression wavered in his eyes because he was looking backward across forty years which seemed a hundred.

"That's what I meant by moving the world," T. Tembarom went on. "You know she's RIGHT, and you've got to do what she says, if you love her."

"And you always do," said the duke—"always and forever. There are very few. They are the elect."

T. Tembarom took it gravely.

"I said to her once that there wasn't more than one of her in the world because there couldn't be enough to make two of that kind. I wasn't joshing either; I meant it. It's her quiet little voice and her quiet, babyfied eyes that get you where you can't move. And it's something else you don't know anything about. It's her never doing anything for herself, but just doing it because it's the right thing for you."

The duke's chin had sunk a little on his breast, and looking back across the hundred years, he forgot for a moment where he was. The one he remembered had been another man's wife, a little angel brought up in a convent by white-souled nuns, passed over by her people to an elderly vaurien of great magnificence, and she had sent the strong, laughing, impassioned young English peer away before it was too late, and with the young, young eyes of her looking upward at him in that way which saw "straight into a thing" and with that quiet little voice. So long ago! So long ago!

"Ah! Heloise!" he sighed unconsciously.

"What did you say?" asked T. Tembarom. The duke came back.

"I was thinking of the time when I was nine and twenty," he answered. "It was not yesterday nor even the day before. The one I knew died when she was twenty-four."

"Died!" said Tembarom. "Good Lord!" He dropped his head and even changed color. "A fellow can't get on to a thing like that. It seems as if it couldn't happen. Suppose—" he caught his breath hard and then pulled himself up—"Nothing could happen to her before she knew that I've proved what I said—just proved it, and done every single thing she told me to do."

"I am sure you have," the duke said.

"It's because of that I began to say this." Tembarom spoke hurriedly that he might thrust away the sudden dark thought. "You're a man, and I'm a man; far away ahead of me as you are, you're a man, too. I was crazy to get her to marry me and come here with me, and she wouldn't."

The duke's eyes lighted anew.

"She had her reasons," he said.

"She laid 'em out as if she'd been my mother instead of a little red-headed angel that you wanted to snatch up and crush up to you so she couldn't breathe. She didn't waste a word. She just told me what I was up against. She'd lived in the village with her grandmother, and she knew. She said I'd got to come and find out for myself what no one else could teach me. She told me about the kind of girls I'd see—beauties that were different from anything I'd ever seen before. And it was up to me to see all of them—the best of them."

"Ladies?" interjected the duke gently.

"Yes. With titles like those in novels, she said, and clothes like those in the Ladies' Pictorial. The kind of girls, she said, that would make her look like a housemaid. Housemaid be darned!" he exclaimed, suddenly growing hot. "I've seen the whole lot of them; I've done my darndest to get next, and there's not one—" he stopped short. "Why should any of them look at me, anyhow?" he added suddenly.

"That was not her point," remarked the duke. "She wanted you to look at them, and you have looked." T. Tembarom's eagerness was inspiring to behold.

"I have, haven't I?" he cried. "That was what I wanted to ask you. I've done as she said. I haven't shirked a thing. I've followed them around when I knew they hadn't any use on earth for me. Some of them have handed me the lemon pretty straight. Why shouldn't they? But I don't believe she knew how tough it might be for a fellow sometimes."

"No, she did not," the duke said. "Also she probably did not know that in ancient days of chivalry ladies sent forth their knights to bear buffeting for their sakes in proof of fealty. Rise up, Sir Knight!" This last phrase of course T. Tembarom did not know the poetic significance of.

To his hearer Palliser's story became an amusing thing, read in the light of this most delicious frankness. It was Palliser himself who played the fool, and not T. Tembarom, who had simply known what he wanted, and had, with businesslike directness, applied himself to finding a method of obtaining it.

The young women he gave his time to must be "Ladies" because Miss Hutchinson had required it from him. The female flower of the noble houses had been passed in review before him to practise upon, so to speak. The handsomer they were, the more dangerously charming, the better Miss Hutchinson would be pleased. And he had been regarded as a presumptuous aspirant. It was a situation for a comedy. But the "Ladies" would not enjoy it if they were told. It was also not the Duke of Stone who would tell them. They could not in the least understand the subtlety of the comedy in which they had unconsciously taken part. Ann Hutchinson's grandmother curtsied to them in her stiff old way when they passed. Ann Hutchinson had gone to the village school and been presented with prizes for needlework and good behavior. But what a girl she must be, the slim bit of a thing with a red head! What a clear-headed and firm little person!

In courts he had learned to wear a composed countenance when he was prompted to smile, and he wore one now. He enjoyed the society of T. Tembarom increasingly every hour. He provided him with every joy.

Their drive was a long one, and they talked a good deal. They talked of the Hutchinsons, of the invention, of the business "deals" Tembarom had entered into at the outset, and of their tremendously encouraging result. It was not mere rumor that Hutchinson would end by being a rich man. The girl would be an heiress. How complex her position would be! And being of the elect who unknowingly bear with them the power that "moves the world," how would she affect Temple Barholm and its surrounding neighborhood?

"I wish to God she was here now!" exclaimed Tembarom, suddenly.

It had been an interesting talk, but now and then the duke had wondered if, as it went on, his companion was as wholly at his ease as was usual with him. An occasional shade of absorption in his expression, as if he were thinking of two things at once despite himself, a hint of restlessness, revealed themselves occasionally. Was there something more he was speculating on the possibility of saying, something more to tell or explain? If there was, let him take his time. His audience, at all events, was possessed of perceptions. This somewhat abrupt exclamation might open the way.

"That is easily understood, my dear fellow," replied the duke.

"There's times when you want a little thing like that just to talk things over with, just to ask, because you—you're dead sure she'd never lose her head and give herself away without knowing she was doing it. She could just keep still and let the waves roll over her and be standing there ready and quiet when the tide had passed. It's the keeping your mouth shut that's so hard for most people, the not saying a darned thing, whatever happens, till just the right time."

"Women cannot often do it," said the duke. "Very few men can."

"You're right," Tembarom answered, and there was a trifle of anxiety in his tone.

"There's women, just the best kind, that you daren't tell a big thing to. Not that they'd mean to give it away—perhaps they wouldn't know when they did it—but they'd feel so anxious they'd get—they'd get—"

"Rattled," put in the duke, and knew who he was thinking of. He saw Miss Alicia's delicate, timid face as he spoke.

T. Tembarom laughed.

"That's just it," he answered. "They wouldn't go back on you for worlds, but—well, you have to be careful with them."

"He's got something on his mind," mentally commented the duke. "He wonders if he will tell it to me."

"And there's times when you'd give half you've got to be able to talk a thing out and put it up to some one else for a while. I could do it with her. That's why I said I wish to God that she was here."

"You have learned to know how to keep still," the duke said. "So have I. We learned it in different schools, but we have both learned."

As he was saying the words, he thought he was going to hear something; when he had finished saying them he knew that he would without a doubt. T. Tembarom made a quick move in his seat; he lost a shade of color and cleared his throat as he bent forward, casting a glance at the backs of the coachman and footman on the high seat above them.

"Can those fellows hear me?" he asked.

"No," the duke answered; "if you speak as you are speaking now."

"You are the biggest man about here," the young man went on. "You stand for everything that English people care for, and you were born knowing all the things I don't. I've been carrying a big load for quite a while, and I guess I'm not big enough to handle it alone, perhaps. Anyhow, I want to be sure I'm not making fool mistakes. The worst of it is that I've got to keep still if I'm right, and I've got to keep still if I'm wrong. I've got to keep still, anyhow."

"I learned to hold my tongue in places where, if I had not held it, I might have plunged nations into bloodshed," the duke said. "Tell me all you choose."

As a result of which, by the time their drive had ended and they returned to Stone Hover, he had told him, and, the duke sat in his corner of the carriage with an unusual light in his eyes and a flush of somewhat excited color on his cheek.

"You're a queer fellow, T. Tembarom," he said when they parted in the drawing-room after taking tea. "You exhilarate me. You make me laugh. If I were an emotional person, you would at moments make me cry. There's an affecting uprightness about you. You're rather a fine fellow too, 'pon my life." Putting a waxen, gout-knuckled old hand on his shoulder, and giving him a friendly push which was half a pat, he added, "You are, by God!"

And after his guest had left him, the duke stood for some minutes gazing into the fire with a complicated smile and the air of a man who finds himself quaintly enriched.

"I have had ambitions in the course of my existence—several of them," he said, "but even in over-vaulting moments never have I aspired to such an altitude as this—to be, as it were, part of a melodrama. One feels that one scarcely deserves it."

CHAPTER XXVII

"Mr. Temple Barholm seems in better spirits," Lady Mallowe said to Captain Palliser as they walked on the terrace in the starlight dusk after dinner.

Captain Palliser took his cigar from his mouth and looked at the glowing end of it.

"Has it struck you that he has been in low spirits?" he inquired speculatively. "One does not usually connect him with depression."

"Certainly not with depression. He's an extraordinary creature. One would think he would perish from lack of the air he is used to breathing—New York air."

"He is not perishing. He's too shrewd," returned Palliser. "He mayn't exactly like all this, but he's getting something out of it."

"He is not getting much of what he evidently wants most. I am out of all patience," said Lady Mallowe.

Her acquaintance with Palliser had lasted through a number of years. They argued most matters from the same basis of reasoning. They were at times almost candid with each other. It may be acknowledged, however, that of the two Lady Mallowe was the more inclined to verge on self-revelation. This was of course because she was the less clever and had more temper. Her temper, she had, now and then, owned bitterly to herself, had played her tricks. Captain Palliser's temper never did this. It was Lady Mallowe's temper which spoke now, but she did not in the least mind his knowing that Joan was exasperating her beyond endurance. He knew the whole situation well enough to be aware of it without speech on her part. He had watched similar situations several times before.

"Her manner toward him is, to resort to New York colloquialisms, 'the limit,'" Palliser said quietly. "Is it your idea that his less good spirits have been due to Lady Joan's ingenuities? They are ingenious, you know."

"They are devilish," exclaimed her mother. "She treads him in the mire and sails about professing to be conducting herself flawlessly. She is too clever for me," she added with bitterness.

Palliser laughed softly.

"But very often you have been too clever for her," he suggested. "For my part, I don't quite see how you got her here."

Lady Mallowe became not almost, but entirely, candid.

"Upon the whole, I don't quite know myself. I believe she really came for some mysterious reason of her own."

"That is rather my impression," said Palliser. "She has got something up her sleeve, and so has he."

"He!" Lady Mallowe quite ejaculated the word. "She always has. That's her abominable secretive way. But he! T. Tembarom with something up his sleeve! One can't imagine it."

"Almost everybody has. I found that out long years ago," said Palliser, looking at his cigar end again as if consulting it. "Since I arrived at the conclusion, I always take it for granted, and look out for it. I've become rather clever in following such things up, and I have taken an unusual interest in T. Tembarom from the first."

Lady Mallowe turned her handsome face, much softened by an enwreathing gauze scarf, toward him anxiously.

"Do you think his depression, or whatever it is, means Joan?" she asked.

"If he is depressed by her, you need not be discouraged," smiled Palliser. "The time to lose hope would be when, despite her ingenuities, he became entirely cheerful. But," he added after a moment of pause, "I have an idea there is some other little thing."

"Do you suppose that some young woman he has left behind in New York is demanding her rights?" said Lady Mallowe, with annoyance. "That is exactly the kind of thing Joan would like to hear, and so entirely natural. Some shop-girl or other."

"Quite natural, as you say; but he would scarcely be running up to London and consulting Scotland Yard about her," Palliser answered.

"Scotland Yard!" ejaculated his companion. "How in the world did you find that out?"

Captain Palliser did not explain how he had done it. Presumably his knowledge was due to the adroitness of the system of "following such things up."

"Scotland Yard has also come to him," he went on. "Did you chance to see a red-faced person who spent a morning with him last week?"

"He looked like a butcher, and I thought he might be one of his friends," Lady Mallowe said.

"I recognized the man. He is an extremely clever detective, much respected for his resources in the matter of following clues which are so attenuated as to be scarcely clues at all."

"Clues have no connection with Joan," said Lady Mallowe, still more annoyed. "All London knows her miserable story."

"Have you—" Captain Palliser's tone was thoughtful, "—has any one ever seen Mr. Strangeways?"

"No. Can you imagine anything more absurdly romantic? A creature without a memory, shut up in a remote wing of a palace like this, as if he were the Man with the Iron Mask. Romance is not quite compatible with T. Tembarom."

"It is so incongruous that it has entertained me to think it over a good deal," remarked Palliser. "He leaves everything to one's imagination. All one knows is that he isn't a relative; that he isn't mad, but only too nervous to see or be seen. Queer situation. I've found there is always a reason for things; the queerer they are, the more sure it is that there's a reason. What is the reason Strangeways is kept here, and where would a detective come in? Just on general principles I'm rather going into the situation. There's a reason, and it would be amusing to find it out. Don't you think so?"

He spoke casually, and Lady Mallowe's answer was casual, though she knew from experience that he was not as casual as he chose to seem. He was clever enough always to have certain reasons of his own which formulated themselves into interests large and small. He knew things about people which were useful. Sometimes quite small things were useful. He was always well behaved, and no one had ever accused him of bringing pressure to bear; but it was often possible for him to sell things or buy things or bring about things in circumstances which would have presented difficulties to other people. Lady Mallowe knew from long experience all about the exigencies of cases when "needs must," and she was not critical. Temple Barholm as the estate of a distant relative and T. Tembarom as its owner were not assets to deal with indifferently. When a man made a respectable living out of people who could be persuaded to let you make investments for them, it was not an unbusinesslike idea to be in the position to advise an individual strongly.

"It's quite natural that you should feel an interest," she answered. "But the romantic stranger is too romantic, though I will own Scotland Yard is a little odd."

"Yes, that is exactly what I thought," said Palliser.

He had in fact thought a good deal and followed the thing up in a quiet, amateur way, though with annoyingly little result. Occasionally he had felt rather a fool for his pains, because he had been led to so few facts of importance and had found himself so often confronted by T. Tembarom's entirely frank grin. His own mental attitude was not a complex one. Lady Mallowe's summing up had been correct enough on the whole. Temple

Barholm ought to be a substantial asset, regarded in its connection with its present owner. Little dealings in stocks—sometimes rather large ones when luck was with him—had brought desirable returns to Captain Palliser throughout a number of years. Just now he was taking an interest in a somewhat imposing scheme, or what might prove an imposing one if it were managed properly and presented to the right persons. If T. Tembarom had been sufficiently lured by the spirit of speculation to plunge into old Hutchinson's affair, as he evidently had done, he was plainly of the temperament attracted by the game of chance. There had been no reason but that of temperament which could have led him to invest. He had found himself suddenly a moneyed man and had liked the game. Never having so much as heard of Little Ann Hutchinson, Captain Palliser not unnaturally argued after this wise. There seemed no valid reason why, if a vague invention had allured, a less vague scheme, managed in a more businesslike manner, should not. This Mexican silver and copper mine was a dazzling thing to talk about. He could go into details. He had, in fact, allowed a good deal of detail to trail through his conversation at times. It had not been difficult to accomplish this in his talks with Lady Mallowe in his host's presence. Lady Mallowe was always ready to talk of mines, gold, silver, or copper. It happened at times that one could manage to secure a few shares without the actual payment of money. There were little hospitalities or social amiabilities now and then which might be regarded as value received. So she had made it easy for Captain Palliser to talk, and T. Tembarom had heard much which would have been of interest to the kind of young man he appeared to be. Sometimes he had listened absorbedly, and on a few occasions he had asked a few questions which laid him curiously bare in his role of speculator. If he had no practical knowledge of the ways and means of great mining companies, he at least professed none. At all events, if there was any little matter he preferred to keep to himself, there was no harm in making oneself familiar with its aspect and significance. A man's arguments, so far as he himself is concerned, assume the character with which his own choice of adjectives and adverbs labels them. That is, if he labels them. The most astute do not. Captain Palliser did not. He dealt merely with reasoning processes which were applicable to the subject in hand, whatsoever its nature. He was a practical man of the world—a gentleman, of course. It was necessary to adjust matters without romantic hair-splitting. It was all by the way.

T. Tembarom had at the outset seemed to present, so to speak, no surface. Palliser had soon ceased to be at all sure that his social ambitions were to be relied on as a lever. Besides which, when the old Duke of Stone took delighted possession of him, dined with him, drove with him, sat and gossiped with him by the hour, there was not much one could offer him. Strangeways had at first meant only eccentricity. A little later he had occasionally faintly stirred curiosity, and perhaps the fact that Burrill enjoyed him as a grievance and a mystery had stimulated the stirring. The veriest chance had led him to find himself regarding the opening up of possible vistas.

From a certain window in a certain wing of the house a much-praised view was to be seen. Nothing was more natural than that on the occasion of a curious sunset Palliser should, in coming from his room, decide to take a look at it. As he passed through a corridor Pearson came out of a room near him.

"How is Mr. Strangeways to-day?" Palliser asked.

"Not quite so well, I am afraid, sir," was the answer.

"Sorry to hear it," replied Palliser, and passed on.

On his return he walked somewhat slowly down the corridor. As he turned into it he thought he heard the murmur of voices. One was that of T. Tembarom, and he was evidently using argument. It sounded as if he were persuading some one to agree with him, and the persuasion was earnest. He was not arguing with Pearson or a housemaid. Why was he arguing with his pensioner? His voice was as low as it was eager, and the other man's replies were not to be heard. Only just after Palliser had passed the door there broke out an appeal which was a sort of cry.

"No! My God, no! Don't send me away? Don't send me away!"

One could not, even if so inclined, stand and listen near a door while servants might chance to be wandering about. Palliser went on his way with a sense of having been slightly startled.

"He wants to get rid of him, and the fellow is giving him trouble," he said to himself. "That voice is not American. Not in the least." It set him thinking and observing. When Tembarom wore the look which was not a look of depression, but of something more puzzling, he thought that he could guess at its reason. By the time he talked with Lady Mallowe he had gone much further than he chose to let her know.

CHAPTER XXVIII

The popularity of Captain Palliser's story of the "Ladies" had been great at the outset, but with the passage of time it had oddly waned. This had resulted from the story's ceasing to develop itself, as the simplest intelligence might have anticipated, by means of the only person capable of its proper development. The person in question was of course T. Tembarom. Expectations, amusing expectations, of him had been raised, and he had singularly failed in the fulfilling of them. The neighborhood had, so to speak, stood upon tiptoe,—the feminine portion of it, at least,—looking over shoulders to get the first glimpses of what would inevitably take place.

As weeks flew by, the standing on tiptoe became a thing of the past. The whole thing flattened out most disappointingly. No attack whatever was made upon the "Ladies." That the Duke of Stone had immensely taken up Mr. Temple Barholm had of course resulted in his being accepted in such a manner as gave him many opportunities to encounter one and all. He appeared at dinners, teas, and garden parties. Miss Alicia, whom he had in some occult manner impressed upon people until they found themselves actually paying a sort of court to her, was always his companion.

"One realizes one cannot possibly leave her out of anything," had been said. "He has somehow established her as if she were his mother or his aunt—or his interpreter. And such clothes, my dear, one doesn't behold. Worth and Paquin and Doucet must go sleepless for weeks to invent them. They are without a flaw in shade or line or texture." Which was true, because Mrs. Mellish of the Bond Street shop had become quite obsessed by her idea and committed extravagances Miss Alicia offered up contrite prayer to atone for, while Tembarom, simply chortling in his glee, signed checks to pay for their exquisite embodiment. That he was not reluctant to avail himself of social opportunities was made manifest by the fact that he never refused an invitation. He appeared upon any spot to which hospitality bade him, and unashamedly placed himself on record as a neophyte upon almost all occasions. His well-cut clothes began in time to wear more the air of garments belonging to him, but his hat made itself remarked by its trick of getting pushed back on his head or tilted on side, and his New York voice and accent rang out sharp and finely nasal in the midst of low-pitched, throaty, or mellow English enunciations. He talked a good deal at times because he found himself talked to by people who either wanted to draw him out or genuinely wished to hear the things he would be likely to say.

That the hero of Palliser's story should so comport himself as to provide either diversion or cause for haughty displeasure would have been only a natural outcome of his ambitions. In a brief period of time, however, every young woman who might have expected to find herself an object of such ambitions realized that his methods of approach and attack were not marked by the usual characteristics of aspirants of his class. He evidently desired to see and be seen. He presented himself, as it were, for inspection and consideration, but while he was attentive, he did not press attentions upon any one. He did not make advances in the ordinary sense of the word. He never essayed flattering or even admiring remarks. He said queer things at which one often could not help but laugh, but he somehow wore no air of saying them with the intention of offering them as witticisms which might be regarded as allurements. He did not ogle, he did not simper or shuffle about nervously and turn red or pale, as eager and awkward youths have a habit of doing under the stress of unrequited admiration. In the presence of a certain slightingness of treatment, which he at the outset met with not infrequently, he conducted himself with a detached good nature which seemed to take but small account of attitudes less unoffending than his own. When the slightingness disappeared from sheer lack of anything to slight, he did not change his manner in any degree.

"He is not in the least forward," Beatrice Talchester said, the time arriving when she and her sisters occasionally talked him over with their special friends, the Granthams, "and he is not forever under one's feet, as the pushing sort usually is. Do you remember those rich people from the place they called Troy—the ones who took Burnaby for a year—and the awful eldest son who perpetually invented excuses for calling, bringing books and ridiculous things?"

"This one never makes an excuse," Amabel Grantham put in.

"But he never declines an invitation. There is no doubt that he wants to see people," said Lady Honora, with the pretty little nose and the dimples. She had ceased to turn up the pretty little nose, and she showed a dimple as she added: "Gwynedd is tremendously taken with him. She is teaching him to play croquet. They spend hours together."

"He's beginning to play a pretty good game," said Gwynedd. "He's not stupid, at all events."

"I believe you are the first choice, if he is really choosing," Amabel Grantham decided. "I should like to ask you a question."

"Ask it, by all means," said Gwynedd.

"Does he ever ask you to show him how to hold his mallet, and then do idiotic things, such as managing to touch your hand?"

"Never," was Gwynedd's answer. "The young man from Troy used to do it, and then beg pardon and turn red."

"I don't understand him, or I don't understand Captain Palliser's story," Amabel Grantham argued. "Lucy and I are quite out of the running, but I honestly believe that he takes as much notice of us as he does of any of you. If he has intentions, he 'doesn't act the part,' which is pure New York of the first water."

"He said, however, that the things that mattered were not only titles, but looks. He asked how many of us were 'lookers.' Don't be modest, Amabel. Neither you nor Lucy are out of the running," Beatrice amiably suggested.

"Ladies first," commented Amabel, pertly. There was no objection to being supported in one's suspicion that, after all, one was a "looker."

"There may be a sort of explanation," Honora put the idea forward somewhat thoughtfully. "Captain Palliser insists that he is much shrewder than he seems. Perhaps he is cautious, and is looking us all over before he commits himself."

"He is a Temple Barholm, after all," said Gwynedd, with boldness. "He's rather good looking. He has the nicest white teeth and the most cheering grin I ever saw, and he's as 'rich as grease is,' as I heard a housemaid say one day. I'm getting quite resigned to his voice, or it is improving, I don't know which. If he only knew the mere A B C of ordinary people like ourselves, and he committed himself to me, I wouldn't lay my hand on my heart and say that one might not think him over."

"I told you she was tremendously taken with him," said her sister. "It's come to this."

"But," said Lady Gwynedd, "he is not going to commit himself to any of us, incredible as it may seem. The one person he stares at sometimes is Joan Fayre, and he only looks at her as if he were curious and wouldn't object to finding out why she treats him so outrageously. He isn't annoyed; he's only curious."

"He's been adored by salesladies in New York," said Honora, "and he can't understand it."

"He's been liked," Amabel Grantham summed him up. "He's a likable thing. He's even rather a dear. I've begun to like him myself."

"I hear you are learning to play croquet," the Duke of Stone remarked to him a day or so later. "How do you like it?"

"Lady Gwynedd Talchester is teaching me," Tembarom answered. "I'd learn to iron shirt-waists if she would give me lessons. She's one of the two that have dimples," he added, reflection in his tone. "I guess that'll count. Shouldn't you think it would?"

"Miss Hutchinson?" queried the duke.

Tembarom nodded.

"Yes, it's always her," he answered without a ray of humor. "I just want to stack 'em up."

"You are doing it," the duke replied with a slightly twisted mouth. There were, in fact, moments when he might have fallen into fits of laughter while Tembarom was seriousness itself. "I must, however, call your attention to the fact that there is sometimes in your manner a hint of a businesslike pursuit of a fixed object which you must beware of. The Lady Gwynedds might not enjoy the situation if they began to suspect. If they decided to flout you,—'to throw you down,' I ought to say—where would little Miss Hutchinson be?"

Tembarom looked startled and disturbed.

"Say," he exclaimed, "do I ever look that way? I must do better than that. Anyhow, it ain't all put on. I'm doing my stunt, of course, but I like them. They're mighty nice to me when you consider what they're up against. And those two with the dimples,—Lady Gwynned and Lady Honora, are just peaches. Any fellow might"—he stopped and looked serious again—"That's why they'd count," he added.

They were having one of their odd long talks under a particularly splendid copper beech which provided the sheltered out-of-door corner his grace liked best. When they took their seats together in this retreat, it was mysteriously understood that they were settling themselves down to enjoyment of their own, and must not be disturbed.

"When I am comfortable and entertained," Moffat, the house steward, had quoted his master as saying, "you may mention it if the castle is in flames; but do not annoy me with excitement and flurry. Ring the bell in the courtyard, and call up the servants to pass buckets; but until the lawn catches fire, I must insist on being left alone."

"What dear papa talks to him about, and what he talks about to dear papa," Lady Celia had more than once murmured in her gently remote, high-nosed way, "I cannot possibly imagine. Sometimes when I have passed them on my way to the croquet lawn I have really seen them both look as absorbed as people in a play. Of course it is very good for papa. It has had quite a marked effect on his digestion. But isn't it odd!"

"I wish," Lady Edith remarked almost wistfully, "that I could get on better with him myself conversationally. But I don't know what to talk about, and it makes me nervous."

Their father, on the contrary, found in him unique resources, and this afternoon it occurred to him that he had never so far heard him express himself freely on the subject of Palliser. If led to do so, he would probably reveal that he had views of Captain Palliser of which he might not have been suspected, and the manner in which they would unfold themselves would more than probably be illuminating. The duke was, in fact, serenely sure that he required neither warning nor advice, and he had no intention of offering either. He wanted to hear the views.

"Do you know," he said as he stirred his tea, "I've been thinking about Palliser, and it has occurred to me more than once that I should like to hear just how he strikes you?"

"What I got on to first was how I struck him," answered Tembarom, with a reasonable air. "That was dead easy."

There was no hint of any vaunt of superior shrewdness. His was merely the level-toned manner of an observer of facts in detail.

"He has given you an opportunity of seeing a good deal of him," the duke added. "What do you gather from him—unless he has made up his mind that you shall not gather anything at all?"

"A fellow like that couldn't fix it that way, however much he wanted to," Tembarom answered again reasonably. "Just his trying to do it would give him away."

"You mean you have gathered things?"

"Oh, I've gathered enough, though I didn't go after it. It hung on the bushes. Anyhow, it seemed to me that way. I guess you run up against that kind everywhere. There's stacks of them in New York—different shapes and sizes."

"If you met a man of his particular shape and size in New York, how would you describe him?" the duke asked.

"I should never have met him when I was there. He wouldn't have come my way. He'd have been on Wall Street, doing high-class bucket-shop business, or he'd have had a swell office selling copper-mines—any old kind of mine that's going to make ten million a minute, the sort of deal he's in now. If he'd been the kind I might have run up against," he added with deliberation, "he wouldn't have been as well dressed or as well spoken. He'd have been either flashy or down at heel. You'd have called him a crook."

The duke seemed pleased with his tea as, after having sipped it, he put it down on the table at his side.

"A crook?" he repeated. "I wonder if that word is altogether American?"

"It's not complimentary, but you asked me," said Tembarom. "But I don't believe you asked me because you thought I wasn't on to him."

"Frankly speaking, no," answered the duke. "Does he talk to you about the mammoth mines and the rubber forests?"

"Say, that's where he wins out with me," Tembarom replied admiringly. "He gets in such fine work that I switch him on to it whenever I want cheering up. It makes me sorter forget things that worry me just to see a man act the part right up to the top notch the way he does it. The very way his clothes fit, the style he's got his hair brushed, and that swell, careless lounge of his, are half of the make-up. You see, most of us couldn't mistake him for anything else but just what he looks like—a gentleman visiting round among his friends and a million miles from wanting to butt in with business. The thing that first got me interested was watching how he slid in the sort of guff he wanted you to get worked up about and think over. Why, if I'd been what I look like to him, he'd have had my pile long ago, and he wouldn't be loafing round here any more."

"What do you think you look like to him?" his host inquired.

"I look as if I'd eat out of his hand," Tembarom answered, quite unbiased by any touch of wounded vanity. "Why shouldn't I? And I'm not trying to wake him up, either. I like to look that way to him and to his sort. It gives me a chance to watch and get wise to things. He's a high-school education in himself. I like to hear him talk. I asked him to come and stay at the house so that I could hear him talk."

"Did he introduce the mammoth mines in his first call?" the duke inquired.

"Oh, I don't mean that kind of talk. I didn't know how much good I was going to get out of him at first. But he was the kind I hadn't known, and it seemed like he was part of the whole thing—like the girls with title that Ann said I must get next to. And an easy way of getting next to the man kind was to let him come and stay. He wanted to, all right. I guess that's the way he lives when he's down on his luck, getting invited to stay at places. Like Lady Mallowe," he added, quite without prejudice.

"You do sum them up, don't you?" smiled the duke.

"Well, I don't see how I could help it," he said impartially. "They're printed in sixty-four point black-face, seems to me."

"What is that?" the duke inquired with interest. He thought it might be a new and desirable bit of slang. "I don't know that one."

"Biggest type there is," grinned Tembarom. "It's the kind that's used for head-lines. That's newspaper-office talk."

"Ah, technical, I see. What, by the way, is the smallest lettering called?" his grace followed up.

"Brilliant," answered Tembarom.

"You," remarked the duke, "are not printed in sixty-four-point black-face so far as they are concerned. You are not even brilliant. They don't find themselves able to sum you up. That fact is one of my recreations."

"I'll tell you why," Tembarom explained with his clearly unprejudiced air. "There's nothing much about me to sum up, anyhow. I'm too sort of plain sailing and ordinary. I'm not making for anywhere they'd think I'd want to go. I'm not hiding anything they'd be sure I'd want to hide."

"By the Lord! you're not!" exclaimed the duke.

"When I first came here, every one of them had a fool idea I'd want to pretend I'd never set eyes on a newsboy or a boot-black, and that I couldn't find my way in New York when I got off Fifth Avenue. I used to see them thinking they'd got to look as if they believed it, if they wanted to keep next. When I just let out and showed I didn't care a darn and hadn't sense enough to know that it mattered, it nearly made them throw a fit. They had to turn round and fix their faces all over again and act like it was 'interesting.' That's what Lady Mallowe calls it. She says it's so 'interesting!'"

"It is," commented the duke.

"Well, you know that, but she doesn't. Not on your life! I guess it makes her about sick to think of it and have to play that it's just what you'd want all your men friends to have done. Now, Palliser—" he paused and grinned again. He was sitting in a most casual attitude, his hands clasped round one up-raised knee, which he nursed, balancing himself. It was a position of informal ease which had an air of assisting enjoyable reflection.

"Yes, Palliser? Don't let us neglect Palliser," his host encouraged him.

"He's in a worse mix-up than the rest because he's got more to lose. If he could work this mammoth-mine song and dance with the right people, there'd be money enough in it to put him on Easy Street. That's where he's aiming for. The company's just where it has to have a boost. It's just GOT to. If it doesn't, there'll be a bust up that may end in fitting out a high-toned promoter or so in a striped yellow-and-black Jersey suit and set him to breaking rocks or playing with oakum. I'll tell you, poor old Palliser gets the Willies sometimes after he's read his mail. He turns the color of ecru baby Irish. That's a kind of lace I got a dressmaker to tell me about when I wrote up receptions and dances for the Sunday Earth. Ecru baby Irish—that's Palliser's color after he's read his letters."

"I dare say the fellow's in a devil of a mess, if the truth were known," the duke said.

"And here's 'T. T.,' hand-made and hand-painted for the part of the kind of sucker he wants." T. Tembarom's manner was almost sympathetic in its appreciation. "I can tell you I'm having a real good time with Palliser. It looked like I'd just dropped from heaven when he first saw me. If he'd been the praying kind, I'd have been just the sort he'd have prayed for when he said his `Now-I-lay-me's' before he went to bed. There wasn't a chance in a hundred that I wasn't a fool that had his head swelled so that he'd swallow any darned thing if you handed it to him smooth enough. First time he called he asked me a lot of questions about New York business. That was pretty smart of him. He wanted to find out, sort of careless, how much I knew—or how little."

The duke was leaning back luxuriously in his chair and gazing at him as he might have gazed at the work of an old master of which each line and shade was of absorbing interest.

"I can see him," he said. "I can see him."

"He found out I knew nothing," Tembarom continued. "And what was to hinder him trying to teach me something, by gee! Nothing on top of the green earth. I was there, waiting with my mouth open, it seemed like."

"And he has tried—in his best manner?" said his grace.

"What he hasn't tried wouldn't be worthy trying," Tembarom answered cheerfully. "Sometimes it seems like a shame to waste it. I've got so I know how to start him when he doesn't know I'm doing it. I tell you, he's fine. Gentlemanly—that's his way, you know. High-toned friend that just happens to know of a good thing and thinks enough of you in a sort of reserved way to feel like it's a pity not to give you a chance to come in on the ground floor, if you've got the sense to see the favor he's friendly enough to do you. It's such a favor that it'd just disgust a man if you could possibly turn it down. But of course you're to take it or leave it. It's not to his interest to push it. Lord, no! Whatever you did his way is that he'd not condescend to say a darned word. High-toned silence, that's all."

The Duke of Stone was chuckling very softly. His chuckles rather broke his words when he spoke.

"By—by—Jove!" he said. "You—you do see it, don't you? You do see it."

Tembarom nursed his knee comfortably.

"Why," he said, "it's what keeps me up. You know a lot more about me than any one else does, but there's a whole raft of things I think about that I couldn't hang round any man's neck. If I tried to hang them round yours, you'd know that I would be having a hell of a time here, if I'd let myself think too much. If I didn't see it, as you call it, if I didn't see so many things, I might begin to get sorry for myself." There was a pause of a second. "Gee!" he said, "Gee! this not hearing a thing about Ann!—"

"Good Lord! my dear fellow," the duke said hastily, "I know. I know."

Tembarom turned and looked at him.

"You've been there," he remarked. "You've been there, I bet."

"Yes, I've been there," answered the duke. "I've been there—and come back. But while it's going on—you have just described it. A man can have a hell of a time."

"He can," Tembarom admitted unreservedly. "He's got to keep going to stand it. Well, Strangeways gives me some work to do. And I've got Palliser. He's a little sunbeam."

A man-servant approaching to suggest a possible need of hot tea started at hearing his grace break into a sudden and plainly involuntary crow of glee. He had not heard that one before either. Palliser as a little sunbeam brightening the pathway of T. Tembarom, was, in the particular existing circumstances, all that could be desired of fine humor. It somewhat recalled the situation of the "Ladies" of the noble houses of Pevensy, Talchester, and Stone unconsciously passing in review for the satisfaction of little Miss Hutchinson. Tembarom laughed a little himself, but he went on with a sort of seriousness,

"There's one thing sure enough. I've got on to it by listening and working out what he would do by what he doesn't know he says. If he could put the screws on me in any way, he wouldn't hold back. It'd be all quite polite and gentlemanly, but he'd do it all the same. And he's dead-sure that everybody's got something they'd like to hide—or get. That's what he works things out from."

"Does he think you have something to hide—or get?" the duke inquired rather quickly.

"He's sure of it. But he doesn't know yet whether it's get or hide. He noses about. Pearson's seen him. He asks questions and plays he ain't doing it and ain't interested, anyhow."

"He doesn't like you, he doesn't like you," the duke said rather thoughtfully. "He has a way of conveying that you are far more subtle than you choose to look. He is given to enlarging on the fact that an air of entire frankness is one of the chief assets of certain promoters of huge American schemes."

Tembarom smiled the smile of recognition.

"Yes," he said, "it looks like that's a long way round, doesn't it? But it's not far to T. T. when you want to hitch on the connection. Anyhow, that's the way he means it to look. If ever I was suspected of being in any mix-up, everybody would remember he'd said that."

"It's very amusin'," said the duke. "It's very amusin'."

They had become even greater friends and intimates by this time than the already astonished neighborhood suspected them of being. That they spent much time together in an amazing degree of familiarity was the talk of the country, in fact, one of the most frequent resources of conversation. Everybody endeavored to find reason for the situation, but none had been presented which seemed of sufficiently logical convincingness. The duke was eccentric, of course. That was easy to hit upon. He was amiably perverse and good-humoredly cynical. He was of course immensely amused by the incongruity of the acquaintance. This being the case, why exactly he had never before chosen for himself a companion equally out of the picture it was not easy to explain. There were plow-boys or clerks out of provincial shops who would surely have been quite as incongruous when surrounded by ducal splendors. He might have got a young man from Liverpool or Blackburn who would have known as little of polite society as Mr. Temple Barholm; there were few, of course, who could know less. But he had never shown the faintest desire to seek one out. Palliser, it is true, suggested it was Tembarom's "cheek" which stood him in good stead. The young man from behind the counter in a Liverpool or Blackburn shop would probably have been frightened to death and afraid to open his mouth in self-revelation, whereas Temple Barholm was so entirely a bounder that he did not know he was one, and was ready to make an ass of himself to any extent. The frankest statement of the situation, if any one had so chosen to put it, would have been that he was regarded as a sort of court fool without cap or bells.

No one was aware of the odd confidences which passed between the weirdly dissimilar pair. No one guessed that the old peer sat and listened to stories of a red-headed, slim-bodied girl in a dingy New York boarding-house, that he liked them sufficiently to encourage their telling, that he had made a mental picture of a certain look in a pair of maternally yearning and fearfully convincing round young eyes, that he knew the burnished fullness and glow of the red hair until he could imagine the feeling of its texture and abundant warmth in the hand. And this subject was only one of many. And of others they talked with interest, doubt, argument, speculation, holding a living thrill.

The tap of croquet mallets sounded hollow and clear from the sunken lawn below the mass of shrubs between them and the players as the duke repeated.

"It's hugely amusin'," dropping his "g," which was not one of his usual affectations.

"Confound it!" he said next, wrinkling the thin, fine skin round his eyes in a speculative smile, "I wish I had had a son of my own just like you."

All of Tembarom's white teeth revealed themselves.

"I'd have liked to have been in it," he replied, "but I shouldn't have been like me."

"Yes, you would." The duke put the tips of his fingers delicately together. "You are of the kind which in all circumstances is like itself." He looked about him, taking in the turreted, majestic age and mass of the castle. "You would have been born here. You would have learned to ride your pony down the avenue. You would have gone to Eton and to Oxford. I don't think you would have learned much, but you would have been decidedly edifying and companionable. You would have had a sense of humor which would have made you popular in society and at court. A young fellow who makes those people laugh holds success in his hand. They want to be made to laugh as much as I do. Good God! how they are obliged to be bored and behave decently under it! You would have seen and known more things to be humorous about than you know now. I don't think you would have been a fool about women, but some of them would have been fools about you, because you've got a way. I had one myself. It's all the more dangerous because it's possibility suggesting without being sentimental. A friendly young fellow always suggests possibilities without being aware of it.

"Would I have been Lord Temple Temple Barholm or something of that sort?" Tembarom asked.

"You would have been the Marquis of Belcarey," the duke replied, looking him over thoughtfully, "and your name would probably have been Hugh Lawrence Gilbert Henry Charles Adelbert, or words to that effect."

"A regular six-shooter," said Tembarom.

The duke was following it up with absorption in his eyes.

"You'd have gone into the Guards, perhaps," he said, "and drill would have made you carry yourself better. You're a good height. You'd have been a well-set-up fellow. I should have been rather proud of you. I can see you riding to the palace with the rest of them, sabres and chains clanking and glittering and helmet with plumes streaming. By Jove! I don't wonder at the effect they have on nursery-maids. On a sunny morning in spring they suggest knights in a fairytale."

"I should have liked it all right if I hadn't been born in Brooklyn," grinned Tembarom. "But that starts you out in a different way. Do you think, if I'd been born the Marquis of Bel—what's his name—I should have been on to Palliser's little song and dance, and had as much fun out of it?"

"On my soul, I believe you would," the duke answered. "Brooklyn or Stone Hover Castle, I'm hanged if you wouldn't have been YOU."

CHAPTER XXIX

After this came a pause. Each man sat thinking his own thoughts, which, while marked with difference in form, were doubtless subtly alike in the line they followed. During the silence T. Tembarom looked out at the late afternoon shadows lengthening themselves in darkening velvet across the lawns.

At last he said:

"I never told you that I've been reading some of the 'steen thousand books in the library. I started it about a month ago. And somehow they've got me going."

The slightly lifted eyebrows of his host did not express surprise so much as questioning interest. This man, at least, had discovered that one need find no cause for astonishment in any discovery that he had been doing a thing for some time for some reason or through some prompting of his own, and had said nothing whatever about it until he was what he called "good and ready." When he was "good and ready" he usually revealed himself to the duke, but he was not equally expansive with others.

"No, you have not mentioned it," his grace answered, and laughed a little. "You frequently fail to mention things. When first we knew each other I used to wonder if you were naturally a secretive fellow; but you are not. You always have a reason for your silences."

"It took about ten years to kick that into me—ten good years, I should say." T. Tembarom looked as if he were looking backward at many episodes as he said it. "Naturally, I guess, I must have been an innocent, blab-mouthed kid. I meant no harm, but I just didn't know. Sometimes it looks as if just not knowing is about the worst disease you can be troubled with. But if you don't get killed first, you find out in time that what you've got to hold on to hard and fast is the trick of 'saying nothing and sawing wood.'"

The duke took out his memorandum-book and began to write hastily. T. Tembarom was quite accustomed to this. He even repeated his axiom for him.

"Say nothing and saw wood," he said. "It's worth writing down. It means 'shut your mouth and keep on working.'"

"Thank you," said the duke. "It is worth writing down. Thank you."

"I did not talk about the books because I wanted to get used to them before I began to talk," Tembarom explained. "I wanted to get somewhere. I'd never read a book through in my life before. Never wanted to. Never had one and never had time. When night came, I was dog-tired and dog-ready to drop down and sleep."

Here was a situation of interest. A young man of odd, direct shrewdness, who had never read a book through in his existence, had plunged suddenly into the extraordinarily varied literary resources of the Temple Barholm library. If he had been a fool or a genius one might have guessed at the impression made on him; being T. Tembarom, one speculated with secret elation. The primitiveness he might reveal, the profundities he might touch the surface of, the unexpected ends he might reach, suggested the opening of vistas.

"I have often thought that if books attracted you the library would help you to get through a good many of the hundred and thirty-six hours a day you've spoken of, and get through them pretty decently," commented the duke.

"That's what's happened," Tembarom answered. "There's not so many now. I can cut 'em off in chunks."

"How did it begin?"

He listened with much pleasure while Tembarom told him how it had begun and how it had gone on.

"I'd been having a pretty bad time one day. Strangeways had been worse—a darned sight worse—just when I thought he was better. I'd been trying to help him to think straight; and suddenly I made a break, somehow, and must have touched exactly the wrong spring. It seemed as if I set him nearly crazy. I had to leave him to Pearson right away. Then it poured rain steady for about eight hours, and I couldn't get out and 'take a walk.' Then I went wandering into the picture-gallery and found Lady Joan there, looking at Miles Hugo. And she ordered me out, or blamed near it."

"You are standing a good deal," said the duke.

"Yes, I am—but so is she." He set his hard young jaw and nursed his knee, staring once more at the velvet shadows. "The girl in the book I picked up—" he began.

"The first book?" his host inquired.

Tembarom nodded.

"The very first. I was smoking my pipe at night, after every one else had gone to bed, and I got up and began to wander about and stare at the names of the things on the shelves. I was thinking over a whole raft of things—a whole raft of them—and I didn't know I was doing it, until something made me stop and read a name again. It was a book called 'Good-by, Sweetheart, Good-by,' and it hit me straight. I wondered what it was about, and I wondered where old Temple Barholm had fished up a thing like that. I never heard he was that kind."

"He was a cantankerous old brute," said the Duke of Stone with candor, "but he chanced to be an omnivorous novel-reader. Nothing was too sentimental for him in his later years."

"I took the thing out and read it," Tembarom went on, uneasily, the emotion of his first novel-reading stirring him as he talked. "It kept me up half the night, and I hadn't finished it then. I wanted to know the end."

"Benisons upon the books of which one wants to know the end!" the duke murmured.

Tembarom's interest had plainly not terminated with "the end." Its freshness made it easily revived. There was a hint of emotional indignation in his relation of the plot.

"It was about a couple of fools who were dead stuck on each other—dead. There was no mistake about that. It was all real. But what do they do but work up a fool quarrel about nothing, and break away from each other. There was a lot of stuff about pride. Pride be damned! How's a man going to be proud and put on airs when he loves a woman? How's a woman going to be proud and stick out about things when she loves a man? At least, that's the way it hit me."

"That's the way it hit me—once," remarked his grace.

"There is only once," said Tembarom, doggedly.

"Occasionally," said his host. "Occasionally."

Tembarom knew what he meant.

"The fellow went away, and neither of them would give in. It's queer how real it was when you read it. You were right there looking on, and swallowing hard every few minutes—though you were as mad as hops. The girl began to die—slow—and lay there day after day, longing for him to come back, and knowing he wouldn't. At the very end, when there was scarcely a breath left in her, a young fellow who was crazy about her himself, and always had been, put out after the hard-headed fool to bring him to her anyhow. The girl had about given in then. And she lay and waited hour after hour, and the youngster came back by himself. He couldn't bring the man he'd gone after. He found him getting married to a nice girl he didn't really care a darn for. He'd sort of set his teeth and done it—just because he was all in and down and out, and a fool. The girl just dropped her head back on the pillow and lay there, dead! What do you think of that?" quite fiercely. "I guess it was sentimental all right, but it got you by the throat."

"'Good-bye, Sweetheart, Good-bye,'" his grace quoted. "First-class title. We are all sentimental. And that was the first, was it?"

"Yes, but it wasn't the last. I began to read the others. I've been reading them ever since. I tell you, for a fellow that knows nothing it's an easy way of finding out a lot of things. You find out what different kinds of people there are, and what different kinds of ways. If you've lived in one place, and been up against nothing but earning your living, you think that's all there is of it—that it's the whole thing. But it isn't, by gee!" His air became thoughtful. "I've begun to kind of get on to what all this means"—glancing about him—"to you people; and how a fellow like T. T. must look to you. I've always sort of guessed, but reading a few dozen novels has helped me to see WHY it's that way. I've yelled right out laughing over it many a time. That fellow called Thackeray—I can't read his things right straight through—but he 's an eye-opener."

"You have tried nothing BUT novels?" his enthralled hearer inquired.

"Not yet. I shall come to the others in time. I'm sort of hungry for these things about PEOPLE. It's the ways they're different that gets me going. There was one that stirred me all up—but it wasn't like that first one. It was about a man "—he spoke slowly, as if searching for words and parallels—"well, I guess he was one of the early savages here. It read as if they were like the first Indians in America, only stronger and fiercer. When Palford was explaining things to me he'd jerk in every now and then something about 'coming over with the Conqueror' or being here 'before the Conqueror.' I didn't know what it meant. I found out in this book I'm telling about. It gave me the whole thing so that you SAW it. Here was this little country, with no one in it but these first savage fellows it'd always belonged to. They thought it was the world." There was a humorous sense of illumination in his half-laugh. "It was their New York, by jings," he put in. "Their little old New York that they'd never been outside of! And then first one lot slams in, and then another, and another, and tries to take it from them. Julius Caesar was the first Mr. Buttinski; and they fought like hell. They were fighters from Fightersville, anyhow. They fought each other, took each other's castles and lands and wives and jewelry—just any old thing they wanted. The only jails were private ones meant for their particular friends. And a man was hung only when one of his neighbors got mad enough at him, and then he had to catch him first and run the risk of being strung up himself, or have his head chopped off and stuck up on a spike somewhere for ornament. But fight! Good Lord! They were at it day and night. Did it for fun, just like folks go to the show. They didn't know what fear was. Never heard of it. They'd go about shouting and bragging and swaggering, with their heads hanging half off. And the one in this book was the bulliest fighter of the lot. I guess I don't know how to pronounce his name. It began with H."

"Was it Hereward the Wake, by chance?" exclaimed his auditor. "Hereward the Last of the English?"

"That's the man," cried Tembarom.

"An engaging ruffian and thief and murderer, and a touching one also," commented the duke. "You liked him?" He really wanted to know.

"I like the way he went after what he wanted to get, and the way he fought for his bit of England. By gee! When he went rushing into a fight, shouting and boasting and swinging his sword, I got hot in the collar. It was his England. What was old Bill doing there anyhow, darn him! Those chaps made him swim in their blood before they let him put the thing over. Good business! I'm glad they gave him all that was coming to him—hot and strong."

His sharp face had reddened and his voice rose high and nasal. There was a look of roused blood in him.

"Are you a fighter from Fightersville?" the duke asked, far from unstirred himself. These things had become myths to most people, but here was Broadway in the midst of them unconsciously suggesting that it might not have done ill in the matter of swinging "Brain-Biter" itself. The modern entity slipped back again through the lengthened links of bygone centuries—back until it became T. Tembarom once more—casual though shrewd; ready and jocular. His eyes resumed their dry New York humor of expression as they fixed themselves on his wholly modern questioner.

"I'll fight," he said, "for what I've got to fight for, but not for a darned thing else. Not a darned thing."

"But you would fight," smiled the duke, grimly. "Did you happen to remember that blood like that has come down to you? It was some drop of it which made you `hot in the collar' over that engaging savage roaring and slashing about him for his `bit of England.'"

Tembarom seemed to think it out interestedly.

"No, I did not," he answered. "But I guess that's so. I guess it's so. Great Jakes! Think of me perhaps being sort of kin to fellows just like that. Some way, you couldn't help liking him. He was always making big breaks and bellowing out `The Wake! The Wake!' in season and out of season; but the way he got there—just got there!"

He was oddly in sympathy with "the early savages here," and as understandingly put himself into their places as he had put himself into Galton's. His New York comprehension of their berserker furies was apparently without limit. Strong partizan as he was of the last of the English, however, he admitted that William of Normandy had "got in some good work, though it wasn't square."

"He was a big man," he ended. "If he hadn't been the kind he was I don't know how I should have stood it when the Hereward fellow knelt down before him, and put his hands between his and swore to be his man. That's the way the book said it. I tell you that must have been tough—tough as hell!"

From "Good-bye, Sweetheart" to "Hereward the Last of the English" was a far cry, but he had gathered a curious collection of ideas by the way, and with characteristic everyday reasoning had linked them to his own experiences.

"The women in the Hereward book made me think of Lady Joan," he remarked, suddenly.

"Torfreda?" the duke asked.

He nodded quite seriously.

"She had ways that reminded me of her, and I kept thinking they must both have had the same look in their eyes—sort of fierce and hungry. Torfreda had black hair and was a winner as to looks; but people were afraid of her and called her a witch. Hereward went mad over her and she went mad over him. That part of it was 'way out of sight, it was so fine. She helped him with his fights and told him what to do, and tried to keep him from drinking and bragging. Whatever he did, she never stopped being crazy about him. She mended his men's clothes, and took care of their wounds, and lived in the forest with him when he was driven out."

"That sounds rather like Miss Hutchinson," his host suggested, "though the parallel between a Harlem flat and an English forest in the eleventh century is not exact."

"I thought that, too," Tembarom admitted. "Ann would have done the same things, but she'd have done them in her way. If that fellow had taken his wife's advice, he wouldn't have ended with his head sticking on a spear."

"Another lady, if I remember rightly," said the duke.

"He left her, the fool!" Tembarom answered. "And there's where I couldn't get away from seeing Lady Joan; Jem Temple Barholm didn't go off with another woman, but what Torfreda went through, this one has gone through, and she's going through it yet. She can't dress herself in sackcloth, and cut off her hair, and hide herself away with a bunch of nuns, as the other one did. She has to stay and stick it out, however bad it is. That's a darned sight worse. The day after I'd finished the book, I couldn't keep my eyes off her. I tried to stop it, but it was no use. I kept hearing that Torfreda one screaming out, 'Lost! Lost! Lost!' It was all in her face."

"But, my good fellow," protested the duke, despite feeling a touch of the thrill again, "unfortunately, she would not suspect you of looking at her because you were recalling Torfreda and Hereward the Wake. Men stare at her for another reason."

"That's what I know about half as well again as I know anything else," answered Tembarom. He added, with a deliberation holding its own meaning, "That's what I'm coming to."

The duke waited. What was it he was coming to?

"Reading that novel put me wise to things in a new way. She's been wiping her feet on me hard for a good while, and I sort of made up my mind I'd got to let her until I was sure where I was. I won't say I didn't mind it, but I could stand it. But that night she caught me looking at her, the way she looked back at me made me see all of a sudden that it would be easier for her if I told her straight that she was mistaken."

"That she is mistaken in thinking—?"

"What she does think. She wouldn't have thought it if the old lady hadn't been driving her mad by hammering it in. She'd have hated me all right, and I don't blame her when I think of how poor Jem was treated; but she wouldn't have thought that every time I tried to be decent and friendly to her I was butting in and making a sick fool of myself. She's got to stay where her mother keeps her, and she's got to listen to her. Oh, hell! She's got to be told!"

The duke set the tips of his fingers together.

"How would you do it?" he inquired.

"Just straight," replied T. Tembarom. "There's no other way."

From the old worldling broke forth an involuntary low laugh, which was a sort of cackle. So this was what he was coming to.

"I cannot think of any devious method," he said, "which would make it less than a delicate thing to do. A beautiful young woman, whose host you are, has flouted you furiously for weeks, under the impression that you are offensively in love with her. You propose to tell her that her judgment has betrayed her, and that, as you say, 'There's nothing doing.'"

"Not a darned thing, and never has been," said T. Tembarom. He looked quite grave and not at all embarrassed. He plainly did not see it as a situation to be regarded with humor.

"If she will listen——" the duke began.

"Oh, she'll listen," put in Tembarom. "I'll make her."

His was a self-contradicting countenance, the duke reflected, as he took him in with a somewhat long look. One did not usually see a face built up of boyishness and maturity, simpleness which was baffling, and a good nature which could be hard. At the moment, it was both of these last at one and the same time.

"I know something of Lady Joan and I know something of you," he said, "but I don't exactly foresee what will happen. I will not say that I should not like to be present."

"There'll be nobody present but just me and her," Tembarom answered.

CHAPTER XXX

The visits of Lady Mallowe and Captain Palliser had had their features. Neither of the pair had come to one of the most imposing "places" in Lancashire to live a life of hermit-like seclusion and dullness. They had arrived with the intention of availing themselves of all such opportunities for entertainment as could be guided in their direction by the deftness of experience. As a result, there had been hospitalities at Temple Barholm such as it had not beheld during the last generation at least. T. Tembarom had looked on, an interested spectator, as these festivities had been adroitly arranged and managed for him. He had not, however, in the least resented acting as a sort of figurehead in the position of sponsor and host.

"They think I don't know I'm not doing it all myself," was his easy mental summing-up. "They've got the idea that I'm pleased because I believe I'm It. But that's all to the merry. It's what I've set my mind on having going on here, and I couldn't have started it as well myself. I shouldn't have known how. They're teaching me. All I hope is that Ann's grandmother is keeping tab."

"Do you and Rose know old Mrs. Hutchinson?" he had inquired of Pearson the night before the talk with the duke.

"Well, not to say exactly know her, sir, but everybody knows of her. She is a most remarkable old person, sir." Then, after watching his face for a moment or so, he added tentatively, "Would you perhaps wish us to make her acquaintance for—for any reason?"

Tembarom thought the matter over speculatively. He had learned that his first liking for Pearson had been founded upon a rock. He was always to be trusted to understand, and also to apply a quite unusual intelligence to such matters as he became aware of without having been told about them.

"What I'd like would be for her to hear that there's plenty doing at Temple Barholm; that people are coming and going all the time; and that there's ladies to burn—and most of them lookers, at that," was his answer.

How Pearson had discovered the exotic subtleties of his master's situation and mental attitude toward it, only those of his class and gifted with his occult powers could explain in detail. The fact exists that Pearson did know an immense number of things his employer had not mentioned to him, and held them locked in his bosom in honored security, like a little gentleman. He made his reply with a polite conviction which carried weight.

"It would not be necessary for either Rose or me to make old Mrs. Hutchinson's acquaintance with a view to informing her of anything which occurs on the estate or in the village, sir," he remarked. "Mrs. Hutchinson knows more of things than any one ever tells her. She sits in her cottage there, and she just knows things and sees through people in a way that'd be almost unearthly, if she wasn't a good old person, and so respectable that there's those that touches their hats to her as if she belonged to the gentry. She's got a blue eye, sir—"

"Has she?" exclaimed Tembarom.

"Yes, sir. As blue as a baby's, sir, and as clear, though she's past eighty. And they tell me there's a quiet, steady look in it that ill-doers downright quail before. It's as if she was a kind of judge that sentenced them without speaking. They can't stand it. Oh, sir! you can depend upon old Mrs. Hutchinson as to who's been here, and even what they've thought about it. The village just flocks to her to tell her the news and get advice about things. She'd know."

It was as a result of this that on his return from Stone Hover he dismissed the carriage at the gates and walked through them to make a visit in the village. Old Mrs. Hutchinson, sitting knitting in her chair behind the abnormally flourishing fuchsias, geraniums, and campanula carpaticas in her cottage-window, looked between the banked-up flower-pots to see that Mr. Temple Barholm had opened her wicket-gate and was walking up the clean bricked path to her front door. When he knocked she called out in the broad Lancashire she had always spoken, "Coom in!" When he entered he took off his hat and looked at her, friendly but hesitant, and with the expression of a young man who has not quite made up his mind as to what he is about to encounter.

"I'm Temple Temple Barholm, Mrs. Hutchinson," he announced.

"I know that," she answered. "Not that tha looks loike th' Temple Barholms, but I've been watchin' thee walk an' drive past here ever since tha coom to th' place."

She watched him steadily with an astonishingly limpid pair of old eyes. They were old and young at the same time; old because they held deeps of wisdom, young because they were so alive and full of question.

"I don't know whether I ought to have come to see you or not," he said.

"Well, tha'st coom," she replied, going on with her knitting. "Sit thee doun and have a bit of a chat."

"Say!" he broke out. "Ain't you going to shake hands with me?" He held his hand out impetuously. He knew he was all right if she'd shake hands.

"Theer's nowt agen that surely," she answered, with a shrewd bit of a smile. She gave him her hand. "If I was na stiff in my legs, it's my place to get up an' mak' thee a curtsey, but th' rheumatics has no respect even for th' lord o' th' manor."

"If you got up and made me a curtsey," Tembarom said, "I should throw a fit. Say, Mrs. Hutchinson, I bet you know that as well as I do."

The shrewd bit of a smile lighted her eyes as well as twinkled about her mouth.

"Sit thee doun," she said again.

So he sat down and looked at her as straight as she looked at him.

"Tha 'd give a good bit," she said presently, over her flashing needles, "to know how much Little Ann's tow'd me about thee."

"I'd give a lot to know how much it'd be square to ask you to tell me about her," he gave back to her, hesitating yet eager.

"What does tha mean by square?" she demanded.

"I mean `fair.' Can I talk to you about her at all? I promised I'd stick it out here and do as she said. She told me she wasn't going to write to me or let her father write. I've promised, and I'm not going to fall down when I've said a thing."

"So tha coom to see her grandmother?"

He reddened, but held his head up.

"I'm not going to ask her grandmother a thing she doesn't want me to be told. But I've been up against it pretty hard lately. I read some things in the New York papers about her father and his invention, and about her traveling round with him and helping him with his business."

"In Germany they wur," she put in, forgetting herself. "They're havin' big doin's over th' invention. What Joe 'u'd do wi'out th' lass I canna tell. She's doin' every bit o' th' managin' an' contrivin' wi' them furriners—but he'll never know it. She's got a chap to travel wi' him as can talk aw th' languages under th' sun."

Her face flushed and she stopped herself sharply.

"I'm talkin' about her to thee!" she said. "I would na ha' believed o' mysen'."

He got up from his chair.

"I guess I oughtn't to have come," he said, restlessly. "But you haven't told me more than I got here and there in the papers. That was what started me. It was like watching her. I could hear her talking and see the way she was doing things till it drove me half crazy. All of a sudden, I just got wild and made up my mind I'd come here. I've wanted to do it many a time, but I've kept away."

"Tha showed sense i' doin' that," remarked Mrs. Hutchinson. "She'd not ha' thowt well o' thee if tha'd coom runnin' to her grandmother every day or so. What she likes about thee is as she thinks tha's got a strong backbone o' thy own."

She looked up at him over her knitting, looked straight into his eyes, and there was that in her own which made him redden and feel his pulse quicken. It was actually something which even remotely suggested that she was not—in the deeps of her strong old mind—as wholly unswerving as her words might imply. It was something more subtle than words. She was not keeping him wholly in the dark when she said "What she likes about thee." If Ann said things like that to her, he was pretty well off.

"Happen a look at a lass's grandmother—when tha conna get at th' lass hersen—is a bit o' comfort," she added. "But don't tha go walkin' by here to look in at th' window too often. She would na think well o' that either."

"Say! There's one thing I'm going to get off my chest before I go," he announced, "just one thing. She can go where she likes and do what she likes, but I'm going to marry her when she's done it—unless something knocks me on the head and finishes me. I'm going to marry her."

"Tha art, art tha?" laconically; but her eyes were still on his, and the something in their depths by no means diminished.

"I'm keeping up my end here, and it's no slouch of a job, but I'm not forgetting what she promised for one minute! And I'm not forgetting what her promise means," he said obstinately.

"Tha'd like me to tell her that?" she said.

"If she doesn't know it, you telling her wouldn't cut any ice," was his reply. "I'm saying it because I want you to know it, and because it does me good to say it out loud. I'm going to marry her."

"That's for her and thee to settle," she commented, impersonally.

"It is settled," he answered. "There's no way out of it. Will you shake hands with me again before I go?"

"Aye," she consented, "I will."

When she took his hand she held it a minute. Her own was warm, and there was no limpness about it. The secret which had seemed to conceal itself behind her eyes had some difficulty in keeping itself wholly in the background.

"She knows aw tha' does," she said coolly, as if she were not suddenly revealing immensities. "She knows who cooms an' who goes, an' what they think o' thee, an' how tha gets on wi' 'em. Now get thee gone, lad, an' dunnot tha coom back till her or me sends for thee."

Within an hour of this time the afternoon post brought to Lady Mallowe a letter which she read with an expression in which her daughter recognized relief. It was in fact a letter for which she had waited with anxiety, and the invitation it contained was a tribute to her social skill at its highest watermark. In her less heroic moments, she had felt doubts of receiving it, which had caused shudders to run the entire length of her spine.

"I'm going to Broome Haughton," she announced to Joan.

"When?" Joan inquired.

"At the end of the week. I am invited for a fortnight."

"Am I going?" Joan asked.

"No. You will go to London to meet some friends who are coming over from Paris."

Joan knew that comment was unnecessary. Both she and her mother were on intimate terms with these hypothetical friends who so frequently turned up from Paris or elsewhere when it was necessary that she should suddenly go back to London and live in squalid seclusion in the unopened house, with a charwoman to provide her with underdone or burnt chops, and eggs at eighteen a shilling, while the shutters of the front rooms were closed, and dusty desolation reigned. She knew every detail of the melancholy squalor of it, the dragging hours, the nights of lying awake listening to the occasional passing of belated cabs, or the squeaks and nibbling of mice in the old walls.

"If you had conducted yourself sensibly you need not have gone," continued her mother. "I could have made an excuse and left you here. You would at least have been sure of good food and decent comforts."

"After your visit, are we to return here?" was Lady Joan's sole reply.

"Don't look at me like that," said Lady Mallowe. "I thought the country would freshen your color at least; but you are going off more every day. You look like the Witch of Endor sometimes."

Joan smiled faintly. This was the brandishing of an old weapon, and she understood all its significance. It meant that the time for opportunities was slipping past her like the waters of a rapid river.

"I do not know what will happen when I leave Broome Haughton," her mother added, a note of rasped uncertainty in her voice. "We may be obliged to come here for a short time, or we may go abroad."

"If I refuse to come, would you let me starve to death in Piers Street?" Joan inquired.

Lady Mallowe looked her over, feeling a sort of frenzy at the sight of her. In truth, the future was a hideous thing to contemplate if no rescue at all was in sight. It would be worse for her than for Joan, because Joan did not care what happened or did not happen, and she cared desperately. She had indeed arrived at a maddening moment.

"Yes," she snapped, fiercely.

And when Joan faintly smiled again she understood why women of the lower orders beat one another until policemen interfere. She knew perfectly well that the girl had somehow found out that Sir Moses Monaldini was to be at Broome Haughton, and that when he left there he was going abroad. She knew also that she had not been able to conceal that his indifference had of late given her some ghastly hours, and that her play for this lagging invitation had been a frantically bold one. That the most ingenious efforts and devices had ended in success only after such delay made it all the more necessary that no straw must remain unseized on.

"I can wear some of your things, with a little alteration," she said. "Rose will do it for me. Hats and gloves and ornaments do not require altering. I shall need things you will not need in London. Where are your keys?"

Lady Joan rose and got them for her. She even flushed slightly. They were often obliged to borrow each other's possessions, but for a moment she felt herself moved by a sort of hard pity.

"We are like rats in a trap," she remarked. "I hope you will get out."

"If I do, you will be left inside. Get out yourself! Get out yourself!" said Lady Mallowe in a fierce whisper.

Her regrets at the necessity of their leaving Temple Barholm were expressed with fluent touchingness at the dinner-table. The visit had been so delightful. Mr. Temple Barholm and Miss Alicia had been so kind. The loveliness of the whole dear place had so embraced them that they felt as if they were leaving a home instead of ending a delightful visit. It was extraordinary what an effect the house had on one. It was as if one had lived in it always—and always would. So few places gave one the same feeling. They should both look forward—greedy as it seemed—to being allowed some time to come again. She had decided from the first that it was not necessary to go to any extreme of caution or subtlety with her host and Miss Alicia. Her method of paving the way for future visits was perhaps more than a shade too elaborate. She felt, however, that it sufficed. For the most part, Lady Joan sat with lids dropped over her burning eyes. She tried to force herself not to listen. This was the kind of thing which made her sick with humiliation. Howsoever rudimentary these people were, they could not fail to comprehend that a foothold in the house was being bid for. They should at least see that she did not join in the bidding. Her own visit had been filled with feelings at war with one another. There had been hours too many in which she would have been glad—even with the dingy horrors of the closed town house before her—to have flown from the hundred things which called out to her on every side. In the long-past three months of happiness, Jem had described them all to her—the rooms, gardens, pleached walks, pictures, the very furniture itself. She could enter no room, walk in no spot she did not seem to know, and passionately love in spite of herself. She loved them so much that there were times when she yearned to stay in the place at any cost, and others when she could not endure the misery it woke in her—the pure misery. Now it was over for the time being, and she was facing something new. There were endless varieties of wretchedness. She had been watching her mother for some months, and had understood her varying moods of temporary elation or prolonged anxiety. Each one had meant some phase of the episode of Sir Moses Monaldini. The people who lived at Broome Haughton were enormously rich Hebrews, who were related to him. They had taken the beautiful old country-seat and were filling it with huge parties of their friends. The party which Lady Mallowe was to join would no doubt offer opportunities of the most desirable kind. Among this special class of people she was a great success. Her amazingly achieved toilettes, her ripe good looks, her air of belonging to the great world, impressed themselves immensely.

T. Tembarom thought he never had seen Lady Joan look as handsome as she looked to-night. The color on her cheek burned, her eyes had a driven loneliness in them. She had a wonderfully beautiful mouth, and its curve drooped in a new way. He wished Ann could get her in a corner and sit down and talk sense to her. He remembered what he had said to the duke. Perhaps this was the time. If she was going away, and her mother meant to drag her back again when she was ready, it would make it easier for her to leave the place knowing she need not hate to come back. But the duke wasn't making any miss hit when he said it wouldn't be easy. She was not like Ann, who would feel some pity for the biggest fool on earth if she had to throw him down hard. Lady Joan would feel neither compunctions nor relentings. He knew the way she could look at a fellow. If he couldn't make her understand what he was aiming at, they would both be worse off than they would be if he left things as they were. But—the hard line showed itself about his mouth—he wasn't going to leave things as they were.

As they passed through the hall after dinner, Lady Mallowe glanced at a side-table on which lay some letters arrived by the late post. An imposing envelope was on the top of the rest. Joan saw her face light as she took it up.

"I think this is from Broome Haughton," she said. "If you will excuse me, I will go into the library and read it. It may require answering at once."

She turned hot and cold, poor woman, and went away, so that she might be free from the disaster of an audience if anything had gone wrong. It would be better to be alone even if things had gone right. The letter was from Sir Moses Monaldini. Grotesque and ignoble as it naturally strikes the uninitiated as seeming, the situation had its touch of hideous pathos. She had fought for her own hand for years; she could not dig, and to beg she was not ashamed; but a time had come when even the most adroit begging began to bore people. They saw through it, and then there resulted strained relations, slight stiffness of manner, even in the most useful and amiable persons, lack of desire to be hospitable, or even condescendingly generous. Cold shoulders were turned, there were ominous threatenings of icy backs presenting themselves. The very tradesmen had found this out, and could not be persuaded that the advertisement furnished by the fact that two beautiful women of fashion ate, drank, and wore the articles which formed the items in their unpaid bills, was sufficient return for the outlay of capital required. Even Mrs. Mellish, when graciously approached by the "relative of Miss Temple Barholm, whose perfect wardrobe you supplied," had listened to all seductions with a civil eye fixed unmovedly and had referred to the "rules of the establishment." Nearer and nearer the edge of the abyss the years had pushed them, and now if something did not happen—something—something—even the increasingly shabby small house in town would become a thing of the past. And what then? Could any one wonder she said to herself that she could have beaten Joan furiously. It would not matter to any one else if they dropped out of the world into squalid oblivion—oh, she knew that—she knew that with bitter certainty!—but oh, how it would matter to them!—at least to herself. It was all very well for Mudie's to pour forth streams of sentimental novels preaching the horrors of girls marrying for money, but what were you to do—what in heaven's name were you to do? So, feeling terrified enough actually to offer up a prayer, she took the imposingly addressed letter into the library.

The men had come into the drawing-room when she returned. As she entered, Joan did not glance up from the book she was reading, but at the first sound of her voice she knew what had occurred.

"I was obliged to dash off a note to Broome Haughton so that it would be ready for the early post," Lady Mallowe said. She was at her best. Palliser saw that some years had slipped from her shoulders. The moment which relieves or even promises to relieve fears does astonishing things. Tembarom wondered whether she had had good news, and Miss Alicia thought that her evening dress was more becoming than any she had ever seen her wear before. Her brilliant air of social ease returned to her, and she began to talk fluently of what was being done in London, and to touch lightly upon the possibility of taking part in great functions. For some time she had rather evaded talk of the future. Palliser had known that the future had seemed to be closing in upon her, and leaving her staring at a high blank wall. Persons whose fortunate names had ceased to fall easily from her lips appeared again upon the horizon. Miss Alicia was impressed anew with the feeling that she had known every brilliant or important personage in the big world of social London; that she had taken part in every dazzling event. Tembarom somehow realized that she had been afraid of something or other, and was for some reason not afraid any more. Such a change, whatsoever the reason for it, ought to have had some effect on her daughter. Surely she would share her luck, if luck had come to her.

But Lady Joan sat apart and kept her eyes upon her book. This was one of the things she often chose to do, in spite of her mother's indignant protest.

"I came here because you brought me," she would answer. "I did not come to be entertaining or polite."

She was reading this evening. She heard every word of Lady Mallowe's agreeable and slightly excited conversation. She did not know exactly what had happened; but she knew that it was something which had buoyed her up with a hopefulness which exhilarated her almost too much—as an extra glass of wine might have done. Once or twice she even lost her head a little and was a trifle swaggering. T. Tembarom would not recognize the slip, but Joan saw Palliser's faint smile without looking up from her book. He observed shades in taste and bearing. Before her own future Joan saw the blank wall of stone building itself higher and higher. If Sir Moses had capitulated, she would be counted out. With what degree of boldness could a mother cast her penniless daughter on the world? What unendurable provision make for her? Dare they offer a pound a week and send her to live in the slums until she chose to marry some Hebrew friend of her step-father's? That she knew would be the final alternative. A cruel little smile touched her lips, as she reviewed the number of things she could not do to earn her living. She could not take in sewing or washing, and there was nothing she could teach. Starvation or marriage. The wall built itself higher and yet higher. What a hideous thing it was for a penniless girl to be brought up merely to be a beauty, and in consequence supposably a great lady. And yet if she was born to a certain rank and had height and figure, a lovely mouth, a delicate nose, unusual eyes and lashes, to train her to be a dressmaker or a housemaid would be a stupid investment of capital. If nothing tragic interfered and the right man wanted such a girl, she had been trained to please him. But tragic things had happened, and before her grew the wall while she pretended to read her book.

T. Tembarom was coming toward her. She had heard Palliser suggest a game of billiards.

"Will you come and play billiards with us?" Tembarom asked. "Palliser says you play splendidly."

"She plays brilliantly," put in Lady Mallowe. "Come, Joan."

"No, thank you," she answered. "Let me stay here and read."

Lady Mallowe protested. She tried an air of playful maternal reproach because she was in good spirits. Joan saw Palliser smiling quietly, and there was that in his smile which suggested to her that he was thinking her an obstinate fool.

"You had better show Temple Barholm what you can do," he remarked. "This will be your last chance, as you leave so soon. You ought never let a last chance slip by. I never do."

Tembarom stood still and looked down at her from his good height. He did not know what Palliser's speech meant, but an instinct made him feel that it somehow held an ugly, quiet taunt.

"What I would like to do," was the unspoken crudity which passed through his mind, "would be to swat him on the mouth. He's getting at her just when she ought to be let alone."

"Would you like it better to stay here and read?" he inquired.

"Much better, if you please," was her reply.

"Then that goes," he answered, and left her.

He swept the others out of the room with a good-natured promptness which put an end to argument. When he said of anything "Then that goes," it usually did so.

CHAPTER XXXI

When she was alone Joan sat and gazed not at her wall but at the pictures that came back to her out of a part of her life which seemed to have been lived centuries ago. They were the pictures that came back continually without being called, the clearness of which always startled her afresh. Sometimes she thought they sprang up to add to her torment, but sometimes it seemed as if they came to save her from herself—her mad, wicked self. After all, there were moments when to know that she had been the girl whose eighteen-year-old heart had leaped so when she turned and met Jem's eyes, as he stood gazing at her under the beech-tree, was something to cling to. She had been that girl and Jem had been—Jem. And she had been the girl who had joined him in that young, ardent vow that they would say the same prayers at the same hour each night together. Ah! how young it had been—how YOUNG! Her throat strained itself because sobs rose in it, and her eyes were hot with the swell of tears.

She could hear voices and laughter and the click of balls from the billiard-room. Her mother and Palliser laughed the most, but she knew the sound of her mother's voice would cease soon, because she would come back to her. She knew she would not leave her long, and she knew the kind of scene they would pass through together when she returned. The old things would be said, the old arguments used, but a new one would be added. It was a pleasant thing to wait here, knowing that it was coming, and that for all her fierce pride and fierce spirit she had no defense. It was at once horrible and ridiculous that she must sit and listen—and stare at the growing wall. It was as she caught her breath against the choking swell of tears that she heard Lady Mallowe returning. She came in with an actual sweep across the room. Her society air had fled, and she was unadornedly furious when she stopped before Joan's chair. For a few seconds she actually glared; then she broke forth in a suppressed undertone:

"Come into the billiard-room. I command it!"

Joan lifted her eyes from her book. Her voice was as low as her mother's, but steadier.

"No," she answered.

"Is this conduct to continue? Is it?" Lady Mallowe panted.

"Yes," said Joan, and laid her book on the table near her. There was nothing else to say. Words made things worse.

Lady Mallowe had lost her head, but she still spoke in the suppressed voice.

"You SHALL behave yourself!" she cried, under her breath, and actually made a passionate half-start toward her. "You violent-natured virago! The very look on your face is enough to drive one mad!"

"I know I am violent-natured," said Joan. "But don't you think it wise to remember that you cannot make the kind of scene here that you can in your own house? We are a bad-tempered pair, and we behave rather like fishwives when we are in a rage. But when we are guests in other people's houses—"

Lady Mallowe's temper was as elemental as any Billingsgate could provide.

"You think you can take advantage of that!" she said. "Don't trust yourself too far. Do you imagine that just when all might go well for me I will allow you to spoil everything?"

"How can I spoil everything?"

"By behaving as you have been behaving since we came here—refusing to make a home for yourself; by hanging round my neck so that it will appear that any one who takes me must take you also."

"There are servants outside," Joan warned her.

"You shall not stop me!" cried Lady Mallowe.

"You cannot stop yourself," said Joan. "That is the worst of it. It is bad enough when we stand and hiss at each other in a stage whisper; but when you lose control over yourself and raise your voice—"

"I came in here to tell you that this is your last chance. I shall never give you another. Do you know how old you are?"

"I shall soon be twenty-seven," Joan answered. "I wish I were a hundred. Then it would all be over."

"But it will not be over for years and years and years," her mother flung back at her. "Have you forgotten that the very rags you wear are not paid for?"

"No, I have not forgotten." The scene was working itself up on the old lines, as Joan had known it would. Her mother never failed to say the same things, every time such a scene took place.

"You will get no more such rags—paid or unpaid for. What do you expect to do? You don't know how to work, and if you did no decent woman would employ you. You are too good-looking and too bad-tempered."

Joan knew she was perfectly right. Knowing it, she remained silent, and her silence added to her mother's helpless rage. She moved a step nearer to her and flung the javelin which she always knew would strike deep.

"You have made yourself a laughing-stock for all London for years. You are mad about a man who disgraced and ruined himself."

She saw the javelin quiver as it struck; but Joan's voice as it answered her had a quality of low and deadly steadiness.

"You have said that a thousand times, and you will say it another thousand—though you know the story was a lie and was proved to be one."

Lady Mallowe knew her way thoroughly.

"Who remembers the denials? What the world remembers is that Jem Temple Barholm was stamped as a cheat and a trickster. No one has time to remember the other thing. He is dead—dead! When a man's dead it's too late."

She was desperate enough to drive her javelin home deeper than she had ever chanced to drive it before. The truth—the awful truth she uttered shook Joan from head to foot. She sprang up and stood before her in heart-wrung fury.

"Oh! You are a hideously cruel woman!" she cried. "They say even tigers care for their young! But you—you can say that to *me*. 'When a man's dead, it's too late.'"

"It *is* too late—it IS too late!" Lady Mallowe persisted. Why had not she struck this note before? It was breaking her will: "I would say anything to bring you to your senses."

Joan began to move restlessly to and fro.

"Oh, what a fool I am!" she exclaimed. "As if you could understand—as if you could care!"

Struggle as she might to be defiant, she was breaking, Lady Mallowe repeated to herself. She followed her as a hunter might have followed a young leopardess with a wound in its flank.

"I came here because it *is* your last chance. Palliser knew what he was saying when he made a joke of it just now. He knew it wasn't a joke. You might have been the Duchess of Merthshire; you might have been Lady St. Maur, with a husband with millions. And here you are. You know what's before you—when I am out of the trap."

Joan laughed. It was a wild little laugh, and she felt there was no sense in it.

"I might apply for a place in Miss Alicia's Home for Decayed Gentlewomen," she said.

Lady Mallowe nodded her head fiercely.

"Apply, then. There will be no place for you in the home I am going to live in," she retorted.

Joan ceased moving about. She was about to hear the one argument that was new.

"You may as well tell me," she said, wearily.

"I have had a letter from Sir Moses Monaldini. He is to be at Broome Haughton. He is going there purposely to meet me. What he writes can mean only one thing. He means to ask me to marry him. I'm your mother, and I'm nearly twenty years older than you; but you see that I'm out of the trap first."

"I knew you would be," answered Joan.

"He detests you," Lady Mallowe went on. "He will not hear of your living with us—or even near us. He says you are old enough to take care of yourself. Take my advice. I am doing you a good turn in giving it. This New York newsboy is mad over you. If he hadn't been we should have been bundled out of the house before this. He never has spoken to a lady before in his life, and he feels as if you were a goddess. Go into the billiard-room this instant, and do all a woman can. Go!" And she actually stamped her foot on the carpet.

Joan's thunder-colored eyes seemed to grow larger as she stared at her. Her breast lifted itself, and her face slowly turned pale. Perhaps—she thought it wildly—people sometimes did die of feelings like this.

"He would crawl at your feet," her mother went on, pursuing what she felt sure was her advantage. She was so sure of it that she added words only a fool or a woman half hysteric with rage would have added. "You might live in the very house you would have lived in with Jem Temple Barholm, on the income he could have given you."

She saw the crassness of her blunder the next moment. If she had had an advantage, she had lost it. Wickedly, without a touch of mirth, Joan laughed in her face.

"Jem's house and Jem's money—and the New York newsboy in his shoes," she flung at her. "T. Tembarom to live with until one lay down on one's deathbed. T. Tembarom!"

Suddenly, something was giving way in her, Lady Mallowe thought again. Joan slipped into a chair and dropped her head and hidden face on the table.

"Oh! Mother! Mother!" she ended. "Oh! Jem! Jem!"

Was she sobbing or trying to choke sobbing back? There was no time to be lost. Her mother had never known a scene to end in this way before.

"Crying!" there was absolute spite in her voice. "That shows you know what you are in for, at all events. But I've said my last word. What does it matter to me, after all? You're in the trap. I'm not. Get out as best you can. I've done with you."

She turned her back and went out of the room—as she had come into it—with a sweep Joan would have smiled at as rather vulgar if she had seen it. As a child in the nursery, she had often seen that her ladyship was vulgar.

But she did not see the sweep because her face was hidden. Something in her had broken this time, as her mother had felt. That bitter, sordid truth, driven home as it had been, had done it. Who had time to remember denials, or lies proved to be lies? Nobody in the world. Who had time to give to the defense of a dead man? There was not time enough to give to living ones. It was true—true! When a man is dead, it is too late. The wall had built itself until it reached her sky; but it was not the wall she bent her head and sobbed over. It was that suddenly she had seen again Jem's face as he had stood with slow-growing pallor, and looked round at the ring of eyes which stared at him; Jem's face as he strode by her without a glance and went out of the room. She forgot everything else on earth. She forgot where she was. She was eighteen again, and she sobbed in her arms as eighteen sobs when its heart is torn from it.

"Oh Jem! Jem!" she cried. "If you were only in the same world with me! If you were just in the same world!"

She had forgotten all else, indeed. She forgot too long. She did not know how long. It seemed that no more than a few minutes had passed before she was without warning struck with the shock of feeling that some one was in the room with her, standing near her, looking at her. She had been mad not to remember that exactly this thing would be sure to happen, by some abominable chance. Her movement as she rose was almost violent, she could not hold herself still, and her face was horribly wet with shameless, unconcealable tears. Shameless she felt them—indecent—a sort of nudity of the soul. If it had been a servant who had intruded, or if it had been Palliser it would have been intolerable enough. But it was T. Tembarom who confronted her with his common face, moved mysteriously by some feeling she resented even more than she resented his presence. He was too grossly ignorant to know that a man of breeding, having entered by chance, would have turned and gone away, professing not to have seen. He seemed to think—the dolt!—that he must make some apology.

"Say! Lady Joan!" he began. "I beg your pardon. I didn't want to butt in."

"Then go away," she commanded. "Instantly—instantly!"

She knew he must see that she spoke almost through her teeth in her effort to control her sobbing breath. But he made no move toward leaving her. He even drew nearer, looking at her in a sort of meditative, obstinate way.

"N-no," he replied, deliberately. "I guess—I won't."

"You won't?" Lady Joan repeated after him. "Then I will."

He made a stride forward and laid his hand on her arm.

"No. Not on your life. You won't, either—if I can help it. And you're going to LET me help it."

Almost any one but herself—any one, at least, who did not resent his very existence—would have felt the drop in his voice which suddenly struck the note of boyish, friendly appeal in the last sentence. "You're going to LET me," he repeated.

She stood looking down at the daring, unconscious hand on her arm.

"I suppose," she said, with cutting slowness, "that you do not even *know* that you are insolent. Take your hand away," in arrogant command.

He removed it with an unabashed half-smile.

"I beg your pardon," he said. "I didn't even know I'd put it there. It was a break—but I wanted to keep you."

That he not only wanted to keep her, but intended to do so was apparent. His air was neither rough nor brutal, but he had ingeniously placed himself in the outlet between the big table and the way to the door. He put his hands in his pockets in his vulgar, unconscious way, and watched her.

"Say, Lady Joan!" he broke forth, in the frank outburst of a man who wants to get something over. "I should be a fool if I didn't see that you're up against it—hard! What's the matter?" His voice dropped again.

There was something in the drop this time which—perhaps because of her recent emotion—sounded to her almost as if he were asking the question with the protecting sympathy of the tone one would use in speaking to a child. How dare he! But it came home to her that Jem had once said "What's the matter?" to her in the same way.

"Do you think it likely that I should confide in you?" she said, and inwardly quaked at the memory as she said it.

"No," he answered, considering the matter gravely. "It's not likely—the way things look to you now. But if you knew me better perhaps it would be likely."

"I once explained to you that I do not intend to know you better," she gave answer.

He nodded acquiescently.

"Yes. I got on to that. And it's because it's up to me that I came out here to tell you something I want you to know before you go away. I'm going to confide in you."

"Cannot even you see that I am not in the mood to accept confidences?" she exclaimed.

"Yes, I can. But you're going to accept this one," steadily. "No," as she made a swift movement, "I'm not going to clear the way till I've done."

"I insist!" she cried. "If you were—"

He put out his hand, but not to touch her.

"I know what you're going to say. If I were a gentleman—Well, I'm not laying claim to that—but I'm a sort of a man, anyhow, though you mayn't think it. And you're going to listen."

She began to stare at him. It was not the ridiculous boyish drop in his voice which arrested her attention. It was a fantastic, incongruous, wholly different thing. He had suddenly dropped his slouch and stood upright. Did he realize that he had slung his words at her as if they were an order given with the ring of authority?

"I've not bucked against anything you've said or done since you've been here," he went on, speaking fast and grimly. "I didn't mean to. I had my reasons. There were things that I'd have given a good deal to say to you and ask you about, but you wouldn't let me. You wouldn't give me a chance to square things for you—if they could be squared. You threw me down every time I tried!"

He was too wildly incomprehensible with his changes from humanness to folly. Remembering what he had attempted to say on the day he had followed her in the avenue, she was inflamed again.

"What in the name of New York slang does that mean?" she demanded.

"Never mind New York," he answered, cool as well as grim. "A fellow that's learned slang in the streets has learned something else as well. He's learned to keep his eyes open. He's on to a way of seeing things. And what I've seen is that you're so doggone miserable that—that you're almost down and out."

This time she spoke to him in the voice with the quality of deadliness in it which she had used to her mother.

"Do you think that because you are in your own house you can be as intrusively insulting as you choose?" she said.

"No, I don't," he answered. "What I think is quite different. I think that if a man has a house of his own, and there's any one in big trouble under the roof of it—a woman most of all—he's a cheap skate if he don't get busy and try to help—just plain, straight help."

He saw in her eyes all her concentrated disdain of him, but he went on, still obstinate and cool and grim.

"I guess 'help' is too big a word just yet. That may come later, and it mayn't. What I'm going to try at now is making it easier for you—just easier."

Her contemptuous gesture registered no impression on him as he paused a moment and looked fixedly at her.

"You just hate me, don't you?" It was a mere statement which couldn't have been more impersonal to himself if he had been made of wood. "That's all right. I seem like a low-down intruder to you. Well, that's all right, too. But what ain't all right is what your mother has set you on to thinking about me. You'd never have thought it yourself. You'd have known better."

"What," fiercely, "is that?"

"That I'm mutt enough to have a mash on you."

The common slangy crassness of it was a kind of shock. She caught her breath and merely stared at him. But he was not staring at her; he was simply looking straight into her face, and it amazingly flashed upon her that the extraordinary words were so entirely unembarrassed and direct that they were actually not offensive.

He was merely telling her something in his own way, not caring the least about his own effect, but absolutely determined that she should hear and understand it.

Her caught breath ended in something which was like a half-laugh. His queer, sharp, incomprehensible face, his queer, unmoved voice were too extraordinarily unlike anything she had ever seen or heard before.

"I don't want to be brash—and what I want to say may seem kind of that way to you. But it ain't. Anyhow, I guess it'll relieve your mind. Lady Joan, you're a looker—you're a beaut from Beautville. If I were your kind, and things were different, I'd be crazy about you—crazy! But I'm not your kind—and things are different." He drew a step nearer still to her in his intentness. "They're this different. Why, Lady Joan! I'm dead stuck on another girl!"

She caught her breath again, leaning forward.

"Another—!"

"She says she's not a lady; she threw me down just because all this darned money came to me," he hastened on, and suddenly he was imperturbable no longer, but flushed and boyish, and more of New York than ever. "She's a little bit of a quiet thing and she drops her h's, but gee—! You're a looker— you're a queen and she's not. But Little Ann Hutchinson—Why, Lady Joan, as far as this boy's concerned"—and he oddly touched himself on the breast—"she makes you look like thirty cents."

Joan quickly sat down on the chair she had just left. She rested an elbow on the table and shaded her face with her hand. She was not laughing; she scarcely knew what she was doing or feeling.

"You are in love with Ann Hutchinson," she said, in a low voice.

"Am I?" he answered hotly. "Well, I should smile!" He disdained to say more.

Then she began to know what she felt. There came back to her in flashes scenes from the past weeks in which she had done her worst by him; in which she had swept him aside, loathed him, set her feet on him, used the devices of an ingenious demon to discomfit and show him at his poorest and least ready. And he had not been giving a thought to the thing for which she had striven to punish him. And he plainly did not even hate her. His mind was clear, as water is clear. He had come back to her this evening to do her a good turn—a good turn. Knowing what she was capable of in the way of arrogance and villainous temper, he had determined to do her—in spite of herself—a good turn.

"I don't understand you," she faltered.

"I know you don't. But it's only because I'm so dead easy to understand. There's nothing to find out. I'm just friendly—friendly—that's all."

"You would have been friends with me!" she exclaimed. "You would have told me, and I wouldn't let you! Oh!" with an impulsive flinging out of her hand to him, "you good—good fellow!"

"Good be darned!" he answered, taking the hand at once.

"You are good to tell me! I have behaved like a devil to you. But oh! if you only knew!"

His face became mature again; but he took a most informal seat on the edge of the table near her.

"I do know—part of it. That's why I've been trying to be friends with you all the time." He said his next words deliberately. "If I was the woman Jem Temple Barholm had loved wouldn't it have driven me mad to see another man in his place—and remember what was done to him. I never even saw him, but, good God! "—she saw his hand clench itself—"when I think of it I want to kill somebody! I want to kill half a dozen. Why didn't they know it couldn't be true of a fellow like that!"

She sat up stiffly and watched him.

"Do—you—feel like that—about him?"

"Do I!" red-hotly. "There were men there that knew him! There were women there that knew him! Why wasn't there just one to stand by him? A man that's been square all his life doesn't turn into a card-sharp in a night. Damn fools! I beg your pardon," hastily. And then, as hastily again: "No, I mean it. Damn fools!"

"Oh!" she gasped, just once.

Her passionate eyes were suddenly blinded with tears. She caught at his clenched hand and dragged it to her, letting her face drop on it and crying like a child.

The way he took her utter breaking down was just like him and like no one else. He put the other hand on her shoulder and spoke to her exactly as he had spoken to Miss Alicia on that first afternoon.

"Don't you mind me, Lady Joan," he said. "Don't you mind me a bit. I'll turn my back. I'll go into the billiard-room and keep them playing until you get away up-stairs. Now we understand each other, it'll be better for both of us."

"No, don't go! Don't!" she begged. "It is so wonderful to find some one who sees the cruelty of it." She spoke fast and passionately. "No one would listen to any defense of him. My mother simply raved when I said what you are saying."

"Do you want "—he put it to her with a curious comprehending of her emotion—"to talk about him? Would it do you good?"

"Yes! Yes! I have never talked to any one. There has been no one to listen."

"Talk all you want," he answered, with immense gentleness. "I'm here."

"I can't understand it even now, but he would not see me!" she broke out. "I was half mad. I wrote, and he would not answer. I went to his chambers when I heard he was going to leave England. I went to beg him to take me with him, married or unmarried. I would have gone on my knees to him. He was gone! Oh, why? Why?"

"You didn't think he'd gone because he didn't love you?" he put it to her quite literally and unsentimentally. "You knew better than that?"

"How could I be sure of anything! When he left the room that awful night he would not look at me! He would not look at me!"

"Since I've been here I've been reading a lot of novels, and I've found out a lot of things about fellows that are not the common, practical kind. Now, he wasn't. He'd lived pretty much like a fellow in a novel, I guess. What's struck me about that sort is that they think they have to make noble sacrifices, and they'll just walk all over a woman because they won't do anything to hurt her. There's not a bit of sense in it, but that was what he was doing. He believed he was doing the square thing by you—and you may bet your life it hurt him like hell. I beg your pardon—but that's the word—just plain hell."

"I was only a girl. He was like iron. He went away alone. He was killed, and when he was dead the truth was told."

"That's what I've remembered "—quite slowly—"every time I've looked at you. By gee! I'd have stood anything from a woman that had suffered as much as that."

It made her cry—his genuineness—and she did not care in the least that the tears streamed down her cheeks. How he had stood things! How he had borne, in that odd, unimpressive way, insolence and arrogance for which she ought to have been beaten and blackballed by decent society! She could scarcely bear it.

"Oh! to think it should have been you," she wept, "just you who understood!"

"Well," he answered speculatively, "I mightn't have understood as well if it hadn't been for Ann. By jings! I used to lie awake at night sometimes thinking `supposing it bad been Ann and me!' I'd sort of work it out as it might have happened in New York—at the office of the Sunday Earth. Supposing some fellow that'd had a grouch against me had managed it so that Galton thought I'd been getting away with money that didn't belong to me—fixing up my expense account, or worse. And Galton wouldn't listen to what I said, and fired me; and I couldn't get a job anywhere else because I was down and out for good. And nobody would listen. And I was killed without clearing myself. And Little Ann was left to stand it—Little Ann! Old Hutchinson wouldn't listen, I know that. And it would be all shut up burning in her big little heart—burning. And T. T. dead, and not a word to say for himself. Jehoshaphat!"—taking out his handkerchief and touching his forehead—"it used to make the cold sweat start out on me. It's doing it now. Ann and me might have been Jem and you. That's why I understood."

He put out his hand and caught hers and frankly squeezed it—squeezed it hard; and the unconventional clutch was a wonderful thing to her.

"It's all right now, ain't it?" he said. "We've got it straightened out. You'll not be afraid to come back here if your mother wants you to." He stopped for a moment and then went on with something of hesitation: "We don't want to talk about your mother. We can't. But I understand her, too. Folks are different from each other in their ways. She's different from you. I'll—I'll straighten it out with her if you like."

"Nothing will need straightening out after I tell her that you are going to marry Little Ann Hutchinson," said Joan, with a half-smile. "And that you were engaged to her before you saw me."

"Well, that does sort of finish things up, doesn't it?" said T. Tembarom.

He looked at her so speculatively for a moment after this that she wondered whether he had something more to say. He had.

"There's something I want to ask you," he ventured.

"Ask anything."

"Do you know any one—just any one—who has a photo—just any old photo—of Jem Temple Barholm?"

She was rather puzzled.

"Yes. I know a woman who has worn one for nearly eight years. Do you want to see it?"

"I'd give a good deal to," was his answer.

She took a flat locket from her dress and handed it to him.

"Women don't wear lockets in these days." He could barely hear her voice because it was so low. "But I've never taken it off. I want him near my heart. It's Jem!"

He held it on the palm of his hand and stood under the light, studying it as if he wanted to be sure he wouldn't forget it.

"It's—sorter like that picture of Miles Hugo, ain't it?" he suggested.

"Yes. People always said so. That was why you found me in the picture-gallery the first time we met."

"I knew that was the reason—and I knew I'd made a break when I butted in," he answered. Then, still looking at the photograph, "You'd know this face again most anywhere you saw it, I guess."

"There are no faces like it anywhere," said Joan.

"I guess that's so," he replied. "And it's one that wouldn't change much either. Thank you, Lady Joan."

He handed back the picture, and she put out her hand again.

"I think I'll go to my room now," she said. "You've done a strange thing to me. You've taken nearly all the hatred and bitterness out of my heart. I shall want to come back here whether my mother comes or not—I shall want to."

"The sooner the quicker," he said. "And so long as I'm here I'll be ready and waiting."

"Don't go away," she said softly. "I shall need you."

"Isn't that great?" he cried, flushing delightedly. "Isn't it just great that we've got things straightened so that you can say that. Gee! This is a queer old world! There's such a lot to do in it, and so few hours in the day. Seems like there ain't time to stop long enough to hate anybody and keep a grouch on. A fellow's got to keep hustling not to miss the things worth while."

The liking in her eyes was actually wistful.

"That's your way of thinking, isn't it?" she said. "Teach it to me if you can. I wish you could. Good-night." She hesitated a second. "God bless you!" she added, quite suddenly—almost fantastic as the words sounded to her. That she, Joan Fayre, should be calling down devout benisons on the head of T. Tembarom—T. Tembarom!

Her mother was in her room when she reached it. She had come up early to look over her possessions—and Joan's—before she began her packing. The bed, the chairs, and tables were spread with evening, morning, and walking-dresses, and the millinery collected from their combined wardrobes. She was examining anxiously a lace appliqued and embroidered white coat, and turned a slightly flushed face toward the opening door.

"I am going over your things as well as my own," she said. "I shall take what I can use. You will require nothing in London. You will require nothing anywhere in future. What is the matter?" she said sharply, as she saw her daughter's face.

Joan came forward feeling it a strange thing that she was not in the mood to fight—to lash out and be glad to do it.

"Captain Palliser told me as I came up that Mr. Temple Barholm had been talking to you," her mother went on. "He heard you having some sort of scene as he passed the door. As you have made your decision, of course I know I needn't hope that anything has happened."

"What has happened has nothing to do with my decision. He wasn't waiting for that," Joan answered her. "We were both entirely mistaken, Mother."

"What are you talking about?" cried Lady Mallowe, but she temporarily laid the white coat on a chair. "What do you mean by mistaken?"

"He doesn't want me—he never did," Joan answered again. A shadow of a smile hovered over her face, and there was no derision in it, only a warming recollection of his earnestness when he had said the words she quoted: "He is what they call in New York 'dead stuck on another girl.'"

Lady Mallowe sat down on the chair that held the white coat, and she did not push the coat aside.

"He told you that in his vulgar slang!" she gasped it out. "You—you ought to have struck him dead with your answer."

"Except poor Jem Temple Barholm," was the amazing reply she received, "he is the only friend I ever had in my life."

CHAPTER XXXII

It was business of serious importance which was to bring Captain Palliser's visit to a close. He explained it perfectly to Miss Alicia a day or so after Lady Mallowe and her daughter left them. He had lately been most amiable in his manner toward Miss Alicia, and had given her much valuable information about companies and stocks. He rather unexpectedly found it imperative that he should go to London and Berlin to "see people"—dealers in great financial schemes who were deeply interested in solid business speculations, such as his own, which were fundamentally different from all others in the impeccable firmness of their foundations.

"I suppose he will be very rich some day," Miss Alicia remarked the first morning she and T. Tembarom took their breakfast alone together after his departure. "It would frighten me to think of having as much money as he seems likely to have quite soon."

"It would scare me to death," said Tembarom. She knew he was making a sort of joke, but she thought the point of it was her tremor at the thought of great fortune.

"He seemed to think that it would be an excellent thing for you to invest in—I'm not sure whether it was the India Rubber Tree Company, or the mahogany forests or the copper mines that have so much gold and silver mixed in them that it will pay for the expense of the digging—" she went on.

"I guess it was the whole lot," put in Tembarom.

"Perhaps it was. They are all going to make everybody so rich that it is quite bewildering. He is very clever in business matters. And so kind. He even said that if I really wished it he might be able to invest my income for me and actually treble it in a year. But of course I told him that my income was your generous gift to me, and that it was far more than sufficient for my needs."

Tembarom put down his coffee-cup so suddenly to look at her that she was fearful that she had appeared to do Captain Palliser some vague injustice.

"I am sure he meant to be most obliging, dear," she explained. "I was really quite touched. He said most sympathetically and delicately that when women were unmarried, and unaccustomed to investment, sometimes a business man could be of use to them. He forgot"—affectionately—"that I had you."

Tembarom regarded her with tender curiosity. She often opened up vistas for him as he himself opened them for the Duke of Stone.

"If you hadn't had me, would you have let him treble your income in a year?" he asked.

Her expression was that of a soft, woodland rabbit or a trusting spinster dove.

"Well, of course, if one were quite alone in the world and had only a small income, it would be nice to have it wonderfully added to in such a short time," she answered. "But it was his friendly solicitude which touched me. I have not been accustomed to such interested delicacy on the part of—of gentlemen." Her hesitance before the last word being the result of training, which had made her feel that it was a little bold for "ladies" to refer quite openly to "gentlemen."

"You sometimes read in the newspapers," said Tembarom, buttering his toast, "about ladies who are all alone in the world with a little income, but they're not often left alone with it long. It's like you said—you've got me; but if the time ever comes when you haven't got me just you make a dead-sure thing of it that you don't let any solicitous business gentleman treble your income in a year. If it's an income that comes to more than five cents, don't you hand it over to be made into fifteen. Five cents is a heap better—just plain five."

"Temple!" gasped Miss Alicia. "You—you surely cannot mean that you do not think Captain Palliser is—sincere!"

Tembarom laughed outright, his most hilarious and comforting laugh. He had no intention of enlightening her in such a manner as would lead her at once to behold pictures of him as the possible victim of appalling catastrophes. He liked her too well as she was.

"Sincere?" he said. "He's sincere down to the ground—in what he's reaching after. But he's not going to treble your income, nor mine. If he ever makes that offer again, you just tell him I'm interested, and that I'll talk it over with him."

"I could not help saying to him that I didn't think you could want any more money when you had so much," she added, "but he said one never knew what might happen. He was greatly interested when I told him you had once said the very same thing yourself."

Their breakfast was at an end, and he got up, laughing again, as he came to her end of the table and put his arm around her shoulders in the unconventional young caress she adored him for.

"It's nice to be by ourselves again for a while," he said. "Let us go for a walk together. Put on the little bonnet and dress that are the color of a mouse. Those little duds just get me. You look so pretty in them."

The sixteen-year-old blush ran up to the roots of her gray side-ringlets. Just imagine his remembering the color of her dress and bonnet, and thinking that anything could make her look pretty! She was overwhelmed with innocent and grateful confusion. There really was no one else in the least like him.

"You do look well, ma'am," Rose said, when she helped her to dress. "You've got such a nice color, and that tiny bit of old rose Mrs. Mellish put in the bonnet does bring it out."

"I wonder if it is wrong of me to be so pleased," Miss Alicia thought. "I must make it a subject of prayer, and ask to be aided to conquer a haughty and vain-glorious spirit."

She was pathetically serious, having been trained to a view of the Great First Cause as figuratively embodied in the image of a gigantic, irascible, omnipotent old gentleman, especially wrought to fury by feminine follies connected with becoming headgear.

"It has sometimes even seemed to me that our Heavenly Father has a special objection to ladies," she had once timorously confessed to Tembarom. "I suppose it is because we are so much weaker than men, and so much more given to vanity and petty vices."

He had caught her in his arms and actually hugged her that time. Their intimacy had reached the point where the affectionate outburst did not alarm her.

"Say!" he had laughed. "It's not the men who are going to have the biggest pull with the authorities when folks try to get into the place where things are evened up. What I'm going to work my passage with is a list of the few 'ladies' I've known. You and Ann will be at the head of it. I shall just slide it in at the box-office window and say, 'Just look over this, will you? These were friends of mine, and they were mighty good to me. I guess if they didn't turn me down, you needn't. I know they're in here. Reserved seats. I'm not expecting to be put with them but if I'm allowed to hang around where they are that'll be heaven enough for me.'"

"I know you don't mean to be irreverent, dear Temple," she gasped. "I am quite sure you don't! It is—it is only your American way of expressing your kind thoughts. And of course"—quite hastily—"the Almighty must understand Americans—as he made so many." And half frightened though she was, she patted his arm with the warmth of comfort in her soul and moisture in her eyes. Somehow or other, he was always so comforting.

He held her arm as they took their walk. She had become used to that also, and no longer thought it odd. It was only one of the ways he had of making her feel that she was being taken care of. They had not been able to have many walks together since the arrival of the visitors, and this occasion was at once a cause of relief and inward rejoicing. The entire truth was that she had not been altogether happy about him of late. Sometimes, when he was not talking and saying amusing New York things which made people laugh, he seemed almost to forget where he was and to be thinking of something which baffled and tried him. The way in which he pulled himself together when he realized that any one was looking at him was, to her mind, the most disturbing feature of his fits of abstraction. It suggested that if he really had a trouble it was a private one on which he would not like her to intrude. Naturally, her adoring eyes watched him oftener than he knew, and she tried to find plausible and not too painful reasons for his mood. He always made light of his unaccustomedness to his new life; but perhaps it made him feel more unrestful than he would admit.

As they walked through the park and the village, her heart was greatly warmed by the way in which each person they met greeted him. They greeted no one else in the same way, and yet it was difficult to explain what the difference was. They liked him—really liked him, though how he had overcome their natural distrust of his newsboy and bootblack record no one but himself knew. In fact, she had reason to believe that even he himself did not know—had indeed never asked himself. They had gradually begun to like him, though none of them had ever accused him of being a gentleman according to their own acceptance of the word. Every man touched his cap or forehead with a friendly grin which spread itself the instant he caught sight of him. Grin and salute were synchronous. It was as if there were some extremely human joke between them. Miss Alicia had delightedly remembered a remark the Duke of Stone had made to her on his return from one of their long drives.

"He is the most popular man in the county," he had chuckled. "If war broke out and he were in the army, he could raise a regiment at his own gates which would follow him wheresoever he chose to lead it—if it were into hottest Hades."

Tembarom was rather silent during the first part of their walk, and when he spoke it was of Captain Palliser.

"He's a fellow that's got lots of curiosity. I guess he's asked you more questions than he's asked me," he began at last, and he looked at her interestedly, though she was not aware of it.

"I thought—" she hesitated slightly because she did not wish to be critical— "I sometimes thought he asked me too many."

"What was he trying to get on to mostly?"

"He asked so many things about you and your life in New York—but more, I think, about you and Mr. Strangeways. He was really quite persistent once or twice about poor Mr. Strangeways."

"What did he ask?"

"He asked if I had seen him, and if you had preferred that I should not. He calls him your Mystery, and thinks your keeping him here is so extraordinary."

"I guess it is—the way he'd look at it," Tembarom dropped in.

"He was so anxious to find out what he looked like. He asked how old he was and how tall, and whether he was quite mad or only a little, and where you picked him up, and when, and what reason you gave for not putting him in some respectable asylum. I could only say that I really knew nothing about him, and that I hadn't seen him because he had a dread of strangers and I was a little timid."

She hesitated again.

"I wonder," she said, still hesitating even after her pause, "I wonder if I ought to mention a rather rude thing I saw him do twice?"

"Yes, you ought," Tembarom answered promptly; "I've a reason for wanting to know."

"It was such a singular thing to do—in the circumstances," she went on obediently. "He knew, as we all know, that Mr. Strangeways must not be disturbed. One afternoon I saw him walk slowly backward and forward before the west room window. He had something in his hand and kept looking up. That was what first attracted my attention—his queer way of looking up. Quite suddenly he threw something which rattled on the panes of glass—it sounded like gravel or small pebbles. I couldn't help believing he thought Mr. Strangeways would be startled into coming to the window."

Tembarom cleared his throat.

"He did that twice," he said. "Pearson caught him at it, though Palliser didn't know he did. He'd have done it three times, or more than that, perhaps, but I casually mentioned in the smoking-room one night that some curious fool of a gardener boy had thrown some stones and frightened Strangeways, and that Pearson and I were watching for him, and that if I caught him I was going to knock his block off—bing! He didn't do it again. Darned fool! What does he think he's after?"

"I am afraid he is rather—I hope it is not wrong to say so—but he is rather given to gossip. And I dare say that the temptation to find something quite new to talk about was a great one. So few new things happen in the neighborhood, and, as the duke says, people are so bored—and he is bored himself."

"He'll be more bored if he tries it again when he comes back," remarked Tembarom.

Miss Alicia's surprised expression made him laugh.

"Do you think he will come back?" she exclaimed. "After such a long visit?"

"Oh, yes, he'll come back. He'll come back as often as he can until he's got a chunk of my income to treble—or until I've done with him."

"Until you've done with him, dear?" inquiringly.

"Oh! well,"—casually—"I've a sort of idea that he may tell me something I'd like to know. I'm not sure; I'm only guessing. But even if he knows it he won't tell me until he gets good and ready and thinks I don't want to hear it. What he thinks he's going to get at by prowling around is something he can get me in the crack of the door with."

"Temple"—imploringly—"are you afraid he wishes to do you an injury?"

"No, I'm not afraid. I'm just waiting to see him take a chance on it," and he gave her arm an affectionate squeeze against his side. He was always immensely moved by her little alarms for him. They reminded him, in a remote way, of Little Ann coming down Mrs. Bowse's staircase bearing with her the tartan comforter.

How could any one—how could any one want to do him an injury? she began to protest pathetically. But he would not let her go on. He would not talk any more of Captain Palliser or allow her to talk of him. Indeed, her secret fear was that he really knew something he did not wish her to be troubled by, and perhaps thought he had said too much. He began to make jokes and led her to other subjects. He asked her to go to the Hibblethwaites' cottage and pay a visit to Tummas. He had learned to understand his accepted privileges in making of cottage visits by this time; and when he clicked any wicket-gate the door was open before he had time to pass up the wicket-path. They called at several cottages, and he nodded at the windows of others where faces appeared as he passed by.

They had a happy morning together, and he took her back to Temple Barholm beaming, and forgetting Captain Palliser's existence, for the time, at least. In the afternoon they drove out together, and after dining they read the last copy of the Sunday Earth, which had arrived that day. He found quite an interesting paragraph about Mr. Hutchinson and the invention. Little Miss Hutchinson was referred to most flatteringly by the writer, who almost inferred that she was responsible not only for the inventor but for the invention itself. Miss Alicia felt quite proud of knowing so prominent a character, and wondered what it could be like to read about oneself in a newspaper.

About nine o'clock he laid his sheet of the Earth down and spoke to her.

"I'm going to ask you to do me a favor," he said. "I couldn't ask it if we weren't alone like this. I know you won't mind."

Of course she wouldn't mind. She was made happier by the mere idea of doing something for him.

"I'm going to ask you to go to your room rather early," he explained. "I want to try a sort of stunt on Strangeways. I'm going to bring him downstairs if he'll come. I'm not sure I can get him to do it; but he's been a heap better lately, and perhaps I can."

"Is he so much better as that?" she said. "Will it be safe?"

He looked as serious as she had ever seen him look—even a trifle more serious.

"I don't know how much better he is," was his answer. "Sometimes you'd think he was almost all right. And then—! The doctor says that if he could get over being afraid of leaving his room it would be a big thing for him. He wants him to go to his place in London so that he can watch him."

"Do you think you could persuade him to go?"

"I've tried my level best, but so far—nothing doing."

He got up and stood before the mantel, his back against it, his hands in his pockets.

"I've found out one thing," he said. "He's used to houses like this. Every now and again he lets something out quite natural. He knew that the furniture in his room was Jacobean—that's what he called it—and he knew it was fine stuff. He wouldn't have known that if he'd been a piker. I'm going to try if he won't let out something else when he sees things here—if he'll come."

"You have such a wonderfully reasoning mind, dear," said Miss Alicia, as she rose. "You would have made a great detective, I'm sure."

"If Ann had been with him," he said, rather gloomily, "she'd have caught on to a lot more than I have. I don't feel very chesty about the way I've managed it."

Miss Alicia went up-stairs shortly afterward, and half an hour later Tembarom told the footmen in the hall that they might go to bed. The experiment he was going to make demanded that the place should be cleared of any disturbing presence. He had been thinking it over for sometime past. He had sat in the private room of the great nerve specialist in London and had talked it over with him. He had talked of it with the duke on the lawn at Stone Hover. There had been a flush of color in the older man's cheek-bones, and his eyes had been alight as he took his part in the discussion. He had added the touch of his own personality to it, as always happened.

"We are having some fine moments, my good fellow," he had said, rubbing his hands. "This is extremely like the fourth act. I'd like to be sure what comes next."

"I'd like to be sure myself," Tembarom answered. "It's as if a flash of lightning came sometimes, and then things clouded up. And sometimes when I am trying something out he'll get so excited that I daren't go on until I've talked to the doctor."

It was the excitement he was dubious about to-night. It was not possible to be quite certain as to the entire safety of the plan; but there might be a chance—even a big chance—of wakening some cell from its deadened sleep. Sir Ormsby way had talked to him a good deal about brain cells, and he had listened faithfully and learned more than he could put into scientific English. Gradually, during the past months, he had been coming upon strangely exciting hints of curious possibilities. They had been mere hints at first, and had seemed almost absurd in their unbelievableness. But each one had linked itself with another, and led him on to further wondering and exploration. When Miss Alicia and Palliser had seen that he looked absorbed and baffled, it had been because he had frequently found himself, to use his own figures of speech, "mixed up to beat the band." He had not known which way to turn; but he had gone on turning because he could not escape from his own excited interest, and the inevitable emotion roused by being caught in the whirl of a melodrama. That was what he'd dropped into—a whacking big play. It had begun for him when Palford butted in that night and told him he was a lost heir, with a fortune and an estate in England; and the curtain had been jerking up and down ever since. But there had been thrills in it, queer as it was. Something doing all the time, by gee!

He sat and smoked his pipe and wished Ann were with him because he knew he was not as cool as he had meant to be. He felt a certain tingling of excitement in his body; and this was not the time to be excited. He waited for some minutes before he went up-stairs. It was true that Strangeways had been much better lately. He had seemed to find it easier to follow conversation. During the past few days, Tembarom had talked to him in a matter-of-fact way about the house and its various belongings. He had at last seemed to waken to an interest in the picture-gallery. Evidently he knew something of picture-galleries and portraits, and found himself relieved by his own clearness of thought when he talked of them.

"I feel better," he said, two or three times. "Things seem clearer—nearer."

"Good business!" exclaimed Tembarom. "I told you it'd be that way. Let's hold on to pictures. It won't be any time before you'll be remembering where you've seen some."

He had been secretly rather strung up; but he had been very gradual in approaching his final suggestion that some night, when everything was quiet, they might go and look at the gallery together.

"What you need is to get out of the way of wanting to stay in one place," he argued. "The doctor says you've got to have a change, and even going from one room to another is a fine thing."

Strangeways had looked at him anxiously for a few moments, even suspiciously, but his face had cleared after the look. He drew himself up and passed his hand over his forehead.

"I believe—perhaps he is right," he murmured.

"Sure he's right!" said Tembarom. "He's the sort of chap who ought to know. He's been made into a baronet for knowing. Sir Ormsby Galloway, by jings! That's no slouch of a name Oh, he knows, you bet your life!"

This morning when he had seen him he had spoken of the plan again. The visitors had gone away; the servants could be sent out of sight and hearing; they could go into the library and smoke and he could look at the books. And then they could take a look at the picture-gallery if he wasn't too tired. It would be a change anyhow.

To-night, as he went up the huge staircase, Tembarom's calmness of being had not increased. He was aware of a quickened pulse and of a slight dampness on his forehead. The dead silence of the house added to the unusualness of things. He could not remember ever having been so anxious before, except on the occasion when he had taken his first day's "stuff" to Galton, and had stood watching him as he read it. His forehead had grown damp then. But he showed no outward signs of excitement when he entered the room and found Strangeways standing, perfectly attired in evening dress.

Pearson, setting things in order at the other side of the room, was taking note of him furtively over his shoulder. Quite in the casual manner of the ordinary man, he had expressed his intention of dressing for the evening, and Pearson had thanked his stars for the fact that the necessary garments were at hand. From the first, he had not infrequently asked for articles such as only the resources of a complete masculine wardrobe could supply; and on one occasion he had suddenly wished to dress for dinner, and the lame excuses it had been necessary to make had disturbed him horribly instead of pacifying him. To explain that his condition precluded the necessity of the usual appurtenances would have been out of the question. He had been angry.

What did Pearson mean? What was the matter? He had said it over and over again, and then had sunk into a hopelessly bewildered mood, and had sat huddled in his dressing-gown staring at the fire. Pearson had been so harrowed by the situation that it had been his own idea to suggest to his master that all possible requirements should be provided. There were occasions when it appeared that the cloud over him lifted for a passing moment, and a gleam of light recalled to him some familiar usage of his past. When he had finished dressing, Pearson had been almost startled by the amount of effect produced by the straight, correctly cut lines of black and white. The mere change of clothes had suddenly changed the man himself—had "done something to him," Pearson put it. After his first glance at the mirror he had straightened himself, as if recognizing the fault of his own carriage. When he crossed the room it was with the action of a man who has been trained to move well. The good looks, which had been almost hidden behind a veil of uncertainty of expression and strained fearfulness, became obvious. He was tall, and his lean limbs were splendidly hung together. His head was perfectly set, and the bearing of his square shoulders was a soldierly thing. It was an extraordinarily handsome man Tembarom and Pearson found themselves gazing at. Each glanced involuntarily at the other.

"Now that's first-rate! I'm glad you feel like coming," Tembarom plunged in. He didn't intend to give him too much time to think.

"Thank you. It will be a change, as you said," Strangeways answered. "One needs change."

His deep eyes looked somewhat deeper than usual, but his manner was that of any well-bred man doing an accustomed thing. If he had been an ordinary guest in the house, and his host had dropped into his room, he would have comported himself in exactly the same way.

They went together down the corridor as if they had passed down it together a dozen times before. On the stairway Strangeways looked at the tapestries with the interest of a familiarized intelligence.

"It is a beautiful old place," he said, as they crossed the hall. "That armor was worn by a crusader." He hesitated a moment when they entered the library, but it was only for a moment. He went to the hearth and took the chair his host offered him, and, lighting a cigar, sat smoking it. If T. Tembarom had chanced to be a man of an analytical or metaphysical order of intellect he would have found, during the past month, many things to lead him far in mental argument concerning the weird wonder of the human mind—of its power where its possessor, the body, is concerned, its sometime closeness to the surface of sentient being, its sometime remoteness. He would have known—awed, marveling at the blackness of the pit into which it can descend—the unknown shades that may enfold it and imprison its gropings.

The old Duke of Stone had sat and pondered many an hour over stories his favorite companion had related to him. What curious and subtle processes had the queer fellow not been watching in the closely guarded quiet of the room where the stranger had spent his days; the strange thing cowering in its darkness; the ray of light piercing the cloud one day and seeming lost again the next; the struggles the imprisoned thing made to come forth—to cry out that it was but immured, not wholly conquered, and that some hour would arrive when it would fight its way through at last. Tembarom had not entered into psychological research. He had been entirely uncomplex in his attitude, sitting down before his problem as a besieger might have sat down before a castle. The duke had sometimes wondered whether it was not a good enough thing that he had been so simple about it, merely continuing to believe the best with an unswerving obstinacy and lending a hand when he could. A never flagging sympathy had kept him singularly alive to every chance, and now and then he had illuminations which would have done credit to a cleverer man, and which the duke had rubbed his hands over in half-amused, half-touched elation. How he had kept his head level and held to his purpose!

T. Tembarom talked but little as he sat in his big chair and smoked. Best let him alone and give him time to get used to the newness, he thought. Nothing must happen that could give him a jolt. Let things sort of sink into him, and perhaps they'd set him to thinking and lead him somewhere. Strangeways himself evidently did not want talk. He never wanted it unless he was excited. He was not excited now, and had settled down as if he was comfortable. Having finished one cigar he took another, and began to smoke it much more slowly than he had smoked his first. The slowness began to arrest Tembarom's attention. This was the smoking of a man who was either growing sleepy or sinking into deep thought, becoming oblivious to what he was doing. Sometimes he held the cigar absently between his strong, fine fingers, seeming to forget it. Tembarom watched him do this until he saw it go out, and its white ash drop on the rug at his feet. He did not notice it, but sat sinking deeper and deeper into his own being, growing more remote. What was going on under his absorbed stillness? Tembarom would not have moved or spoken "for a block of Fifth Avenue," he said internally. The dark eyes seemed to become darker until there was only a pin's point of light to be seen in their pupils. It was as if he were looking at something at a distance—at a strangely long distance. Twice he turned his head and appeared to look slowly round the room, but not as normal people look—as if it also was at the strange, long distance from him, and he were somewhere outside its walls. It was an uncanny thing to be a spectator to.

"How dead still the room is!" Tembarom found himself thinking.

It was "dead still." And it was a queer deal sitting, not daring to move—just watching. Something was bound to happen, sure! What was it going to be?

Strangeways' cigar dropped from his fingers and appeared to rouse him. He looked puzzled for a moment, and then stooped quite naturally to pick it up.

"I forgot it altogether. It's gone out," he remarked.

"Have another," suggested Tembarom, moving the box nearer to him.

"No, thank you." He rose and crossed the room to the wall of book-shelves. And Tembarom's eye was caught again by the fineness of movement and line the evening clothes made manifest. "What a swell he looked when he moved about like that! What a swell, by jings!"

He looked along the line of shelves and presently took a book down and opened it. He turned over its leaves until something arrested his attention, and then he fell to reading. He read several minutes, while Tembarom watched him. The silence was broken by his laughing a little.

"Listen to this," he said, and began to read something in a language totally unknown to his hearer. "A man who writes that sort of thing about a woman is an old bounder, whether he's a poet or not. There's a small, biting spitefulness about it that's cattish."

"Who did it?" Tembarom inquired softly. It might be a good idea to lead him on.

"Horace. In spite of his genius, he sometimes makes you feel he was rather a blackguard."

"Horace!" For the moment T. Tembarom forgot himself. "I always heard he was a sort of Y.M.C.A. old guy—old Horace Greeley. The Tribune was no yellow journal when he had it."

He was sorry he had spoken the next moment. Strangeways looked puzzled.

"The Tribune," he hesitated. "The Roman Tribune?"

"No, New York. He started it—old Horace did. But perhaps we're not talking of the same man."

Strangeways hesitated again.

"No, I think we're not," he answered politely.

"I've made a break," thought Tembarom. "I ought to have kept my mouth shut. I must try to switch him back."

Strangeways was looking down at the back of the book he held in his hand.

"This one was the Latin poet, Quintus Horatius Flaccus, 65 B. C. You know him," he said.

"Oh, that one!" exclaimed Tembarom, as if with an air of immense relief. "What a fool I was to forget! I'm glad it's him. Will you go on reading and let me hear some more? He's a winner from Winnersville—that Horace is."

Perhaps it was a sort of miracle, accomplished by his great desire to help the right thing to happen, to stave off any shadow of the wrong thing. Whatsoever the reason, Strangeways waited only a moment before turning to his book again. It seemed to be a link in some chain slowly forming itself to drag him back from his wanderings. And T. Tembarom, lightly sweating as a frightened horse will, sat smoking another pipe and listening intently to "Satires" and "Lampoons," read aloud in the Latin of 65 B. C.

"By gee!" he said faithfully, at intervals, when he saw on the reader's face that the moment was ripe. "He knew it all—old Horace—didn't he?"

He had steered his charge back. Things were coming along the line to him. He'd learned Latin at one of these big English schools. Boys always learned Latin, the duke had told him. They just had to. Most of them hated it like thunder, and they used to be caned when they didn't recite it right. Perhaps if he went on he'd begin to remember the school. A queer part of it was that he did not seem to notice that he was not reading his own language.

He did not, in fact, seem to remember anything in particular, but went on quite naturally for some minutes. He had replaced Horace on the shelf and was on the point of taking down another volume when he paused, as if recalling something else.

"Weren't we going to see the picture-gallery?" he inquired. "Isn't it getting late? I should like to see the portraits."

"No hurry," answered T. Tembarom. "I was just waiting till you were ready. But we'll go right away, if you like."

They went without further ceremony. As they walked through the hall and down the corridors side by side, an imaginative person might have felt that perhaps the eyes of an ancient darkling portrait or so looked down at the pair curiously: the long, loosely built New Yorker rather slouching along by the soldierly, almost romantic figure which, in a measure, suggested that others not unlike it might have trod the same oaken floor, wearing ruff and doublet, or lace jabot and sword. There was a far cry between the two, but they walked closely in friendly union. When they entered the picture-gallery Strangeways paused a moment again, and stood peering down its length.

"It is very dimly lighted. How can we see?" he said.

"I told Pearson to leave it dim," Tembarom answered. "I wanted it just that way at first."

He tried—and succeeded tolerably well—to say it casually, as he led the way ahead of them. He and the duke had not talked the scheme over for nothing. As his grace had said, they had "worked the thing up." As they moved down the gallery, the men and women in their frames looked like ghosts staring out to see what was about to happen.

"We'll turn up the lights after a while," T. Tembarom explained, still casually. "There's a picture here I think a good deal of. I've stood and looked at it pretty often. It reminded me of some one the first day I set eyes on it; but it was quite a time before I made up my mind who it was. It used to drive me half dotty trying to think it out."

"Which one was it?" asked Strangeways.

"We're coming to it. I want to see if it reminds you of any one. And I want you to see it sudden." "It's got to be sudden," he had said to the duke. "If it's going to pan out, I believe it's got to be sudden." "That's why I had the rest of 'em left dim. I told Pearson to leave a lamp I could turn up quick," he said to Strangeways.

The lamp was on a table near by and was shaded by a screen. He took it from the shadow and lifted it suddenly, so that its full gleam fell upon the portrait of the handsome youth with the lace collar and the dark, drooping eyes. It was done in a second, with a dramatically unexpected swiftness. His heart jumped up and down.

"Who's that?" he demanded, with abruptness so sharp-pitched that the gallery echoed with the sound. "Who's that?"

He heard a hard, quick gasp, a sound which was momentarily a little horrible, as if the man's soul was being jerked out of his body's depths.

"Who is he?" he cried again. "Tell me."

After the gasp, Strangeways stood still and stared. His eyes were glued to the canvas, drops of sweat came out on his forehead, and he was shuddering. He began to back away with a look of gruesome struggle. He backed and backed, and stared and stared. The gasp came twice again, and then his voice seemed to tear itself loose from some power that was holding it back.

"Th—at!" he cried. "It is—it—is Miles Hugo!"

The last words were almost a shout, and he shook as if he would have fallen. But T. Tembarom put his hand on his shoulder and held him, breathing fast himself. Gee! if it wasn't like a thing in a play!

"Page at the court of Charles the Second," he rattled off. "Died of smallpox when he was nineteen. Miles Hugo! Miles Hugo! You hold on to that for all your worth. And hold on to me. I'll keep you steady. Say it again."

"Miles Hugo." The poor majestic-looking fellow almost sobbed it. "Where am I? What is the name of this place?"

"It's Temple Barholm in the county of Lancashire, England. Hold on to that, too—like thunder!"

Strangeways held the young man's arm with hands that clutched. He dragged at him. His nightmare held him yet; Tembarom saw it, but flashes of light were blinding him.

"Who"—he pleaded in a shaking and hollow whisper—"are you?"

Here was a stumper! By jings! By jings! And not a minute to think it out. But the answer came all right—all right!

"My name's Tembarom. T. Tembarom." And he grinned his splendid grin from sheer sense of relief. "I'm a New Yorker—Brooklyn. I was just forked in here anyhow. Don't you waste time thinking over me. You sit down here and do your durndest with Miles Hugo."

CHAPTER XXXIII

Tembarom did not look as though he had slept particularly well, Miss Alicia thought, when they met the next morning; but when she asked him whether he had been disappointed in his last night's experiment, he answered that he had not. The experiment had come out all right, but Strangeways had been a good deal worked up, and had not been able to sleep until daylight. Sir Ormsby Galloway was to arrive in the afternoon, and he'd probably give him some-thing quieting. Had the coming downstairs seemed to help him to recall anything? Miss Alicia naturally inquired. Tembarom thought it had. He drove to Stone Hover and spent the morning with the duke; he even lunched with him. He returned in time to receive Sir Ormsby Galloway, however, and until that great personage left, they were together in Mr. Strangeways' rooms.

"I guess I shall get him up to London to the place where Sir Ormsby wants him," he said rather nervously, after dinner. "I'm not going to miss any chances. If he'll go, I can get him away quietly some time when I can fix it so there's no one about to worry him."

She felt that he had no inclination to go much into detail. He had never had the habit of entering into the details connected with his strange charge. She believed it was because he felt the subject too abnormal not to seem a little awesome to her sympathetic timidity. She did not ask questions because she was afraid she could not ask them intelligently. In fact, the knowledge that this unknown man was living through his struggle with his lost past in the remote rooms of the west wing, almost as though he were a secret prisoner, did seem a little awesome when one awoke in the middle of the dark night and thought of it.

During the passage of the next few weeks, Tembarom went up to London several times. Once he seemed called there suddenly, as it was only during dinner that he told her he was going to take a late train, and should leave the house after she had gone to bed. She felt as though something important must have happened, and hoped it was nothing disturbing.

When he had said that Captain Palliser would return to visit them, her private impression, despite his laugh, had been that it must surely be some time before this would occur. But a little more than three weeks later he appeared, preceded only half an hour by a telegram asking whether he might not spend a night with them on his way farther north. He could not at all understand why the telegram, which he said he had sent the day before, had been delayed.

A certain fatigued haggardness in his countenance caused Miss Alicia to ask whether he had been ill, and he admitted that he had at least not been well, as a result of long and too hurried journeys, and the strenuousness of extended and profoundly serious interviews with his capitalist and magnates.

"No man can engineer gigantic schemes to success without feeling the reaction when his load drops from his shoulders," he remarked.

"You've carried it quite through?" inquired Tembarom.

"We have set on foot one of the largest, most substantially capitalized companies in the European business world," Palliser replied, with the composure which is almost indifference.

"Good!" said Tembarom cheerfully.

He watched his guest a good deal during the day. He was a bad color for a man who had just steered clear of all shoals and reached the highest point of success. He had a haggard eye as well as a haggard face. It was a terrified eye when its desperate determination to hide its terrors dropped from it for an instant, as a veil might drop. A certain restlessness was manifest in him, and he talked more than usual. He was going to make a visit in Northumberland to an elderly lady of great possessions. It was to be vaguely gathered that she was somewhat interested in the great company—the Cedric. She was a remarkable old person who found a certain agreeable excitement in dabbling in stocks. She was rich enough to be in a position to regard it as a sort of game, and he had been able on several occasions to afford her entertainment. He would remain a few days, and spend his time chiefly in telling her the details of the great scheme and the manner in which they were to be developed.

"If she can play with things that way, she'll be sure to want stock in it," Tembarom remarked.

"If she does, she must make up her mind quickly," Palliser smiled, "or she will not be able to get it. It is not easy to lay one's hands on even now."

Tembarom thought of certain speculators of entirely insignificant standing of whom he had chanced to see and hear anecdotes in New York. Most of them were youths of obscure origin who sold newspapers or blacked boots, or "swapped" articles the value of which lay in the desire they could excite in other persons to possess them. A popular method known as "bluff" was their most trusted weapon, and even at twelve and fifteen years of age Tembarom had always regarded it as singularly obvious. He always detested "bluff," whatsoever its disguise, and was rather mystified by its ingenious faith in itself.

"He's got badly stung," was his internal comment as he sucked at his pipe and smiled urbanely at Palliser across the room as they sat together. "He's come here with some sort of deal on that he knows he couldn't work with any one but just such a fool as he thinks I am. I guess," he added in composed reflectiveness, "I don't really know how big a fool I do look."

Whatsoever the deal was, he would be likely to let it be known in time.

"He'll get it off his chest if he's going away to-morrow," decided Tembarom. "If there's anything he's found out, he'll use it. If it doesn't pan out as he thinks it will he'll just float away to his old lady."

He gave Palliser every chance, talking to him and encouraging him to talk, even asking him to let him look over the prospectus of the new company and explain details to him, as he was going to explain them to the old lady in Northumberland. He opened up avenues; but for a time Palliser made no attempt to stroll down them. His walk would be a stroll, Tembarom knew, being familiar with his methods. His aspect would be that of a man but little concerned. He would be capable of a slightly rude coldness if he felt that concern on his part was in any degree counted as a factor. Tembarom was aware, among other things, that innocent persons would feel that it was incumbent upon them to be very careful in their treatment of him. He seemed to be thinking things over before he decided upon the psychological moment at which he would begin, if he began. When a man had a good deal to lose or to win, Tembarom realized that he would be likely to hold back until he felt something like solid ground under him.

After Miss Alicia had left them for the night, perhaps he felt, as a result of thinking the matter over, that he had reached a foothold of a firmness at least somewhat to be depended upon.

"What a change you have made in that poor woman's life!" he said, walking to the side-table and helping himself to a brandy and soda. "What a change!"

"It struck me that a change was needed just about the time I dropped in," answered his host.

"All the same," suggested Palliser, tolerantly, "you were immensely generous. She wasn't entitled to expect it, you know."

"She didn't expect anything, not a darned thing," said Tembarom. "That was what hit me."

Palliser smiled a cold, amiable smile. His slim, neatly fitted person looked a little shrunken and less straight than was its habit, and its slackness suggested itself as being part of the harry and fatigue which made his face and eyes haggard under his pale, smooth hair.

"Do you purpose to provide for the future of all your indigent relatives even to the third and fourth generation, my dear chap?" he inquired.

"I won't refuse till I'm asked, anyhow," was the answer.

"Asked!" Palliser repeated. "I'm one of them, you know, and Lady Mallowe is another. There are lots of us, when we come out of our holes. If it's only a matter of asking, we might all descend on you."

Tembarom, smiling, wondered whether they hadn't descended already, and whether the descent had so far been all that they had anticipated.

Palliser strolled down his opened avenue with an incidental air which was entirely creditable to his training of himself. T. Tembarom acknowledged that much.

"You are too generous," said Palliser. "You are the sort of fellow who will always need all he has, and more. The way you go among the villagers! You think you merely slouch about and keep it quiet, but you don't. You've set an example no other landowner can expect to live up to, or intends to. It's too lavish. It's pernicious, dear chap. I have heard all about the cottage you are doing over for Pearson and his bride. You had better invest in the Cedric."

Tembarom wanted him to go on, if there was anything in it. He made his face look as he knew Palliser hoped it would look when the psychological moment came. Its expression was not a deterrent; in fact, it had a character not unlikely to lead an eager man, or one who was not as wholly experienced as he believed he was, to rush down a steep hill into the sea, after the manner of the swine in the parable.

Heaven knew Palliser did not mean to rush, and was not aware when the rush began; but he had reason to be so much more eager than he professed to be that momentarily he swerved, despite himself, and ceased to be casual.

"It is an enormous opportunity," he said—"timber lands in Mexico, you know. If you had spent your life in England, you would realize that timber has become a desperate necessity, and that the difficulties which exist in the way of supplying the demand are almost insuperable. These forests are virtually boundless, and the company which controls them—"

"That's a good spiel!" broke in Tembarom.

It sounded like the crudely artless interruption of a person whose perceptions left much to be desired. T. Tembarom knew what it sounded like. If Palliser lost his temper, he would get over the ground faster, and he wanted him to get over the ground.

"I'm afraid I don't understand," he replied rather stiffly.

"There was a fellow I knew in New York who used to sell type-writers, and he had a thing to say he used to reel off when any one looked like a customer. He used to call it his 'spiel.'"

Palliser's quick glance at him asked questions, and his stiffness did not relax itself.

"Is this New York chaff?" he inquired coldly.

"No," Tembarom said. "You're not doing it for ten per. He was"

"No, not exactly," said Palliser. "Neither would you be doing it for ten per if you went into it." His voice changed. He became slightly haughty. "Perhaps it was a mistake on my part to think you might care to connect yourself with it. You have not, of course, been in the position to comprehend such matters."

"If I was what I look like, that'd stir me up and make me feel bad," thought T. Tembarom, with cheerful comprehension of this, at least. "I'd have to rush in and try to prove to him that I was as accustomed to big business as he is, and that it didn't rattle me. The way to do it that would come most natural would be to show I was ready to buy as big a block of stock as any other fellow."

But the expression of his face did not change. He only gave a half-awkward sort of laugh.

"I guess I can learn," he said.

Palliser felt the foothold become firmer. The bounder was interested, but, after a bounder's fashion, was either nervous or imagined that a show of hesitation looked shrewd. The slight hit made at his inexperience in investment had irritated him and made him feel less cock-sure of himself. A slightly offended manner might be the best weapon to rely upon.

"I thought you might care to have the thing made clear to you," he continued indifferently. "I meant to explain. You may take the chance or leave it, as you like, of course. That is nothing to me at this stage of the game. But, after all, we are as I said, relatives of a sort, and it is a gigantic opportunity. Suppose we change the subject. Is that the Sunday Earth I see by you on the table?" He leaned forward to take the paper, as though the subject really were dropped; but, after a seemingly nervous suck or two at his pipe, Tembarom came to his assistance. It wouldn't do to let him quiet down too much.

"I'm no Van Morganbilt," he said hesitatingly, "but I can see that it's a big opportunity—for some one else. Let's have a look over the prospectus again."

Palliser paused in his unconcerned opening of the copy of the Sunday Earth. His manner somewhat disgustedly implied indecision as to whether it was worth while to allow oneself to be dropped and taken up by turns.

"Do you really mean that?" he asked with a certain chill of voice.

"Yes. I don't mind trying to catch on to what's doing in any big scheme."

Palliser did not lay aside his suggestion of cold semi-reluctance more readily than any man who knew his business would have laid it aside. His manner at the outset was quite perfect. His sole ineptitude lay in his feeling a too great confidence in the exact quality of his companion's type, as he summed it up. He did not calculate on the variations from all type sometimes provided by circumstances.

He produced his papers without too obvious eagerness. He spread them upon the table, and coolly examined them himself before beginning his explanation. There was more to explain to a foreigner and one unused to investment than there would be to a man who was an Englishman and familiar with the methods of large companies, he said. He went into technicalities, so to speak, and used rapidly and lightly some imposing words and phrases, to which T. Tembarom listened attentively, but without any special air of illumination. He dealt with statistics and the resulting probabilities. He made apparent the existing condition of England's inability to supply an enormous and unceasing demand for timber. He had acquired divers excellent methods of stating his case to the party of the second part.

"He made me feel as if a fellow had better hold on to a box of matches like grim death, and that the time wasn't out of sight when you'd have to give fifty-seven dollars and a half for a toothpick," Tembarom afterwards said to the duke.

What Tembarom was thinking as he listened to him was that he was not getting over the ground with much rapidity, and that it was time something was doing. He had not watched him for weeks without learning divers of his idiosyncrasies.

"If he thought I wanted to know what he thinks I'd a heap rather NOT know, he'd never tell me," he speculated. "If he gets a bit hot in the collar, he may let it out. Thing is to stir him up. He's lost his nerve a bit, and he'll get mad pretty easy."

He went on smoking and listening, and asking an unenlightened question now and then, in a manner which was as far from being a deterrent as the largely unilluminated expression of his face was.

"Of course money is wanted," Palliser said at length. "Money is always wanted, and as much when a scheme is a success as when it isn't. Good names, with a certain character, are wanted. The fact of your inheritance is known everywhere; and the fact that you are an American is a sort of guaranty of shrewdness."

"Is it?" said T. Tembarom. "Well," he added slowly, "I guess Americans are pretty good business men."

Palliser thought that this was evolving upon perfectly natural lines, as he had anticipated it would. The fellow was flattered and pleased. You could always reach an American by implying that he was one of those who specially illustrate enviable national characteristics.

He went on in smooth, casual laudation:

"No American takes hold of a scheme of this sort until he knows jolly well what he's going to get out of it. You were shrewd enough," he added significantly, "about Hutchinson's affair. You 'got in on the ground floor' there. That was New York forethought, by Jove!"

Tembarom shuffled a little in his chair, and grinned a faint, pleased grin.

"I'm a man of the world, my boy—the business world," Palliser commented, hoping that he concealed his extreme satisfaction. "I know New York, though I haven't lived there. I'm only hoping to. Your air of ingenuous ignorance is the cleverest thing about you," which agreeable implication of the fact that he had been privately observant and impressed ought to have fetched the bounder if anything would.

T. Tembarom's grin was no longer faint, but spread itself. Palliser's first impression was that he had "fetched" him. But when he answered, though the very crudeness of his words seemed merely the result of his betrayal into utter tactlessness by soothed vanity, there was something—a shade of something—not entirely satisfactory in his face and nasal twang.

"Well, I guess," he said, "New York DID teach a fellow not to buy a gold brick off every con man that came along."

Palliser was guilty of a mere ghost of a start. Was there something in it, or was he only the gross, blundering fool he had trusted to his being? He stared at him a moment, and saw that there WAS something under the words and behind his professedly flattered grin—something which must be treated with a high hand.

"What do you mean?" he exclaimed haughtily. "I don't like your tone. Do you take ME for what you call a 'con man'?"

"Good Lord, no!" answered Tembarom; and he looked straight at Palliser and spoke slowly. "You're a gentleman, and you're paying me a visit. You could no more try on a game to do me in my own house than—well, than I could TELL you if I'd got on to you if I saw you doing it. You're a gentleman."

Palliser glared back into his infuriatingly candid eyes. He was a far cry from being a dullard himself; he was sharp enough to "catch on" to the revelation that the situation was not what he had thought it, the type was more complex than he had dreamed. The chap had been playing a part; he had absolutely been "jollying him along," after the New York fashion. He became pale with humiliated rage, though he knew his only defense was to control himself and profess not to see through the trick. Until he could use his big lever, he added to himself.

"Oh, I see," he commented acridly. "I suppose you don't realize that your figures of speech are unfortunate."

"That comes of New York streets, too," Tembarom answered with deliberation. "But you can't live as I've lived and be dead easy—not DEAD easy."

Palliser had left his chair, and stood in contemptuous silence.

"You know how a fellow hates to be thought DEAD easy"—Tembarom actually went to the insolent length of saying the words with a touch of cheerful confidingness—"when he's NOT. And I'm not. Have another drink."

There was a pause. Palliser began to see, or thought he began to see, where he stood. He had come to Temple Barholm because he had been driven into a corner and had a dangerous fight before him. In anticipation of it he had been following a clue for some time, though at the outset it had been one of incredible slightness. Only his absolute faith in his theory that every man had something to gain or lose, which he concealed discreetly, had led him to it. He held a card too valuable to be used at the beginning of a game. Its power might have lasted a long time, and proved an influence without limit. He forbore any mental reference to blackmail; the word was absurd. One used what fell into one's hands. If Tembarom had followed his lead with any degree of docility, he would have felt it wiser to save his ammunition until further pressure was necessary. But behind his ridiculous rawness, his foolish jocularity, and his professedly candid good humor, had been hidden the Yankee trickster who was fool enough to think he could play his game through. Well, he could not.

During the few moments' pause he saw the situation as by a photographic flashlight. He leaned over the table and supplied himself with a fresh brandy and soda from the tray of siphons and decanters. He gave himself time to take the glass up in his hand.

"No," he answered, "you are not 'dead easy.' That's why I am going to broach another subject to you."

Tembarom was refilling his pipe.

"Go ahead," he said.

"Who, by the way, is Mr. Strangeways?"

He was deliberate and entirely unemotional. So was T. Tembarom when, with match applied to his tobacco, he replied between puffs as he lighted it:

"You can search me. You can search him, too, for that matter. He doesn't know who he is himself."

"Bad luck for him!" remarked Palliser, and allowed a slight pause again. After it he added, "Did it ever strike you it might be good luck for somebody else?"

"Somebody else?" Tembarom puffed more slowly, perhaps because his pipe was lighted.

Palliser took some brandy in his soda.

"There are men, you know," he suggested, "who can be spared by their relatives. I have some myself, by Jove!" he added with a laugh. "You keep him rather dark, don't you?"

"He doesn't like to see people."

"Does he object to people seeing him? I saw him once myself."

"When you threw the gravel at his window?"

Palliser stared contemptuously.

"What are you talking about? I did not throw stones at his window," he lied. "I'm not a school-boy."

"That's so," Tembarom admitted.

"I saw him, nevertheless. And I can tell you he gave me rather a start."

"Why?"

Palliser half laughed again. He did not mean to go too quickly; he would let the thing get on Tembarom's nerves gradually.

"Well, I'm hanged if I didn't take him for a man who is dead."

"Enough to give any fellow a jolt," Tembarom admitted again.

"It gave me a `jolt.' Good word, that. But it would give you a bigger one, my dear fellow, if he was the man he looked like."

"Why?" Tembarom asked laconically.

"He looked like Jem Temple Barholm."

He saw Tembarom start. There could be no denying it.

"You thought that? Honest?" he said sharply, as if for a moment he had lost his head. "You thought that?"

"Don't be nervous. Perhaps I couldn't have sworn to it. I did not see him very close."

T. Tembarom puffed rapidly at his pipe, and only, ejaculated:

"Oh!"

"Of course he's dead. If he wasn't,"—with a shrug of his shoulders,—"Lady Joan Fayre would be Lady Joan Temple Barholm, and the pair would be bringing up an interesting family here." He looked about the room, and then, as if suddenly recalling the fact, added, "By George! you'd be selling newspapers, or making them—which was it?—in New York!"

It was by no means unpleasing to see that he had made his hit there. T. Tembarom swung about and walked across the room with a suddenly perturbed expression.

"Say," he put it to him, coming back, "are you in earnest, or are you just saying it to give me a jolt?"

Palliser studied him. The American sharpness was not always so keen as it sometimes seemed. His face would have betrayed his uneasiness to the dullest onlooker.

"Have you any objection to my seeing him in his own room?" Palliser inquired.

"It does him harm to see people," Tembarom said, with nervous brusqueness. "It worries him."

Palliser smiled a quiet but far from agreeable smile. He enjoyed what he put into it.

"Quite so; best to keep him quiet," he returned. "Do you know what my advice would be? Put him in a comfortable sanatorium. A lot of stupid investigations would end in nothing, of course, but they'd be a frightful bore."

He thought it extraordinarily stupid in T. Tembarom to come nearer to him with an anxious eagerness entirely unconcealed, if he really knew what he was doing.

"Are you sure that if you saw him close you'd KNOW, so that you could swear to him?" he demanded.

"You're extremely nervous, aren't you?" Palliser watched him with smiling coolness. "Of course Jem Temple Barholm is dead; but I've no doubt that if I saw this man of yours, I could swear he had remained dead—if I were asked."

"If you knew him well, you could make me sure. You could swear one way or another. I want to be SURE," said Tembarom.

"So should I in your place; couldn't be too sure. Well, since you ask me, I COULD swear. I knew him well enough. He was one of my most intimate enemies. What do you say to letting me see him?"

"I would if I could," Tembarom replied, as if thinking it over. "I would if I could."

Palliser treated him to the far from pleasing smile again.

"But it's quite impossible at present?" he suggested. "Excitement is not good for him, and all that sort of thing. You want time to think it over."

Tembarom's slowly uttered answer, spoken as if he were still considering the matter, was far from being the one he had expected.

"I want time; but that's not the reason you can't see him right now. You can't see him because he's not here. He's gone."

Then it was Palliser who started, taken totally unaware in a manner which disgusted him altogether. He had to pull himself up.

"He's gone!" he repeated. "You are quicker than I thought. You've got him safely away, have you? Well, I told you a comfortable sanatorium would be a good idea."

"Yes, you did." T. Tembarom hesitated, seeming to be thinking it over again. "That's so." He laid his pipe aside because it had gone out.

He suddenly sat down at the table, putting his elbows on it and his face in his hands, with a harried effect of wanting to think it over in a sort of withdrawal from his immediate surroundings. This was as it should be. His Yankee readiness had deserted him altogether.

"By Jove! you are nervous!" Palliser commented. "It's not surprising, though. I can sympathize with you." With a markedly casual air he himself sat down and drew his documents toward him. "Let us talk of something else," he said. He preferred to be casual and incidental, if he were allowed. It was always better to suggest things and let them sink in until people saw the advantage of considering them and you. To manage a business matter without open argument or too frank a display of weapons was at once more comfortable and in better taste.

"You are making a great mistake in not going into this," he suggested amiably. "You could go in now as you went into Hutchinson's affair, 'on the ground floor.' That's a good enough phrase, too. Twenty thousand pounds would make you a million. You Americans understand nothing less than millions."

But T. Tembarom did not take him up. He muttered in a worried way from behind his shading hands, "We'll talk about that later."

"Why not talk about it now, before anything can interfere?" Palliser persisted politely, almost gently.

Tembarom sprang up, restless and excited. He had plainly been planning fast in his temporary seclusion.

"I'm thinking of what you said about Lady Joan," he burst forth. "Say, she's gone through all this Jem Temple Barholm thing once; it about half killed her. If any one raised false hopes for her, she'd go through it all again. Once is enough for any woman."

His effect at professing heat and strong feeling made a spark of amusement show itself in Palliser's eye. It struck him as being peculiarly American in its affectation of sentiment and chivalry.

"I see," he said. "It's Lady Joan you're disturbed about. You want to spare her another shock, I see. You are a considerate fellow, as well as a man of business."

"I don't want her to begin to hope if—"

"Very good taste on your part." Palliser's polite approval was admirable, but he tapped lightly on the paper after expressing it. "I don't want to seem to press you about this, but don't you feel inclined to consider it? I can assure you that an investment of this sort would be a good thing to depend on if the unexpected happened. If you gave me your check now, it would be Cedric stock to-morrow, and quite safe. Suppose you—"

"I—I don't believe you were right—about what you thought." The sharp-featured face was changing from pale to red. "You'd have to be able to swear to it, anyhow, and I don't believe you can." He looked at Palliser in eager and anxious uncertainty. "If you could," he dragged out, "I shouldn't have a check-book. Where would you be then?"

"I should be in comfortable circumstances, dear chap, and so would you if you gave me the money to-night, while you possess a check-book. It would be only a sort of temporary loan in any case, whatever turned up. The investment would quadruple itself. But there is no time to be lost. Understand that."

T. Tembarom broke out into a sort of boyish resentment.

"I don't believe he did look like him, anyhow," he cried. "I believe it's all a bluff." His crude-sounding young swagger had a touch of final desperation in it as he turned on Palliser. "I'm dead sure it's a bluff. What a fool I was not to think of that! You want to bluff me into going into this Cedric thing. You could no more swear he was like him than—than I could."

The outright, presumptuous, bold stripping bare of his phrases infuriated Palliser too suddenly and too much. He stepped up to him and looked into his eyes.

"Bluff you, you young bounder!" he flung out at him. "You're losing your head. You're not in New York streets here. You are talking to a gentleman. No," he said furiously, "I couldn't swear that he was like him, but what I can swear in any court of justice is that the man I saw at the window was Jem Temple Barholm, and no other man on earth."

When he had said it, he saw the astonishing dolt change his expression utterly again, as if in a flash. He stood up, putting his hands in his pockets. His face changed, his voice changed.

"Fine!" he said. "First-rate! That's what I wanted to get on to."

CHAPTER XXXIV

After this climax the interview was not so long as it was interesting. Two men as far apart as the poles, as remote from each other in mind and body, in training and education or lack of it, in desires and intentions, in points of view and trend of being, as nature and circumstances could make them, talked in a language foreign to each other of a wildly strange thing. Palliser's arguments and points of aspect were less unknown to T. Tembarom than his own were to Palliser. He had seen something very like them before, though they had developed in different surroundings and had been differently expressed. The colloquialism "You're not doing that for your health" can be made to cover much ground in the way of the stripping bare of motives for action. This was what, in excellent and well-chosen English, Captain Palliser frankly said to his host. Of nothing which T. Tembarom said to him in his own statement did he believe one word or syllable. The statement in question was not long or detailed. It was, of course, Palliser saw, a ridiculously impudent flinging together of a farrago of nonsense, transparent in its effort beyond belief. Before he had listened five minutes with the distinctly "nasty" smile, he burst out laughing.

"That is a good `spiel,' my dear chap," he said. "It's as good a `spiel' as your typewriter friend used to rattle off when he thought he saw a customer; but I'm not a customer."

Tembarom looked at him interestedly for about ten seconds. His hands were thrust into his trousers pockets, as was his almost invariable custom. Absorption and speculation, even emotion and excitement, were usually expressed in this unconventional manner.

"You don't believe a darned word of it," was his sole observation.

"Not a darned word," Palliser smiled. "You are trying a `bluff,' which doesn't do credit to your usual sharpness. It's a bluff that is actually silly. It makes you look like an ass."

"Well, it's true," said Tembarom; "it's true."

Palliser laughed again.

"I only said it made you look like an ass," he remarked. "I don't profess to understand you altogether, because you are a new species. Your combination of ignorance and sharpness isn't easy to calculate on. But there is one thing I have found out, and that is, that when you want to play a particular sharp trick you are willing to let people take you for a fool. I'll own you've deceived me once or twice, even when I suspected you. I've heard that's one of the most successful methods used in the American business world. That's why I only say you look like an ass. You are an ass in some respects; but you are letting yourself look like one now for some shrewd end. You either think you'll slip out of danger by it when I make this discovery public, or you think you'll somehow trick me into keeping my mouth shut."

"I needn't trick you into keeping your mouth shut," Tembarom suggested. "There's a straightway to do that, ain't there?" And he indelicately waved his hand toward the documents pertaining to the Cedric Company.

It was stupid as well as gross, in his hearer's opinion. If he had known what was good for him he would have been clever enough to ignore the practical presentation of his case made half an hour or so earlier.

"No, there is not," Palliser replied, with serene mendacity. "No suggestion of that sort has been made. My business proposition was given out on an entirely different basis. You, of course, choose to put your personal construction upon it."

"Gee whiz!" ejaculated T. Tembarom. "I was 'way off, wasn't I?"

"I told you that professing to be an ass wouldn't be good enough in this case. Don't go on with it," said Palliser, sharply.

"You're throwing bouquets. Let a fellow be natural," said Tembarom.

"That is bluff, too," Palliser replied more sharply still. "I am not taken in by it, bold as it is. Ever since you came here, you have been playing this game. It was your fool's grin and guffaw and pretense of good nature that first made me suspect you of having something up your sleeve. You were too unembarrassed and candid."

"So you began to look out," Tembarom said, considering him curiously, "just because of that." Then suddenly he laughed outright, the fool's guffaw.

It somehow gave Palliser a sort of puzzled shock. It was so hearty that it remotely suggested that he appeared more secure than seemed possible. He tried to reply to him with a languid contempt of manner.

"You think you have some tremendously sharp `deal' in your hand," he said, "but you had better remember you are in England where facts are like sledge-hammers. You can't dodge from under them as you can in America. I dare say you won't answer me, but I should like to ask you what you propose to do."

"I don't know what I'm going to do any more than you do," was the unilluminating answer. "I don't mind telling you that."

"And what do you think he will do?"

"I've got to wait till I find out. I'm doing it. That was what I told you. What are you going to do?" he added casually.

"I'm going to Lincoln's Inn Fields to have an interview with Palford & Grimby."

"That's a good enough move," commented Tembarom, "if you think you can prove what you say. You've got to prove things, you know. I couldn't, so I lay low and waited, just like I told you."

"Of course, of course," Palliser himself almost grinned in his derision. "You have only been waiting."

"When you've got to prove a thing, and haven't much to go on, you've got to wait," said T. Tembarom—"to wait and keep your mouth shut, whatever happens, and to let yourself be taken for a fool or a horse-thief isn't as gilt-edged a job as it seems. But proof's what it's best to have before you ring up the curtain. You'd have to have it yourself. So would Palford & Grimby before it'd be stone-cold safe to rush things and accuse a man of a penitentiary offense."

He took his unconventional half-seat on the edge of the table, with one foot on the floor and the other one lightly swinging.

"Palford & Grimby are clever old ducks, and they know that much. Thing they'd know best would be that to set a raft of lies going about a man who's got money enough to defend himself, and to make them pay big damages for it afterward, would be pretty bum business. I guess they know all about what proof stands for. They may have to wait; so may you, same as I have."

Palliser realized that he was in the position of a man striking at an adversary whose construction was of India-rubber. He struck home, but left no bruise and drew no blood, which was an irritating thing. He lost his temper.

"Proof!" he jerked out. "There will be proof enough, and when it is made public, you will not control the money you threaten to use."

"When you get proof, just you let me hear about it," T. Tembarom said. "And all the money I'm threatening on shall go where it belongs, and I'll go back to New York and sell papers if I have to. It won't come as hard as you think."

The flippant insolence with which he brazened out his pretense that he had not lied, that his ridiculous romance was actual and simple truth, suggested dangerous readiness of device and secret knowledge of power which could be adroitly used.

"You are merely marking time," said Palliser, rising, with cold determination to be juggled with no longer. "You have hidden him away where you think you can do as you please with a man who is an invalid. That is your dodge.

You've got him hidden somewhere, and his friends had better get at him before it is too late."

"I'm not answering questions this evening, and I'm not giving addresses, though there are no witnesses to take them down. If he's hidden away, he's where he won't be disturbed," was T. Tembarom's rejoinder. "You may lay your bottom dollar on that."

Palliser walked toward the door without speaking. He had almost reached it when he whirled about involuntarily, arrested by a shout of laughter.

"Say," announced Tembarom, "you mayn't know it, but this lay-out would make a first-rate turn in a vaudeville. You think I'm lying, I look like I'm lying, I guess every word I say sounds like I'm lying. To a fellow like you, I guess it couldn't help but sound that way. And I'm not lying. That's where the joke comes in. I'm not lying. I've not told you all I know because it's none of your business and wouldn't help; but what I have told you is the stone-cold truth."

He was keeping it up to the very end with a desperate determination not to let go his hold of his pose until he had made his private shrewd deal, whatsoever it was. At least, so it struck Palliser, who merely said:

"I 'm leaving the house by the first train to-morrow morning." He fixed a cold gray eye on the fool's grin.

"Six forty-five," said T. Tembarom. "I'll order the carriage. I might go up myself."

The door closed.

Tembarom was looking cheerful enough when he went into his bedroom. He had become used to its size and had learned to feel that it was a good sort of place. It had the hall bedroom at Mrs. Bowse's boarding-house "beaten to a frazzle." There was about everything in it that any man could hatch up an idea he'd like to have. He had slept luxuriously on the splendid carved bed through long nights, he had lain awake and thought out things on it, he had lain and watched the fire-light flickering on the ceiling, as he thought about Ann and made plans, and "fixed up" the Harlem flat which could be run on fifteen per. He had picked out the pieces of furniture from the Sunday Earth advertisement sheet, and had set them in their places. He always saw the six-dollar mahogany-stained table set for supper, with Ann at one end and himself at the other. He had grown actually fond of the old room because of the silence and comfort of it, which tended to give reality to his dreams. Pearson, who had ceased to look anxious, and who had acquired fresh accomplishments in the form of an entirely new set of duties, was waiting, and handed him a telegram.

"This just arrived, sir," he explained. "James brought it here because he thought you had come up, and I didn't send it down because I heard you on the stairs."

"That's right. Thank you, Pearson," his master said.

He tore the yellow envelop, and read the message. In a moment Pearson knew it was not an ordinary message, and therefore remained more than ordinarily impassive of expression. He did not even ask of himself what it might convey.

Mr. Temple Barholm stood still a few seconds, with the look of a man who must think and think rapidly.

"What is the next train to London, Pearson?" he asked.

"There is one at twelve thirty-six, sir," he answered. "It's the last till six in the morning. You have to change at Crowley."

"You're always ready, Pearson," returned Mr. Temple Barholm. "I want to get that train."

Pearson was always ready. Before the last word was quite spoken he had turned and opened the bedroom door.

"I'll order the dog-cart; that's quickest, sir," he said. He was out of the room and in again almost immediately. Then he was at the wardrobe and taking out what Mr. Temple Barholm called his "grip," but what Pearson knew as a Gladstone bag. It was always kept ready packed for unexpected emergencies of travel.

Mr. Temple Barholm sat at the table and drew pen and paper toward him. He looked excited; he looked more troubled than Pearson had seen him look before.

"The wire's from Sir Ormsby Galloway, Pearson," he said.

"It's about Mr. Strangeways. He's done what I used to be always watching out against: he's disappeared."

"Disappeared, sir!" cried Pearson, and almost dropped the Gladstone bag. "I beg pardon, sir. I know there's no time to lose." He steadied the bag and went on with his task without even turning round.

His master was in some difficulty. He began to write, and after dashing off a few words, stopped, and tore them up.

"No," he muttered, "that won't do. There's no time to explain." Then he began again, but tore up his next lines also.

"That says too much and not enough. It'd frighten the life out of her."

He wrote again, and ended by folding the sheet and putting it into an envelop.

"This is a message for Miss Alicia," he said to Pearson. "Give it to her in the morning. I don't want her to worry because I had to go in a hurry. Tell her everything's going to be all right; but you needn't mention that anything's happened to Mr. Strangeways."

"Yes, sir," answered Pearson.

Mr. Temple Barholm was already moving about the room, doing odd things for himself rapidly, and he went on speaking.

"I want you and Rose to know," he said, "that whatever happens, you are both fixed all right—both of you. I've seen to that."

"Thank you, sir," Pearson faltered, made uneasy by something new in his tone. "You said whatever happened, sir—"

"Whatever old thing happens," his master took him up.

"Not to you, sir. Oh, I hope, sir, that nothing—"

Mr. Temple Barholm put a cheerful hand on his shoulder.

"Nothing's going to happen that'll hurt any one. Things may change, that's all. You and Rose are all right, Miss Alicia's all right, I'm all right. Come along. Got to catch that train."

In this manner he took his departure.

Miss Alicia had from necessity acquired the habit of early rising at Rowcroft vicarage, and as the next morning was bright, she was clipping roses on a terrace before breakfast when Pearson brought her the note.

"Mr. Temple Barholm received a telegram from London last night, ma'am," he explained, "and he was obliged to take the midnight train. He hadn't time to do any more than leave a few lines for you, but he asked me to tell you that nothing disturbing had occurred. He specially mentioned that everything was all right."

"But how very sudden!" exclaimed Miss Alicia, opening her note and beginning to read it. Plainly it had been written hurriedly indeed. It read as though he had been in such haste that he hadn't had time to be clear.

Dear little Miss Alicia:

I've got to light out of here as quick as I can make it. I can't even stop to tell you why. There's just one thing—don't get rattled, Miss Alicia. Whatever any one says or does, just don't let yourself get rattled.

Yours affectionately,

T. TEMBAROM.

"Pearson," Miss Alicia exclaimed, again looking up, "are you sure everything is all right?"

"That was what he said, ma'am. `All right,' ma'am."

"Thank you, Pearson. I am glad to hear it."

She walked to and fro in the sunshine, reading the note and rereading it.

"Of course if he said it was all right, it was all right," she murmured. "It is only the phrasing that makes me slightly nervous. Why should he ask me not to get rattled?" The term was by this time as familiar to her as any in Dr. Johnson's dictionary. "Of course he knows I do get rattled much too easily; but why should I be in danger of getting rattled now if nothing has happened?" She gave a very small start as she remembered something. "Could it be that Captain Palliser—But how could he? Though I do not like Captain Palliser."

Captain Palliser, her distaste for whom at the moment quite agitated her, was this morning an early riser also, and as she turned in her walk she found him coming toward her.

"I find I am obliged to take an early train to London this morning," he said, after their exchange of greetings. "It is quite unexpected. I spoke to Mr. Temple Barholm about it last night."

Perhaps the unexpectedness, perhaps a certain suggestion of coincidence, caused Miss Alicia's side ringlets to appear momentarily tremulous.

"Then perhaps we had better go in to breakfast at once," she said.

"Is Mr. Temple Barholm down?" he inquired as they seated themselves at the breakfast-table.

"He is not here," she answered. "He, too, was called away unexpectedly. He went to London by the midnight train."

She had never been so aware of her unchristian lack of liking for Captain Palliser as she was when he paused a moment before he made any comment. His pause was as marked as a start, and the smile he indulged in was, she felt, most singularly disagreeable. It was a smile of the order which conceals an unpleasant explanation of itself.

"Oh," he remarked, "he has gone first, has he?"

"Yes," she answered, pouring out his coffee for him. "He evidently had business of importance."

They were quite alone, and she was not one of the women one need disturb oneself about. She had been browbeaten into hypersensitive timidity early in life, and did not know how to resent cleverly managed polite bullying. She would always feel herself at fault if she was tempted to criticize any one. She was innocent and nervous enough to betray herself to any extent, because she would feel it rude to refuse to answer questions, howsoever far they exceeded the limits of polite curiosity. He had learned a good deal from her in the past. Why not try what could be startled out of her now? Thus Captain Palliser said:

"I dare say you feel a little anxious at such an extraordinarily sudden departure," he suggested amiably. "Bolting off in the middle of the night was sudden, if he did not explain himself."

"He had no time to explain," she answered.

"That makes it appear all the more sudden. But no doubt he left you a message. I saw you were reading a note when I joined you on the terrace."

Lightly casual as he chose to make the words sound, they were an audacity he would have known better than to allow himself with any one but a timid early-Victorian spinster whose politeness was hypersensitive in its quality.

"He particularly desired that I should not be anxious," she said. "He is always considerate."

"He would, of course, have explained everything if he had not been so hurried?"

"Of course, if it had been necessary," answered Miss Alicia, nervously sipping her tea.

"Naturally," said Captain Palliser. "His note no doubt mentioned that he went away on business connected with his friend Mr. Strangeways?"

There was no question of the fact that she was startled.

"He had not time enough," she said. "He could only write a few lines. Mr. Strangeways?"

"We had a long talk about him last night. He told me a remarkable story," Captain Palliser went on. "I suppose you are quite familiar with all the details of it?"

"I know how he found him in New York, and I know how generous he has been to him."

"Have you been told nothing more?"

"There was nothing more to tell. If there was anything, I am sure he had some good reason for not telling me," said Miss Alicia, loyally. "His reasons are always good."

Palliser's air of losing a shade or so of discretion as a result of astonishment was really well done.

"Do you mean to say that he has not even hinted that ever since he arrived at Temple Barholm he has strongly suspected Strangeways' identity—that he has even known who he is?" he exclaimed.

Miss Alicia's small hands clung to the table-cloth.

"He has not known at all. He has been most anxious to discover. He has used every endeavor," she brought out with some difficulty.

"You say he has been trying to find out?" Palliser interposed.

"He has been more than anxious," she protested. "He has been to London again and again; he has gone to great expense; he has even seen people from Scotland Yard. I have sometimes almost thought he was assuming more responsibility than was just to himself. In the case of a relative or an old friend, but for an entire stranger—Oh, really, I ought not to seem to criticize. I do not presume to criticize his wonderful generosity and determination and goodness. No one should presume to question him."

"If he knows that you feel like this—" Palliser began.

"He knows all that I feel," Miss Alicia took him up with a pretty, rising spirit. "He knows that I am full of unspeakable gratitude to him for his beautiful kindness to me; he knows that I admire and respect and love him in a way I could never express, and that I would do anything in the world he could wish me to do."

"Naturally," said Captain Palliser. "I was only about to express my surprise that since he is aware of all this he has not told you who he has proved Strangeways to be. It is a little odd, you know."

"I think "—Miss Alicia was even gently firm in her reply—"that you are a little mistaken in believing Mr. Temple Barholm has proved Mr. Strangeways to be anybody. When he has proof, he will no doubt think proper to tell me about it. Until then I should prefer—"

Palliser laughed as he finished her sentence.

"Not to know. I was not going to betray him, Miss Alicia. He evidently has one of his excellent reasons for keeping things to himself. I may mention, however, that it is not so much he who has proof as I myself."

"You!" How could she help quite starting in her seat when his gray eyes fixed themselves on her with such a touch of finely amused malice?

"I offered him the proof last night, and it rather upset him," he said. "He thought no one knew but himself, and he was not inclined to tell the world. He was upset because I said I had seen the man and could swear to his identity. That was why he went away so hurriedly. He no doubt went to see Strangeways and talk it over."

"See Mr. Strangeways? But Mr. Strangeways—" Miss Alicia rose and rang the bell.

"Tell Pearson I wish to see him at once," she said to the footman.

Palliser took in her mood without comment. He had no objection to being present when she made inquiries of Pearson.

"I hear the wheels of the dog-cart," he remarked. "You see, I must catch my train."

Pearson stood at the door.

"Is not Mr. Strangeways in his room, Pearson?" Miss Alicia asked.

"Mr. Temple Barholm took him to London when he last went, ma'am," answered Pearson. "You remember he went at night. The doctor thought it best."

"He did not tell you that, either?" said Palliser, casually.

"The dog-cart is at the door, sir," announced Pearson.

Miss Alicia's hand was unsteady when the departing guest took it.

"Don't be disturbed," he said considerately, "but a most singular thing has happened. When I asked so many questions about Temple Barholm's Man with the Iron Mask I asked them for curious reasons. That must be my apology. You will hear all about it later, probably from Palford & Grimby."

When he had left the room Miss Alicia stood upon the hearth-rug as the dog-cart drove away, and she was pale. Her simple and easily disturbed brain was in a whirl. She could scarcely remember what she had heard, and could not in the least comprehend what it had seemed intended to imply, except that there had been concealed in the suggestions some disparagement of her best beloved.

Singular as it was that Pearson should return without being summoned, when she turned and found that he mysteriously stood inside the threshold again, as if she had called him, she felt a great sense of relief.

"Pearson," she faltered, "I am rather upset by certain things which Captain Palliser has said. I am afraid I do not understand."

She looked at him helplessly, not knowing what more to say. She wished extremely that she could think of something definite.

The masterly finish of Pearson's reply lay in its neatly restrained hint of unobtrusively perceptive sympathy.

"Yes, Miss. I was afraid so. Which is why I took the liberty of stepping into the room again. I myself do not understand, but of course I do not expect to. If I may be so bold as to say it, Miss, whatever we don't understand, we both understand Mr. Temple Barholm. My instructions were to remind you, Miss, that everything would be all right."

Miss Alicia took up her letter from the table where she had laid it down.

"Thank you, Pearson," she said, her forehead beginning to clear itself a little. "Of course, of course. I ought not to—He told me not to—get rattled," she added with plaintive ingenuousness, "and I ought not to, above all things."

"Yes, Miss. It is most important that you should not."

CHAPTER XXXV

The story of the adventures, experiences, and journeyings of Mr. Joseph Hutchinson, his daughter, and the invention, if related in detail, would prove reading of interest; but as this is merely a study of the manner in which the untrained characteristics and varied limitations of one man adjusted or failed to adjust themselves to incongruous surroundings and totally unprepared-for circumstances, such details, whatsoever their potential picturesqueness, can be touched upon but lightly. No new idea of value to the world of practical requirements is presented to the public at large without the waking of many sleeping dogs, and the stirring of many snapping fish, floating with open ears and eyes in many pools. An uneducated, blustering, obstinate man of one idea, having resentfully borne discouragement and wounded egotism for years, and suddenly confronting immense promise of success, is not unlikely to be prey easily harpooned. Joseph Hutchinson's rebound from despair to high and well-founded hope made of him exactly what such a man is always made by such rebound. The testimony to his genius and judgment which acknowledgment of the value of his work implied was naturally, in his opinion, only a proper tribute which the public had been a bull-headed fool not to lay at his feet years before. So much time lost, and so much money for it, as well as for him, and served 'em all damned well right, he said. If Temple Barholm hadn't come into his money, and hadn't had more sense than the rest of them, where would they all have been? Perhaps they'd never have had the benefit of the thing he'd been telling them about for years. He prided himself immensely on the possession of a business shrewdness which was an absolute defense against any desire on the part of the iniquitous to overreach him. He believed it to be a peculiarly Lancashire characteristic, and kept it in view constantly.

"Lancashire's not easy to do," he would say hilariously, "Them that can do a Lancashire chap has got to look out that they get up early in the morning and don't go to bed till late."

Smooth-mannered and astute men of business who knew how to make a man talk were given diffuse and loud-voiced explanations of his methods and long-acknowledged merits and characteristics. His life, his morals, and his training, or rather lack of it, were laid before them as examples of what a man might work himself up to if "he had it in him." Education didn't do it. He had never been to naught but a village school, where he'd picked up precious little but the three R's. It had to be born in a man. Look at him! His invention promised to bring him in a fortune like a duke's, if he managed it right and kept his eyes open for sharpers. This company and that company were after him, but Lancashire didn't snap up things without going into 'em, and under 'em, and through 'em, for the matter of that.

The well-mannered gentlemen of business stimulated him greatly by their appreciative attention. He sometimes lost his head a trifle and almost bullied them, but they did not seem to mind it. Their apparently old-time knowledge of and respect for Lancashire business sagacity seemed invariably a marked thing. Men of genius and powerful character combined with practical shrewdness of outlook they intimated, were of enormous value to the business world. They were to be counted upon as important factors. They could see and deal with both sides of a proposal as those of weaker mind could not.

"That they can," Hutchinson would admit, rolling about in his chair and thrusting his hands in his pockets. "They've got some bottom to stand on." And he would feel amenable to reason.

Little Ann found her duties and responsibilities increasing daily. Many persons seemed to think it necessary to come and talk business, and father had so much to think of and reason out, so that he could be sure that he didn't make any mistakes. In a quiet, remote, and darkened corner of her mind, in which were stored all such things as it was well to say little or nothing about, there was discreetly kept for reference the secretly acquired knowledge that father did not know so much about business ways and business people as he thought he did. Mother had learned this somewhat important fact, and had secluded it in her own private mental store-room with much affectionate delicacy.

"Father's a great man and a good man, Ann love," she had confided to her, choosing an occasion when her husband was a hundred miles away, "and he IS right-down Lancashire in his clever way of seeing through people that think themselves sharp; but when a man is a genius and noble-minded he sometimes can't see the right people's faults and wickedness. He thinks they mean as honest as he does. And there's times when he may get taken in if some one, perhaps not half as clever as he is, doesn't look after him. When the invention's taken up, and everybody's running after him to try to cheat him out of his rights, if I'm not there, Ann, you must just keep with him and watch every minute. I've seen these sharp, tricky ones right-down flinch and quail when there was a nice, quiet-behaved woman in the room, and she just fixed her eye steady and clear-like on them and showed she'd took in every word and was like to remember. You know what I mean, Ann; you've got that look in your own eye."

She had. The various persons who interviewed Mr. Hutchinson became familiar with the fact that he had an unusual intimacy with and affection for his daughter. She was present on all occasions. If she had not been such a quiet and entirely unobtrusive little thing, she might have been an obstacle to freedom of expression. But she seemed a childish, unsophisticated creature, who always had a book with her when she waited in an office, and a trifle of sewing to occupy herself with when she was at home. At first she so obliterated herself that she was scarcely noticed; but in course of time it became observed by some that she was curiously pretty. The face usually bent over her book or work was tinted like a flower, and she had quite magnificent red hair. A stout old financier first remarked her eyes. He found one day that she had quietly laid her book on her lap, and that they were resting upon him like unflinching crystals as he talked to her father. Their serenity made him feel annoyed and uncomfortable. It was a sort of recording serenity. He felt as though she would so clearly remember every word he had said that she would be able to write it down when she went home; and he did not care to have it written down. So he began to wander somewhat in his argument, and did not reach his conclusions.

"I was glad, Father, to see how you managed that gentleman this afternoon," Little Ann said that night when Hutchinson had settled himself with his pipe after an excellent dinner.

"Eh?" he exclaimed. "Eh?"

"The one," she exclaimed, "that thought he was so sure he was going to persuade you to sign that paper. I do wonder he could think you'd listen to such a poor offer, and tie up so much. Why, even I could see he was trying to take advantage, and I know nothing in the world about business."

The financier in question had been a brilliant and laudatory conversationalist, and had so soothed and exhilarated Mr. Hutchinson that such perils had beset him as his most lurid imaginings could never have conceived in his darkest moments of believing that the entire universe had ceased all other occupation to engage in that of defrauding him of his rights and dues. He had been so uplifted by the admiration of his genius so properly exhibited, and the fluency with which his future fortunes had been described, that he had been huffed when the arguments seemed to dwindle away. Little Ann startled him, but it was not he who would show signs of dismay at the totally unexpected expression of adverse opinion. He had got into the habit of always listening, though inadvertently, as it were, to Ann as he had inadvertently listened to her mother.

"Rosenthal?" he said. "Are you talking about him?"

"Yes, I am," Little Ann answeered, smiling approvingly over her bit of sewing. "Father, I wish you'd try and teach me some of the things you know about business. I've learned a little by just listening to you talk; but I should so like to feel as if I could follow you when you argue. I do so enjoy hearing you argue. It's just an education."

"Women are not up to much at business," reflected Hutchinson. "If you'd been a boy, I'd have trained you same as I've trained myself. You're a sharp little thing, Ann, but you're a woman. Not but what a woman's the best thing on earth," he added almost severely in his conviction—"the best thing on earth in her place. I don't know what I'd ever have done without you, Ann, in the bad times."

He loved her, blundering old egotist, just as he had loved her mother. Ann always knew it, and her own love for him warmed all the world about them both. She got up and went to him to kiss him, and pat him, and stuff a cushion behind his stout back.

"And now the good times have come," she said, bestowing on him two or three special little pats which were caresses of her own invention, "and people see what you are and always have been, as they ought to have seen long ago, I don't want to feel as if I couldn't keep up with you and understand your plans. Perhaps I've got a little bit of your cleverness, and you might teach me to use it in small ways. I've got a good memory you know, Father love, and I might recollect things people say and make bits of notes of them to save you trouble. And I can calculate. I once got a copy of Bunyan's `Pilgrim's Progress' for a prize at the village school just for sums."

The bald but unacknowledged fact that Mr. Hutchinson had never exhibited gifts likely to entitle him to receive a prize for "sums" caused this suggestion to be one of some practical value. When business men talked to him of per cents., and tenth shares or net receipts, and expected him to comprehend their proportions upon the spot without recourse to pencil and paper, he felt himself grow hot and nervous and red, and was secretly terrified lest the party of the second part should detect that he was tossed upon seas of horrible uncertainty. T. Tembarom in the same situation would probably have said, "This is the place where T. T. sits down a while to take breath and count things up on his fingers. I am not a sharp on arithmetic, and I need time—lots of it."

Mr. Hutchinson's way was to bluster irritatedly.

"Aye, aye, I see that, of course, plain enough. I see that." And feel himself breaking into a cold perspiration. "Eh, this English climate is a damp un," he would add when it became necessary to mop his red forehead somewhat with his big clean handkerchief.

Therefore he found it easy to receive Little Ann's proposition with favor.

"There's summat i' that," he acknowledged graciously, dropping into Lancashire. "That's one of the little things a woman can do if she's sharp at figures. Your mother taught me that much. She always said women ought to look after the bits of things as was too small for a man to bother with."

"Men have the big things to look after. That's enough for anybody," said Little Ann. "And they ought to leave something for women to do. If you'll just let me keep notes for you and remember things and answer your letters, and just make calculations you're too busy to attend to, I should feel right-down happy, Father."

"Eh!" he said relievedly, "tha art like thy mother."

"That would make me happy if there was nothing else to do it," said Ann, smoothing his shoulder.

"You're her girl," he said, warmed and supported.

"Yes, I'm her girl, and I'm yours. Now, isn't there some little thing I could begin with? Would you mind telling me if I was right in what I thought you thought about Mr. Rosenthal's offer?"

"What did you think I thought about it?" He was able to put affectionate condescension into the question.

She went to her work-basket and took out a sheet of paper. She came back and sat cozily on the arm of his chair.

"I had to put it all down when I came home," she said. "I wanted to make sure I hadn't forgotten. I do hope I didn't make mistakes."

She gave it to him to look at, and as he settled himself down to its careful examination, she kept her blue eyes upon him. She herself did not know that it was a wonderful little document in its neatly jotted down notes of the exact detail most important to his interests.

There were figures, there were calculations of profits, there were records of the gist of his replies, there were things Hutchinson himself could not possibly have fished out of the jumbled rag-bag of his uncertain recollections.

"Did I say that?" he exclaimed once.

"Yes, Father love, and I could see it upset him. I was watching his face because it wasn't a face I took to."

Joseph Hutchinson began to chuckle—the chuckle of a relieved and gratified stout man.

"Tha kept thy eyes open, Little Ann," he said. "And the way tha's put it down is a credit to thee. And I'll lay a sovereign that tha made no mistakes in what tha thought I was thinking."

He was a little anxious to hear what it had been. The memorandum had brought him up with a slight shock, because it showed him that he had not remembered certain points, and had passed over others which were of dangerous importance. Ann slipped her warm arm about his neck, as she nearly always did when she sat on the arm of his chair and talked things over with him. She had never thought, in fact she was not even aware, that her soft little instincts made her treat him as the big, good, conceited, blundering child nature had created him.

"What I was seeing all the time was the way you were taking in his trick of putting whole lots of things in that didn't really matter, and leaving out things that did," she explained. "He kept talking about what the invention would make in England, and how it would make it, and adding up figures and per cents. and royalties until my head was buzzing inside. And when he thought he'd got your mind fixed on England so that you'd almost forget there was any other country to think of, he read out the agreement that said `All rights,' and he was silly enough to think he could get you to sign it without reading it over and over yourself, and showing it to a clever lawyer that would know that as many tricks can be played by things being left out of a paper as by things being put in."

Small beads of moisture broke out on the bald part of Joseph Hutchinson's head. He had been first so flattered and exhilarated by the quoting of large figures, and then so flustrated and embarrassed by his inability to calculate and follow argument, and again so soothed and elated and thrilled by his own importance in the scheme and the honors which his position in certain companies would heap upon him, that an abyss had yawned before him of which he had been wholly unaware. He was not unaware of it now. He was a vainglorious, ignorant man, whose life had been spent in common work done under the supervision of those who knew what he did not know. He had fed himself upon the comforting belief that he had learned all the tricks of any trade. He had been openly boastful of his astuteness and experience, and yet, as Ann's soft little voice went on, and she praised his cleverness in seeing one point after another, he began to quake within himself before the dawning realization that he had seen none of them, that he had been carried along exactly as Rosenthal had intended that he should be, and that if luck had not intervened, he had been on the brink of signing his name to an agreement that would have implied a score of concessions he would have bellowed like a bull at the thought of making if he had known what he was doing.

"Aye, lass," he gulped out when he could speak—"aye, lass, tha wert right enow. I'm glad tha wert there and heard it, and saw what I was thinking. I didn't say much. I let the chap have rope enow to hang himself with. When he comes back I'll give him a bit o' my mind as'll startle him. It was right-down clever of thee to see just what I had i' my head about all that there gab about things as didn't matter, an' the leavin' out them as did—thinking I wouldn't notice. Many's the time I've said, 'It is na so much what's put into a contract as what's left out.' I'll warrant tha'st heard me say it thysen."

"I dare say I have," answered Ann, "and I dare say that was why it came into my mind."

"That was it," he answered. "Thy mother was always tellin' me of things I'd said that I'd clean forgot myself."

He was beginning to recover his balance and self-respect. It would have been so like a Lancashire chap to have seen and dealt shrewdly with a business schemer who tried to outwit him that he was gradually convinced that he had thought all that had been suggested, and had comported himself with triumphant though silent astuteness. He even began to rub his hands.

"I'll show him," he said, "I'll send him off with a flea in his ear."

"If you'll help me, I'll study out the things I've written down on this paper," Ann said, "and then I'll write down for you just the things you make up your mind to say. It will be such a good lesson for me, if you don't mind, Father. It won't be much to write it out the way you'll say it. You know how you always feel that in business the fewer words the better, and that, however much a person deserves it, calling names and showing you're angry is only wasting time. One of the cleverest things you ever thought was that a thief doesn't mind being called one if he's got what he wanted out of you; he'll only laugh to see you in a rage when you can't help yourself. And if he hasn't got what he wanted, it's only waste of strength to work yourself up. It's you being what you are that makes you know that temper isn't business."

"Well," said Hutchinson, drawing a long and deep breath, "I was almost hot enough to have forgot that, and I'm glad you've reminded me. We'll go over that paper now, Ann. I'd like to give you your lesson while we've got a bit o' time to ourselves and what I've said is fresh in your mind. The trick is always to get at things while they're fresh in your mind."

The little daughter with the red hair was present during Rosenthal's next interview with the owner of the invention. The fellow, he told himself, had been thinking matters over, had perhaps consulted a lawyer; and having had time for reflection, he did not present a mass of mere inflated and blundering vanity as a target for adroit aim. He seemed a trifle sulky, but he did not talk about himself diffusely, and lose his head when he was smoothed the right way. He had a set of curiously concise notes to which he referred, and he stuck to his points with a bulldog obstinacy which was not to be shaken. Something had set him on a new tack. The tricks which could be used only with a totally ignorant and readily flattered and influenced business amateur were no longer in order. This was baffling and irritating.

The worst feature of the situation was that the daughter did not read a book, as had seemed her habit at other times. She sat with a tablet and pencil on her knee, and, still as unobtrusively as ever, jotted down notes.

"Put that down, Ann," her father said to her more than once. "There's no objections to having things written down, I suppose?" he put it bluntly to Rosenthal. "I've got to have notes made when I'm doing business. Memory's all well enough, but black and white's better. No one can go back of black and white. Notes save time."

There was but one attitude possible. No man of business could resent the recording of his considered words, but the tablet and pencil and the quietly bent red head were extraordinary obstacles to the fluidity of eloquence. Rosenthal found his arguments less ready and his methods modifying themselves. The outlook narrowed itself. When he returned to his office and talked the situation over with his partner, he sat and bit his nails in restless irritation.

"Ridiculous as it seems, outrageously ridiculous, I've an idea," he said, "I've more than an idea that we have to count with the girl."

"Girl? What girl?"

"Daughter. Well-behaved, quiet bit of a thing, who sits in a corner and listens while she pretends to sew or read. I'm certain of it. She's taken to making notes now, and Hutchinson's turned stubborn. You need not laugh, Lewis. She's in it. We've got to count with that girl, little female mouse as she looks."

This view, which was first taken by Rosenthal and passed on to his partner, was in course of time passed on to others and gradually accepted, sometimes reluctantly and with much private protest, sometimes with amusement. The well-behaved daughter went with Hutchinson wheresoever his affairs called him. She was changeless in the unobtrusiveness of her demeanor, which was always that of a dutiful and obedient young person who attended her parent because he might desire her humble little assistance in small matters.

"She's my secretary," Hutchinson began to explain, with a touch of swagger. "I've got to have a secretary, and I'd rather trust my private business to my own daughter than to any one else. It's safe with her."

It was so safe with her steady demureness that Hutchinson found himself becoming steady himself. The "lessons" he gave to Little Ann, and the notes made as a result, always ostensibly for her own security and instruction, began to form a singularly firm foundation for statement and argument. He began to tell himself that his memory was improving. Facts were no longer jumbled together in his mind. He could better follow a line of logical reasoning. He less often grew red and hot and flustered.

"That's the thing I've said so often—that temper's got naught to do wi' business, and only upsets a man when he wants all his wits about him. It's the truest thing I ever worked out," he not infrequently congratulated himself. "If a chap can keep his temper, he'll be like to keep his head and drive his bargain. I see it plainer every day o' my life."

CHAPTER XXXVI

It was in the course of the "lessons" that he realized that he had always argued that the best way to do business was to do it face to face with people. To stay in England, and let another chap make your bargains for you in France or Germany or some other outlandish place, where frog-eating foreigners ran loose, was a fool's trick. He'd said it often enough. "Get your eye on 'em, and let them know you've got it on them, and they'd soon find out they were dealing with Lancashire, and not with foreign knaves and nincompoops." So, when it became necessary to deal with France, Little Ann packed him up neatly, so to speak, and in the role of obedient secretarial companion took him to that country, having for weeks beforehand mentally confronted the endless complications attending the step. She knew, in the first place, what the effect of the French language would be upon his temper: that it would present itself to him as a wall deliberately built by the entire nation as a means of concealing a deep duplicity the sole object of which was the baffling, thwarting, and undoing of Englishmen, from whom it wished to wrest their honest rights. Apoplexy becoming imminent, as a result of his impotent rage during their first few days in Paris, she paid a private visit to a traveler's agency, and after careful inquiry discovered that it was not impossible to secure the attendance and service of a well-mannered young man who spoke most of the languages employed by most of the inhabitants of the globe. She even found that she might choose from a number of such persons, and she therefore selected with great care.

"One that's got a good temper, and isn't easy irritated," she said to herself, in summing up the aspirants, "but not one that's easy-tempered because he's silly. He must have plenty of common sense as well as be willing to do what he's told."

When her father discovered that he himself had been considering the desirability of engaging the services of such a person, and had, indeed already, in a way, expressed his intention of sending her to "the agency chap" to look him up, she was greatly relieved.

"I can try to teach him what you've taught me, Father," she said, "and of course he'll learn just by being with you."

The assistant engaged was a hungry young student who had for weeks, through ill luck, been endeavoring to return with some courage the gaze of starvation, which had been staring him in the face.

His name was Dudevant, and with desperate struggles he had educated himself highly, having cherished literary ambitions from his infancy. At this juncture it had become imperative that he should, for a few months at least, obtain food. Ann had chosen well by instinct. His speech had told her that he was intelligent, his eyes had told her that he would do anything on earth to earn his living.

From the time of his advent, Joseph Hutchinson had become calmer and had ceased to be in peril of apoplectic seizure. Foreign nations became less iniquitous and dangerous, foreign languages were less of a barrier, easier to understand. A pleasing impression that through great facility he had gained a fair practical knowledge of French, German, and Italian, supported and exhilarated him immensely.

"It's right-down wonderful how a chap gets to understand these fellows' lingo after he's listened to it a bit," he announced to Ann. "I wouldn't have believed it of myself that I could see into it as quick as I have. I couldn't say as I understand everything they say just when they're saying it; but I understand it right enough when I've had time to translate like. If foreigners didn't talk so fast and run their words one into another, and jabber as if their mouths was full of puddin', it'd be easier for them as is English. Now, there's `wee' and `nong.' I know 'em whenever I hear 'em, and that's a good bit of help."

"Yes," answered Ann, "of course that's the chief thing you want to know in business, whether a person is going to say `yes' or `no.'"

He began to say "wee" and "nong" at meals, and once broke forth "Passy mor le burr" in a tone so casually Parisian that Ann was frightened, because she did not understand immediately, and also because she saw looming up before her a future made perilous by the sudden interjection of unexpected foreign phrases it would be incumbent upon her and Dudevant to comprehend instantaneously without invidious hesitation.

"Don't you understand? Pass the butter. Don't you understand a bit o' French like that?" he exclaimed irritatedly. "Buy yourself one o' these books full of easy sentences and learn some of 'em, lass. You oughtn't to be travelin' about with your father in foreign countries and learnin' nothin'. It's not every lass that's gettin' your advantages."

Ann had not mentioned the fact that she spent most of her rare leisure moments in profound study of phrase-books and grammars, which she kept in her trunk and gave her attention to before she got up in the morning, after she went to her room at night, and usually while she was dressing. You can keep a book open before you when you are brushing your hair. Dudevant gave her a lesson or so whenever time allowed. She was as quick to learn as her father thought he was, and she was desperately determined. It was really not long before she understood much more than "wee and nong" when she was present at a business interview.

"You are a wonderful young lady," Dudevant said, with that well-known yearning in his eyes. "You are most wonderful."

"She's just a wonder," Mrs. Bowse and her boarders had said. And the respectful yearning in the young Frenchman's eyes and voice were well known to her because she had seen it often before, and remembered it, in Jem Bowles and Julius Steinberger. That this young man had without an hour of delay fallen abjectly in love with her was a circumstance with which she dealt after her own inimitably kind and undeleterious method, which in itself was an education to any amorous youth.

"I can understand all you tell me," she said when he reached the point of confiding his hard past to her. "I can understand it because I knew some one who had to fight for himself just that way, only perhaps it was harder because he wasn't educated as you are."

"Did he—confide in you?" Dudevant ventured, with delicate hesitation. "You are so kind I am sure he did, Mademoiselle."

"He told me about it because he knew I wanted to hear," she answered. "I was very fond of him," she added, and her kind gravity was quite unshaded by any embarrassment. "I was right-down fond of him."

His emotion rendered him for a moment indiscreet, to her immediate realization and regret, as was evident by his breaking off in the midst of his question.

"And now—are you?"

"Yes, I always shall be, Mr. Dudevant."

His adoration naturally only deepened itself as all hope at once receded, as it could not but recede before the absolute pellucid truth of her.

"However much he likes me, he will get over it in time. People do, when they know how things stand," she was thinking, with maternal sympathy.

It did him no bitter harm to help her with her efforts at learning what she most needed, and he found her intelligence and modest power of concentration remarkable. A singularly clear knowledge of her own specialized requirements was a practical background to them both. She had no desire to shine; she was merely steadily bent on acquiring as immediately as possible a comprehension of nouns, verbs, and phrases that would be useful to her father. The manner in which she applied herself, and assimilated what it was her quietly fixed intention to assimilate, bespoke her possession of a brain the powers of which being concentrated on large affairs might have accomplished almost startling results. There was, however, nothing startling in her intentions, and ambition did not touch her. Yet, as she went with

Hutchinson from one country to another, more than one man of affairs had it borne in upon him that her young slimness and her silence represented an unanticipated knowledge of points under discussion which might wisely be considered as a factor in all decisions for or against. To realize that a soft-cheeked, child-eyed girl was an element to regard privately in discussions connected with the sale of, or the royalties paid on, a valuable patent appeared in some minds to be a situation not without flavor. She was the kind of little person a man naturally made love to, and a girl who was made love to in a clever manner frequently became amenable to reason, and might be persuaded to use her influence in the direction most desired. But such male financiers as began with this idea discovered that they had been led into errors of judgment through lack of familiarity with the variations of type. One personable young man of title, who had just been disappointed in a desirable marriage with a fortune, being made aware that the invention was likely to arrive at amazing results, was sufficiently rash to approach Mr. Hutchinson with formal proposals. Having a truly British respect for the lofty in place, and not being sufficiently familiar with titled personages to discriminate swiftly between the large and the small, Joseph Hutchinson was somewhat unduly elated.

"The chap's a count, lass," he said. "Tha'u'd go back to Manchester a countess."

"I've heard they're nearly all counts in these countries," commented Ann. "And there's countesses that have to do their own washing, in a manner of speaking. You send him to me, Father."

When the young man came, and compared the fine little nose of Miss Hutchinson with the large and bony structure dominating the countenance of the German heiress he had lost, also when he gazed into the clearness of the infantile blue eyes, his spirits rose. He felt himself en veine; he was equal to attacking the situation. He felt that he approached it with alluring and chivalric delicacy. He almost believed all that he said.

But the pellucid blueness of the gaze that met his was confusingly unstirred by any shade of suitable timidity or emotion. There was something in the lovely, sedate little creature, something so undisturbed and matter of fact, that it frightened him, because he suddenly felt like a fool whose folly had been found out.

"That's downright silly," remarked Little Ann, not allowing him to escape from her glance, which unhesitatingly summed up him and his situation. "And you know it is. You don't know anything about me, and you wouldn't like me if you did. And I shouldn't like you. We're too different. Please go away, and don't say anything more about it. I shouldn't have patience to talk it over."

"Father," she said that night, "if ever I get married at all, there's only one person I'm going to marry. You know that." And she would say no more.

By the time they returned to England, the placing of the invention in divers countries had been arranged in a manner which gave assurance of a fortune for its owners on a foundation not likely to have established itself in more adverse circumstances. Mr. Hutchinson had really driven some admirable bargains, and had secured advantages which to his last hour he would believe could have been achieved only by Lancashire shrewdness and Lancashire ability to "see as far through a mile-stone as most chaps, an' a bit farther." The way in which he had never allowed himself to be "done" caused him at times to chuckle himself almost purple with self-congratulation.

"They got to know what they was dealing with, them chaps. They was sharp, but Joe was a bit sharper," he would say.

They found letters waiting for them when they reached London.

"There's one fro' thy grandmother," Hutchinson said, in dealing out the package. "She's written to thee pretty steady for an old un."

This was true. Letters from her had followed them from one place to another. This was a thick one in an envelop of good size.

"Aren't tha going to read it?" he asked.

"Not till you've had your dinner, Father. You've had a long day of it with that channel at the end. I want to see you comfortable with your pipe."

The hotel was a good one, and the dinner was good. Joseph Hutchinson enjoyed it with the appetite of a robust man who has had time to get over a not too pleasant crossing. When he had settled down into a stout easy-chair with the pipe, he drew a long and comfortable breath as he looked about the room.

"Eh, Ann, lass," he said, "thy mother 'd be fine an' set up if she could see aw this. Us having the best that's to be had, an' knowin' we can have it to the end of our lives, that's what it's come to, tha knows. No more third-class railway-carriages for you and me. No more `commercial' an' `temperance' hotels. Th' first cut's what we can have—th' upper cut. Eh, eh, but it's a good day for a man when he's begun to be appreciated as he should be."

"It's a good day for those that love him," said Little Ann. "And I dare say mother knows every bit about it."

"I dare say she does," admitted Hutchinson, with tender lenience. "She was one o' them as believed that way. And I never knowed her to be wrong in aught else, so I'm ready to give in as she was reet about that. Good lass she was, good lass."

He had fallen into a contented and utterly comfortable doze in his chair when Ann sat down to read her grandmother's letter. The old woman always wrote at length, giving many details and recording village events with shrewd realistic touches. Throughout their journeyings, Ann had been followed by a record of the estate and neighborhood of Temple Barholm which had lacked nothing of atmosphere. She had known what the new lord of the manor did, what people said, what the attitude of the gentry had become; that the visit of the Countess of Mallowe and her daughter had extended itself until curiosity and amusement had ceased to comment, and passively awaited results. She had heard of Miss Alicia and her reincarnation, and knew much of the story of the Duke of Stone, whose reputation as a "dommed clever owd chap" had earned for him a sort of awed popularity. There had been many "ladies." The new Temple Barholm had boldly sought them out and faced them in their strongholds with the manner of one who would confront the worst and who revealed no tendency to flinch. The one at Stone Hover with the "pretty color" and the one with the dimples had appeared frequently upon the scene. Then there had been Lady Joan Fayre, who had lived at his elbow, sitting at his table, driving in his carriages with the air of cold aloofness which the cottagers "could na abide an' had no patience wi'." She had sometimes sat and wondered and wondered about things, and sometimes had flushed daisy-red instead of daisy-pink; and sometimes she had turned rather pale and closed her soft mouth firmly. But, though she had written twice a week to her grandmother, she had recorded principally the successes and complexities of the invention, and had asked very few questions. Old Mrs. Hutchinson would tell her all she must know, and her choice of revelation would be made with a far-sightedness which needed no stimulus of questioning. The letter she had found awaiting her had been long on its way, having missed her at point after point and followed her at last to London. It looked and felt thick and solid in its envelop. Little Ann opened it, stirred by the suggestion of quickened pulse-beats with which she had become familiar. As she bent over it she looked sweetly flushed and warmed.

Joseph Hutchinson's doze had almost deepened into sleep when he was awakened by the touch of her hand on his shoulder. She was standing by him, holding some sheets of her grandmother's letter, and several other sheets were lying on the table. Something had occurred which had changed her quiet look.

"Has aught happened to your grandmother?" he asked.

"No, Father, but this letter that's been following me from one place to another has got some queer news in it."

"What's up, lass? Tha looks as if summat was up."

"The thing that's happened has given me a great deal to think of," was her answer. "It's about Mr. Temple Barholm and Mr. Strangeways."

He became wide-awake at once, sitting up and turning in his chair in testy anxiety.

"Now, now," he exclaimed, "I hope that cracked chap's not gone out an' out mad an' done some mischief. I towd Temple Barholm it was a foolish thing to do, taking all that trouble about him. Has he set fire to th' house or has he knocked th' poor lad on th' head?"

"No, he hasn't, Father. He's disappeared, and Mr. Temple Barholm's disappeared, too."

"Disappeared?" Hutchinson almost shouted. "What for, i' the Lord's name?"

"Nobody knows for certain, and people are talking wild. The village is all upset, and all sorts of silly things are being said."

"What sort o' things?"

"You know what servants at big houses are—how they hear bits of talk and make much of it," she explained. "They've been curious and chattering among themselves about Mr. Strangeways from the first. It was Burrill that said he believed he was some relation that was being hid away for some good reason. One night Mr. Temple Barholm and Captain Palliser were having a long talk together, and Burrill was about—"

"Aye, he'd be about if he thought there was a chance of him hearing summat as was none of his business," jerked out Hutchinson, irately.

"They were talking about Mr. Strangeways, and Burrill heard Captain Palliser getting angry; and as he stepped near the door he heard him say out loud that he could swear in any court of justice that the man he had seen at the west room window—it's a startling thing, Father—was Mr. James Temple Barholm." For the moment her face was pale.

Hereupon Hutchinson sprang up.

"What!" His second shout was louder than his first. "Th' liar! Th' chap's dead, an' he knows it. Th' dommed mischief-makin' liar!"

Her eyes were clear and speculatively thoughtful, notwithstanding her lack of color.

"There have been people that have been thought dead that have come back to their friends alive. It's happened many a time," she said. "It wouldn't be so strange for a man that had no friends to be lost in a wild, far-off place where there was neither law nor order, and where every man was fighting for his own life and the gold he was mad after. Particularly a man that was shamed and desperate and wanted to hide himself. And, most of all, it would be easy, if he was like Mr. Strangeways, and couldn't remember, and had lost himself."

As her father listened, the angry redness of his countenance moderated its hue. His eyes gradually began to question and his under jaw fell slightly.

"Si' thee, lass," he broke out huskily, "does that mean to say tha believes it?"

"It's not often you can believe what you don't know," she answered. "I don't know anything about it. There's just one thing I believe, because I know it. I believe what grandmother does. Read that."

She handed him the final sheet of old Mrs. Hutchinson's letter. It was written with very black ink and in an astonishingly bold and clear hand. It was easy to read the sentences with which she ended.

There's a lot said. There's always more saying than doing. But it's right-down funny to see how the lad has made hard and fast friends just going about in his queer way, and no one knowing how he did it. I like him myself. He's one of those you needn't ask questions about. If there's anything said that isn't to his credit, it's not true. There's no ifs, buts, or ands about that, Ann.

Little Ann herself read the words as her father read them.

"That's the thing I believe, because I know it," was all she said.

"It's the thing I'd swear to mysel'," her father answered bluffly. "But, by Judd—"

She gave him a little push and spoke to him in homely Lancashire phrasing, and with some soft unsteadiness of voice.

"Sit thee down, Father love," she said, "and let me sit on thy knee."

He sat down with emotional readiness, and she sat on his stout knee like a child. It was a thing she did in tender or troubled moments as much in these days as she had done when she was six or seven. Her little lightness and soft young ways made it the most natural thing in the world, as well as the prettiest. She had always sat on his knee in the hours when he had been most discouraged over the invention. She had known it made him feel as though he were taking care of her, and as though she depended utterly on him to steady the foundations of her world. What could such a little bit of a lass do without "a father"?

"It's upset thee, lass," he said. "It's upset thee."

He saw her slim hands curl themselves into small, firm fists as they rested on her lap.

"I can't bear to think that ill can be said of him, even by a wastrel like Captain Palliser," she said. "He's MINE."

It made him fumble caressingly at her big knot of soft red hair.

"Thine, is he?" he said. "Thine! Eh, but tha did say that just like thy mother would ha' said it; tha brings the heart i' my throat now and again. That chap's i' luck, I can tell him—same as I was once."

"He's mine now, whatever happens," she went on, with a firmness which no skeptic would have squandered time in the folly of hoping to shake. "He's done what I told him to do, and it's ME he wants. He's found out for himself, and so have I. He can have me the minute he wants me—the very minute."

"He can?" said Hutchinson. "That settles it. I believe tha'd rather take him when he was i' trouble than when he was out of it. Same as tha'd rather take him i' a flat in Harlem on fifteen dollar a week than on fifteen hundred."

"Yes, Father, I would. It'd give me more to do for him."

"Eh, eh," he grunted tenderly, "thy mother again. I used to tell her as the only thing she had agen me was that I never got i' jail so she could get me out an' stand up for me after it. There's only one thing worrits me a bit: I wish the lad hadn't gone away."

"I've thought that out, though I've not had much time to reason about things," said Little Ann. "If he's gone away, he's gone to get something; and whatever it happens to be, he'll be likely to bring it back with him, Father."

CHAPTER XXXVII

Old Mrs. Hutchinson's letter had supplied much detail, but when her son and grand-daughter arrived in the village of Temple Barholm they heard much more, the greater part of it not in the least to be relied upon.

"The most of it's lies, as folks enjoys theirsels pretendin' to believe," the grand-mother commented. "It's servants'-hall talk and cottage gossip, and plenty made itself up out o' beer drunk in th' tap-room at th' Wool Park. In a place where naught much happens, people get into th' way 'o springin' on a bit o' news, and shakin' and worryin' it like a terrier does a rat. It's nature. That lad's given 'em lots to talk about ever since he coom. He's been a blessin' to 'em. If he'd been gentry, he'd not ha' been nigh as lively. Th' village lads tries to talk through their noses like him. Little Tummas Hibblethwaite does it i' broad Lancashire."

The only facts fairly authenticated were that the mysterious stranger had been taken away very late one night, some time before the interview between Mr. Temple Barholm and Captain Palliser, of which Burrill knew so much because he had "happened to be about." When a domestic magnate of Burrill's type "happens to be about" at a crisis, he is not unlikely to hear a great deal. Burrill, it was believed, knew much more than he deigned to make public. The entire truth was that Captain Palliser himself, in one of his hasty appearances in the neighborhood of Temple Barholm, had bestowed a few words of cold caution on him.

"Don't talk too much," he had said. "Proof is required before talk is safe. The American was sharp enough to say that to me himself. He was sharp enough, too, to keep his man hidden. I was the only person that saw him who could have recognized him, and I saw him by chance. Palford & Grimby require proof. We are in search of it. Servants will talk; but if you don't want to run the risk of getting yourself into trouble, don't make absolute statements."

This had been a disappointment to Burrill, who had seen himself developing in magnitude; but he was a timid man, and therefore felt it wise to convey his knowledge merely through the conviction carried by a dignified silence after his first indiscreet revelation of having "happened to be about" had been made. It would have been some solace to him to intimate to Miss Alicia by his bearing and the manner of his services that she had been discovered, so to speak, in the character of a sort of accomplice; that her position was a perilously uncertain one, which would probably end in utter downfall, leaving her in her old and proper place as an elderly, insignificant, and unattractive poor relation, without a feature to recommend her. But being, as before remarked, a timid man, and recalling the interview between himself and his employer held outside the dining-room door, and having also a disturbing memory of the sharp, cool, boyish eye and the tone of the casual remark that he had "a head on his shoulders" and that it was "up to him to make the others understand," it seemed as well to restrain his inclinations until the proof Palford & Grimby required was forthcoming.

It was perhaps the moderate and precautionary attitude of Palford & Grimby, during their first somewhat startled though reserved interview with Captain Palliser, which had prevented the vaguely wild rumors from being regarded as more than villagers' exaggerated talk among themselves. The "gentry," indeed, knew much less of the cottagers than the cottagers knew of the gentry; consequently events furnishing much excitement among the village people not infrequently remained unheard of by those in the class above them. A story less incredible might have been more considered; but the highly colored reasons given for the absence of the owner of Temple Barholm would, if heard of, have been more than likely to be received and passed over with a smile.

The manner of Mr. Palford and also of Mr. Grimby during the deliberately unmelodramatic and carefully connected relation of Captain Palliser's singular story, was that of professional gentlemen who for reasons of good breeding were engaged in restraining outward expression of conviction that they were listening to utter nonsense. Palliser himself was aware of this, and upon the whole did not wonder at it in entirely unimaginative persons of extremely sober lives. In fact, he had begun by giving them some warning as to what they might expect in the way of unusualness.

"You will, no doubt, think what I am about to tell you absurd and incredible," he had prefaced his statements. "I thought the same myself when my first suspicions were aroused. I was, in fact, inclined to laugh at my own idea until one link connected itself with another."

Neither Mr. Grimby nor Mr. Palford was inclined to laugh. On the contrary, they were extremely grave, and continued to find it necessary to restrain their united tendency to indicate facially that the thing must be nonsense. It transcended all bounds, as it were. The delicacy with which they managed to convey this did them much credit. This delicacy was equaled by the moderation with which Captain Palliser drew their attention to the fact that it was not the thing likely-to-happen on which were founded the celebrated criminal cases of legal history; it was the incredible and almost impossible events, the ordinarily unbelievable duplicities, moral obliquities and coincidences, which made them what they were and attracted the attention of the world. This, Mr. Palford and his partner were obviously obliged to admit. What they did not admit was that such things never having occurred in one's own world, they had been mentally relegated to the world of newspaper and criminal record as things that could not happen to oneself. Mr. Palford cleared his throat in a seriously cautionary way.

"This is, of course, a matter suggesting too serious an accusation not to be approached in the most conservative manner," he remarked.

"Most serious consequences have resulted in cases implying libelous assertions which have been made rashly," added Mr. Grimby. "As Mr. Temple Barholm intimated to you, a man of almost unlimited means has command of resources which it might not be easy to contend with if he had reason to feel himself injured."

The fact that Captain Palliser had in a bitterly frustrated moment allowed himself to be goaded into losing his temper, and "giving away" to Tembarom the discovery on which he had felt that he could rely as a lever, did not argue that a like weakness would lead him into more dangerous indiscretion. He had always regarded himself as a careful man whose defenses were well built about him at such crises in his career as rendered entrenchment necessary. There would, of course, be some pleasure in following the matter up and getting more than even with a man who had been insolent to him; but a more practical feature of the case was that if, through his alert observation and shrewd aid, Jem Temple Barholm was restored to his much-to-be-envied place in the world, a far from unnatural result would be that he might feel suitable gratitude and indebted-ness to the man who, not from actual personal liking but from a mere sense of justice, had rescued him. As for the fears of Messrs. Palford & Grimby, he had put himself on record with Burrill by commanding him to hold his tongue and stating clearly that proof was both necessary and lacking. No man could be regarded as taking risks whose attitude was so wholly conservative and non-accusing. Servants will gossip. A superior who reproves such gossip holds an unattackable position. In the private room of Palford & Grimby, however, he could confidently express his opinions without risk.

"The recognition of a man lost sight of for years, and seen only for a moment through a window, is not substantial evidence," Mr. Grimby had proceeded. "The incident was startling, but not greatly to be relied upon."

"I knew him." Palliser was slightly grim in his air of finality. "He was a man most men either liked or hated. I didn't like him. I detested a trick he had of staring at you under his drooping lids. By the way, do you remember the portrait of Miles Hugo which was so like him?"

Mr. Palford remembered having heard that there was a certain portrait in the gallery which Mr. James Temple Barholm had been said to resemble. He had no distinct recollection of the ancestor it represented.

"It was a certain youngster who was a page in the court of Charles the Second and who died young. Miles Hugo Charles James was his name. He is my strongest clue. The American seemed rather keen the first time we talked together. He was equally keen about Jem Temple Barholm. He wanted to know what he looked like, and whether it was true that he was like the portrait."

"Indeed!" exclaimed Palford and Grimby, simultaneously.

"It struck me that there was something more than mere curiosity in his manner," Palliser enlarged. "I couldn't make him out then. Later, I began to see that he was remarkably anxious to keep every one from Strangeways. It was a sort of Man in the Iron Mask affair. Strangeways was apparently not only too excitable to be looked at or spoken to, but too excitable to be spoken of. He wouldn't talk about him."

"That is exceedingly curious," remarked Mr. Palford, but it was not in response to Palliser. A few moments before he had suddenly looked thoughtful. He wore now the aspect of a man trying to recall something as Palliser continued.

"One day, after I had been to look at a sunset through a particular window in the wing where Strangeways was kept, I passed the door of his sitting-room, and heard the American arguing with him. He was evidently telling him he was to be taken elsewhere, and the poor devil was terrified. I heard him beg him for God's sake not to send him away. There was panic in his voice. In connection with the fact that he has got him away secretly—at midnight-it's an ugly thing to recall."

"It would seem to have significance." Grimby said it uneasily.

"It set me thinking and looking into things," Palliser went on. "Pearson was secretive, but the head man, Burrill, made casual enlightening remarks. I gathered some curious details, which might or might not have meant a good deal. When Strangeways suddenly appeared at his window one evening a number of things fitted themselves together. My theory is that the American—Tembarom, as he used to call himself—may not have been certain of the identity at first, but he wouldn't have brought Strangeways with him if he had not had some reason to suspect who he was. He daren't lose sight of him, and he wanted time to make sure and to lay his plans. The portrait of Miles Hugo was a clue which alarmed him, and no doubt he has been following it. If he found it led to nothing, he could easily turn Strangeways over to the public charge and let him be put into a lunatic asylum. If he found it led to a revelation which would make him a pauper again, it would be easy to dispose of him."

"Come! Come! Captain Palliser! We mustn't go too far!" ejaculated Mr. Grimby, alarmedly. It shocked him to think of the firm being dragged into a case dealing with capital crime and possible hangmen! That was not its line of the profession.

Captain Palliser's slight laugh contained no hint of being shocked by any possibilities whatever.

"There are extremely private asylums and so-called sanatoriums where the discipline is strict, and no questions are asked. One sometimes reads in the papers of cases in which mild-mannered keepers in defending themselves against the attacks of violent patients are obliged to use force—with disastrous results. It is in such places that our investigations should begin."

"Dear me! Dear me!" Mr. Grimby broke out. "Isn't that going rather far? You surely don't think—"

"Mr. Tembarom's chief characteristic was that he was a practical and direct person. He would do what he had to do in exactly that businesslike manner. The inquiries I have been making have been as to the whereabouts of places in which a superfluous relative might be placed without attracting attention."

"That is really astute, but—but—what do you think, Palford?" Mr. Grimby turned to his partner, still wearing the shocked and disturbed expression.

"I have been recalling to mind a circumstance which probably bears upon the case," said Mr. Palford. "Captain Palliser's mention of the portrait reminded me of it. I remember now that on Mr. Temple Barholm's first visit to the picture-gallery he seemed much attracted by the portrait of Miles Hugo. He stopped and examined it curiously. He said he felt as if he had seen it before. He turned to it once or twice; and finally remarked that he might have seen some one like it at a great fancy-dress ball which had taken place in New York."

"Had he been invited to the ball?" laughed Palliser.

"I did not gather that," replied Mr. Palford gravely. "He had apparently watched the arriving guests from some railings near by—or perhaps it was a lamp-post—with other news-boys."

"He recognized the likeness to Strangeways, no doubt, and it gave him what he calls a 'jolt,'" said Captain Palliser. "He must have experienced a number of jolts during the last few months."

Palford & Grimby's view of the matter continued to be marked by extreme distaste for the whole situation and its disturbing and irritating possibilities. The coming of the American heir to the estate of Temple Barholm had been trying to the verge of extreme painfulness; but, sufficient time having lapsed and their client having troubled them but little, they had outlived the shock of his first appearance and settled once more into the calm of their accustomed atmosphere and routine. That he should suddenly reappear upon their dignified horizon as a probable melodramatic criminal was a fault of taste and a lack of consideration beyond expression. To be dragged-into vulgar detective work, to be referred to in news-papers in a connection which would lead to confusing the firm with the representatives of such branches of the profession as dealt with persons who had committed acts for which in vulgar parlance they might possibly "swing," if their legal defenders did not "get them off," to a firm whose sole affairs had been the dealing with noble and ancient estates, with advising and supporting personages of stately name, and with private and weighty family confidences. If the worst came to the worst, the affair would surely end in the most glaring and odious notoriety: in head-lines and daily reports even in London, in appalling pictures of every one concerned in every New York newspaper, even in baffled struggles to keep abominable woodcuts of themselves—Mr. Edward James Palford and Mr. James Matthew Grimby—from being published in sensational journalistic sheets! Professional duty demanded that the situation should be dealt with, that investigation should be entered into, that the most serious even if conservative steps should be taken at once. With regard to the accepted report of Mr. James Temple Barholm's tragic death, it could not be denied that Captain Palliser's view of the naturalness of the origin of the mistake that had been made had a logical air.

"In a region full of rioting derelicts crazed with the lawless excitement of their dash after gold," he had said, "identities and names are easily lost. Temple Barholm himself was a derelict and in a desperate state. He was in no mood to speak of himself or try to make friends. He no doubt came and went to such work as he did scarcely speaking to any one. A mass of earth and debris of all sorts suddenly gives way, burying half-a-dozen men. Two or three are dug out dead, the others not reached. There was no time to spare to dig for dead men. Some one had seen Temple Barholm near the place; he was seen no more. Ergo, he was buried with the rest. At that time, those who knew him in England felt it was the best thing that could have happened to him. It would have been if his valet had not confessed his trick, and old Temple Barholm had not died. My theory is that he may have left the place days before the accident without being missed. His mental torment caused some mental illness, it does not matter what. He lost his memory and wandered about—the Lord knows how or where he lived; he probably never knew himself. The American picked him up and found that he had money. For reasons of his own, he professed to take care of him. He must have come on some clue just when he heard of his new fortune. He was naturally panic-stricken; it must have been a big blow at that particular moment. He was sharp enough to see what it might mean, and held on to the poor chap like grim death, and has been holding on ever since."

"We must begin to take steps," decided Palford & Grimby. "We must of course take steps at once, but we must begin with discretion."

After grave private discussion, they began to take the steps in question and with the caution that it seemed necessary to observe until they felt solid ground under their feet. Captain Palliser was willing to assist them. He had been going into the matter himself. He went down to the neighborhood of Temple Barholm and quietly looked up data which might prove illuminating when regarded from one point or another. It was on the first of these occasions that he saw and warned Burrill. It was from Burrill he heard of Tummas Hibblethwaite.

"There's an impident little vagabond in the village, sir," he said, "that Mr. Temple Barholm used to go and see and take New York newspapers to. A cripple the lad is, and he's got a kind of craze for talking about Mr. James Temple Barholm. He had a map of the place where he was said to be killed. If I may presume to mention it, sir," he added with great dignity, "it is my opinion that the two had a good deal of talk together on the subject."

"I dare say," Captain Palliser admitted indifferently, and made no further inquiry or remark.

He sauntered into the Hibblethwaite cottage, however, late the next afternoon.

Tummas was in a bad temper, for reasons quite sufficient for himself, and he regarded him sourly.

"What has tha coom for?" he demanded. "I did na ask thee."

"Don't be cheeky!" said Captain Palliser. "I will give you a sovereign if you'll let me see the map you and Mr. Temple Barholm used to look at and talk so much about."

He laid the sovereign down on the small table by Tummas's sofa, but Tummas did not pick it up.

"I know who tha art. Tha'rt Palliser, an' tha wast th' one as said as him as was killed in th' Klondike had coom back alive."

"You've been listening to that servants' story, have you?" remarked Palliser. "You had better be careful as to what you say. I suppose you never heard of libel suits. Where would you find yourself if you were called upon to pay Mr. Temple Barholm ten thousand pounds' damages? You'd be obliged to sell your atlas."

"Burrill towd as he heard thee say tha'd swear in court as it was th' one as was killed as tha'd seen."

"That's Burrill's story, not mine. And Burrill had better keep his mouth shut," said Palliser. "If it were true, how would you like it? I've heard you were interested in 'th' one as was killed.'"

Tummas's eyes burned troublously.

"I've got reet down taken wi' th' other un," he answered. "He's noan gentry, but he's th' reet mak'. I—I dunnot believe as him as was killed has coom back."

"Neither do I," Palliser answered, with amiable tolerance. "The American gentleman had better come back himself and disprove it. When you used to talk about the Klondike, he never said anything to make you feel as if he doubted that the other man was dead?"

"Not him," answered Tummas.

"Eh! Tummas, what art tha talkin' about?" exclaimed Mrs. Hibblethwaite, who was mending at the other end of the room. "I heerd him say mysel, 'Suppose th' story hadn't been true an' he was alive somewhere now, it'd make a big change, would na' it?' An' he laughed."

"I never heerd him," said Tummas, in stout denial.

"Tha's losin' tha moind," commented his mother. "As soon as I heerd th' talk about him runnin' away an' takin' th' mad gentleman wi' him I remembered it. An' I remembered as he sat still after it and said nowt for a minute or so, same as if he was thinkin' things over. Theer was summat a bit queer about it."

"I never heerd him," Tummas asserted, obstinately, and shut his mouth.

"He were as ready to talk about th' poor gentleman as met with th' accident as tha wert thysel', Tummas," Mrs. Hibblethwaite proceeded, moved by the opportunity offered for presenting her views on the exciting topic. "He'd ax thee aw sorts o' questions about what tha'd found out wi' pumpin' foak. He'd ax me questions now an' agen about what he was loike to look at, an' how tall he wur. Onct he axed me if I remembered what soart o' chin he had an' how he spoke."

"It wur to set thee goin' an' please me," volunteered Tummas, grudgingly. "He did it same as he'd look at th' map to please me an' tell me tales about th' news-lads i' New York."

It had not seemed improbable that a village cripple tied to a sofa would be ready enough to relate all he knew, and perhaps so much more that it would be necessary to use discretion in selecting statements of value. To drop in and give him a sovereign and let him talk had appeared simple. Lads of his class liked to be listened to, enjoyed enlarging upon and rendering dramatic such material as had fallen into their hands. But Tummas was an eccentric, and instinct led him to close like an oyster before a remote sense of subtly approaching attack. It was his mother, not he, who had provided information; but it was not sufficiently specialized to be worth much.

"What did tha say he'd run away fur?" Tummas said to his parent later. "He's not one o' th' runnin' away soart."

"He has probably been called away by business," remarked Captain Palliser, as he rose to go after a few minutes' casual talk with Mrs. Hibblethwaite. "It was a mistake not to leave an address behind him. Your mother is mistaken in saying that he took the mad gentleman with him. He had him removed late at night some time before he went himself."

"Tak tha sov'rin'," said Tummas, as Palliser moved away. "I did na show thee th' atlas. Tha did na want to see it."

"I will leave the sovereign for your mother," said Palliser. "I'm sorry you are not in a better humor."

His interest in the atlas had indeed been limited to his idea that it would lead to subjects of talk which might cast illuminating side-lights and possibly open up avenues and vistas. Tummas, however, having instinctively found him displeasing, he had gained but little.

Avenues and vistas were necessary—avenues through which the steps of Palford and Grimby might wander, vistas which they might explore with hesitating, investigating glances. So far, the scene remained unpromisingly blank. The American Temple Barholm had simply disappeared, as had his mysterious charge. Steps likely to lead to definite results can scarcely be taken hopefully in the case of a person who has seemed temporarily to cease to exist. You cannot interrogate him, you cannot demand information, whatsoever the foundations upon which rest your accusations, if such accusation can be launched only into thin air and the fact that there is nobody to reply to—to acknowledge or indignantly refute them—is in itself a serious barrier to accomplishment. It was also true that only a few weeks had elapsed since the accused had, so to speak, dematerialized. It was also impossible to calculate upon what an American of his class and peculiarities would be likely to do in any circumstances whatever.

In private conference, Palford and Grimby frankly admitted to each other that they would almost have preferred that Captain Palliser should have kept his remarkable suspicions to himself, for the time being at least. Yet when they had admitted this they were confronted by the disturbing possibility—

suggested by Palliser—that actual crime had been or might be committed. They had heard unpleasant stories of private lunatic asylums and their like. Things to shudder at might be going on at the very moment they spoke to each other. Under this possibility, no supineness would be excusable. Efforts to trace the missing man must at least be made. Efforts were made, but with no result. Painful as it was to reflect on the subject of the asylums, careful private inquiry was made, information was quietly collected, there were even visits to gruesomely quiet places on various polite pretexts.

"If a longer period of time had elapsed," Mr. Palford remarked several times, with some stiffness of manner, "we should feel that we had more solid foundation for our premises."

"Perfectly right," Captain Palliser agreed with him, "but it is lapse of time which may mean life or death to Jem Temple Barholm; so it's perhaps as well to be on the safe side and go on quietly following small clues. I dare say you would feel more comfortable yourselves."

Both Mr. Palford and Mr. Grimby, having made an appointment with Miss Alicia, arrived one afternoon at Temple Barholm to talk to her privately, thereby casting her into a state of agonized anxiety which reduced her to pallor.

"Our visit is merely one of inquiry, Miss Temple Barholm," Mr. Palford began. "There is perhaps nothing alarming in our client's absence."

"In the note which he left me he asked me to—feel no anxiety," Miss Alicia said.

"He left you a note of explanation? I wish we had known this earlier!" Mr. Palford's tone had the note of relieved exclamation. Perhaps there was an entirely simple solution of the painful difficulty.

But his hope had been too sanguine.

"It was not a note of explanation, exactly. He went away too suddenly to have time to explain."

The two men looked at each other disturbedly.

"He had not mentioned to you his intention of going?" asked Mr. Grimby.

"I feel sure he did not know he was going when he said good-night. He remained with Captain Palliser talking for some time." Miss Alicia's eyes held wavering and anxious question as she looked from one to the other. She wondered how much more than herself her visitors knew. "He found a telegram when he went to his room. It contained most disquieting news about Mr. Strangeways. He—he had got away from the place where—"

"Got away!" Mr. Palford was again exclamatory. "Was he in some institution where he was kept under restraint?"

Miss Alicia was wholly unable to explain to herself why some quality in his manner filled her with sudden distress.

"Oh, I think not! Surely not! Surely nothing of that sort was necessary. He was very quiet always, and he was getting better every day. But it was important that he should be watched over. He was no doubt under the care of a physician in some quiet sanatorium."

"Some quiet sanatorium!" Mr. Palford's disturbance of mind was manifest. "But you did not know where?"

"No. Indeed, Mr. Temple Barholm talked very little of Mr. Strangeways. I believe he knew that it distressed me to feel that I could be of no real assistance as—as the case was so peculiar."

Each perturbed solicitor looked again with rapid question at the other. Miss Alicia saw the exchange of glances and, so to speak, broke down under the pressure of their unconcealed anxiety. The last few weeks with their suggestion of accusation too vague to be met had been too much for her.

"I am afraid—I feel sure you know something I do not," she began. "I am most anxious and unhappy. I have not liked to ask questions, because that would have seemed to imply a doubt of Mr. Temple Barholm. I have even remained at home because I did not wish to hear things I could not understand. I do not know what has been said. Pearson, in whom I have the greatest confidence, felt that Mr. Temple Barholm would prefer that I should wait until he returned."

"Do you think he will return?" said Mr. Grimby, amazedly.

"Oh!" the gentle creature ejaculated. "Can you possibly think he will not? Why? Why?"

Mr. Palford had shared his partner's amazement. It was obvious that she was as ignorant as a babe of the details of Palliser's extraordinary story. In her affectionate consideration for Temple Barholm she had actually shut herself up lest she should hear anything said against him which she could not refute. She stood innocently obedient to his wishes, like the boy upon the burning deck, awaiting his return and his version of whatsoever he had been accused of. There was something delicately heroic in the little, slender old thing, with her troubled eyes and her cap and her quivering sideringlets.

"You," she appealed, "are his legal advisers, and will be able to tell me if there is anything he would wish me to know. I could not allow myself to listen to villagers or servants; but I may ask you."

"We are far from knowing as much as we desire to know," Mr. Palford replied.

"We came here, in fact," added Grimby, "to ask questions of you, Miss Temple Barholm."

"The fact that Miss Temple Barholm has not allowed herself to be prejudiced by village gossip, which is invariably largely unreliable, will make her an excellent witness," Mr. Palford said to his partner, with a deliberation which held suggestive significance. Each man, in fact, had suddenly realized that her ignorance would leave her absolutely unbiased in her answers to any questions they might put, and that it was much better in cross-examining an emotional elderly lady that such should be the case.

"Witness!" Miss Alicia found the word alarming. Mr. Palford's bow was apologetically palliative.

"A mere figure of speech, madam," he said.

"I really know so little every one else doesn't know." Miss Alicia's protest had a touch of bewilderment in it. What could they wish to ask her?

"But, as we understand it, your relations with Mr. Temple Barholm were most affectionate and confidential."

"We were very fond of each other," she answered.

"For that reason he no doubt talked to you more freely than to other people," Mr. Grimby put it. "Perhaps, Palford, it would be as well to explain to Miss Temple Barholm that a curious feature of this matter is that it—in a way—involves certain points concerning the late Mr. Temple Barholm."

Miss Alicia uttered a pathetic exclamation.

"Poor Jem—who died so cruelly!"

Mr. Palford bent his head in acquiescence.

"Perhaps you can tell me what the present Mr. Temple Barholm knew of him—how much he knew?"

"I told him the whole story the first time we took tea together," Miss Alicia replied; and, between her recollection of that strangely happy afternoon and her wonder at its connection with the present moment, she began to feel timid and uncertain.

"How did it seem to impress him?"

She remembered it all so well—his queer, dear New York way of expressing his warm-hearted indignation at the cruelty of what had happened.

"Oh, he was very much excited. He was so sorry for him. He wanted to know everything about him. He asked me what he looked like."

"Oh!" said Palford. "He wanted to know that?"

"He was so full of sympathy," she replied, her explanation gaining warmth. "When I told him that the picture of Miles Hugo in the gallery was said to look like Jem as a boy, he wanted very much to see it. Afterward we went and saw it together. I shall always remember how he stood and looked at it. Most young men would not have cared. But he always had such a touching interest in poor Jem."

"You mean that he asked questions about him—about his death, and so forth?" was Mr. Palford's inquiry.

"About all that concerned him. He was interested especially in his looks and manner of speaking and personality, so to speak. And in the awful accident which ended his life, though he would not let me talk about that after he had asked his first questions."

"What kind of questions?" suggested Grimby.

"Only about what was known of the time and place, and how the sad story reached England. It used to touch me to think that the only person who seemed to care was the one who—might have been expected to be almost glad the tragic thing had happened. But he was not."

Mr. Palford watched Mr. Grimby, and Mr. Grimby gave more than one dubious and distressed glance at Palford.

"His interest was evident," remarked Palford, thoughtfully. "And unusual under the circumstances."

For a moment he hesitated, then put another question: "Did he ever seem—I should say, do you remember any occasion when he appeared to think that—there might be any reason to doubt that Mr. James Temple Barholm was one of the men who died in the Klondike?"

He felt that through this wild questioning they had at least reached a certain testimony supporting Captain Palliser's views; and his interest reluctantly increased. It was reluctant because there could be no shadow of a question that this innocent spinster lady told the absolute truth; and, this being the case, one seemed to be dragged to the verge of depths which must inevitably be explored. Miss Alicia's expression was that of one who conscientiously searched memory.

"I do not remember that he really expressed doubt," she answered, carefully. "Not exactly that, but—"

"But what?" prompted Palford as she hesitated. "Please try to recall exactly what he said. It is most important."

The fact that his manner was almost eager, and that eagerness was not his habit, made her catch her breath and look more questioning and puzzled than before.

"One day he came to my sitting-room when he seemed rather excited," she explained. "He had been with Mr. Strangeways, who had been worse than usual. Perhaps he wanted to distract himself and forget about it. He asked me questions and talked about poor Jem for about an hour. And at last he said, 'Do you suppose there's any sort of chance that it mightn't be true—that story that came from the Klondike?' He said it so thoughtfully that I was startled and said, 'Do you think there could be such a chance—do you?' And he drew a long breath and answered, 'You want to be sure about things like that; you've got to be sure.' I was a little excited, so he changed the subject very soon afterward, and I never felt quite certain of what he was really thinking. You see what he said was not so much an expression of doubt as a sort of question."

A touch of the lofty condemnatory made Mr. Palford impressive.

"I am compelled to admit that I fear that it was a question of which he had already guessed the answer," he said.

At this point Miss Alicia clasped her hands quite tightly together upon her knees.

"If you please," she exclaimed, "I must ask you to make things a little clear to me. What dreadful thing has happened? I will regard any communication as a most sacred confidence."

"I think we may as well, Palford?" Mr. Grimby suggested to his partner.

"Yes," Palford acquiesced. He felt the difficulty of a blank explanation. "We are involved in a most trying position," he said. "We feel that great discretion must be used until we have reached more definite certainty. An extraordinary—in fact, a startling thing has occurred. We are beginning, as a result of cumulative evidence, to feel that there was reason to believe that the Klondike story was to be doubted—"

"That poor Jem—!" cried Miss Alicia.

"One begins to be gravely uncertain as to whether he has not been in this house for months, whether he was not the mysterious Mr. Strangeways!"

"Jem! Jem!" gasped poor little Miss Temple Barholm, quite white with shock.

"And if he was the mysterious Strangeways," Mr. Grimby assisted to shorten the matter, "the American Temple Barholm apparently knew the fact, brought him here for that reason, and for the same reason kept him secreted and under restraint."

"No! No!" cried Miss Alicia. "Never! Never! I beg you not to say such a thing. Excuse me—I cannot listen! It would be wrong—ungrateful. Excuse me!" She got up from her seat, trembling with actual anger in her sense of outrage. It was a remarkable thing to see the small, elderly creature angry, but this remarkable thing had happened. It was as though she were a mother defending her young.

"I loved poor Jem and I love Temple, and, though I am only a woman who never has been the least clever, I know them both. I know neither of them could lie or do a wicked, cunning thing. Temple is the soul of honor."

It was quite an inspirational outburst. She had never before in her life said so much at one time. Of course tears began to stream down her face, while Mr. Palford and Mr. Grimby gazed at her in great embarrassment.

"If Mr. Strangeways was poor Jem come back alive, Temple did not know—he never knew. All he did for him was done for kindness' sake. I—I—" It was inevitable that she should stammer before going to this length of violence, and that the words should burst from her: "I would swear it!"

It was really a shock to both Palford and Grimby. That a lady of Miss Temple Barholm's age and training should volunteer to swear to a thing was almost alarming. It was also in rather unpleasing taste.

"Captain Palliser obliged Mr. Temple Temple Barholm to confess that he had known for some time," Mr. Palford said with cold regret. "He also informed him that he should communicate with us without delay."

"Captain Palliser is a bad man." Miss Alicia choked back a gasp to make the protest.

"It was after their interview that Mr. Temple Barholm almost immediately left the house."

"Without any explanation whatever," added Grimby.

"He left a few lines for me," defended Miss Alicia.

"We have not seen them." Mr. Palford was still as well as cold. Poor little Miss Alicia took them out of her pocket with an unsteady hand. They were always with her, and she could not on such a challenge seem afraid to allow them to be read. Mr. Palford took them from her with a slight bow of thanks. He adjusted his glasses and read aloud, with pauses between phrases which seemed somewhat to puzzle him.

"Dear little Miss Alicia:

"I've got to light out of here as quick as I can make it. I can't even stop to tell you why. There's just one thing—don't get rattled, Miss Alicia. Whatever any one says or does, don't get rattled.

"Yours affectionately,

"T. TEMBAROM."

There was a silence, Mr. Palford passed the paper to his partner, who gave it careful study. Afterward he refolded it and handed it back to Miss Alicia.

"In a court of law," was Mr. Palford's sole remark, "it would not be regarded as evidence for the defendant."

Miss Alicia's tears were still streaming, but she held her ringleted head well up.

"I cannot stay! I beg your pardon, I do indeed!" she said. "But I must leave you. You see," she added, with her fine little touch of dignity, "as yet this house is still Mr. Temple Barholm's home, and I am the grateful recipient of his bounty. Burrill will attend you and make you quite comfortable." With an obeisance which was like a slight curtsey, she turned and fled.

In less than an hour she walked up the neat bricked path, and old Mrs. Hutchinson, looking out, saw her through the tiers of flower-pots in the window. Hutchinson himself was in London, but Ann was reading at the other side of the room.

"Here's poor little owd Miss Temple Barholm aw in a flutter," remarked her grandmother. "Tha's got some work cut out for thee if tha's going to quiet her. Oppen th' door, lass."

Ann opened the door, and stood by it with calm though welcoming dimples.

"Miss Hutchinson "—Miss Alicia began all at once to realize that they did not know each other, and that she had flown to the refuge of her youth without being at all aware of what she was about to say. "Oh! Little Ann!" she broke down with frank tears. "My poor boy! My poor boy!"

Little Ann drew her inside and closed the door.

"There, Miss Temple Barholm," she said. "There now Just come in and sit down. I'll get you a good cup of tea. You need one."

CHAPTER XXXVIII

The Duke of Stone had been sufficiently occupied with one of his slighter attacks of rheumatic gout to have been, so to speak, out of the running in the past weeks. His indisposition had not condemned him to the usual dullness, however. He had suffered less pain than was customary, and Mrs. Braddle had been more than usually interesting in conversation on those occasions when, in making him very comfortable in one way or another, she felt that a measure of entertainment would add to his well-being. His epicurean habit of mind tended toward causing him to find a subtle pleasure in the hearing of various versions of any story whatever. His intimacy with T. Tembarom had furnished forth many an agreeable mental repast for him. He had had T. Tembarom's version of himself, the version of the county, the version of the uneducated class, and his own version. All of these had had varying shades of their own. He had found a cynically fine flavor in Palliser's version, which he had gathered through talk and processes of exclusion and inclusion.

"There is a good deal to be said for it," he summed it up. "It's plausible on ordinary sophisticated grounds. T. Tembarom would say, 'It looks sort of that way.'"

As Mrs. Braddle had done what she could in the matter of expounding her views of the uncertainties of the village attitude, he had listened with stimulating interest. Mrs. Braddle's version on the passing of T. Tembarom stood out picturesquely against the background of the version which was his own—the one founded on the singular facts he had shared knowledge of with the chief character in the episode. He had not, like Miss Alicia, received a communication from Tembarom. This seemed to him one of the attractive features of the incident. It provided opportunity for speculation. Some wild development had called the youngster away in a rattling hurry. Of what had happened since his departure he knew no more than the villagers knew. What had happened for some months before his going he had watched with the feeling of an intelligently observant spectator at a play. He had been provided with varied emotions by the fantastic drama. He had smiled; he had found himself moved once or twice, and he had felt a good deal of the thrill of curious uncertainty as to what the curtain would rise and fall on. The situation was such that it was impossible to guess. Results could seem only to float in the air. One thing might happen; so might another, so might a dozen more. What he wished really to attain was some degree of certainty as to what was likely to occur in any case to the American Temple Barholm.

He felt, the first time he drove over to call on Miss Alicia, that his indisposition and confinement to his own house had robbed him of something. They had deprived him of the opportunity to observe shades of development and to hear the expressing of views of the situation as it stood. He drove over with views of his own and with anticipations. He had reason to know that he would encounter in the dear lady indications of the feeling that she had reached a crisis. There was a sense of this crisis impending as one mounted the terrace steps and entered the hall. The men-servants endeavored to wipe from their countenances any expression denoting even a vague knowledge of it. He recognized their laudable determination to do so. Burrill was monumental in the unconsciousness of his outward bearing.

Miss Alicia, sitting waiting on Fate in the library, wore precisely the aspect he had known she would wear. She had been lying awake at night and she had of course wept at intervals, since she belonged to the period the popular female view of which had been that only the unfeeling did not so relieve themselves in crises of the affections. Her eyelids were rather pink and her nice little face was tired.

"It is very, very kind of you to come," she said, when they shook hands. "I wonder "—her hesitance was touching in its obvious appeal to him not to take the wrong side,—"I wonder if you know how deeply troubled I have been?"

"You see, I have had a touch of my abominable gout, and my treasure of a Braddle has been nursing me and gossiping," he answered. "So, of course I know a great deal. None of it true, I dare say. I felt I must come and see you, however."

He looked so neat and entirely within the boundaries of finished and well-dressed modernity and every-day occurrence, in his perfectly fitting clothes, beautifully shining boots, and delicate fawn gaiters, that she felt a sort of support in his mere aspect. The mind connected such almost dapper freshness and excellent taste only with unexaggerated incidents and a behavior which almost placed the stamp of absurdity upon the improbable in circumstance. The vision of disorderly and illegal possibilities seemed actually to fade into an unreality.

"If Mr. Palford and Mr. Grimby knew him as I know him—as—as you know him—" she added with a faint hopefulness.

"Yes, if they knew him as we know him that would make a different matter of it," admitted the duke, amiably. But, thought Miss Alicia, he might only have put it that way through consideration for her feelings, and because he was an extremely polished man who could not easily reveal to a lady a disagreeable truth. He did not speak with the note of natural indignation which she thought she must have detected if he had felt as she felt herself. He was of course a man whose manner had always the finish of composure. He did not seem disturbed or even very curious—only kind and most polite.

"If we only knew where he was!" she began again. "If we only knew where Mr. Strangeways was!"

"My impression is that Messrs. Palford & Grimby will probably find them both before long," he consoled her. "They are no doubt exciting themselves unnecessarily."

He was not agitated at all; she felt it would have been kinder if he had been a little agitated. He was really not the kind of person whose feelings appeared very deep, being given to a light and graceful cynicism of speech which delighted people; so perhaps it was not natural that he should express any particular emotion even in a case affecting a friend—surely he had been Temple's friend. But if he had seemed a little distressed, or doubtful or annoyed, she would have felt that she understood better his attitude. As it was, he might almost have been on the other side—a believer or a disbeliever—or merely a person looking on to see what would happen. When they sat down, his glance seemed to include her with an interest which was sympathetic but rather as if she were a child whom he would like to pacify. This seemed especially so when she felt she must make clear to him the nature of the crisis which was pending, as he had felt when he entered the house.

"You perhaps do not know"—the appeal which had shown itself in her eyes was in her voice—"that the solicitors have decided, after a great deal of serious discussion and private inquiry in London, that the time has come when they must take open steps."

"In the matter of investigation?" he inquired.

"They are coming here this afternoon with Captain Palliser to—to question the servants, and some of the villagers. They will question me," alarmedly.

"They would be sure to do that,"—he really seemed quite to envelop her with kindness—"but I beg of you not to be alarmed. Nothing you could have to say could possibly do harm to Temple Barholm." He knew it was her fear of this contingency which terrified her.

"You do feel sure of that?" she burst forth, relievedly. "You do—because you know him?"

"I do. Let us be calm, dear lady. Let us be calm."

"I will! I will!" she protested. "But Captain Palliser has arranged that a lady should come here—a lady who disliked poor Temple very much. She was most unjust to him."

"Lady Joan Fayre?" he suggested, and then paused with a remote smile as if lending himself for the moment to some humor he alone detected in the situation.

"She will not injure his cause, I think I can assure you."

"She insisted on misunderstanding him. I am so afraid—"

The appearance of Pearson at the door interrupted her and caused her to rise from her seat. The neat young man was pale and spoke in a nervously lowered voice.

"I beg pardon, Miss. I beg your Grace's pardon for intruding, but—"

Miss Alicia moved toward him in such a manner that he himself seemed to feel that he might advance.

"What is it, Pearson? Have you anything special to say?"

"I hope I am not taking too great a liberty, Miss, but I did come in for a purpose, knowing that his Grace was with you and thinking you might both kindly advise me. It is about Mr. Temple Barholm, your Grace—" addressing him as if in involuntary recognition of the fact that he might possibly prove the greater support.

"Our Mr. Temple Barholm, Pearson? We are being told there are two of them." The duke's delicate emphasis on the possessive pronoun was delightful, and it so moved and encouraged sensitive little Pearson that he was emboldened to answer with modest firmness:

"Yes,—ours. Thank you, your Grace."

"You feel him yours too, Pearson?" a shade more delightfully still.

"I—I take the liberty, your Grace, of being deeply attached to him, and more than grateful."

"What did you want to ask advice about?"

"The family solicitors. Captain Palliser and Lady Joan Fayre and Mr. and Miss Hutchinson are to be here shortly, and I have been told I am to be questioned. What I want to know, your Grace, is—" He paused, and looked no longer pale but painfully red as he gathered himself together for his anxious outburst—"Must I speak the truth?"

Miss Alicia started alarmedly.

The duke looked down at the delicate fawn gaiters covering his fine instep. His fleeting smile was not this time an external one.

"Do you not wish to speak the truth, Pearson?"

Pearson's manner could have been described only as one of obstinate frankness.

"No, your Grace. I do not! Your Grace may misunderstand me—but I do not!"

His Grace tapped the gaiters with the slight ebony cane he held in his hand.

"Is this "—he put it with impartial curiosity—"because the truth might be detrimental to our Mr. Temple Barholm?"

"If you please, your Grace," Pearson made a firm step forward, "what is the truth?"

"That is what Messrs. Palford & Grimby seem determined to find out. Probably only our Mr. Temple Barholm can tell them."

"Your Grace, what I'm thinking of is that if I tell the truth it may seem to prove something that's not the truth."

"What kinds of things, Pearson?" still impartially.

"I can be plain with your Grace. Things like this: I was with Mr. Temple Barholm and Mr. Strangeways a great deal. They'll ask me about what I heard. They'll ask me if Mr. Strangeways was willing to go away to the doctor; if he had to be persuaded and argued with. Well, he had and he hadn't, your Grace. At first, just the mention of it would upset him so that Mr. Temple Barholm would have to stop talking about it and quiet him down. But when he improved—and he did improve wonderfully, your Grace—he got into the way of sitting and thinking it over and listening quite quiet. But if I'm asked suddenly—"

"What you are afraid of is that you may be asked point-blank questions without warning?" his Grace put it with the perspicacity of experience.

"That's why I should be grateful for advice. Must I tell the truth, your Grace, when it will make them believe things I'd swear are lies—I'd swear it, your Grace."

"So would I, Pearson." His serene lightness was of the most baffling, but curiously supporting, order. "This being the case, my advice would be not to go into detail. Let us tell white lies—all of us—without a shadow of hesitancy. Miss Temple Barholm, even you must do your best."

"I will try—indeed, I will try!" And the Duke felt her tremulously ardent assent actually delicious.

"There! we'll consider that settled, Pearson," he said.

"Thank you, your Grace. Thank you, Miss," Pearson's relieved gratitude verged on the devout. He turned to go, and as he did so his attention was arrested by an approach he remarked through a window.

"Mr. and Miss Hutchinson are arriving now, Miss," he announced, hastily.

"They are to be brought in here," said Miss Alicia.

The duke quietly left his seat and went to look through the window with frank and unembarrassed interest in the approach. He went, in fact, to look at Little Ann, and as he watched her walk up the avenue, her father lumbering beside her, he evidently found her aspect sufficiently arresting.

"Ah!" he exclaimed softly, and paused. "What a lot of very nice red hair," he said next. And then, "No wonder! No wonder!"

"That, I should say," he remarked as Miss Alicia drew near, "is what I once heard a bad young man call 'a deserving case.'"

He was conscious that she might have been privately a little shocked by such aged flippancy, but she was at the moment perturbed by something else.

"The fact is that I have never spoken to Hutchinson," she fluttered. "These changes are very confusing. I suppose I ought to say Mr. Hutchinson, now that he is such a successful person, and Temple—"

"Without a shadow of a doubt!" The duke seemed struck by the happiness of the idea. "They will make him a peer presently. He may address me as 'Stone' at any moment. One must learn to adjust one's self with agility. 'The old order changeth.' Ah! she is smiling at him and I see the dimples."

Miss Alicia made a clean breast of it.

"I went to her—I could not help it!" she confessed. "I was in such distress and dare not speak to anybody. Temple had told me that she was so wonderful. He said she always understood and knew what to do."

"Did she in this case?" he asked, smiling.

Miss Alicia's manner was that of one who could express the extent of her admiration only in disconnected phrases.

"She was like a little rock. Such a quiet, firm way! Such calm certainty! Oh, the comfort she has been to me! I begged her to come here to-day. I did not know her father had returned."

"No doubt he will have testimony to give which will be of the greatest assistance," the duke said most encouragingly. "Perhaps he will be a sort of rock."

"I—I don't in the least know what he will be!" sighed Miss Alicia, evidently uncertain in her views.

But when the father and daughter were announced she felt that his Grace was really enchanting in the happy facility of his manner. He at least adjusted himself with agility. Hutchinson was of course lumbering. Lacking the support of T. Tembarom's presence and incongruity, he himself was the incongruous feature. He would have been obliged to bluster by way of sustaining himself, even if he had only found himself being presented to Miss Alicia; but when it was revealed to him that he was also confronted with the greatest personage of the neighborhood, he became as hot and red as he had become during certain fateful business interviews. More so, indeed.

"Th' other chaps hadn't been dukes;" and to Hutchinson the old order had not yet so changed that a duke was not an awkwardly impressive person to face unexpectedly.

The duke's manner of shaking hands with him, however, was even touched with an amiable suggestion of appreciation of the value of a man of genius. He had heard of the invention, in fact knew some quite technical things about it. He realized its importance. He had congratulations for the inventor and the world of inventions so greatly benefited.

"Lancashire must be proud of your success, Mr. Hutchinson." How agreeably and with what ease he said it!

"Aye, it's a success now, your Grace," Hutchinson answered, "but I might have waited a good bit longer if it hadn't been for that lad an' his bold backing of me."

"Mr. Temple Barholm?" said the duke.

"Aye. He's got th' way of making folks see things that they can't see even when they're hitting them in th' eyes. I'd that lost heart I could never have done it myself."

"But now it is done," smiled his Grace. "Delightful!"

"I've got there—same as they say in New York—I've got there," said Hutchinson.

He sat down in response to Miss Alicia's invitation. His unease was wonderfully dispelled. He felt himself a person of sufficient importance to address even a duke as man to man.

"What's all this romancin' talk about th' other Temple Barholm comin' back, an' our lad knowin' an' hidin' him away? An' Palliser an' th' lawyers an' th' police bein' after 'em both?"

"You have heard the whole story?" from the duke.

"I've heard naught else since I come back."

"Grandmother knew a great deal before we came home," said Little Ann.

The duke turned his attention to her with an engaged smile. His look, his bow, his bearing, in the moment of their being presented to each other, had seemed to Miss Alicia the most perfect thing. His fine eye had not obviously wandered while he talked to her father, but it had in fact been taking her in with an inclusiveness not likely to miss agreeable points of detail.

"What is her opinion, may I ask?" he said. "What does she say?"

"Grandmother is very set in her ways, your Grace." The limpidity of her blue eye and a flickering dimple added much to the quaint comprehensiveness of her answer. "She says the world's that full of fools that if they were all killed the Lord would have to begin again with a new Adam and Eve."

"She has entire faith in Mr. Temple Barholm—as you have," put forward his Grace.

"Mine's not faith exactly. I know him," Little Ann answered, her tone as limpid as her eyes.

"There's more than her has faith in him," broke forth Hutchinson. "Danged if I don't like th' way them village chaps are taking it. They're ready to fight over it. Since they've found out what it's come to, an' about th' lawyers comin' down, they're talkin' about gettin' up a kind o' demonstration."

"Delightful!" ejaculated his Grace again. He leaned forward. "Quite what I should have expected. There's a good deal of beer drunk, I suppose."

"Plenty o' beer, but it'll do no harm." Hutchinson began to chuckle. "They're talkin' o' gettin' out th' fife an' drum band an' marchin' round th' village with a calico banner with 'Vote for T. Tembarom' painted on it, to show what they think of him."

The duke chuckled also.

"I wonder how he's managed it?" he laughed. "They wouldn't do it for any of the rest of us, you know, though I've no doubt we're quite as deserving. I am, I know."

Hutchinson stopped laughing and turned on Miss Alicia.

"What's that young woman comin' down here for?" he inquired.

"Lady Joan was engaged to Mr. James Temple Barholm," Miss Alicia answered.

"Eh! Eh!" Hutchinson jerked out. "That'll turn her into a wildcat, I'll warrant. She'll do all th' harm she can. I'm much obliged to you for lettin' us come, ma'am. I want to be where I can stand by him."

"Father," said Little Ann, "what you have got to remember is that you mustn't fly into a passion. You know you've always said it never did any good, and it only sends the blood to your head."

"You are not nervous, Miss Hutchinson?" the duke suggested.

"About Mr. Temple Barholm? I couldn't be, your Grace. If I was to see two policemen bringing him in handcuffed I shouldn't be nervous. I should know the handcuffs didn't belong to him, and the policemen would look right-down silly to me."

Miss Alicia fluttered over to fold her in her arms.

"Do let me kiss you," she said. "Do let me, Little Ann!"

Little Ann had risen at once to meet her embrace. She put a hand on her arm.

"We don't know anything about this really," she said. "We've only heard what people say. We haven't heard what he says. I'm going to wait." They were all looking at her,—the duke with such marked interest that she turned toward him as she ended. "And if I had to wait until I was as old as grandmother I'd wait—and nothing would change my mind."

"And I've been lying awake at night!" softly wailed Miss Alicia.

CHAPTER XXXIX

It was Mr. Hutchinson who, having an eye on the window, first announced an arriving carriage.

"Some of 'em's comin' from the station," he remarked. "There's no young woman with 'em, that I can see from here."

"I thought I heard wheels." Miss Alicia went to look out, agitatedly. "It is the gentlemen. Perhaps Lady Joan—" she turned desperately to the duke. "I don't know what to say to Lady Joan. I don't know what she will say to me. I don't know what she is coming for, Little Ann, do keep near me!"

It was a pretty thing to see Little Ann stroke her hand and soothe her.

"Don't be frightened, Miss Temple Barholm. All you've got to do is to answer questions," she said.

"But I might say things that would be wrong—things that would harm him."

"No, you mightn't, Miss Temple Barholm. He's not done anything that could bring harm on him."

The Duke of Stone, who had seated himself in T. Tembarom's favorite chair, which occupied a point of vantage, seemed to Mr. Palford and Mr. Grimby when they entered the room to wear the aspect of a sort of presidiary audience. The sight of his erect head and clear-cut, ivory-tinted old face, with its alert, while wholly unbiased, expression, somewhat startled them both. They had indeed not expected to see him, and did not know why he had chosen to come. His presence might mean any one of several things, and the fact that he enjoyed a reputation for quite alarming astuteness of a brilliant kind presented elements of probable embarrassment. If he thought that they had allowed themselves to be led upon a wild-goose chase, he would express his opinions with trying readiness of phrase.

His manner of greeting them, however, expressed no more than a lightly agreeable detachment from any view whatsoever. Captain Palliser felt this curiously, though he could not have said what he would have expected from him if he had known it would be his whim to appear.

"How do you do? How d' you do?" His Grace shook hands with the amiable ease which scarcely commits a man even to casual interest, after which he took his seat again.

"How d' do, Miss Hutchinson?" said Palliser. "How d' do, Mr. Hutchinson? Mr. Palford will be glad to find you here."

Mr. Palford shook hands with correct civility.

"I am, indeed," he said. "It was in your room in New York that I first saw Mr. Temple Temple Barholm."

"Aye, it was," responded Hutchinson, dryly.

"I thought Lady Joan was coming," Miss Alicia said to Palliser.

"She will be here presently. She came down in our train, but not with us."

"What—what is she coming for?" faltered Miss Alicia.

"Yes," put in the duke, "what, by the way, is she coming for?"

"I wrote and asked her to come," was Palliser's reply. "I have reason to believe she may be able to recall something of value to the inquiry which is being made."

"That's interesting," said his Grace, but with no air of participating particularly. "She doesn't like him, though, does she? Wouldn't do to put her on the jury."

He did not wait for any reply, but turned to Mr. Palford.

"All this is delightfully portentous. Do you know it reminds me of a scene in one of those numerous plays where the wrong man has murdered somebody—or hasn't murdered somebody—and the whole company must be cross-examined because the curtain cannot be brought down until the right man is unmasked. Do let us come into this, Mr. Palford; what we know seems so inadequate."

Mr. Palford and Mr. Grimby each felt that there lurked in this manner a possibility that they were being regarded lightly. All the objections to their situation loomed annoyingly large.

"It is, of course, an extraordinary story," Mr. Palford said, "but if we are not mistaken in our deductions, we may find ourselves involved in a cause celebre which will set all England talking."

"I am not mistaken," Palliser presented the comment with a short and dry laugh.

"Tha seems pretty cock-sure!" Hutchinson thrust in.

"I am. No one knew Jem Temple Barbolm better than I did in the past. We were intimate—enemies." And he laughed again.

"Tha says tha'll swear th' chap tha saw through th' window was him?" said Hutchinson.

"I'd swear it," with composure.

The duke was reflecting. He was again tapping with his cane the gaiter covering his slender, shining boot.

"If Mr. Temple Temple Barholm had remained here his actions would have seemed less suspicious?" he suggested.

It was Palliser who replied.

"Or if he hadn't whisked the other man away. He lost his head and played the fool."

"He didn't lose his head, that chap. It's screwed on th' right way—his head is," grunted Hutchinson.

"The curious fellow has a number of friends," the duke remarked to Palford and Grimby, in his impartial tone. "I am hoping you are not thinking of cross-examining me. I have always been convinced that under cross-examination I could be induced to innocently give evidence condemnatory to both sides of any case whatever. But would you mind telling me what the exact evidence is so far?"

Mr. Palford had been opening a budget of papers.

"It is evidence which is cumulative, your Grace," he said. "Mr. Temple Temple Barholm's position would have been a far less suspicious one—as you yourself suggested—if he had remained, or if he hadn't secretly removed Mr.—Mr. Strangeways."

"The last was Captain Palliser's suggestion, I believe," smiled the duke. "Did he remove him secretly? How secretly, for instance?"

"At night," answered Palliser. "Miss Temple Barholm herself did not know when it happened. Did you?" turning to Miss Alicia, who at once flushed and paled.

"He knew that I was rather nervous where Mr. Strangeways was concerned. I am sorry to say he found that out almost at once. He even told me several times that I must not think of him—that I need hear nothing about him." She turned to the duke, her air of appeal plainly representing a feeling that he would understand her confession. "I scarcely like to say it, but wrong as it was I couldn't help feeling that it was like having a—a lunatic in the house. I was afraid he might be more—ill—than Temple realized, and that he might some time become violent. I never admitted so much of course, but I was."

"You see, she was not told," Palliser summed it up succinctly.

"Evidently," the duke admitted. "I see your point." But he seemed to disengage himself from all sense of admitting implications with entire calmness, as he turned again to Mr. Palford and his papers.

"You were saying that the exact evidence was—?"

Mr. Palford referred to a sheet of notes.

"That—whether before or shortly after his arrival here is not at all certain—Mr. Temple Temple Barholm began strongly to suspect the identity of the person then known as Strangeways—"

Palliser again emitted the short and dry laugh, and both the duke and Mr. Palford looked at him inquiringly.

"He had `got on to' it before he brought him," he answered their glances. "Be sure of that."

"Then why did he bring him?" the duke suggested lightly.

"Oh, well," taking his cue from the duke, and assuming casual lightness also, "he was obliged to come himself, and was jolly well convinced that he had better keep his hand on the man, also his eye. It was a good-enough idea. He couldn't leave a thing like that wandering about the States. He could play benefactor safely in a house of the size of this until he was ready for action."

The duke gave a moment to considering the matter—still detachedly.

"It is, on the whole, not unlikely that something of the sort might suggest itself to the criminal mind," he said. And his glance at Mr. Palford intimated that he might resume his statement.

"We have secured proof that he applied himself to secret investigation. He is known to have employed Scotland Yard to make certain inquiries concerning the man said to have been killed in the Klondike. Having evidently reached more than suspicion he began to endeavor to persuade Mr. Strangeways to let him take him to London. This apparently took some time. The mere suggestion of removal threw the invalid into a state of painful excitement—"

"Did Pearson tell you that?" the duke inquired.

"Captain Palliser himself in passing the door of the room one day heard certain expressions of terrified pleading," was Mr. Palford's explanation.

"I heard enough," Palliser took it up carelessly, "to make it worth while to question Pearson—who must have heard a great deal more. Pearson was ordered to hold his tongue from the first, but he will have to tell the truth when he is asked."

The duke did not appear to resent his view.

"Pearson would be likely to know what went on," he remarked. "He's an intelligent little fellow."

"The fact remains that in spite of his distress and reluctance Mr. Strangeways was removed privately, and there our knowledge ends. He has not been seen since—and a few hours after, Captain Palliser expressed his conviction, that the person he had seen through the West Room window was Mr. James Temple Barholm, Mr. Temple Temple Barholm left the house taking a midnight train, and leaving no clue as to his where-abouts or intentions."

"Disappeared!" said the duke. "Where has he been looked for?"

The countenance of both Mr. Palford and his party expressed a certain degree of hesitance.

"Principally in asylums and so-called sanatoriums," Mr. Grimby admitted with a hint of reluctance.

"Places where the curiosity of outsiders is not encouraged," said Palliser languidly. "And where if a patient dies in a fit of mania there are always respectable witnesses to explain that his case was hopeless from the first."

Mr. Hutchinson had been breathing hard occasionally as he sat and listened, and now he sprang up uttering a sound dangerously near a violent snort.

"Art tha accusin' that lad o' bein' black villain enough to be ready to do bloody murder?" he cried out.

"He was in a very tight place, Hutchinson," Palliser shrugged his shoulders as he said it. "But one makes suggestions at this stage—not accusations."

That Hutchinson had lost his head was apparent to his daughter at least.

"Tha'd be in a tight place, my fine chap, if I had my way," he flung forth irately. "I'd like to get thy head under my arm."

The roll of approaching wheels reached Miss Alicia.

"There's another carriage," was her agitated exclamation. "Oh, dear! It must be Lady Joan!"

Little Ann left her seat to make her father return to his.

"Father, you'd better sit down," she said, gently pushing him in the right direction. "When you can't prove a thing's a lie, it's just as well to keep quiet until you can." And she kept quiet herself, though she turned and stood before Palliser and spoke with clear deliberateness. "What you pretend to believe is not true, Captain Palliser. It's just not true," she gave to him.

They were facing and looking at each other when Burrill announced Lady Joan Fayre. She entered rather quickly and looked round the room with a sweeping glance, taking them all in. She went to the duke first, and they shook hands.

"I am glad you are here!" she said.

"I would not have been out of it, my dear young lady," he answered, "'for a farm' That's a quotation."

"I know," she replied, giving her hand to Miss Alicia, and taking in Palliser and the solicitors with a bow which was little more than a nod. Then she saw Little Ann, and walked over to her to shake hands.

"I am glad you are here. I rather felt you would be," was her greeting. "I am glad to see you."

"Whether tha 'rt glad to see me or not I'm glad I'm here," said Hutchinson bluntly. "I've just been speaking a bit o' my mind."

"Now, Father love!" Little Ann put her hand on his arm.

Lady Joan looked him over. Her hungry eyes were more hungry than ever. She looked like a creature in a fever and worn by it.

"I think I am glad you are here too," she answered.

Palliser sauntered over to her. He had approved the duke's air of being at once detached and inquiring, and he did not intend to wear the aspect of the personage who plays the unpleasant part of the pursuer and avenger. What he said was:

"It was good of you to come, Lady Joan."

"Did you think I would stay away?" was her answer. "But I will tell you that I don't believe it is true."

"You think that it is too good to be true?"

Her hot eyes had records in them it would have been impossible for him to read or understand. She had been so torn; she had passed through such hours since she had been told this wild thing.

"Pardon my not telling you what I think," she said. "Nothing matters, after all, if he is alive!"

"Except that we must find him," said Palliser.

"If he is in the same world with me I shall find him," fiercely. Then she turned again to Ann. "You are the girl T. Tembarom loves?" she put it to her.

"Yes, my lady."

"If he was lost, and you knew he was on the earth with you, don't you know that you would find him?"

"I should know he'd come back to me," Little Ann answered her. "That's what—" her small face looked very fine as in her second of hesitation a spirited flush ran over it, "that's what your man will do," quite firmly.

It was amazing to see how the bitter face changed, as if one word had brought back a passionate softening memory.

"My man!" Her voice mellowed until it was deep and low. "Did you call T. Tembarom that, too? Oh, I understand you! Keep near me while I talk to these people." She made her sit down by her.

"I know every detail of your letters." She addressed Palliser as well as Palford & Grimby, sweeping all details aside. "What is it you want to ask me?"

"This is our position, your ladyship," Mr. Palford fumbled a little with his papers in speaking. "Mr. Temple Temple Barholm and the person known as Mr. Strangeways have been searched for so far without result. In the meantime we realize that the more evidence we obtain that Mr. Temple Temple Barholm identified Strangeways and acted from motive, the more solid the foundation upon which Captain Palliser's conviction rests. Up to this point we have only his statement which he is prepared to make on oath. Fortunately, however, he on one occasion overheard something said to you which he believes will be corroborative evidence."

"What did you overhear?" she inquired of Palliser.

Her tone was not pacific considering that, logically, she must be on the side of the investigators. But it was her habit, as Captain Palliser remembered, to seem to put most people on the defensive. He meant to look as uninvolved as the duke, but it was not quite within his power. His manner was sufficiently deliberate.

"One evening, before you left for London, I was returning from the billiard-room, and heard you engaged in animated conversation with—our host. My attention was arrested, first because—" a sketch of a smile ill-concealed itself, "you usually scarcely deigned to speak to him, and secondly because I heard Jem Temple Barholm's name."

"And you—?" neither eyes nor manner omitted the word listened.

But the slight lift of his shoulders was indifferent enough.

"I listened deliberately. I was convinced that the fellow was a criminal impostor, and I wanted evidence."

"Ah! come now," remarked the duke amiably. "Now we are getting on. Did you gain any?"

"I thought so. Merely of the cumulative order, of course," Palliser answered with moderation. "Those were early days. He asked you," turning to Lady Joan again, "if you knew any one—any one—who had any sort of a photograph of Jem. You had one and you showed it to him!"

She was quite silent for a moment. The hour came back to her—the extraordinary hour when he had stood in his lounging fashion before her, and through some odd, uncivilized but absolutely human force of his own had made her listen to him—and had gone on talking in his nasal voice until with one common, crude, grotesque phrase he had turned her hideous world upside down—changed the whole face of it—sent the stone wall rising before her crumbling into dust, and seemed somehow to set her free. For the moment he had lifted a load from her the nature of which she did not think he could understand—a load of hatred and silence. She had clutched his hand, she had passionately wept on it, she could have kissed it. He had told her she could come back and not be afraid. As the strange episode rose before her detail by detail, she literally stared at Palliser.

"You did, didn't you?" he inquired.

"Yes," she answered.

Her mind was in a riot, because in the midst of things which must be true, something was false. But with the memory of a myriad subtle duplicities in her brain, she had never seen anything which could have approached a thing like that. He had made her feel more human than any one in the world had ever made her feel—but Jem. He had been able to do it because he was human himself—human. "I'm friendly," he had said with his boy's laugh—"just friendly."

"I saw him start, though you did not," Palliser continued. "He stood and studied the locket intently."

She remembered perfectly. He had examined it so closely that he had unconsciously knit his brows.

"He said something in a rather low voice," Palliser took it up. "I could not quite catch it all. It was something about 'knowing the face again.' I can see you remember, Lady Joan. Can you repeat the exact words?"

He did not understand the struggle he saw in her face. It would have been impossible for him to understand it. What she felt was that if she lost hold on her strange belief in the honesty of this one decent thing she had seen and felt so close to her that it cleared the air she breathed, it would be as if she had fallen into a bottomless abyss. Without knowing why she did it, she got up from her chair as if she were a witness in a court.

"Yes, I can," she said. "Yes, I can; but I wish to make a statement for myself. Whether Jem Temple Barholm is alive or dead, Captain Palliser, T. Tembarom has done him no harm."

The duke sat up delicately alert. He had evidently found her worth looking at and listening to from the outset.

"Hear! Hear!" he said pleasantly.

"What were the exact words?" suggested Palliser.

Miss Alicia who had been weeping on Little Ann's shoulder—almost on her lap—lifted her head to listen. Hutchinson set his jaw and grunted, and Mr. Palford cleared his throat mechanically.

"He said," and no one better than herself realized how ominously "cumulative" the words sounded, "that a man would know a face like that again—wherever he saw it."

"Wherever he saw it!" ejaculated Mr. Grimby.

There ensued a moment of entire pause. It was inevitable. Having reached this point a taking of breath was necessary. Even the duke ceased to appear entirely detached. As Mr. Palford turned to his papers again there was perhaps a slight feeling of awkwardness in the air. Miss Alicia had dropped, terror smitten, into new tears.

The slight awkwardness was, on the whole, rather added to by T. Tembarom—as if serenely introduced by the hand of drama itself—opening the door and walking into the room. He came in with a matter-of-fact, but rather obstinate, air, and stopped in their midst, looking round at them as if collectedly taking them all in.

Hutchinson sprang to his feet with a kind of roar, his big hands plunging deep into his trousers pockets.

"Here he is! Danged if he isn't!" he bellowed. "Now, lad, tha let 'em have it!"

What he was to let them have did not ensue, because his attitude was not one of assault.

"Say, you are all here, ain't you!" he remarked obviously. "Good business!"

Miss Alicia got up from the sofa and came trembling toward him as one approaches one risen from the dead, and he made a big stride toward her and took her in his arms, patting her shoulder in reproachful consolation.

"Say, you haven't done what I told you—have you?" he soothed. "You've let yourself get rattled."

"But I knew it wasn't true," she sobbed. "I knew it wasn't."

"Of course you did, but you got rattled all the same." And he patted her again.

The duke came forward with a delightfully easy and—could it be almost jocose?—air of bearing himself. Palford and Grimby remarked it with pained dismay. He was so unswerving in his readiness as he shook hands.

"How well done of you!" he said. "How well arranged! But I'm afraid you didn't arrange it at all. It has merely happened. Where did you come from?"

"From America; got back yesterday." T. Tembarom's hand-shake was a robust hearty greeting. "It's all right."

"From America!" The united voices of the solicitors exclaimed it.

Joseph Hutchinson broke into a huge guffaw, and he stamped in exultation.

"I'm danged if he has na' been to America!" he cried out. "To America!"

"Oh!" Miss Alicia gasped hysterically, "they go backward and forward to America like—like lightning!"

Little Ann had not risen at his entrance, but sat still with her hands clasped tightly on her lap. Her face had somehow the effect of a flower gradually breaking into extraordinary bloom. Their eyes had once met and then she remained, her soul in hers which were upon him, as she drank in every word he uttered. Her time had not yet come.

Lady Joan had remained standing by the chair, which a few moments before her manner had seemed to transform into something like a witness stand in a court of justice. Her hungry eyes had grown hungrier each second, and her breath came and went quickly. The very face she had looked up at on her last talk with T. Tembarom—the oddly human face—turned on her as he came to her. It was just as it had been that night—just as commonly uncommon and believable.

"Say, Lady Joan! You didn't believe all that guff, did you—You didn't?" he said.

"No—no—no! I couldn't!" she cried fiercely.

He saw she was shaking with suspense, and he pushed her gently into a chair.

"You'd better sit down a minute. You're about all in," he said.

She might have been a woman with an ague as she caught his arm, shaking it because her hands themselves so shook.

"Is it true?" was her low cry. "Is he alive—is he alive?"

"Yes, he's alive." And as he answered he drew close and so placed himself before her that he shielded her from the others in the room. He seemed to manage to shut them out, so that when she dropped her face on her arms against the chair-back her shuddering, silent sobbing was hidden decently. It was not only his body which did it, but some protecting power which was almost physically visible. She felt it spread before her.

"Yes, he's alive," he said, "and he's all right—though it's been a long time coming, by gee!"

"He's alive." They all heard it. For a man of Palliser's make to stand silent in the midst of mysterious slowly accumulating convictions that some one—perilously of his own rarely inept type—was on the verge of feeling appallingly like a fool—was momentarily unendurable. And nothing had been explained, after all.

"Is this what you call 'bluff' in New York?" he demanded. "You've got a lot to explain. You admit that Jem Temple Barholm is alive?" and realized his asinine error before the words were fully spoken.

The realization was the result of the square-shouldered swing with which T. Tembarom turned round, and the expression of his eyes as they ran over him.

"Admit!" he said. "Admit hell! He's up-stairs," with a slight jerk of his head in the direction of the ceiling.

The duke alone did not gasp. He laughed slightly.

"We've just got here. He came down from London with me, and Sir Ormsby Galloway." And he said it not to Palliser but to Palford and Grimby.

"The Sir Ormsby Galloway?" It was an ejaculation from Mr. Palford himself.

T. Tembarom stood square and gave his explanation to the lot of them, so to speak, without distinction.

"He's the big nerve specialist. I've had him looking after the case from the first—before I began to suspect anything. I took orders, and orders were to keep him quiet and not let any fool butt in and excite him. That's what I've been giving my mind to. The great stunt was to get him to go and stay at Sir Ormsby's place." He stopped a moment and suddenly flared forth as if he had had about enough of it. He almost shouted at them in exasperation. "All I'm going to tell you is that for about six months I've been trying to prove that Jem Temple Barholm was Jem Temple Barholm, and the hardest thing I had to do was to get him so that he could prove it himself." He strode over to the hearth and rang a bell. "It's not my place to give orders here now," he said, "but Jem commissioned me to see this thing through. Sir Ormsby'll tell you all you want to hear."

He turned and spoke solely to the duke.

"This is what happened," he said. "I dare say you'll laugh when you hear it. I almost laughed myself. What does Jem do, when he thinks things over, but get some fool notion in his head about not coming back here and pushing me out. And he lights out and leaves the country—leaves it—to get time to think it over some more."

The duke did not laugh. He merely smiled—a smile which had a shade of curious self-questioning in it.

"Romantic and emotional—and quite ridiculous," he commented slowly. "He'd have awakened to that when he had thought it out 'some more.' The thing couldn't be done."

Burrill had presented himself in answer to the bell, and awaited orders. His Grace called Tembarom's attention to him, and Tembarom included Palliser with Palford and Grimby when he gave his gesture of instruction.

"Take these gentlemen to Sir Ormsby Galloway, and then ask Mr. Temple Barholm if he'll come down-stairs," he said.

It is possible that Captain Palliser felt himself more irritatingly infolded in the swathing realization that some one was in a ridiculous position, and it is certain that Mr. Palford felt it necessary to preserve an outwardly flawless dignity as the duke surprisingly left his chair and joined them.

"Let me go, too," he suggested; "I may be able to assist in throwing light." His including movement in Miss Alicia's direction was delightfully gracious and friendly. It was inclusive of Mr. Hutchinson also.

"Will you come with us, Miss Temple Barholm?" he said. "And you too, Mr. Hutchinson. We shall go over it all in its most interesting detail, and you must be eager about it. I am myself."

His happy and entirely correct idea was that the impending entrance of Mr. James Temple Barholm would "come off" better in the absence of audience.

Hutchinson almost bounced from his chair in his readiness. Miss Alicia looked at Tembarom.

"Yes, Miss Alicia," he answered her inquiring glance. "You go, too. You'll get it all over quicker."

Rigid propriety forbade that Mr. Palford should express annoyance, but the effort to restrain the expression of it was in his countenance. Was it possible that the American habit of being jocular had actually held its own in a matter as serious as this? And could even the most cynical and light-minded of ducal personages have been involved in its unworthy frivolities? But no one looked jocular—Tembarom's jaw was set in its hard line, and the duke, taking up the broad ribbon of his rimless monocle to fix the glass in his eye, wore the expression of a man whose sense of humor was temporarily in abeyance.

"Are we to understand that your Grace—?"

"Yes," said his Grace a trifle curtly, "I have known about it for some time."

"But why was nobody told?" put in Palliser.

"Why should people be told? There was nothing sufficiently definite to tell. It was a waiting game." His Grace wasted no words. "I was told. Mr. Temple Barholm did not know England or English methods. His idea—perhaps a mistaken one—was that an English duke ought to be able to advise him. He came to me and made a clean breast of it. He goes straight at things, that young fellow. Makes what he calls a 'bee line.' Oh! I've been in it—I 've been in it, I assure you."

It was as they crossed the hall that his Grace slightly laughed.

"It struck me as a sort of wild-goose chase at first. He had only a ghost of a clue—a mere resemblance to a portrait. But he believed in it, and he had an instinct." He laughed again. "The dullest and most unmelodramatic neighborhood in England has been taking part in a melodrama—but there has been no villain in it—only a matter-of-fact young man, working out a queer thing in his own queer, matter-of-fact way."

When the door closed behind them, Tembarom went to Lady Joan. She had risen and was standing before the window, her back to the room. She looked tall and straight and tensely braced when she turned round, but there was endurance, not fierceness in her eyes.

"Did he leave the country knowing I was here—waiting?" she asked. Her voice was low and fatigued. She had remembered that years had passed, and that it was perhaps after all only human that long anguish should blot things out, and dull a hopeless man's memory.

"No," answered Tembarom sharply. "He didn't. You weren't in it then. He believed you'd married that Duke of Merthshire fellow. This is the way it was: Let me tell it to you quick. A letter that had been wandering round came to him the night before the cave-in, when they thought he was killed. It told him old Temple Barholm was dead. He started out before daylight, and you can bet he was strung up till he was near crazy with excitement. He believed that if he was in England with plenty of money he could track down that cardsharp lie. He believed you'd help him. Somewhere, while he was traveling he came across an old paper with a lot of dope about your being engaged."

Joan remembered well how her mother had worked to set the story afloat—how they had gone through the most awful of their scenes—almost raving at each other, shut up together in the boudoir in Hill Street.

"That's all he remembers, except that he thought some one had hit him a crack on the head. Nothing had hit him. He'd had too much to stand up under and something gave way in his brain. He doesn't know what happened after that. He'd wake up sometimes just enough to know he was wandering about trying to get home. It's been the limit to try to track him. If he'd not come to himself we could never have been quite sure. That's why I stuck at it. But he DID come to himself. All of a sudden. Sir Ormsby will tell you that's what nearly always happens. They wake up all of a sudden. It's all right; it's all right. I used to promise him it would be—when I wasn't sure that I wasn't lying." And for the first time he broke into the friendly grin—but it was more valiant than spontaneous. He wanted her to know that it was "all right."

"Oh!" she cried, "oh! you—"

She stopped because the door was opening.

"It's Jem," he said sharply. "Ann, let's go." And that instant Little Ann was near him.

"No! no! don't go," cried Lady Joan.

Jem Temple Barholm came in through the doorway. Life and sound and breath stopped for a second, and then the two whirled into each other's arms as if a storm had swept them there.

"Jem!" she wailed. "Oh, Jem! My man! Where have you been?"

"I've been in hell, Joan—in hell!" he answered, choking,—"and this wonderful fellow has dragged me out of it."

But Tembarom would have none of it. He could not stand it. This sort of thing filled up his throat and put him at an overwhelming disadvantage. He just laid a hand on Jem Temple Barholm's shoulder and gave him an awkwardly friendly push.

"Say, cut me out of it!" he said. "You get busy," his voice rather breaking. "You've got a lot to say to her. It was up to me before;—now, it's up to you."

Little Ann went with him into the next room.

The room they went into was a smaller one, quiet, and its oriel windows much overshadowed by trees. By the time they stood together in the center of it Tembarom had swallowed something twice or thrice, and had recovered himself. Even his old smile had come back as he took one of her hands in each of his, and holding them wide apart stood and looked down at her.

"God bless you, Little Ann," he said. "I just knew I should find you here. I'd have bet my last dollar on it."

The hands he held were trembling just a little, and the dimples quivered in and out. But her eyes were steady, and a lovely increasing intensity glowed in them.

"You went after him and brought him back. He was all wrought up, and he needed some one with good common sense to stop him in time to make him think straight before he did anything silly," she said.

"I says to him," T. Tembarom made the matter clear; "'Say, you've left something behind that belongs to you! Comeback and get it.' I meant Lady Joan. And I says, `Good Lord, man, you're acting like a fellow in a play. That place doesn't belong to me. It belongs to you. If it was mine, fair and square, Little Willie'd hang on to it. There'd be no noble sacrifice in his. You get a brace on.'"

"When they were talking in that silly way about you, and saying you'd run away," said Little Ann, her face uplifted adoringly as she talked, "I said to father, `If he's gone, he's gone to get something. And he'll be likely to bring it back.'"

He almost dropped her hands and caught her to him then. But he saved himself in time.

"Now this great change has come," he said, "everything will be different. The men you'll know will look like the pictures in the advertisements at the backs of magazines—those fellows with chins and smooth hair. I shall look like a chauffeur among them."

But she did not blench in the least, though she remembered whose words he was quoting. The intense and lovely femininity in her eyes only increased. She came closer to him, and so because of his height had to look up more.

"You will always make jokes—but I don't care. I don't care for anything but you," she said. "I love your jokes; I love everything about you: I love your eyes—and your voice—and your laugh. I love your very clothes." Her voice quivered as her dimples did. "These last months I've sometimes felt as if I should die of loving you."

It was a wonderful thing—wonderful. His eyes—his whole young being had kindled as he looked down drinking in every word.

"Is that the kind of quiet little thing you are?" he said.

"Yes, it is," she answered firmly.

"And you're satisfied—you know, who it is I want?—You're ready to do what you said you would that last night at Mrs. Bowse's?"

"What do you think?" she said in her clear little voice.

He caught her then in a strong, hearty, young, joyous clutch.

"You come to me, Little Ann. You come right to me," he said.

CHAPTER XL

Many an honest penny was turned, with the assistance of the romantic Temple Barholm case, by writers of paragraphs for newspapers published in the United States. It was not merely a romance which belonged to England but was excitingly linked to America by the fact that its hero regarded himself as an American, and had passed through all the picturesque episodes of a most desirably struggling youth in the very streets of New York itself, and had "worked his way up" to the proud position of society reporter "on" a huge Sunday paper. It was generally considered to redound largely to his credit that refusing "in spite of all temptations to belong to other nations," he had been born in Brooklyn, that he had worn ragged clothes and shoes with holes in them, that he had blacked other people's shoes, run errands, and sold newspapers there. If he had been a mere English young man, one recounting of his romance would have disposed of him; but as he was presented to the newspaper public every characteristic lent itself to elaboration. He was, in fact, flaringly anecdotal. As a newly elected President who has made boots or driven a canal-boat in his unconsidered youth endears himself indescribably to both paragraph reader and paragraph purveyor, so did T. Tembarom endear himself. For weeks, he was a perennial fount. What quite credible story cannot be related of a hungry lad who is wildly flung by chance into immense fortune and the laps of dukes, so to speak? The feeblest imagination must be stirred by the high color of such an episode, and stimulated to superb effort. Until the public had become sated with reading anecdotes depicting the extent of his early privations, and dwelling on illustrations which presented lumber-yards in which he had slept, and the facades of tumble-down tenements in which he had first beheld the light of day, he was a modest source of income. Any lumber-yard or any tenement sufficiently dilapidated would serve as a model; and the fact that in the shifting architectural life of New York the actual original scenes of the incidents had been demolished and built upon by new apartment-houses, or new railroad stations, or new factories seventy-five stories high, was an unobstructing triviality. Accounts of his manner of conducting himself in European courts to which he had supposedly been bidden, of his immense popularity in glittering circles, of his finely democratic bearing when confronted by emperors surrounded by their guilty splendors, were the joy of remote villages and towns. A thrifty and young minor novelist hastily incorporated him in a serial, and syndicated it upon the spot under the title of "Living or Dead." Among its especial public it was a success of such a nature as betrayed its author into as hastily writing a second romance, which not being rendered stimulating by a foundation of fact failed to repeat his triumph.

T. Tembarom, reading in the library at Temple Barholm the first newspapers sent from New York, smiled widely.

"You see they've got to say something, Jem," he explained. "It's too big a scoop to be passed over. Something's got to be turned in. And it means money to the fellows, too. It's good copy."

"Suppose," suggested Jem, watching him with interest, "you were to write the facts yourself and pass them on to some decent chap who'd be glad to get them."

"Glad!" Tembarom flushed with delight. "Any chap would be'way up in the air at the chance. It's the best kind of stuff. Wouldn't you mind? Are you sure you wouldn't?" He was the warhorse snuffing battle from afar.

Jem Temple Barholm laughed outright at the gleam in his eyes.

"No, I shouldn't care a hang, dear fellow. And the fact that I objected would not stop the story."

"No, it wouldn't, by gee! Say, I'll get Ann to help me, and we'll send it to the man who took my place on the Earth. It'll mean board and boots to him for a month if he works it right. And it'll be doing a good turn to Galton, too. I shall be glad to see old Galton when I go back."

"You are quite sure you want to go back?" inquired Jem. A certain glow of feeling was always in his eyes when he turned them on T. Tembarom.

"Go back! I should smile! Of course I shall go back. I've got to get busy for Hutchinson and I've got to get busy for myself. I guess there'll be work to do that'll take me half over the world; but I'm going back first. Ann's going with me."

But there was no reference to a return to New York when the Sunday Earth and other widely circulated weekly sheets gave prominence to the marriage of Mr. Temple Temple Barholm and Miss Hutchinson, only child and heiress of Mr. Joseph Hutchinson, the celebrated inventor. From a newspaper point of view, the wedding had been rather unfairly quiet, and it was necessary to fill space with a revival of the renowned story, with pictures of bride and bridegroom, and of Temple Barholm surrounded by ancestral oaks. A thriving business would have been done by the reporters if an ocean greyhound had landed the pair at the dock some morning, and snap-shots could have been taken as they crossed the gangway, and wearing apparel described. But hope of such fortune was swept away by the closing paragraph, which stated that Mr. and Mrs. Temple Barholm would "spend the next two months in motoring through Italy and Spain in their 90 h.p. Panhard."

It was T. Tembarom who sent this last item privately to Galton.

"It's not true," his letter added, "but what I'm going to do is nobody's business but mine and my wife's, and this will suit people just as well." And then he confided to Galton the thing which was the truth.

The St. Francesca apartment-house was a very new one, situated on a corner of an as yet sparsely built but rapidly spreading avenue above the "100th Streets"—many numbers above them. There was a frankly unfinished air about the neighborhood, but here and there a "store" had broken forth and valiantly displayed necessities, and even articles verging upon the economically ornamental. It was plainly imperative that the idea should be suggested that there were on the spot sources of supply not requiring the immediate employment of the services of the elevated railroad in the achievement of purchase, and also that enterprise rightly encouraged might develop into being equal to all demands. Here and there an exceedingly fresh and clean "market store," brilliant with the highly colored labels adorning tinned soups and meats and edibles in glass jars, alluringly presented itself to the passer-by. The elevated railroad perched upon iron supports, and with iron stairways so tall that they looked almost perilous, was a prominent feature of the landscape. There were stretches of waste ground, and high backgrounds of bits of country and woodland to be seen. The rush of New York traffic had not yet reached the streets, and the avenue was of an agreeable suburban cleanliness and calm. People who lived in upper stories could pride themselves on having "views of the river." These they laid stress upon when it was hinted that they "lived a long way uptown."

The St. Francesca was built of light-brown stone and decorated with much ornate molding. It was fourteen stories high, and was supplied with ornamental fire-escapes. It was "no slouch of a building." Everything decorative which could be done for it had been done. The entrance was almost imposing, and a generous lavishness in the way of cement mosaic flooring and new and thick red carpet struck the eye at once. The grill-work of the elevator was of fresh, bright blackness, picked out with gold, and the colored elevator-boy wore a blue livery with brass buttons. Persons of limited means who were willing to discard the excitements of "downtown" got a good deal for their money, and frequently found themselves secretly surprised and uplifted by the atmosphere of luxury which greeted them when they entered their red-carpeted hall. It was wonderful, they said, congratulating one another privately, how much comfort and style you got in a New York apartment-house after you passed the "150ths."

On a certain afternoon T. Tembarom, with his hat on the back of his head and his arms full of parcels, having leaped off the "L" when it stopped at the nearest station, darted up and down the iron stairways until he reached the ground, and then hurried across the avenue to the St. Francesca. He made long strides, and two or three times grinned as if thinking of something highly amusing; and once or twice he began to whistle and checked himself. He looked approvingly at the tall building and its solidly balustraded entrance-steps as he approached it, and when he entered the red-carpeted hall he gave greeting to a small mulatto boy in livery.

"Hello, Tom! How's everything?" he inquired, hilariously. "You taking good care of this building? Let any more eight-room apartments? You've got to keep right on the job, you know. Can't have you loafing because you've got those brass buttons."

The small page showed his teeth in gleeful appreciation of their friendly intimacy.

"Yassir. That's so," he answered. "Mis' Barom she's waitin' for you. Them carpets is come, sir. Tracy's wagon brought 'em 'bout an hour ago. I told her I'd help her lay 'em if she wanted me to, but she said you was comin' with the hammer an' tacks. 'Twarn't that she thought I was too little. It was jest that there wasn't no tacks. I tol' her jest call me in any time to do anythin' she want done, an' she said she would."

"She'll do it," said T. Tembarom. "You just keep on tap. I'm just counting on you and Light here," taking in the elevator-boy as he stepped into the elevator, "to look after her when I'm out."

The elevator-boy grinned also, and the elevator shot up the shaft, the numbers of the floors passing almost too rapidly to be distinguished. The elevator was new and so was the boy, and it was the pride of his soul to land each passenger at his own particular floor, as if he had been propelled upward from a catapult. But he did not go too rapidly for this passenger, at least, though a paper parcel or so was dropped in the transit and had to be picked up when he stopped at floor fourteen.

The red carpets were on the corridor there also, and fresh paint and paper were on the walls. A few yards from the elevator he stopped at a door and opened it with a latch-key, beaming with inordinate delight.

The door opened into a narrow corridor leading into a small apartment, the furniture of which was not yet set in order. A roll of carpet and some mats stood in a corner, chairs and tables with burlaps round their legs waited here and there, a cot with a mattress on it, evidently to be transformed into a "couch," held packages of bafflingly irregular shapes and sizes. In the tiny kitchen new pots and pans and kettles, some still wrapped in paper, tilted themselves at various angles on the gleaming new range or on the closed lids of the doll-sized stationary wash-tubs.

Little Ann had been very busy, and some of the things were unpacked. She had been sweeping and mopping floors and polishing up remote corners, and she had on a big white pinafore-apron with long sleeves, which transformed her into a sort of small female chorister. She came into the narrow corridor with a broom in her hand, her periwinkle-blue gaze as thrilled as an excited child's when it attacks the arrangement of its first doll's house. Her hair was a little ruffled where it showed below the white kerchief she had tied over her head. The warm, daisy pinkness of her cheeks was amazing.

"Hello!" called out Tembarom at sight of her. "Are you there yet? I don't believe it."

"Yes, I'm here," she answered, dimpling at him.

"Not you!" he said. "You couldn't be! You've melted away. Let's see." And he slid his parcels down on the cot and lifted her up in the air as if she had been a baby. "How can I tell, anyhow?" he laughed out. "You don't weigh anything, and when a fellow squeezes you he's got to look out what he's doing."

He did not seem to "look out" particularly when he caught her to him in a hug into which she appeared charmingly to melt. She made herself part of it, with soft arms which went at once round his neck and held him.

"Say!" he broke forth when he set her down. "Do you think I'm not glad to get back?"

"No, I don't, Tem," she answered, "I know how glad you are by the way I'm glad myself."

"You know just everything!" he ejaculated, looking her over, "just every darned thing—God bless you! But don't you melt away, will you? That's what I'm afraid of. I'll do any old thing on earth if you'll just stay."

That was his great joke,—though she knew it was not so great a joke as it seemed,—that he would not believe that she was real, and believed that she might disappear at any moment. They had been married three weeks, and she still knew when she saw him pause to look at her that he would suddenly seize and hold her fast, trying to laugh, sometimes not with entire success.

"Do you know how long it was? Do you know how far away that big place was from everything in the world?" he had said once. "And me holding on and gritting my teeth? And not a soul to open my mouth to! The old duke was the only one who understood, anyhow. He'd been there."

"I'll stay," she answered now, standing before him as he sat down on the end of the "couch." She put a firm, warm-palmed little hand on each side of his face, and held it between them as she looked deep into his eyes. "You look at me, Tem—and see."

"I believe it now," he said, "but I shan't in fifteen minutes."

"We're both right-down silly," she said, her soft, cosy laugh breaking out. "Look round this room and see what we've got to do. Let's begin this minute. Did you get the groceries?"

He sprang up and began to go over his packages triumphantly.

"Tea, coffee, sugar, pepper, salt, beefsteak," he called out.

"We can't have beefsteak often," she said, soberly, "if we're going to do it on fifteen a week."

"Good Lord, no!" he gave back to her, hilariously. "But this is a Fifth Avenue feed."

"Let's take them into the kitchen and put them into the cupboard, and untie the pots and pans." She was suddenly quite absorbed and businesslike. "We must make the room tidy and tack down the carpet, and then cook the dinner."

He followed her and obeyed her like an enraptured boy. The wonder of her was that, despite its unarranged air, the tiny place was already cleared and set for action. She had done it all before she had swept out the undiscovered corners. Everything was near the spot to which it belonged. There was nothing to move or drag out of the way.

"I got it all ready to put straight," she said, "but I wanted you to finish it with me. It wouldn't have seemed right if I'd done it without you. It wouldn't have been as much OURS."

Then came active service. She was like a small general commanding an army of one. They put things on shelves; they hung things on hooks; they found places in which things belonged; they set chairs and tables straight; and then, after dusting and polishing them, set them at a more imposing angle; they unrolled the little green carpet and tacked down its corners; and transformed the cot into a "couch" by covering it with what Tracy's knew as a "throw" and adorning one end of it with cotton-stuffed cushions. They hung little photogravures on the walls and strung up some curtains before the good-sized window, which looked down from an enormous height at the top of four-storied houses, and took in beyond them the river and the shore beyond. Because there was no fireplace Tembarom knocked up a shelf, and, covering it with a scarf (from Tracy's), set up some inoffensive ornaments on it and flanked them with photographs of Jem Temple Barholm, Lady Joan in court dress, Miss Alicia in her prettiest cap, and the great house with its huge terrace and the griffins.

"Ain't she a looker?" Tembarom said of Lady Joan. "And ain't Jem a looker, too? Gee! they're a pair. Jem thinks this honeymoon stunt of ours is the best thing he ever heard of—us fixing ourselves up here just like we would have done if nothing had ever happened, and we'd HAD to do it on fifteen per. Say," throwing an arm about her, "are you getting as much fun out of it as if we HAD to, as if I might lose my job any minute, and we might get fired out of here because we couldn't pay the rent? I believe you'd rather like to think I might ring you into some sort of trouble, so that you could help me to get you out of it."

"That's nonsense," she answered, with a sweet, untruthful little face. "I shouldn't be very sensible if I wasn't glad you COULDN'T lose your job. Father and I are your job now."

He laughed aloud. This was the innocent, fantastic truth of it. They had chosen to do this thing—to spend their honey-moon in this particular way, and there was no reason why they should not. The little dream which had been of such unattainable proportions in the days of Mrs. Bowse's boarding-house could be realized to its fullest. No one in the St. Francesca apartments knew that the young honey-mooners in the five-roomed apartment were other than Mr. and Mrs. T. Barholm, as recorded on the tablet of names in the entrance. Hutchinson knew, and Miss Alicia knew, and Jem Temple Barholm, and Lady Joan. The Duke of Stone knew, and thought the old-fashionedness of the idea quite the last touch of modernity.

"Did you see any one who knew you when you were out?" Little Ann asked.

"No, and if I had they wouldn't have believed they'd seen me, because the papers told them that Mr. and Mrs. Temple Barholm are spending their honeymoon motoring through Spain in their ninety-horse-power Panhard."

"Let's go and get dinner," said Little Ann.

They went into the doll's-house kitchen and cooked the dinner. Little Ann broiled steak and fried potato chips, and T. Tembarom produced a wonderful custard pie he had bought at a confectioner's. He set the table, and put a bunch of yellow daisies in the middle of it.

"We couldn't do it every day on fifteen per week," he said. "If we wanted flowers we should have to grow them in old tomato-cans."

Little Ann took off her chorister's-gown apron and her kerchief, and patted and touched up her hair. She was pink to her ears, and had several new dimples; and when she sat down opposite him, as she had sat that first night at Mrs. Bowse's boarding-house supper, Tembarom stared at her and caught his breath.

"You ARE there?" he said, "ain't you?"

"Yes, I am," she answered.

When they had cleared the table and washed the dishes, and had left the toy kitchen spick and span, the ten million lights in New York were lighted and casting their glow above the city. Tembarom sat down on the Adams chair before the window and took Little Ann on his knee. She was of the build which settles comfortably and with ease into soft curves whose nearness is a caress. Looked down at from the fourteenth story of the St. Francesca apartments, the lights strung themselves along lines of streets, crossing and recrossing one another; they glowed and blazed against masses of buildings, and they hung at enormous heights in mid-air here and there, apparently without any support. Everywhere was the glow and dazzle of their brilliancy of light, with the distant bee hum of a nearing elevated train, at intervals gradually deepening into a roar. The river looked miles below them, and craft with sparks or blaze of light went slowly or swiftly to and fro.

"It's like a dream," said Little Ann, after a long silence. "And we are up here like birds in a nest."

He gave her a closer grip.

"Miss Alicia once said that when I was almost down and out," he said. "It gave me a jolt. She said a place like this would be like a nest. Wherever we go,—and we'll have to go to lots of places and live in lots of different ways,— we'll keep this place, and some time we'll bring her here and let her try it. I've just got to show her New York."

"Yes, let us keep it," said Little Ann, drowsily, "just for a nest."

There was another silence, and the lights on the river far below still twinkled or blazed as they drifted to and fro.

"You are there, ain't you?" said Tembarom in a half-whisper.

"Yes—I am," murmured Little Ann.

But she had had a busy day, and when he looked down at her, she hung softly against his shoulder, fast asleep.

Milton Keynes UK
Ingram Content Group UK Ltd.
UKHW041921151124
451262UK00007B/1120

9 789362 514530